GHOSTS
OF
WINTER

SHIFTERS OF CAERTON : BOOK 2

BY

H.B. LYNE

Published by Weaver of Words Press
UK

Originally Published in 2014
as Echoes of the Past: Ghosts of Winter
Published as part of the Shifters of Caerton Series 2019

This edition published in 2020

2

Book Cover design by Olivia Pro Design
Interior Formatting by Evenstar Books Ltd.

ISBN 978-1-913673-02-4
(paperback)
ISBN 978-1-913673-03-1
(ebook)

hblyne.com

ARE WE A PERFECT MATCH?

Ghosts of Winter is dark urban fantasy. In these pages you won't find sparkly vampires or teenage heroines with perfect hair.

I write dark, gritty, emotionally compelling stories filled with flawed protagonists, anti-heroes and deliciously dark villains.

There will be plot twists that bring out your most colourful language and yes, I write in British English.

If any of these things bother you, turn back now.

If however, darkness is your poison, then read on and lose yourself in the shadows for a while.

Acknowledgements

Chris, Agena, Arran, Phil and Andy; my friends and partners in creation.

The rich mythologies of this diverse and wonderful world.

My family, for their constant support and encouragement.

My editor, Zoe Markham, whose advice and encouragement have made me a stronger writer.

PROLOGUE

FIGHTS-EYES-OPEN

EYES STRODE INTO THE BETTING SHOP. Shadow's Step sat drumming his fingers behind one of the little glass windows. Lily pottered about behind him tidying the office area in advance of closing time. A couple of punters stood transfixed by horse racing on the noisy televisions.

Eyes passed through the shop and into the house behind it. He heard raised voices in the kitchen. Fortune, it was always Fortune.

'Why didn't she tell one of us before now?' the Alpha was bellowing, as Eyes entered.

'What's wrong?' Eyes asked.

'Where's Weaver now?' Fortune went on, apparently not noticing Eyes' arrival.

'The university,' Flames-First-Guardian responded. 'I told her to give us some space to handle this. I'm absolutely certain it's the Phoenix Guard and I don't know how long we have.'

Eyes looked from face to face, confusion and worry seeping into every pore of his body.

'Get back to the petrol station!' Fortune yelled at Flames. 'Do what you have to do.'

Flames nodded and left through the back door without a word. Wind Talker hesitated for a moment and then strode after his mentor. Speaks-With-Stone sat hunched at the table, her face and shoulders heavy with the gravity of the situation.

Fortune ran his hands through his thick hair and stared up at the ceiling. Eyes waited as patiently as he could bear it before he spoke again.

'Fortune?' he asked softly. Fortune's head whipped to him, his eyes wide with shock.

There was a moment of complete silence before the explosion. The sound of the shop window shattering splintered the air and Eyes leapt away from the door and slid across the kitchen table. Screams rang out and the room rapidly filled with fire and smoke. Fortune disappeared from view and Stone sprang from her chair, her body growing swiftly as she moved and sprouting thick fur all over. Her clothes disappeared, as if they had melted into her skin, and in place of her human face was the thick muzzle of a predator, the Agrius. She overturned the huge pine table with one clawed hand and bounded towards a shadowy figure moving into the kitchen through the thick smoke.

Howls and snarls ripped through the smoke and Eyes cursed his blindness. He shifted into his Agrius form, as Stone had, and raced forwards, desperate to find someone to rip apart. He managed two strides before he was roughly tackled from the side and forced to the ground. He started to fight back, but realised in the scramble that it was Fortune who held him and was trying to shield him as someone stepped closer through the smoke, an unknown scent.

'Get out,' Fortune snarled in his ear. 'Run. Find the others. Stay safe. Look after them.'

There was a thud nearby and Eyes gasped in horror as Stone's lifeless eyes stared back at him, blood spattered over her face and hair.

Fortune leapt up, dragging Eyes with him, and heaved him out through the back door. Eyes went skidding across the gravel in the yard and crashed against the wooden fence. He jumped to his feet, suppressing a roar of fury. He looked back at the building; it was engulfed in flames. Fortune filled the doorway and two huge pairs of bestial hands grabbed him and dragged him back inside. It would take at least two of them to take the Alpha down.

Eyes' body shook with rage, he wanted to run back into the fray and fight but the words of his Alpha echoed in his mind, and with a snarl of frustration he sprung across the narrow back street and crouched in the shadow of the building opposite. He huddled in the darkness, watching half of his pack burn and feeling every blow of the fight. The thoughts and feelings of his pack mates swirled inside his mind; pain, fear and blind rage. He knew he had to leave to find the others, but he was riveted to the spot.

Then there was nothing. They were all gone, the connection severed.

'No!' he yelled, though it came out as a distorted growl. He clamped his clawed hand across his muzzle and shrank down into the shadows. Grins-Too-Widely was dead. That was all he knew for certain, and he tried to convince himself that Fortune and Shadow were still fighting, but the cold, sick feeling in his gut lingered and some other sense told him that Stone and Grins-Too-Widely were not the only ones to perish.

He kept still, his mind working furiously to formulate a plan. He had to get clear of the area, whoever did this meant to destroy the whole pack, he needed to get somewhere safe and he needed to find the others.

With his mind made up he shifted from Agrius into his wolf form and set off at a sprint for the petrol station, to find Flames and Wind Talker. They couldn't have got far before the betting shop was attacked, but perhaps they had continued to the fall-back position. He would start there and gather the rest as soon as he could. He was nearly there when a huge explosion rent the air, the shock wave knocked him to the ground. *Hide*, a voice inside screamed. Eyes found himself truly afraid for the first time in his life and he leapt over a wall to find cover. He looked into the darkening sky and saw the vast plume of smoke billowing into the air where the petrol station stood. No one could have survived that explosion and he felt the truth settle on him; his fellow youngsters may have survived, he would have to find them, just as Fortune instructed, but their elders were all gone. They were alone now, and all the odds were stacked against them.

CHAPTER ONE

STALKER-OF-NIGHT'S-SHADOW

One Hour Later

STALKER LOOKED AROUND AT HER PACK MATES; three savage-looking shifters in their Agrius forms, seven feet tall and covered in thick fur of varying hues; half human, half bear. The dust was settling from their fight with the demons that had risen from the wreckage of the Blue Moon betting shop; fire, fear and devastation. The rain that Wind Talker had summoned was easing off, returning to the fine drizzle that nature had intended for that night. Stalker shifted, her limbs shortening, her fur receding to be replaced by pale skin and clothes. Her heavy muzzle shrank back and became her human face, her short brown hair wet from the rain.

They stood in the middle of the street next to a gaping hole in the veil between all of the realms, where their old home had stood an hour previously. They were in

Hepethia, the realm of shapeshifters. Below them, deep in the black pit, was the demon realm, and above them in the dark sky was a hole into the realm of fae. All species could find their way into Hepethia, which shifters could shape over time with their thoughts and actions, but it was the role of shifters to prevent demons from interfering in the human world.

'We'll need to mend the veil, but it'll take preparation.' Wind Talker sighed, the last to move away from the pit. He was tall, with a proud bearing, shrewd eyes and sandy-coloured hair, and he wore across his chest a satchel that used to belong to his mentor, Flames-First-Guardian.

The four of them set off away from the bomb site. Fights-Eyes-Open put an arm around Stalker as they walked. His sharp suit and dark hair were immaculate, protected from the fray when they merged with his thick fur.

'We can do this. We can form a new pack. Retake what was ours and avenge the Blue Moon,' he said with true conviction. The four of them walked slowly down the street; no one said anything, but Stalker silently believed Eyes was right.

'Wait,' Wind Talker called out, coming to a halt. Stalker and the others stopped to look at him. 'I think I can patch the veil now, keep the demons at bay. But it won't hold for more than a few days.'

He rummaged through his bag and pulled out a knife with a bone handle that had belonged to Flames-First-Guardian, their fallen pack mate. He ran back to the pit behind them and Stalker watched him carefully as he cut his palm and began moving his bleeding hand through the air, making the shapes of runes of their kind. She recognised the one for protection and another for healing. He muttered an incantation under his breath and the others just stood watching, still in shock. Stalker wondered how Wind Talker could have it all so together, when she felt as though she had lost limbs.

A few moments later, Wind Talker wiped the blood off the knife and stowed it away in the bag. 'That should do it.'

'Thank you,' Weaver-of-Sky's-Loom said softly. She was a slight young woman with long blond hair and glasses perched on her narrow nose. The smell of smoke clung to her hair and clothes. 'We need to find cover.'

'Flames had a house.' Wind Talker rummaged through the many pockets of the bag over his shoulder, and fished out a set of keys which he held up with a small smile.

Fights-Eyes-Open nodded curtly.

'Take us there,' he said, with all of the authority of their old Alpha, Fortune.

They crossed the veil back into the human world. Stalker felt the familiar tug behind her navel as she willed herself to step between worlds and felt the fabric of reality ripple and fold around them. They emerged in a dark alley close to where the betting shop had been.

Wind Talker led the way quickly across St. Mark's. Stalker was still hot and anxious from their battle with the demons and every unexpected sound caused her to startle. They came to a halt at an average terrace of small, brick houses; Grove Street, a few blocks north of Stalker's own little flat. Wind Talker led them about half way down the street and came to a halt. Stalker stared at the modest house with a black front door; even the dull, brass number

32 nailed in the middle was unremarkable.

After trying a few keys that all looked alike, Wind Talker found the right one and opened the door. A stale odour met them as they filed inside into a narrow hallway with dark, peeling wallpaper. Straight ahead was an equally narrow staircase, and to the right was a door leading to a room at the front of the house. Next to the stairs was a passage through to the back room, presumably the kitchen. The four of them huddled in the hallway, unsure what to do. Stalker felt uneasy. This house belonged to a man who had died a little over and hour ago, and being here without his prior permission felt a bit like grave-robbing.

Wind Talker led them down the hallway towards the back of the house. Stalker was the last to enter and closed the door behind her. The back room was indeed a small kitchen. There were a few empty cupboards, a cooker, a fridge-freezer with nothing but a few frozen steaks in the freezer compartment, and a small table sat against one wall with four chairs crammed around it. There was a back door with small glass panes in it. Stalker peered out but it was pitch black and she couldn't make out what was on the other side of the door.

Stalker gently took the keys from Wind Talker's hand, found the right one to unlock the door and led them outside. Light from the kitchen illuminated the small space and Stalker's eyes adjusted to the low light. It was a small, square garden with high walls of red brick on all sides, and rough paving covered most of the ground. It was terribly overgrown, with weeds bursting up between the paving stones and climbing the walls. In the middle of the garden was a three-foot square of neatly tended earth;

the soil was densely packed and nothing grew there.

'That's odd,' Stalker whispered. 'Why is this patch not neglected like the rest?'

'I don't know. We need to cross over and see what state the place is in on the other side of the veil,' Wind Talker said.

They all agreed and crossed the veil back into Hepethia. The garden felt darker and more oppressive on this side. The walls were much higher, towering over them, and the whole garden was packed with plants climbing the walls and swamping the small space. It would make a very private place to conduct rituals.

Inside the house was completely bare, it was as if it had been stripped and sterilised. There was nothing about the place that would indicate they were in Hepethia; it was a perfect reflection of the house in the normal world.

Stalker felt a surge of helplessness within. They were alone, with so little knowledge and so few resources. How did this happen? What were they going to do now? She whimpered and felt fresh tears hot on her face. Weaver took her hand and held it, and without speaking a word the two of them stepped back across the veil and found themselves in the tiny living room of the house. There was an old gas fire and a worn out couch, which they sat down on. A moment later Wind Talker and Eyes crossed over and sat on the floor in front of them.

'We'll be OK,' Weaver said. 'I know it seems overwhelming right now, but we can do this. We're not on our own, we all have other friends and contacts who can help us if we need them, but mostly we'll get by on our own. We've been trained well.'

A ripple of nods went around the small group but Stalker felt no relief. She had only known what she was for two weeks; it seemed like a lifetime since her frightening first change, but it had really been such a short time.

Her phone started ringing in her pocket and everyone looked at her. She gave them an apologetic look and pulled it out, knowing who it would be. The name on the screen proved her right and there was an icon indicating that she had three missed calls from him. She stood up and moved into the kitchen, answering on her way.

'Hi Rhys,' she whispered. She closed the doors as she moved through the house in the hope of having a little privacy.

'Are you OK? Did you get home OK?' he asked, sounding desperately worried.

'Yeah, I'm fine. Thank you.'

'I saw the news. What the hell is going on? They're saying it's terrorists. But that doesn't make any sense. Why would terrorists blow up a petrol station and a betting shop in St. Mark's?!' He scoffed, a mix of panic and disbelief in his voice.

Stalker had been with Rhys when she felt the pack telepathy break; they had just shared a passionate kiss when she had recoiled from him with the pain coursing through her body and mind. She had to cover her reaction and retreat from him quickly without explanation and now her mind raced with possible tales she could tell him.

'Yeah, I know. It is totally weird. I'm fine though, so please don't worry.' She chewed her lip, unsure if she had said the right or wrong thing.

'It's Friday tomorrow. Are you working?' he asked, his

voice returning to normal.

Stalker thought furiously, she hadn't been back to work since her first change, though she was due back the following week.

'No, I have the day off tomorrow. I'm really busy though. I have classes all weekend, so I'll have to let you know when I'm next free.' She spoke quickly, suddenly worried about having to teach self-defence to a group of locals if they believed terrorists had attacked their city.

'Oh.' Rhys sounded disappointed.

'I'm so sorry about tonight, I really am, I had such a good time and I really wish things had been different.' Her voice cracked as her thoughts turned again to her pack mates who had perished in the fires. 'I really want to see you again, I just have a lot on my plate right now and I don't know when I'll have time.' She cringed at her own words, knowing that no amount of reassurance was going to change the fact that it seemed she was backing away from him.

'OK, well let me know if there's anything I can do. Take care, Ariana.' His voice sounded so distant and she felt a wave of anguish sweep over her as he spoke her human name.

'I will, Rhys, I'll see you soon and I'll text you tomorrow. Bye.' She hoped that she had repaired some of the damage as she ended the call. But somehow she felt it was too late.

Chapter Two

Fights-Eyes-Open

Eyes checked every room in the house. There wasn't much to see. There was one small bedroom with a single bed and no bedding and a bathroom that desperately needed cleaning. A small, awkward staircase led up to the attic, but the door was locked.

The pack gathered in the living room. Weaver and Stalker held each other on the sofa and Wind Talker sat on the floor, rummaging through the bag he had been carrying since Eyes had found him a few blocks from the petrol station.

Eyes rubbed his face, there was so much to do, but he was exhausted and he had to get home to his family. He knew that Chloe, his wife, would be beside herself right now, with unexplained fires and explosions in the city.

'Will you three be OK here tonight? I have to get home,' he said anxiously. His eyes went to Wind Talker first, who glanced up and simply gave a curt nod before returning to his task.

'We'll be fine, Eyes,' Weaver answered in her warm and calm voice.

'OK,' he said, nodding. 'I'll come back here first thing in the morning. I hope you all get some rest. It'll be a busy day tomorrow.'

They all nodded in agreement and Eyes left the house. He jogged all the way across St. Mark's to where the Blue Moon betting shop had been. The press were still there in force and the police van from earlier still sat at the kerb opposite the rubble. His car was parked a hundred yards away from the scene, outside the police tape and he felt relief wash over him when he unlocked it and slipped inside. The last thing he needed was to be connected to the betting shop or the explosions. Questions would have been asked if his car had been recorded as being close to the scene. He drove carefully out of St. Mark's and into Crossway.

His house was only a few blocks from the edge of the territory that the Blue Moon had claimed. Beyond the border lay Fenwick, the territory of the Witches, who had undoubtedly played a part in the attack on his pack. He pulled up outside his house. Lights were on inside and he dashed up the path and in through the front door.

'Chloe?' he called. 'Chloe? Where are you?'

'Here!' She came running from the family room to meet him in the wide hallway. Eyes breathed a sigh of relief and ran forward to embrace her. He held her head against his chest and breathed in the scent of her perfume. Her auburn hair brushed against his cheek and he kissed the top of her head several times. 'They're saying it might be terrorists,' she said, pulling away from him and dragging him into the family room. The TV was on, the volume set low and Eyes glanced at the baby monitor on the bureau next to it. He could just hear the faint, snuffled breathing of his daughter over the monitor.

'It can't be terrorists,' he said quietly. 'Don't worry, it's all over now.'

The news channel was broadcasting from the two locations and a ticker ran along the bottom of the screen with other news headlines, while the anchor woman talked with well-practised calm concern. Eyes watched carefully for a few minutes, checking the backgrounds for signs of anyone he knew. There were none.

He collapsed on the sofa, letting his head fall back onto the soft cushions. Chloe curled up next to him and rested her head on his shoulder. He drifted off to sleep to the sound of the TV and his wife's gentle breathing, with the occasional murmur on the monitor from his precious daughter, Amy.

Eyes dreamed of fire, of Speaks-With-Stone's cold, dead face, Fortune yelling at him to run and of running in fear and panic away from the fight. *Coward.* The word haunted his nightmare.

He woke with a start some time in the early hours of the morning, covered in a fine sheen of sweat. The TV was off, Chloe was gone but she had covered him with a blanket and taken his shoes off. Eyes sat up slowly and took a few deep breaths. He ran his hands through his hair and fought back the disturbing ideas and memories from his dreams. He hadn't acted out of cowardice; he had followed orders and rounded up the survivors.

He slipped through the dark house, checked that all the doors were locked and went silently up the stairs. He found Chloe in their bed, with Amy sprawled out next to her, her blond curly hair spread out like a halo. With a resigned sigh, Eyes slipped across the hall to the spare room and slept the rest of the night there, mercifully with no more nightmares.

The next morning Eyes went into business mode. The panic and fear of the previous evening was behind them and now the fledgling pack faced the daunting task of getting themselves established.

He ate a rushed breakfast with Chloe and Amy, kissed them both goodbye and set off for Grove Street. He let himself into the house and found the rest of his pack eating steak in the kitchen and raised an eyebrow.

'It's all there was in the freezer,' Weaver explained. 'We'll go to the butcher today for bacon and sausages.'

'OK, no judgement from me, it was just an odd sight.' Eyes winked at her.

'I need to find Flames's notes today. I need to work out how to repair the tear in the veil,' Wind Talker told them. 'It's not something he got around to teaching me.'

Eyes thought he could detect an edge of sadness and humility to his pack mate's voice; he was relieved to notice it and nodded in solemn acknowledgement.

'Me and Weaver are going to the DIY shop in Northgate to buy supplies this morning, we can go via the butcher on the way back.' Stalker said. 'This was just a bolt hole for Flames, but we should make it a home and base.'

Eyes nodded in agreement, he was thankful for their initiative. Once breakfast was done, Weaver and Stalker set off and Wind Talker held up the set of keys that had let them into the house.

'I bet one of these gets us into the attic,' he said, jingling them. Eyes smiled and followed Wind Talker up the stairs.

They tried half a dozen of the little keys on the packed ring before Wind Talker found the one that turned in the lock. With a smile, he opened the door. A shower of dust fell like light snow as the door swung open. There was no natural light in the poorly converted attic space, but Eyes found a switch next to the door and a dim bulb slowly came to a warm glow. The floor had been badly boarded and boxes were piled up all around the cramped attic.

The two shifters stepped as softly as they could into the attic and started to look around. Eyes opened the nearest box, it was full of dusty papers. Each page was covered in tiny scrawled writing, which he recognised as belonging to Flames-First-Guardian.

'Wind Talker,' he whispered, though he wasn't sure why he was keeping his voice low. 'I think these are records of some kind.' He leafed through a few pages and Wind Talker came to look over his shoulder.

'They're songs of the bards,' Wind Talker said quietly, his voice full of awe.

'What does that mean?'

'Records of packs,' Wind Talker replied. 'Scroll Keepers like Flames keep a written record of all of the songs, poems and myths that shifters tell of their deeds. These will probably be Blue Moon songs, but there may be others too.'

'I see. We'll need the deeds to this house,' Eyes said. He closed the box. As tempting as it was to dive into those records, they had urgent matters to attend to. 'And a will. What was his human name?'

'I don't know,' Wind Talker said stiffly.

'Ah.' Eyes rubbed his face with his hands; this wasn't going to be simple.

Propped up in front of one of the piles of boxes was a cork board with a map of Caerton pinned to it. Eyes moved over to it and picked it up.

Wind Talker followed and looked over his shoulder.

'What is it?'

'A map of the city. What are these markings?' Eyes asked, pointing at the strange runes, some with crosses through them, dotted around St. Mark's, Northgate, Redfield and Crossway; the areas of the city that the Blue Moon had claimed as their territory.

Wind Talker looked carefully at the map, squinting in the low light. He tapped one of the markings.

'That was a rat's nest,' he said abruptly. 'I helped clear it out in my first week with the Blue Moon. It was a restaurant with a problem; the rat demons had infested the place and we exterminated them. I think these are all problem areas, the ones with crosses through are the ones that have been dealt with.'

Eyes looked over the map carefully, there were a lot more markings with no crosses than there were crossed off ones. With a sigh, Eyes put it down; it was a starting point for them to get on with the routine maintenance of the territory, once they were established.

They searched for what seemed like hours, though it was really little more than one, going through boxes one by one. Wind Talker kept getting engrossed in piles of notes, which frustrated Eyes, but he silently plugged away. Eyes shuffled a pile of boxes away from the edge of the room and pulled them towards him. He blinked away the dust that billowed up and saw a small bureau hidden in the shadows behind the boxes. He tried the handle, but it was locked.

'Can you pass me the keys, please?' he asked Wind Talker, who approached a moment later with the keys in hand.

'Here.' Wind Talker handed the keys to Eyes. 'What's this?'

'What we're looking for, I hope,' Eyes said as he went through the keys for a suitably small one. He found it and tried it in the lock, it clicked and the little door fell open. Inside were a few neatly folded papers, Eyes took them and quickly flicked through them. 'Oh, thank goodness, the house deeds.'

There were a few other important documents, but no will, much to Eyes' frustration. He was going to have to forge one if they were going to hang onto the house. 'Why wouldn't he leave a will?' Eyes asked, not really expecting an answer. 'He owned property, surely he must have considered what he would want to happen to it in the event of his death?'

'He probably never imagined that his pack would all be killed along with him, and assumed they would take care of things like that. Do you have a will?' Wind Talker was leafing through papers nearby and peered up at Eyes with a strange look. Eyes ignored the look and simply nodded in reply.

'I'm going downstairs to make some phone calls. I

know how to get around this, but I'm going to have to get my hands dirty. If the authorities find out about this I'll be dis-barred,' he grumbled to himself as he strode towards the stairs.

'You'll be fine,' Wind Talker called after him. 'First day on our own and already having a lawyer in the pack is turning out to be useful.'

Eyes heard him barking with laughter behind him as he trudged down the stairs. He had been an honest man all his life, he had worked hard to earn his law degree and pass the bar, and he was an up and coming star in chambers. Now it all hung on the brink, he was going to have to carve out a life of lies and criminality in order to hide his pack's activities.

He sat at the kitchen table, a notepad and pen in front of him and his phone in his hand as he built up the courage to make the calls he needed to make.

Eyes knew that he needed to alert some of the other packs of the city to their survival. They would need to assert themselves, make it known that St. Mark's, at least, was still claimed territory. Not to mention the fact that he was feeling the need for some guidance from a more experienced Alpha on how to step up and lead the new pack.

There was only one person he could think of to call. Theodore Harris. He was the Alpha of the Glass Wolves, a well-established and powerful pack that claimed Burnside. It was an area of the city close to the centre that included the financial and business district. The crown court building was on their territory and so Eyes had been introduced to Theodore by Fortune within days of his first change, in order to establish permission to be on their territory for business purposes. He had a direct line to Theodore at Harris Intermediaries and there was an answer after just one ring.

'Harris,' a cool voice stated.

'Hello. It's Martin Davison.' Fights-Eyes-Open announced himself by his human name, part habit, part security.

There was a long silence at the other end of the phone; Eyes guessed that Theodore was somewhat surprised to hear from him, having probably assumed him dead.

'Good to hear from you,' Theodore said at last, his voice perfectly neutral.

'I'd like to talk in person if possible,' Eyes said, hoping he would be granted a meeting.

'Of course, yes I think that would be best. Can you come to my office this afternoon? I'll be here until six.'

'That's fine. I'll head over after lunch. Thank you.' Eyes breathed a sigh of relief and for a moment didn't care if Theodore heard it.

'Very well, I'll see you early this afternoon.' Theodore ended the call without another word and Eyes put his phone down on the table, his hand shaking slightly. He took a steadying breath and immediately regretted allowing Theodore to sense any weakness or desperation from him. He would have to put it behind him and go into the meeting with a positive and authoritative attitude.

The next order of business was getting the house bequeathed to Wind Talker. It made the most sense, as Flames had been his mentor. There was a solicitor that he had often come up against in cases, a man known for getting the job done, no matter who the client. Eyes knew he wasn't always on the level, but right now that was exactly what he needed. He looked up the contact details online on his phone and made the call.

'It's Martin Davison for Jeremy Wilson please,' he told the receptionist, a sour taste filling his mouth. She connected him to his contact, who answered the phone with an edge of curiosity to his voice.

'What can I do for you, Mr. Davison?'

'I need some paperwork drawing up, as quickly as possible. I understand it's something you can help me with.'

There was a long silence. Eyes tapped his pen hard on the pad as he waited. He was confident that Jeremy was the man to contact, so there was little cause for concern, but he hated to be kept waiting, he felt toyed with.

'What sort of paperwork?' Jeremy asked cautiously.

'A last will and testament. It's a small estate, just a property in St. Mark's, to which my client has the deeds. I need this doing today, you understand.'

'Yes, of course. Can you email me the details and a scanned copy of the deeds?'

'No problem. I think I have your email address already.' Eyes let out a silent breath. 'What's the fee?' he asked, stiffly.

'I'll have a think on that and let you know. For now, let's just say you owe me.' Jeremy was grinning, Eyes could hear it in his voice and it made his skin crawl.

'Fine,' he replied curtly.

'I can have it finished by 4pm and send it by bike messenger to chambers.' Jeremy spoke quickly, as if already in action.

'No. Can you send it to the property in the will please? 32 Grove Street, St. Mark's. That's where I'll be.'

'Of course,' Jeremy replied. 'Nice doing business with you, Martin.'

Eyes hung up the phone and slid it across the table in indignation.

'Everything okay?' Weaver's voice caught him by surprise, and Eyes looked over to the door to see her and Stalker filing along the hall with their hands full of carrier bags.

'Fine,' he said with a sigh. 'Fine thanks, just having to sully myself with a disreputable contact in order to secure this place for us. I now owe a bad man a favour and I don't like that. What did you get?' he asked, pointing at the bags.

'Stuff,' Weaver said, grinning.

Stalker dumped her bags down on the kitchen floor and wiped her hands on her trousers.

'Some gardening and DIY supplies,' she clarified. 'But also some food.'

'And cushions!' Weaver said, pulling out a large, black floor cushion with silver embroidery on it. 'To make the living room more comfy.'

Eyes stifled a small laugh as she strode through to the living room to deposit the cushion and evidently several more from the bags she took with her.

'We also got front door keys cut for each of us,' Stalker said, fishing them out of her pocket and placing them on the table. Eyes took one and idly added it to his own key ring.

'Who's going to do the gardening?' he asked Stalker.

'Me,' she replied defiantly.

'You?' He didn't quite believe her.

'Me.' She looked a bit disgruntled at his disbelief. 'Well, someone has to do it.'

Weaver returned and the three of them sorted through the shopping, putting away the stacks of meat, bread and eggs. There were a few tins of beans and vegetables and a packet of pasta, but Eyes suspected they would sit in the cupboard for quite some time.

He went back to the table, laid out the house deed and took pictures of each page with his phone. He quickly composed an email to Jeremy with the correct names and address and attached the photos. His skin crawled and a heavy lump rose in his throat as his thumb hovered over the "send" key. It had to be done, he knew that, he had no choice if he was going to protect the property. He sent the email with resignation and slowly put his phone away. On the bright side, he felt a hint of amusement at learning Flames's real name, assuming that the name on the house deed was genuine, and decided, all things considered, he would keep that information to himself.

Eyes glanced at Stalker as she unpacked the new tools and headed out into the garden with a determined look on her face. Eyes watched her through the window for a while. He felt terrible for her. She was so newly changed, they all were, but Stalker especially was still very connected to her humanity and seemed more overwhelmed by the events of the previous day than the rest of them. He knew he was going to worry about her for a long time to come.

CHAPTER THREE

STALKER-OF-NIGHT'S-SHADOW

STALKER KNELT BY THE FAR WALL OF THE GARDEN, digging out weeds. She had already started pulling the climbing plants off the wall and had cleared a large section. A pile of debris was building up behind her.

She could feel eyes on her, but she knew it was just Fights-Eyes-Open watching from the kitchen window. He worried about her, she knew that, but she worried about him too. She knew that he must be feeling torn in two all the time, between this life and his human family. Whatever she did or didn't have with Rhys, at least it wasn't an established relationship with children.

The thought of Rhys suddenly jogged her memory and she tossed her trowel down onto the stone, took out her phone and hurriedly wrote a message.

Hi. How are you today? All is well here. St. Mark's is buzzing with the events of last night xx

When she and Weaver had gone out she had heard a dozen different conversations about the explosions. People rushed about their business with their heads down, and the driver of the bus they caught home gave them the most terrified look she had seen on any passing human since her change. Everyone seemed convinced that it had been the work of terrorists, despite the headlines of the day reassuring people that there was no evidence of this being the case.

Stalker's phone buzzed with a reply.

> I'm fine, thanks, glad to hear from you. Hope to see you soon xx

She smiled, half with sadness and regret, half with hope as she slipped her phone back into her pocket.

At lunchtime Weaver cooked sausages for the pack and they ate in the small kitchen, talking over what they needed to do.

'We need to assess our new territory around Grove Street,' Eyes stated. Everyone agreed.

'We can't lay claim to everything that belonged to the Blue Moon,' Wind Talker said as he chewed. 'We have to be realistic about what we can control at this point. We should claim a small area for now and gradually expand it.'

'True,' Stalker said. 'But we need to make sure we let the Wrecking Crew know we're here. We should claim as much as we can north of here towards Redfield, before they try to expand any further south.'

The others nodded in agreement.

'We should find a fae ally,' Weaver said quietly, and

a little ripple of sadness went around the group. Stalker felt the loss of Grins-Too-Widely; he had enabled them to communicate telepathically and bound the pack together. Without him, she felt very isolated, even with her pack mates right there around the table with her.

'Do we need one?' Eyes asked, a deep frown on his brow. 'It isn't strictly necessary for us to function, and not all allies grant the same abilities to those that pledge to them, so we might not get our telepathy back.'

'We don't have to have one, no,' Weaver replied. 'But we're starting from scratch here and need as much support as we can muster. It would show strength to the other packs if we had some influence in Hepethia.'

Stalker mused over Weaver's words. She didn't know much about the politics and still had a lot to learn about the spiritual aspect of their lives, but what Weaver said made sense.

'Okay,' Eyes said, his face set in an expression of steely resolve. 'I have an appointment early this afternoon, so we'll just mark our immediate territory and then sort out searching for an ally later.'

When lunch was finished, they crossed the veil and set out from the house, taking to the streets cautiously. It was a grey day and thick clouds rolled overhead, but it was mercifully dry. The street was quiet, with just small noises of movement here and there, and its houses were hunkered down and packed together. The occasional fluttering behind dark windows indicated that demons of paranoia and fear were present. As the pack neared the end of the road, Stalker heard something large moving just out of sight.

They rounded the corner slowly and silently, Stalker taking the lead. She stopped in her tracks and halted the others behind her as a huge, hulking demon lumbered up the road towards them. It was easily ten feet tall and almost as wide, and about the length of a lorry. It moved on clanking limbs and was constructed of metal and shards of glass and was stained with blood. It had no face to speak of but seemed to sense its way. Stalker could tell it was a fear demon, there was something terrifying about it, blood and death and violence all wrapped up in this relentless tank of a demon.

'Can you sense its name, Wind Talker?' Eyes whispered.

'The-Baron-of-Blooded-Shards,' Wind Talker whispered back. 'A fear demon, probably the most powerful of the fear demons around here.'

Stalker frowned, 'How do you know that?'

'It's an innate ability,' Wind Talker replied. 'Artemis blessed me with it.'

Stalker felt a stab of regret. She hadn't known about it. It made her wonder what else she didn't know about her precious, remaining pack mates.

The Baron lumbered past them, apparently unaware of them. Stalker knew that it must have sensed them though, it just thought of them as nothing more than ants and not worthy of its attention. They stood and watched it go by before setting off again, just to finish a circuit around the block. Stalker wondered how much shaping of this area the Blue Moon had done. The streets here were a part of the chaotic maze that they had generated across St. Mark's. They provided residence for many fae and demons, and confused any of the more dangerous demons that found their way across the river from unclaimed St. Catherine's. She wondered what the area had looked like in its natural state, before the Blue Moon had interfered with it.

The pack returned to the house. It wasn't much, but they had at least assessed their immediate environment and left their scents on the place so that others would know it was claimed. Stalker didn't feel reassured. Having a powerful fear demon in their territory didn't bode well.

'Can you research the fear demons of the region for me, Wind Talker?' Eyes asked once safely back in the world of humans. Wind Talker nodded and took himself upstairs to hunt through some of Flames-First-Guardian's notes. He would undoubtedly need to talk to some local fae and demons too, and Stalker guessed he would do that across the veil and in the garden.

'I'm going to tidy up the garden,' she said. 'I assume you don't need me for anything else, Eyes?'

'No, you go ahead. I have to go out for a bit now but I'll be back by four.'

Stalker nodded and went out into the garden and crossed the veil back into Hepethia. It was remarkably peaceful, even though there were neighbouring houses packed tight all around their little terraced house. The walls were so high that a great deal of privacy was assured, and she wondered if all the houses had such gardens, or if these walls had been built by Flames.

As she thought about it, the walls seemed to grow even taller, and her gaze snapped up to their high tops. She was startled and looked carefully, unsure whether she had imagined it or not. The walls had previously come up to the same height as the guttering, now they were a foot or so taller. She wasn't imagining it. She looked at the houses on either side, nothing but their uppermost walls and roofs were visible. Stalker imagined what it would be like if they were angled away from their garden, so that there was no chance of anyone seeing into it from the windows or rooftops. At her command, the houses bent away from her, crunching and groaning as the bricks changed shape.

'Oh my god!' she exclaimed, excitement bursting up into her chest.

Weaver came running out of the house, concern etched onto her face.

'What is it?' she urged.

'I changed the houses,' Stalker said with glee in her voice. 'Look!' She pointed at the neighbouring houses on all sides, bent over, crouched behind the high walls.

'That's incredible,' Weaver said slowly, turning on the spot to look at the changes. 'I've never been able to shape Hepethia before. It takes so much concentration to do it on purpose. Usually it just sort of happens around what shifters do.'

'Try it,' Stalker urged. 'Maybe we have a short window of opportunity to make immediate changes to our territory?'

Weaver gave her an appraising nod and went to the wall furthest from the house. She reached up and touched the red bricks. Very slowly, a sort of ladder started to form. Bricks rumbled and scraped against one another with some of them moving to protrude out of the flat wall. Stalker grinned, elated at the look of surprise and wonder on Weaver's face. Weaver grasped one of the bricks and climbed swiftly up the wall. She pulled herself up onto the top of the wall and stood up. Stalker followed, nimbly dancing her way up the wall. Weaver grasped her hand as she looked out over the landscape.

Stalker followed her gaze. Inside the neighbouring gardens, the places that had long been out of sight of the garden of 32 Grove Street, was the strangest sight. Instead of grass or paving, or anything Stalker had ever seen anywhere on earth, there were beautiful rocks of green, blue and white. Some areas were flat, but the rocks jutted up out of the ground, like stalagmites. 'What are we looking at?' Stalker gasped.

'Crystals,' Weaver replied in a whisper. 'Hepethia's natural form.'

'It's beautiful.' Stalker was captivated; she felt she could look at the crystals all day. 'So that's what Hepethia looks like before shifters go bending it to their will?'

'Yes,' Weaver said, her voice still sounding distant.

Stalker looked back down into their own garden. Weeds swamped the place, they climbed the walls and grew over a foot tall between paving slabs. She focused her attention on them and willed them to recede into the ground. They obeyed her, shrinking away to a much more manageable level. With a grin back at the captivated Weaver, Stalker jumped down from the wall, and after the first few feet of freefall she drifted gracefully to the ground.

Weaver clambered down the rough ladder she had created and grabbed Stalker's shoulders.

'How did you do that?'

'This,' Stalker replied, lifting her clay pendant out from inside her top. 'Shadow gave it to me.' A sudden lump rose in her throat and her fingers trembled slightly as she hurriedly tucked it back into her t-shirt. Weaver gave her shoulders a gentle squeeze. 'It doesn't feel real yet. I keep forgetting that he's gone, that they're all gone.'

'I know,' Weaver said sadly. 'Same here. I keep expecting Flames to come marching in barking "What are you lot doing in my house?"'

Stalker let a small laugh bubble up in her throat. She could just picture it. The laugh died on her lips and the sadness resumed.

'My necklace has a trick, too,' Weaver said, a conspiratorial grin on her lips. She looked into Stalker's eyes and slowly her pupils shrank, the shape of her eyes shifted and the irises turned bright green. Her eyes alone had shifted into those of a cat, Weaver's Artemis-given form.

'Woah,' Stalker gasped.

'I can change bits of myself, not only my whole body,' Weaver said, grinning. 'Any part I choose, into the equivalent cat's feature.'

'That's so cool,' Stalker grinned at her.

'Come on,' Weaver said softly. 'Let's go back across.' She took Stalker's hand and they crossed the veil together.

Stalker sighed when she saw the garden in the state she had left it earlier, with piles of dug up weeds all over the paving. She got down to work with Weaver, stuffing the pulled up weeds into bin bags and giving the paved area a sweep.

As they worked, Stalker felt something watching her and she carefully looked around, not wanting to startle anything that may be lurking. It was early afternoon and the sun was trying to break through the thick clouds above, there were no real shadows to speak of in the garden. Yet there by the door, a dark shadow shimmered slightly in the corner between the door and the garden wall. She looked at it carefully, but felt a hint of disappointment when she realised that it was not Pursuit-of-Midnight-Solitude, her Path of Night patron, the one who had led her to her true name and was her guardian in dark places. This was a minor shadow demon, but she had an affinity with the whole family of shadow and darkness demons and she brushed the dirt off her hands and gave it her full attention.

Weaver stopped working and watched Stalker as she stepped towards the door.

'Yes? Can I help you?' she asked in a quiet, calm voice.

'Blue Moon,' the shadow whispered.

'They're gone.' Stalker choked back the tears.

'Now! Blue Moon!' the demon hissed and then vanished.

Stalker ran to the door but the demon was gone.

'What does that mean?' she called out, but no reply came.

'What did it say?' Weaver asked calmly. She crossed the small garden in a second and placed warm hands on Stalker's shoulders as they locked their eyes on one another. Stalker instantly felt calmer and slowly recounted the demon's brief words.

A deep frown creased Weaver's brow.

'What date is it?' she asked. Stalker had to think for a minute, she had lost track.

'The thirtieth of November. Why?'

Weaver let go of Stalker's shoulders, sighed and

rubbed a hand across her head.

'I'd forgotten,' she said with a slight break in her voice. 'We were going to have a meal to celebrate the start of the full moon last night. It isn't just any full moon today.'

'What do you mean?' Stalker felt heavy with grief.

'There are normally three full moons in each season, but sometimes there are four and when that's the case, the third is called a blue moon. That's what today is. The third of four full moons of autumn.'

Stalker let her head hang heavily. Tears began to fall and she wiped them away quickly with her muddy hands.

'I can't believe this is happening.' Stalker struggled to speak between sobs. 'I can't believe they're all gone. Shadow's Step, he was like a brother to me. He's gone and now we're all alone and who will help us?' Panic was rising in her chest and she looked imploringly at Weaver, who always seemed so cool and level-headed. For a moment Weaver looked just as scared and sad as Stalker felt, but her expression quickly changed to one of firm resolve.

'We're going to be fine,' she said. 'We have to be fine. One thing at a time. Right now we have to put things in order; claim our territory, find allies and arrange income and cover for the pack. If we focus on the practicalities it will help get us through these early days.'

Stalker felt calm begin to replace panic and she took a few deep breaths.

'You're right. We'll manage.'

'We will. A good next step for you, my lovely sister, would be to wash your face.' Weaver gave her a cheeky smile and Stalker looked quickly at her reflection in the kitchen window and saw the smears of dirt across her cheeks from where she had wiped her tears with her grubby hands. She broke into a small laugh. *One thing at a time,* she told herself, *one thing at a time.*

34

Chapter Four

Fights-Eyes-Open

Eyes drove into the centre of Caerton and parked in the car park underneath the court buildings. He made his way quickly through the streets of glass skyscrapers to Free River Tower, the huge building that housed Harris Intermediaries and stood sentinel at the heart of Burnside, the financial and business centre of the city. Free River Tower was the tallest structure in Caerton, an impressive skyscraper of gleaming glass and shining steel. It was an oval shape, with a level roof.

Eyes straightened his tie as he stepped into the revolving front door. He strode across the polished marble floor to the vast reception desk and glanced at the large, brass plaque on the wall behind it, which listed the businesses in the building and on which floor to find them. It came as no surprise to find Harris Intermediaries listed at the top of the building, the top five floors. Theodore's office had to be on the top floor. It's where Eyes would put his office if he were in Theodore's position.

Eyes smiled awkwardly at the security guard at the desk as he signed in and the guard issued him with a guest pass. He went to the lifts to the right of the lobby and dashed into one that was about to close. The lift was empty and he took a steadying breath as he hit the button numbered 50. The lift began to move steadily up the vast tower block and Eyes waited, his mind churning with how much to tell Theodore and how much to keep to himself. He wanted to appear strong and capable, but at the same time, he was here at least in part for help. It was going to be a difficult balance to strike.

After a minute or so, the lift arrived at the top floor and Eyes stepped out into a bright corridor opposite large double doors in a glass wall. The glass was tinted to a deep shade of blue so Eyes could see nothing on the other side. To his right the corridor stretched away, with glass doors at regular intervals, and to his left was an open reception area with crystal clear, floor-to-ceiling windows overlooking the city. He walked towards the desk, there was no sign of anyone here and he looked around for signs of life.

Voices came from behind him and the huge double doors opposite the lift opened wide. Out stepped a young woman, who looked incredibly tense and after her came the man himself, Theodore Harris. He was a tall and very well-built man with short hair and rimless glasses on his broad nose; he looked rather like a large gorilla stuffed into a very nice suit. The effect was striking. Eyes stepped towards him to greet him and Theodore approached with a hand extended, which Eyes took and shook firmly.

'Martin. Good to see you.' Theodore greeted him warmly and led him into his office. The assistant glanced at Eyes and then hurried past him to her desk. Eyes could feel the power oozing off Theodore, making him immediately subservient to the older shifter. He knew that humans must find him ten times as intimidating.

As soon as the office doors closed Theodore's demeanour changed. He turned to look at Eyes, his face hard and wary. Eyes cleared his throat and straightened his back and shoulders, rising to his full height, though he still stood a good few inches shorter than the impressive Alpha before him.

'Thank you for seeing me,' Eyes managed to say, with no betrayal from his voice.

'I was surprised to get your call,' Theodore stated as he strode across his office. It was huge, with one wall entirely glass, looking out across the entire city from the top floor of the tower. A vast desk stood in the middle of the room, with a big comfortable chair behind it, which he slid into, indicating a much more modest chair opposite for Eyes.

'I thought that might be the case.' Eyes took the offered seat and tried not to allow himself to feel small. He looked around the office with a stab of envy.

'I heard that the Blue Moon had all been killed.'

'Not quite.' Eyes swallowed hard and tried not to let Theodore's bluntness rattle him too much. 'Four of us survived. That's why I'm here. To let you know that there is still a pack in St. Mark's. I'd appreciate it if you made it known in your dealings with... others.' He knew Theodore would understand that he meant all supernaturals. Theodore nodded and pressed his fingers together in front of his face.

'That's not the entire reason you're here. You could have told me as much over the phone.' He was staring Eyes down, challenging him to admit his need for help. Eyes took a deep breath.

'We encountered a powerful fear demon on our territory.' He was sure to emphasise the last two words. 'The-Baron-of-Blooded-Shards. Do you know of him?'

'Yes,' Theodore replied. 'He's a demon of fear caused by violence. No doubt he was drawn to St. Mark's after last night.'

Eyes nodded, that much made sense. 'Caerton is plagued by fear demons. It seems most areas have a problem with them. It didn't used to be a problem, but things are changing.' Theodore spoke openly and Eyes began to relax.

'Why do you think that is?' Eyes asked, his curiosity roused. There was something in Theodore's eyes, a glint of some big secret and Eyes felt it was coming to him whether he was ready to hear it or not.

'Your predecessors knew, but I expect they didn't burden the youngsters with this information.' He paused, watching Eyes carefully for a moment. Eyes leaned forward, shaking off the use of the word "youngsters", focussing on what Theodore had to tell him. 'The city's patron, The-King-of-Glass-and-Steel, is missing.'

Eyes snorted, but immediately regretted it. Theodore was entirely serious.

'How can the city's own essence be missing?' he asked, completely taken aback.

'I don't know. It's possible that he became too

powerful and has moved on. But there would normally be signs of that before it happened. All of the packs are aware of this, so it is only fair for me to inform you of it. The rise in prevalence of fear demons is indicative of a general problem in the city. There's no one commanding the demon and fae families and they're likely to drift out of balance. Fear is the first one to do so. I believe that the Baron is not the only one of his kind in Caerton.'

Eyes let out a sudden breath, not realising he had been holding it. He closed his eyes for a moment; this was not what he had wanted to get from this meeting. As if his new pack didn't have enough to do, now it would appear that there were much bigger problems than their own to face.

'Right,' he said, trying to find some assertiveness. 'Do you have any advice for me? Anything else I should be aware of?'

'Get out of the Blue Moon's shadow,' Theodore said with a wry smile. Eyes didn't quite know how to take that. 'Start fresh. It'll be tough, much harder than you realise now. But I wish you the best of luck. I mean that.' His face softened and Eyes believed him. Theodore was one of the most powerful of their kind in the city, in all respects, and Eyes respected him, even if he didn't entirely trust him.

Eyes left the building after the brief meeting feeling determined to get on top of his pack's situation. The sun was slipping lower in the sky as he set off back towards Grove Street and the air grew cold around him. It was the last day of November; winter would be upon them soon, which would bring them further challenges. He glanced up at the bright lights strung across the roads from the buildings. The "Happy Diwali" lights had recently been replaced by "Merry Christmas" ones. He felt a pang of panic at the thought of the approaching holidays and wondered how he was going to juggle pack life with family life.

As Eyes drove into St. Mark's he decided that he would need to lead the pack from the front, to put action first. He parked a few streets away from Grove Street and found a quiet alley. It was almost dark and he didn't have long before he needed to be back at the house. He slipped into the shadows and stepped across the veil into Hepethia. He knew what Fortune would have made of this highly dangerous move, but he needed to set an example and demonstrate his own strength and bravery in order to inspire the pack. His pulse was racing as he edged out of the alley and peered around the dimly lit street.

He shifted into his wolf form; his pelt was sleek and dark grey with white accents around his neck and the tip of his tail. He ran as quickly and as quietly as he could through the dark and threatening streets. Darkness and fear demons shrank away from him and he kept to the lit areas, knowing all too well what might happen if he strayed, alone, into the territories of those demons that were too strong.

As he neared Grove Street he heard movement behind him and turned to look for its source. A huge, seamless demon was speeding towards him, not dissimilar from a Chinese Dragon. It was black with yellow and orange shapes mottled on its long body. It was undulating along the street, weaving between the street lamps, keeping to their pools of light. He took a few steps back, towards the shadow and the street lamp dragon swept past him. He breathed a sigh of relief and set off after it, slowly.

After no more than a few yards, the dragon stopped and turned back to face him. It reared up and let out a fearsome roar that shook the street and ruffled Eyes' fur. It was going to strike.

Eyes shifted into his Agrius form. His bones and muscles stretched, he stood upright with thick, dark grey fur all over his body and a muzzle for a face. His teeth grew longer and sharper, the claws on his forelegs became deadly talons on strong hands, while his hind legs became muscular and powerful. He was the perfect fusion of man and bear; ferocious, powerful and strong but also fast and agile. He bellowed back at the dragon in a display of dominance, though his heart hammered in his huge chest and he had no idea if his plan would work.

The dragon took a humbled step back, watched him for a moment and then turned and resumed its course along the street away from him. Eyes watched him go and let out a shaking sigh of relief. He got lucky this time. That wouldn't always be the case.

Eyes sprinted the short distance remaining to 32 Grove Street and ran in through the front door, stepping back across the veil and shifting back into his human form as he did so.

He appeared in the human world at the same moment as a sharp knock came at the door. He turned and whipped it open. A stunned bicycle courier stood with his hand still raised in a knocking motion.

'Erm, delivery for Martin Davison?' the courier stammered uncertainly.

'That's me,' Eyes said, trying to steady his breathing

quickly.

The courier held out a padded envelope and an electronic signature device. Eyes quickly signed for the packet and gave the courier a brief smile. 'Thanks,' he said curtly and closed the door.

He ripped open the packet and pulled out the documents, they looked like they would do the trick and he breathed a sigh of relief.

The pack had appeared in doorways and from upstairs to see what the commotion was and he leaned heavily on the inside of the door.

'You all right?' Weaver asked from the kitchen doorway, a pair of rubber gloves on and a cloth in her hand. It was an odd sight and Eyes moved quickly up the hall and into the kitchen. The whole room was gleaming and Weaver looked very pleased with herself.

'Fine,' Eyes said absently, marvelling at Weaver's thorough cleaning. The kitchen had been in urgent need of this attention and he was pleased that she had taken on the task. He swept back to the front room, Wind Talker retreated back in there ahead of him and Stalker followed from the stairs. There were piles of notes scattered all over the floor and Flames's old satchel was propped up by the sofa.

'I've been researching local demons,' Wind Talker said, clearing some papers away from the sofa so that Eyes could sit down. 'Flames didn't keep very well-ordered notes. I'm still working on it.'

'No problem. Get what you can from them. I have some things to tell you all,' Eyes said, declining the offered seat. Weaver and Stalker sank onto the sofa instead and sat looking up at him. Wind Talker stood behind them, his hands on the back of the sofa, all three faces watching Eyes attentively.

'First of all, here is a last will and testament for Flames,' he said, holding out the document. 'It bequeaths this house to you.' He passed the will to Wind Talker. His pack mate took the document with a curious look and scanned it.

'It needs signing,' Wind Talker said, looking up at Eyes.

'Yes it does. As well as witnessing. This isn't going to be on the level, obviously, as he is already dead.' The last word stuck in his throat and he cleared it quickly with a small cough. He took a pen from his inside pocket and took the will back from Wind Talker. Resting on the arm of the sofa, Eyes took a deep breath and scrawled something illegible for Flames's signature and dated the document for a month previously. His hand shook slightly as he held out the paper and pen towards Weaver and Stalker. 'One of you needs to sign this.'

They looked at each other for a moment, then Weaver took them and proceeded to sign and date it. Eyes took them back and tucked everything into the inside pocket of his jacket. He gave a silent plea to Artemis that no one would ever come looking for it, that Flames had lived so far off radar that no human authority would notice his passing or identify his remains and come snooping.

With a cleansing breath, Eyes proceeded to report everything that Theodore had told him. Shocked gasps came from the women at the news of the King-of-Glass-and-Steel going missing, but Wind Talker didn't look entirely surprised.

'We have a lot to do,' Eyes continued without waiting for responses. 'The first order of business must be agreeing on an Alpha.' He stood up to his full height and puffed out his chest. 'I believe I can fulfil the role. I believe it is what Fortune intended for me. Last time I saw him he told me to find you and look after you. I know he meant for me to lead you.'

Stalker and Weaver nodded in agreement, but Wind Talker straightened up and crossed his arms over his chest, clearing his throat.

'With all due respect,' he said. 'I'm the eldest here. I'm the most experienced and I should take the role.'

Stalker craned her neck to look at him, but Eyes looked to Weaver for her response. She gave him a small smile and a nod of encouragement.

'Wind Talker– ' Eyes took a step toward him. 'You are our only, truly capable ritualist; you will have a great many responsibilities in that role. I think it's best if you remain focussed on that.'

'There's no reason I can't do both,' Wind Talker snapped. 'There are other Alphas in the city who are also lead ritualists.' Anger bristled off him and left a slight buzz in the air. Eyes felt it, but was not intimidated.

'I'm sure you would be perfectly competent in both roles at once,' he said, emphasising the word "competent" and Wind Talker's lip curled in response. 'But why settle for competent? When you could excel in your role as pack ritualist.'

Wind Talker trembled slightly as he struggled with the rage. He centred himself and Eyes watched him carefully, ready for a fight if need be. Weaver cleared her throat and stood up, walking to Eyes' side.

'I second the proposal to appoint Fights-Eyes-Open as our Alpha,' she said, her quiet voice ringing with warmth and authority. It was hard not to listen to her voice and to trust it implicitly. Eyes gave her a smile in gratitude for her support and waited to see what Stalker would say. The youngest of them looked around at everyone, her face twisted into a slight frown. At last she stood, positioned between Eyes and the sofa, behind which Wind Talker still stood.

'I agree. I think Eyes would make a good Alpha.' She moved to stand with Weaver. Eyes tilted his chin up towards Wind Talker with resolve.

'I think that settles the matter,' he said, striding around the sofa towards his still visibly angry pack mate. 'I trust that you can accept to be my beta and serve the pack with your affinity for rituals and dealing with fae and demons, and your superior knowledge of shifter business.' He extended a hand and locked eyes with Wind Talker, daring him to object. He didn't, the surly shifter took the offered hand and shook it, then drew him into a brotherly embrace, much to Eyes' surprise and relief. He would easily have bested Wind Talker in combat, but he preferred to start his tenure in a more amicable fashion.

'Very well,' Eyes said, stepping back. 'Get a good night's sleep everyone. Tomorrow we find ourselves an ally.'

Chapter Five

Stalker-of-Night's-Shadow

Stalker woke early the next morning, it was still dark and she cursed the winter under her breath as she shifted from her fox form into human and looked around the little living room. Weaver, Wind Talker and herself had spent the last two nights sleeping around the little space heater. At least they had cushions now to make themselves more comfortable. Wind Talker was still asleep, a large badger stretched out in front of the sofa. But Weaver was gone and Stalker made her way into the kitchen to find food and her pack mate.

Weaver was sat at the kitchen table scribbling. Stalker knew this was a bad sign and quietly observed over her pack-sister's shoulder to see what she was drawing. Stalker frowned; it was clearly some sort of demon, but nothing she could identify. It was a vaguely human figure, but with long bony fingers and many layers of clothing that looked like they came from a bygone era. It didn't have a human face though, it had almost a bird's face with a long, pointed beak and huge eyes. It was stepping out of a hole in the ground and above it shone the gibbous moon.

Stalker got a glass of water and sat down quietly opposite Weaver.

'Are you all right?' she asked softly, breaking the silence.

Weaver looked up at her and tossed her pencil down on the table.

'I had a vision,' she sighed.

'So I gathered.' Stalker waved a hand over the sketches. 'Any idea what it means?'

'No,' Weaver scoffed. 'Artemis has a way of making these visions as cryptic as possible. I don't even know what this thing is.'

Wind Talker entered the kitchen, looking half asleep. He grunted a greeting to them and Stalker returned it with a grin.

'Morning sunshine,' she called out to him, and he flinched away from her voice, causing a small ripple of laughter between Stalker and Weaver.

'Where's Eyes?' he asked blearily.

'He went to get his car late last night and then went home to his family,' Weaver replied. 'He'll be back soon.'

Wind Talker fixed himself some coffee and then joined them at the table. He pulled one of Weaver's sketches across the table to look at it.

'Is that a plague doctor?' he asked between sips of hot black coffee.

Weaver and Stalker looked at one another and then back at him.

'What's a plague doctor?' Stalker asked, frowning.

'They were the people who tried to treat plague sufferers. You know, during the big European plague in the middle of the fourteenth century. They wore robes and masks like this.' The two women looked at him blankly, though Stalker supposed he was right, she had no reason to think otherwise. But what on earth did it have to do with anything they might face now?

'It must be,' Weaver said softly, looking over her sketches again. 'Artemis sent me a vision of this man, or demon or whatever it is. Why would she send me a vision of something from over six hundred years ago?'

Stalker had a terrible feeling creeping over her skin.

'Oh please, please don't let there be an outbreak of plague. Please. That is the last thing we need.' She dropped her head to the table and covered it with her arms. It was all she could think it could mean.

'Is this a waxing or waning moon, Weaver?' Wind Talker asked and Stalker reluctantly raised her head.

'I have no idea. The visions aren't that specific. But if it's waning then it could be about to happen in a few days. It's a full moon now.'

Stalker moaned and dropped her head back down.

At the same time the front door opened and slammed shut.

'Hello?' Eyes called out from the hall to announce his presence.

'In the kitchen,' Wind Talker called back. Eyes came into the kitchen, but Stalker didn't look up. This was all too much. She wanted to retreat into a tiny ball and never have to deal with any of this. She listened silently while

Weaver told the Alpha about her vision and Wind Talker repeated what he knew about plague doctors.

'Right. And what's the matter with Stalker?' the Alpha asked. She lifted her head and tried to smile.

'I'm fine. Just, you know, overwhelmed.' She waved her hands about in front of her face, as if batting away flies.

'OK,' Eyes responded brightly, dismissing her negativity. 'Well we'll have to come back to Weaver's vision later. We have a lot to do today.'

A knock at the door interrupted him. They all looked at each other, frowning. Wind Talker stood up and walked briskly to the door, the others following him and peering around him in the narrow hallway. Stalker was at the back and could only just make out that there were two people in the street outside.

'Hi,' a young, male voice greeted them. 'We're friends of Flames-First-Guardian. We've come to pay our respects.'

'By all means.' Wind Talker opened the door wider and the pack retreated back down the hall and into the tiny living room to clear the way. Stalker tried to remember Flames ever mentioning any friends but drew a blank. She waited by the fire with Weaver for the guests to make their way into the room and tried hard not to stare when she saw them.

A man and a woman entered, both dressed in many layers of mostly black clothing. The man wore huge combat boots and his wrists were covered in bangles with tiny charms on. He had chipped black nail polish on his fingernails and wore a long, leather coat. He walked with a slight stoop and smiled as he entered, though it was a sombre sort of smile, given the circumstances.

'Hi,' he spoke softly. 'I'm Scribe-of-the-Fallen. This is Last-Breath-Echoes.' He held out a hand to the woman entering the room behind him. She was quite short and painfully thin with very pale skin and small features. She had long black hair in a braid that hung over her shoulder and wore a lot of jewellery. Stalker watched her carefully as she moved and noticed her making tiny flicks with her fingers against the door frame as she passed through it, they were the smallest of movements and Stalker had to watch even more closely to be sure she wasn't imagining it.

Last-Breath-Echoes waved absently and looked around the room at everyone, a far-away look in her wide, black-rimmed eyes. Stalker just knew that these two had to be the other Scroll Keepers of Caerton. They had the same sort of other-worldliness about them that Flames had had and the rather pressing need to get out in the sunshine.

'Have you come across Flames-First-Guardian's records yet?' Scribe asked. 'I hate to impose, but we have a duty, you know, to make sure they're safe and to continue his work.'

'Of course,' Eyes replied. 'We've found a lot of paperwork, some of it is pertinent to our pack and our territory, you understand.'

'Of course, yes,' Scribe answered quickly. 'It's probably best if we give you some more time to get organised and go through it and you can pass it along to one of us if you find anything that you think the Scroll Keepers should have. Is that acceptable?'

Eyes glanced at Wind Talker for confirmation, which he gave with a curt nod.

'There's a hole upstairs,' Last-Breath-Echoes said dreamily, looking up as if staring through the ceiling. 'Did you know?'

'I'm sorry?' Wind Talker said.

'Let me show you.' The ethereal Scroll Keeper wandered away, clearly expecting someone to follow her. Wind Talker filed out after her and Eyes gave Stalker a quick look to indicate that she should follow them. She walked quickly from the room and followed Wind Talker up the stairs without a word. Last-Breath-Echoes led them up the stairs and along the corridor to the tiny staircase up into the converted attic space.

Echoes ran her hand along one of the eaves and started humming what sounded like a folk tune. Stalker watched her carefully as she walked around the edges of the small space, leaning sideways with the slope of the roof. As she approached the second corner, diagonally opposite the door, Echoes paused and felt with her hand across a section of the roof. Her hand disappeared from view and Stalker suppressed a gasp of surprise. When Echoes retracted her hand she was holding a long, shallow card-board box, the sort of thing you might package a scarf in for a gift.

'Huh.' She shrugged and held it out for one of them to take. Wind Talker took it without taking his eyes off Echoes.

'Thank you,' he said with a strange sense of wonder to his voice.

Stalker smirked and followed Last-Breath-Echoes back down the stairs, Wind Talker followed behind her.

When they arrived back in the living room the others were sat in uncomfortable silence.

'Everything OK?' Stalker asked.

'Yes, fine,' Eyes said a little too quickly, jumping up from the sofa.

Scribe stood up and smiled stiffly.

'We'll need to make funeral arrangements,' he said softly, trying not to look anyone in the eye. 'Echoes here works in the city mortuary, she's already taken possession of, well, of what was left.'

There was a painful ripple around the room. Stalker felt suddenly fiercely protective of the remains of her pack and hated the idea of anyone prodding and poking them. It seemed that the others felt similarly from the rigid jaws and clenched fists appearing on her pack mates.

'There was something left of one of the Phoenix Guard,' Scribe went on cautiously. 'There was really nothing that could be identified at the petrol station, but there was definitely one of them taken down at the betting shop. What would you like us to do with it?'

Stalker looked at Eyes, fighting the rage that boiled in her chest and trying to focus on her Alpha for strength and leadership. He sighed and ran his hands through his hair, just like Fortune used to do. She pressed her hand to her mouth to suppress a sob.

'May I have it?' Wind Talker asked, and everyone turned to look at him.

'Yes,' Echoes chimed in, smiling serenely. 'I'll get a message to one of you when everything is in place. I'm so sorry for what happened to your pack.' A sad crease reached her brow and Stalker wondered if that was as expressive as she ever got.

'Thank you,' Eyes said, barely above a whisper.

Scribe and Echoes moved towards the door and Wind Talker followed to see them out.

Stalker shook out her tense arms, and she noticed Weaver doing the same. She leaned on the door frame and watched Wind Talker seeing out their guests. There was something wrong with Scribe's shadow as he walked down the hall, it seemed to move a split-second later than him, it sent a cold shiver down her spine. Her thoughts ran back to the strange flicks of her fingers that accompanied Echoes through the doorway and Stalker squinted to look at the wood on which she was leaning. There were tiny scratches in the peeling paint, fresh from Echoes' sharp nails. She thought of Flames and his strange mannerisms and the air of unease that followed him. Perhaps it was something to do with being so closely connected to death that turned these Scroll Keepers odd.

Wind Talker closed the door and walked slowly back down the hall, still holding the box that Echoes had found in the attic. He was looking down at it and opened it as he walked. Stalker watched absently, her mind still on the Scroll Keepers. Her reverie was shattered as she saw Wind Talker start convulsing, dropping the box and whatever was in it and erupting into his savage Agrius form right there in the hall with an almighty roar.

Eyes and Weaver ran out from the living room and together with Stalker they pounced on Wind Talker to contain him. This was the true monster within, bursting out through Wind Talker's skin and he thrashed and roared with madness. Between the three of them they wrestled Wind Talker to the ground and pinned him down until the rage ran its course and he lay shaking under them in the hallway in his human form. Gradually they moved off him and let him sit up.

'What the hell just happened?' Eyes asked him.

Wind Talker crawled along the floor, his head turned to one side so as not to look where he was going and he reached blindly with one hand as he approached the box, quickly flipping the lid closed and hiding its contents from view.

'That,' he panted, 'is one interesting painting.'

'Painting?' Weaver asked, reaching for the box.

'Don't open it!' Wind Talker yelled.

She ignored him and lifted the lid, Stalker winced, waiting for the same reaction, but nothing happened. Weaver sat on the floor looking into the box with her head cocked to one side.

'Huh,' Stalker uttered and crawled over to have a look too. She steeled herself against whatever she was about to see. It was a long, thin painting on canvas, mounted on a wooden frame. Looking at it made her head ache instantly; it was a cacophony of swirling colours forming spirals that almost seemed to move as she tilted her head this way and that.

Wind Talker jumped to his feet and made grumbling noises behind her and she tried hard not to laugh. He came up behind them and looked cautiously over Stalker's shoulder, one eye closed. Nothing happened.

'Huh,' he echoed Stalker's previous sentiment. 'There's a demon in it.'

Everyone looked at him.

'It's fine,' he reassured them and bent to pick up the box. The pack moved into the kitchen and Wind Talker put the box on the table for them all to examine more closely. 'It's dormant now; it used all of its energy on me back there. It's The-Madness-of-Spirals-of-Bright-Agony.'

'You're going to have to explain to me what that means,' said Eyes, leaning over to peer closely at the painting.

'I would if I could, but that's all I know. But as an initial bit of guesswork I'd say it's a demon of the insanity aspect of someone called Spirals-of-Bright-Agony.' Wind Talker poked the painting and raised an eyebrow.

Weaver made a few guttural noises and Stalker turned to look at her. Her friend looked very worried, bordering on scared.

'What's the matter?' she asked, touching Weaver's shoulder gently.

'Well, it's got to be something to do with the Spiral Hand, hasn't it?' Weaver said, her voice wavering.

Wind Talker jerked reflexively and Stalker watched as his face went ashen. Eyes looked about as confused as she felt.

'Yes,' Wind Talker whispered. 'I'd say you've hit the nail on the head. I should have realised right away.'

'What's the Spiral Hand?' Stalker asked, looking from Weaver to Wind Talker, confusion and fear mounting in her already worry-filled head.

Wind Talker closed his eyes and turned his face to the ceiling. He rubbed his face with his hands before looking Stalker straight in the eye.

'A very, very, dangerous cult.'

Chapter Six

Stalker looked at Wind Talker and back at Weaver, waiting for more of an explanation. Weaver sat down at the table and quietly closed the lid on the painting. Stalker felt the atmosphere in the room lift slightly and realised that the demon in the painting may have been dormant, but it was still exuding negative energy. Just shutting it away helped alleviate that slightly. No wonder Flames-First-Guardian had hidden it in the attic.

'The Spiral Hand is a chaos cult,' Weaver said softly, staring out of the kitchen window into the tiny garden. 'They don't worship Artemis, or any of the Gods from any of the pantheons of the realms. They worship chaos, fear, anger and every other dangerous demon.'

'Right,' Eyes said, sounding a little impatient.

'They blend in.' Wind Talker chipped in. 'They work by disrupting normal shifter activity, essentially undercover. They can be anyone, anywhere.'

Stalker reflexively looked at each of her pack mates, uncontrollable suspicion creeping up on her. She shook her head and shrugged her shoulders to get rid of it. She was being ridiculous. Wind Talker must be exaggerating for effect. But Weaver looked so scared and Eyes was frowning, deep in thought.

'What are they trying to achieve?' Stalker asked.

'They want to strengthen the demons that they worship by spreading chaos and fear,' Weaver replied. 'It's about power. They don't want to expose the true nature of the world to humanity, but they do want humans to live in fear.'

'Why? What do they get out of it?' Stalker asked. Her mind was racing.

'Power,' Wind Talker replied, his voice low and laced with worry. 'They ally themselves with the forces that, they believe, are most likely to win come Ragnarök, the apocalypse, whatever you want to call it. They want to survive.'

'Why would Flames have that painting?' Stalker asked, though she really didn't want to.

'I don't know,' Wind Talker answered. 'Perhaps he killed this Spirals-of-Bright-Agony and kept the painting as a token of the victory. Or perhaps to keep it secure and prevent it falling into the wrong hands.'

Stalker nodded in agreement, that must be the case. She felt deeply unnerved by the knowledge that there were shifters who would go against everything she had been taught about their role in the world.

'Could the Phoenix Guard have been made up of Spiral Hand?' Stalker asked.

Wind Talker shook his head firmly.

'No,' he said. 'They're a pack of Furies, like the Witches and the Rutherford Estate.'

'Furies?' Eyes asked, raising an eyebrow. 'Like from Greek myth?'

'That's right,' Wind Talker said. 'There are three sects, each named after one of the Greek Furies; Alecto, the never-ending; Tisiphone, the voice of revenge; and Megaira, envious anger. At a guess, the Phoenix Guard was aligned with Megaira.'

Stalker ran her hands over her face. It was a lot to take in. She had become used to the idea that the Furies, as she now knew they were called, had different ideas about how to dominate the demons and run the city, and even about how to interact with humans. That was a clash of ideologies, essentially political in nature. Even though Fortune had been adamant that the war between them was long term and that their differences were irreconcilable, Stalker felt that if both sides could stop killing one another long enough to talk there might be hope of peace. But the Spiral Hand sounded like a group of religious fanatics, intent upon destroying the world. She was very new to all of this and had very little experience or knowledge, but she knew bad news when she heard it.

'I really don't think it's helpful to spend too much time or energy speculating on this.' Eyes spoke up. 'We have a lot to do to get ourselves up and running. Let's try to stay focussed on things that we have some control over.'

There was a murmur of consent from the others.

'Does anyone have any ideas of where to start with looking for an ally?' the Alpha asked.

'I was thinking about this,' Wind Talker said authoritatively. 'How about the river? Our territory can easily run to the river from here, it's not that far and we should find a fae that's powerful enough for us there.'

'Agreed,' Eyes said with a nod of his head.

'I think I can repair the veil today,' Wind Talker added. 'We should do it sooner rather than later.'

'Let's do that first, then,' Eyes said with a firm nod.

The pack crossed the veil into Hepethia and set off for the ruins of the betting shop, trying to keep as low a profile as possible and avoid unwelcome attention from any demons who were unlikely to be friendly.

Stalker's muscles were tense and she kept her eyes sharp. When they had visited the site after the fire and discovered the hole in the veil, three very large, powerful demons had come crawling up from some hell dimension. She didn't know what they were going to find now. Wind Talker had patched the hole in a hurry before they left. It didn't bear thinking about what might have happened if the patch had failed already.

As they approached the site, there was a marked increase in activity. Minor fear and chaos demons scurried away from them, the shadows moved strangely and the smell of smoke still hung on the air. Police tape was still strung across the street and beyond it was the black hole in the terrace.

The pack ducked under the tape and walked cautiously down the middle of the street. The sky above rolled with white clouds and Stalker could feel the eyes of a hundred demons and fae on them. Her eyes darted to every movement but nothing came forward. As her gaze fell on the hole great sadness welled up inside her and she burst into tears. Weaver took her hand and squeezed it. Eyes placed a warm hand on her shoulder and Wind Talker looked visibly moved to be back here too.

The patch had held. Stalker could feel that there was still a tear in the veil, but it wasn't hanging wide open. She peered carefully into the hole in the ground. She could see right down into the core of the earth and into some other hellish realm that lay beneath the surface of Hepethia. Looking up into the sky there was a similar hole in reality and through it she glimpsed shimmering gold and light. All around the hole was a thin, clear film. The patch. It formed a sort of tunnel between worlds, anything could still move freely through the tunnel, but they couldn't get out at this stop, like a lift shaft with a set of doors that wouldn't open.

'Nice work, Wind Talker,' she whispered.

'Thank you,' he replied, with a small smile. 'I did my best in a hurry. The real fix will be harder.'

He directed the rest of them to take up positions around the hole, which for Stalker meant picking her way carefully across the blackened rubble, right along the edge of the hole, to the other side of the terrace. She stood alone, guarding the site from demons that might want to interfere in their work. On the other side of the maw, Wind Talker was setting up his ritual while Weaver and Eyes took up positions a little further away to guard him. There was no sound. It was like looking through a slightly blurry window and Stalker had to fight the urge to reach out and touch the patch.

She turned her attention to the street. A small, tabby

cat was slinking its way towards her on the other side of the street. She watched it carefully, it wasn't a shifter. It stopped a few feet away and sat down to wash itself. After a few minutes it stood up, stretched and trotted across the road towards her. In the pale sunlight, the cat shimmered slightly, betraying its fae nature.

'Hello,' it said silkily, rubbing up against her legs. Stalker was slightly surprised, but bent to stroke the glossy fur.

'Hello,' she replied.

'Terrible business,' the cat sighed.

'Yes,' Stalker said sadly.

'You were one of them. What are you now?' The cat asked her.

'I'm not sure yet,' she replied honestly. 'Were you here when it happened?' Stalker asked, a sudden spark of hope flaring inside her.

'I was,' the cat replied.

'Did you see what happened? Who did this?' Stalker felt desperate for answers and here was a creature that could provide them.

'Didn't you ever hear what curiosity did?' The cat asked. It stood and began to walk away.

'Yes, of course!' Stalker snapped in frustration. 'Killed the cat.'

'Exactly,' the cat said quietly, glancing over its shoulder before it blinked out of existence. Stalker's heart hammered in her chest. She felt angry and sad and more than a touch confused.

'What does that mean?' she shouted.

No reply came.

Stalker looked around for a sign of the fae, but it was gone. She caught sight of Wind Talker across the hole. He was sitting cross-legged on the floor, deep in meditation. Behind the patch she saw the layers of reality slowly being drawn together. Wind Talker was like a surgeon, patiently sewing together each layer like flesh and skin, all with his mind. It occurred to Stalker how powerful shifters could be. Their actions could tear holes in the fabric of reality, but they could also mend them. It was a huge responsibility.

'Well, well,' a soft voice interrupted her reverie. Stalker spun on the spot and came face to face with a shadowy figure, roughly human in size and shape, but almost featureless. It shimmered and shifted about, preventing her from latching onto any one aspect of it.

'What are you?' she hissed.

'Well, that would be telling,' it replied, a smirk in its voice. 'But I do love to tell.'

Stalker was sick and tired of riddles. She reached for a sword, but realised she didn't have her dha with her, and she snarled in frustration.

'What do you want?'

'I wondered when you would be back,' the figure said, gesturing across the hole to the others. 'I was waiting a little longer than I had anticipated. But these things are usually worth the wait.'

'Well we're here now. What do you want?' Stalker asked again, losing patience.

'Blue Moon, Blue Moon, obedient to the crazy lune,' it sing-songed.

Stalker felt anger rise in her chest.

'What are you saying about my pack?' she growled.

'I'm not supposed to say, it's a big, big secret.' There was a grin in its voice, though Stalker could see no mouth.

'Tell me!' Stalker felt herself starting to shift, the rage was taking hold. What was this thing trying to tell her? Was it some sort of demon of deception or corruption? Whatever it was, she knew it was a threat and it was hinting at disparaging comments about her beloved fallen pack mates. Her body shook and began to shift.

'Now, now,' it said, startled at her angry response. 'No need for that, I'm sure. Don't you want to know the truth?'

But Stalker was tipping over the edge, no longer quite capable of rational thought, and she launched herself at the demon. She ripped into it with her fierce claws and teeth, pulling it easily to pieces. How quickly it came apart, like it was ready to spill its guts. As she shifted down into her human form, the rage having subsided with the kill, she realised that she had done something very wrong.

Chapter Seven

Weaver came running to her, skirting dangerously close to the hole, which was visibly much smaller now.

'Are you okay?' she asked as she skidded to a halt.

'Fine,' Stalker replied, still shaken. 'It was some sort of deception demon, it was lying about the Blue Moon and I think it was going to attack and stop us from mending the veil.' She knew she was lying and a nasty lump sat in her throat. She didn't think Weaver could tell, if she could she showed no sign of it and simply gave her a quick nod.

'You did the right thing then, taking care of it.'

Stalker tried to smile.

'Has Wind Talker nearly finished?' she asked, looking over to him and seeing that the veil was nearly repaired.

'Yes,' Weaver replied. 'It won't be long now. I'll keep you company.'

They stood in silence, watching the street for signs of interference. After a few minutes, Stalker felt the patch dissolve and turned to look. It fell like a cloth falling from a table, a small ripple and then a clear view across the rubble of the old betting shop. Wind Talker was on his feet, his hands raised and his eyes on the sky.

Stalker bent and touched the ground. It was burned but whole, the sky was filled with ordinary clouds. You would never have known there had been a gaping wound across all the worlds here. She took Weaver's hand and they picked their way across the rubble to meet the others.

'Well done.' Eyes patted Wind Talker on the back. 'Next stop, the river.'

With barely a pause, the four of them set off west, towards the snaking river that ran through Caerton and had formed the western border of their old territory.

Stalker ran over in her mind the strange encounters she had had, first with the cat and then the demon. Guilt gnawed at her along with the nagging sensation that all was not as it seemed.

As they approached the river bank, Stalker could hear the lively activity across the river, in St. Catherine's. She remembered fighting the chaos demon near Red Bridge with Eyes and Fortune and felt a stirring of painful emotions at the memory. Fortune leading the fight with his huge war hammer, the exhilaration of fighting together with members of her pack for the first time and the pride and joy of Fortune singing her praises afterwards.

This side of the river was quiet, Hepethia had not yet caught up to the fact that the Blue Moon were gone and as yet there was no pack working to keep the population under control.

Wind Talker moved carefully up to the bank of the

river, which was concrete here. Closer to the outlet into the estuary the banks were mud and silt. The tide was fairly high and the river flowed past them, foam clinging to the concrete wall below as rubbish floated past. Stalker wrinkled her nose against the polluted stench.

Wind Talker looked up and down the water, there was no sign of activity. He took a knife from his bag and held out his forearm, his sleeve was already pushed up and with a swift movement he sliced a deep cut into his arm and twisted it to make the crimson blood drip into the murky water.

Below them, the water started churning and bubbling. Eyes and Weaver took a reflexive step back but Stalker leaned forward to get a better look. Blood kept dripping from Wind Talker's arm and Stalker looked up and down the river for signs of a reaction from the river elementals, beyond the bubbles below. Movement caught her eye, something was speeding up the river towards them, she could see the ripples on the water forming a V shape as something swam quickly just under the surface. It stopped a few feet out from the bank where she and Wind Talker stood and then burst up through the surface, sending water cascading over it as it rose up to eye level.

Stalker jerked into a defensive stance. An old woman hovered before them, perched on a fountain of bloody, murky water. Her skin was green and she wore rags. Her teeth were black and broken, her nails were long claws and her hair was a tangled mess of wiry black that clung to her face and hung down her back. Stalker flinched away from the hideous hag, but Wind Talker stood firm.

'What do you want?' The demon hissed at him.

Stalker flinched, but held her stance. They had been looking for a fae, a creature of water and nature, not this thing before them. She glared at Wind Talker, wondering whether he was expecting this demon or not. Wind Talker glanced at Stalker, there was a hint of uncertainty in his eyes, but he blinked and it was gone. He cleared his throat and stood tall and proud.

'Jenny-of-the-River, greetings. We come to petition you to serve as our ally.'

Stalker looked at Eyes, his face was full of worry, and Weaver was hanging her head. Stalker had a terrible feeling about this. Their old patron, Grins-Too-Widely, had been an ancient fox shifter who had grown so old that he had lost his humanity and become a creature of Hepethia. He had worn a permanent grin on his face that made him extremely creepy to look at, but she only ever got a positive vibe from him. That was not what she was getting from Jenny-of-the-River.

The demon grinned, her black teeth gnashing together greedily.

'I'd be delighted to serve a fine young pack such as yourselves.' Her voice dripped with sickly fluid in her throat and Stalker cringed. 'All I ask in return is the blood of the occasional child.'

Wind Talker nodded as though this were a perfectly reasonable request.

'No,' Eyes stated firmly and turned to leave.

'Alpha,' Wind Talker called, halting Eyes in his tracks. 'I believe we should consider this offer.'

Weaver looked at him, her eyes wide with horror. Stalker shook her head and tried to make sense of why he would be willing to go down that route.

'I don't think we can do that, Wind Talker,' she said softly. 'Come on, let's go and look somewhere else.'

The ritualist looked back at Jenny, and with an apologetic sigh he bowed his head to her.

'I regret, we cannot accept those terms.'

Jenny hissed and spittle flew from her mouth, splattering Stalker in the face. She winced and wiped her skin with her sleeve. Jenny's fierce eyes blazed and Stalker tensed again, certain for a moment that an attack would come, but the demon released a rattling breath and sank back down into the river. The pack set off away from the bank and Stalker fell into step next to Wind Talker.

'You can't have been serious,' she said, looking at him carefully as they walked.

'Of course I was serious,' he replied. 'Whoever we get to be our ally will require some display of loyalty and service from us in return. If we want a powerful ally we may have to settle for something that we might have found unsavoury in our old lives.'

Stalker gawked at him.

'Well, let's not drop down to the murder of children as a first step,' she huffed. 'Let's see what other offers we get first.'

Wind Talker shrugged in half-agreement and Stalker dropped the subject, reeling in shock from his coldness.

The four of them walked in silence for a few minutes, Stalker had no ideas for what they might try next. It was just starting to rain, but in true Hepethia style the drops of rain were even more effective at getting them wet than their human world counterparts, and within moments

Stalker was soaked to the skin. She thought about how wet Caerton was, it was part and parcel of living on the estuary. She looked up at the sky overhead, the clouds were dark grey and purple and rolling over one another. There was a flash of lightning on the horizon and a few seconds later the rumble of thunder reached them.

'Huh,' she said with the realisation of what should have been obvious to all of them. The others turned to look at her. 'How about a weather elemental?' she asked.

'That is a really good idea.' Eyes gave her an appraising nod.

'Where will we find one?' she asked, and almost as one, the four of them turned to look up at the telecoms tower in Redfield, just north of St. Mark's. It was by far the tallest structure in north Caerton and on both sides of the veil it was a dominant metal tower with a glowing red light at its tip. The Blue Moon must have willed it into being in Hepethia, and Stalker couldn't help wondering why.

They set off at a run towards it, eager to get there and potentially find themselves an ally. They crossed Hepethia quickly and found themselves at the base of the tower. It stood alone in the middle of an industrial wasteland, surrounded by a rusted mesh fence that was easy to get past at one of the flimsy joints.

Stalker looked up and saw lightning flash overhead as thunder crashed above them at the same time; they were right below the storm. Stalker grabbed hold of the nearest section of the metal tower and started climbing. The others were quick to follow and they climbed with varying degrees of skill up the great tower.

Stalker reached the top first, followed by Weaver.

Eyes clambered up somewhat ungainly and Wind Talker was the last to arrive, almost losing his footing at the last moment, but with a hand from Eyes found his feet on the solid surface at the top. They were standing on a platform with a tall spike jutting out of the middle up into the sky, the red light blinking at the top. Stalker looked out over Hepethia. From this great height she could see for miles. Some areas were recognisable landmarks from Caerton, like the river, snaking its way north towards the estuary. Others were a warped version of their human world counterparts, like the maze-like streets of St. Mark's. But patches gleamed even in the dull sunlight, the crystals of Hepethia shone in a rainbow of colours dotted around the landscape where shifters had had no reason to influence the area.

Stalker turned her attention upward. Thick clouds billowed and rolled overhead, but the storm had paused. Wrapped around the light at the top of the spire was a twisting, almost translucent creature that shifted form the way clouds did.

Wind Talker squinted up at it and gasped.

'What? What is it?' Eyes asked.

'The-Lord-of-Storms-and-Rain,' Wind Talker whispered in awe. 'Or in other words, Thor.'

Stalker whistled softly, impressed. She was familiar enough with Norse myths to know of the god of thunder. His father, Odin, was among her patrons, as she was a member of Odin's Warriors. She never expected to meet Odin, or Artemis or any other deity. They were supposed to be distant beings living in other realms. What was Thor doing here in Hepethia?

They watched as the The-Lord-of-Storms-and-Rain conducted the storm around the tower as if it were an orchestra. Around the edges of the platform were small beings of static energy scuttling about, they were almost invisible but Stalker caught fleeting glimpses of many tiny limbs and they sparked as they moved. She got the impression that they were biding their time, hoping to get the chance to pounce on the shapeshifters.

The Lord circled above and when he finally caught sight of them he rushed down and landed on the platform with a surprising thud. He took a roughly man-like form, but still towered above them all in height.

'What are you doing here?' he bellowed at them with a strong gust of wind.

'Lord-of-Storms-and-Rain, we are seeking a patron and would be honoured if you would consider the role.' Wind Talker spoke in his most commanding voice, though Stalker sensed a hint of humility. She thought Wind Talker was being rather ambitious in making this request, but she remained silent, intrigued to see how this would play out.

The god swirled around them and didn't respond. He swept over them and covered them briefly, leaving Stalker and the others feeling very cold and wet.

'You!' He twisted around and a long arm with a pointing finger darted out of his cloud-like body directly at Stalker.

'Me?' she asked meekly.

'You can fly!' He started laughing and Stalker tensed up, suddenly certain that he was going to throw her off the tower. But he just hovered there, pointing at her chest. She glanced down and caught sight of her necklace, resting against her skin. Her fingers went to it and she smiled in recognition.

'Sort of,' she replied. The others looked at her with mixed expressions of surprise and relief.

She jumped up and hovered in the air about a foot from the platform. The-Lord-of-Storms-and-Rain howled with laughter and clapped his hands, flashes of lightning burst around them and claps of thunder accompanied each clap of his hands.

The levitation only lasted a few seconds, however, and Stalker drifted silently back to the platform. The god stopped laughing abruptly and scowled at her. Stalker's thoughts cleared and she was struck with the idea of shifting form. Her unique ability to take any animal form was sure to have an impact on this deity. With a little focus, she shifted into a beautiful, graceful snowy owl and soared around the spire of the tower. The Lord-of-Storms-and-Rain cheered her on again and when she landed on her human feet he seemed satisfied.

'I am a being of the sky. Not a groundling like yourselves. More shapeshifters really ought to dedicate more of their time to learning how to join me up here.' His voice barked and he spread his arms wide, looking up into the thunderous clouds.

'May we request then that you suggest one of your orchestra to serve us?' Stalker asked, taking the lead for the pack and playing on the favour he showed her.

The Lord turned his shapeless face to her and out of nowhere a bolt of lightning struck the tower, sending a burst of electrical current through the metal structure. Stalker felt the shock and heat rushing through her flesh, and rage started to shake her body but she closed her eyes and breathed deeply. Odin's gift of restraint ran through her hot veins and the rage didn't take control. Slowly she opened her eyes again.

The others were shaking fiercely and before her eyes Fights-Eyes-Open shifted into his Agrius form with a roar and attacked the powerful deity before them, quickly followed by Wind Talker and Weaver. Stalker was the only one to retain control and the fight could not be prevented. With a groan, Stalker forced her body into the small form of a bat and darted underneath the Lord-of-Storms-and-Rain to support her pack against this formidable foe. Perhaps she could at least prevent the god from swatting her pack like flies.

She flitted around him to distract him while the others clawed and bit at him. Despite his cloud-like form he was definitely solid and a few good blows were landed by her pack as the rage took control of their bodies and compelled them to attack.

The static fae remained on the sidelines, but seemed to be cheering their Lord on in their squeaky voices. Stalker slipped past him, avoiding his crushing fists, but the others weren't so lucky. The Lord slammed a fist into Eyes and electrocuted the Alpha, sending him flying back from the fight. He went skidding across the metal and at the last second grabbed the edge of the platform, narrowly avoiding a lethal fall.

Weaver also took a hefty blow and Wind Talker's hair ended up standing on end with the static from a few very near misses. Stalker kept up the distraction and hoped that one of her pack mates would be able to take advantage of her actions.

Weaver crept up on the Lord from behind and leapt onto his back, digging her huge claws into his shoulders. The deity roared and reared up like a huge horse, his arms flailing and trying to get purchase on the pesky shifter at his back. Wind Talker and Eyes dashed in low and hit him hard in the chest and the Lord writhed away from them, rising up into the air. Weaver leapt down before he got too high and the pack stood tall and proud, looking up at him as he twisted back up his spire, retreating from them.

'You can have my son, Bound-and-Chained-Lightning,' he bellowed down at them. 'You will find him there.' A long arm spiked out from his reeling form and a flash of lighting darted down from the sky. The pack looked quickly across Hepethia to see where it would strike. It impacted half a mile away to the south, in the heart of St. Mark's. 'He is a grave disappointment to me, restrained to the earth through sheer incompetence. But maybe he will be good for something. If you can free him he will serve you.'

The pack retreated quickly to the edge of the platform and shifted back into their human selves. The static fae were getting very excited and Stalker wasn't sure they would hold back much longer.

'We thank you for your cooperation,' Eyes barked at him with a curt nod of the head before beginning the long climb down. Weaver followed but Wind Talker looked over the edge with trepidation. Stalker looked back up at the Lord, with what she hoped was a pleading expression. The deity huffed, showering her with fresh rain, before a cloud fae came swirling down from the mass above and scooped up Wind Talker, collected Weaver and Eyes on its way past and floated the rest of the pack gently to the ground. Stalker, however, took a running jump and felt the wind rushing past her as she dropped like a bullet towards the ground. Her heart raced with exhilaration as she fell. Ten feet from impact her talisman kicked in and she gradually slowed down and drifted gently to land next to her pack mates, smiling serenely.

'Thank you,' Eyes said with evident relief.

'No problem,' Stalker replied.

'I didn't know you could levitate,' Wind Talker said, looking at her with wonder.

'I've hardly had chance to test it. Shadow's Step gave me the amulet the morning of the attack.' She stroked the clay gently. Weaver gave her a sad sort of look and Stalker gave her a small smile to let her know she was okay. 'It just works for a few seconds no matter what height I jump from.'

'We should go,' Eyes interjected.

The pack set off at a run, heading south to the spot where the lightning had struck. The air was still buzzing with static when they got there. There were tiny ripples coming off a mound of pure crystal. It gleamed silvery blue in the late afternoon light and the sides jutted up from the smooth ground to form a wall over six feet high. The afternoon was drawing late and the tumultuous sky overheard was darkening, the storm was abating, the Lord having tired himself in the fight, but the rain persisted.

Stalker approached the mound and clucked her tongue in thought.

'I guess we need to get inside,' she said quietly. Weaver came up beside her and placed a hand on the crystal.

Stalker copied her and felt the cool, hard surface against her palm. She pressed hard against it and felt a little give. She glanced at Weaver, who looked surprised and quickly retracted her hand. Stalker persisted and felt the crystal softening and warming. She watched in wonder as it slowly melted away from her palm and a small opening appeared. It wasn't a mound at all, it was an impact crater. She looked around at the others, unable to hide her excitement and beamed at them. Eyes watched carefully, a small smile playing on his lips. Wind Talker frowned, caution written on his broad face.

Stalker took a step into the opening and stopped short, her gaze settling on the snake-like elemental curled up and glowing bright blue-white. It was about six feet long and the light radiating from it rippled along its supple body. It had huge chains shackled around it and rooted into the crystal floor.

'That must be him,' she whispered, looking over her shoulder at Wind Talker for confirmation. He peered around her and gave a single nod of his head and the four of them filed carefully in through the doorway and stood and watched the elemental for a minute.

Eventually he raised his head and looked at them with lamp-like eyes, obviously not surprised to see them.

'Hello.' The fae's voice was little more than a crackle of electricity, but the one word somehow came through clearly.

'Hello,' Wind Talker replied and took a few steps closer. 'Bound-and-Chained-Lightning, are you all right?'

Stalker was taken aback by the concern in Wind Talker's voice and she smiled to herself.

'Who? Me?' The elemental lifted himself up more, looking at Wind Talker with wide eyes the colour of a tropical sea. 'I don't know. Am I?'

Wind Talker glanced back over his shoulder and gave a shrug to Eyes, clearly unsure how to proceed. Eyes moved up to stand next to him and looked thoughtfully at the elemental.

'Do you know what you are?' Eyes asked him.

'Lightning?' the elemental asked in a childlike voice. 'Electricity?'

He seemed to be confused. Stalker and Weaver moved closer. Stalker felt so sorry for him, he was caught in a confusing limbo state between the two forces that made him, with powers pulling him in two directions at once. She could relate.

'Can you tell me what I am?' he asked, his eyes almost seemed sad. He was hard to read.

'Power,' Stalker replied without thinking, looking into his deep blue eyes.

There was a sudden shimmer from the elemental, he shook all over and flexed from nose to tail. Everyone jumped back as sparks flew off him and scattered across the floor. He flared up bright white, filling the whole crystal cage with blinding light and Stalker covered her eyes and turned away.

The light dulled and she looked back at him. He had grown; his chains had tightened around him but were still intact.

'Thank you,' he said, his voice suddenly older and with more of a crackle to it. 'Things feel clearer now.'

Stalker grinned from ear to ear and looked back at her

pack. They were smiling too.

'We're a new pack and need an ally. Are you willing to support us in establishing ourselves?' Eyes asked, stepping forward and speaking kindly but with an edge of authority.

'Yes. If you will free me,' the elemental replied.

'Consider it done,' Eyes said with a firm nod.

Stalker looked around at the crystalline cage and the chains that bound this beautiful fae to the ground. It was raw Hepethia, alien and incredible. Making one small hole in the wall had taken a great deal of focus and mental energy, to break Bound-and-Chained-Lightning free would be a massive effort. She grasped Weaver's hand and they exchanged determined glances.

'We'll need to all work together,' she said quietly.

'Can we change this?' Eyes asked, raising a sceptical eyebrow.

'I think so,' Stalker replied, trying to keep the doubt from her voice. She focused her thoughts on breaking the crystal chains that snaked around Bound-and-Chained-Lightning, willing the fae to be free from its bonds. The chains began to shimmer and shake and the fae within them flexed. A crackle of electricity issued from it and it suddenly glowed brighter. Stalker was distracted for a moment, in awe of the beauty of the fae before them, but she quickly refocused. The chains were trembling and clinking slightly, making strangely melodic sounds.

She felt Weaver's hand tighten on hers and a smile burst onto her lips; they were doing it. The chains began to creak and strain and suddenly a single link snapped, splintering into two pieces that scattered across the smooth floor. Another quickly followed and the fae rapidly expanded, free to move more than it ever had. With one last flex, the remaining chains snapped and Stalker reflexively shielded her face as the small pieces went flying in all directions.

Bound-and-Chained-Lightning soared into the air and seemed to explode into a thousand stars, scattering tiny sparks over the shifters below. Stalker squinted, shielding her eyes with her hand as she tried to watch the fae. The explosive flare died down and in place of the snake was a beautiful silver dragon flying in a figure of eight above them. He was a wingless, Chinese dragon, all rippling muscles and a bobbing head. He flickered constantly, like lightning behind clouds. Stalker drew a slow breath and looked around at the others.

'He's beautiful,' Weaver whispered.

'His name has changed,' Wind Talker said, his voice full of wonder. 'Unchained Lightning,' he added slowly.

'I love it,' Stalker said, a bright smile lighting her face.

'Unchained Lightning,' Eyes called out. The fae stopped circling and looked down at them. 'Will you honour our agreement and help us?'

'The honour is mine,' the fae replied, and he landed in front of them with a soft thud.

'Excellent,' Eyes said. 'Then let's begin.'

Chapter Eight

Fights-Eyes-Open

THE PACK ARRIVED BACK AT 32 GROVE STREET buzzing with adrenaline. They tumbled through the front door into the narrow hallway. Stalker was the first to stop laughing and chattering, going very still in the midst of their celebrations. Eyes noticed and placed a gentle hand on her shoulder. She was sniffing the air and she took a small step down the hall away from him. He felt it then, the prickle on the back of his neck that told him something wasn't quite right.

The others fell quiet and Eyes watched as Stalker edged towards the kitchen, her hands lightly brushing the walls either side of her.

'What's happening?' Wind Talker whispered from the back.

'Something's wrong,' Eyes whispered back.

Stalker shifted into her fox form as she approached the kitchen door, and she sniffed carefully around the back of the house. Eyes followed her, glancing cautiously up the stairs as he passed them. He pointed up with a firm look back at Weaver and Wind Talker, and they obediently slipped quietly up the stairs to check the rest of the house.

Stalker was sniffing at the back door and she turned her head back to look at him with imploring eyes. Eyes went quickly to the back door and unlocked it, and they went out into the back garden.

Eyes looked carefully for physical signs of an intruder, but there were none.

'I'm crossing over,' he told Stalker. 'Do you want to join me?'

She nodded and the two of them crossed over into Hepethia. Unchained Lightning was there, curled up and taking up a good portion of the small garden. Eyes bowed to the fae, who looked up lazily before dropping his head again. He was clearly tired from his efforts in breaking free of his prison.

Stalker sniffed around the garden and then shifted form.

'Someone's been here, but the scent is really faint. I can't tell if I even know it, never mind who it is.' She confirmed what Eyes suspected.

'Unchained Lightning, mighty fae of power, have you sensed anyone else's presence since arriving here?'

The fae opened a sleepy eye and closed it again.

'No.' He rumbled, like far off thunder.

A quiver of the veil caught Eyes' attention and Wind Talker and Weaver stepped across to join them.

'What's going on? We found no sign of an intruder in the house,' Wind Talker said, striding over from the kitchen doorway.

'We're not sure,' Eyes replied.

'All I can tell is that it was a shifter,' Stalker said, frustration showing in her voice.

'That's fine.' Eyes tried to reassure her. 'No one expects you to have all of the answers all of the time. There seems to be nothing we can do about it right now, we'll just have to be vigilant. There was nothing missing?' he asked, turning to Wind Talker.

'Not that I could see from a quick glance,' he replied. 'I can look more carefully though.'

'Yes please,' Eyes said swiftly.

Stalker shuffled her feet a little, looking down at them and Eyes was reminded of himself as an insolent teenager. He remembered that she still was a teenager. The realisation sent a painful pang through his heart. She was too young to have to deal with all of this. He cleared his throat, needing to move them all on from this unsettling discovery of an intruder. 'We have another important matter to discuss. We need a name.'

Weaver looked at him with her piercing blue eyes.

'We're not the Blue Moon any more? Are we?' she asked.

'No,' he replied. 'No we're not. That pack was destroyed. Theodore advised me to get out from under their shadow and start fresh. I can't put my finger on why, but it feels like good advice.'

Wind Talker nodded, his face hard to read. Eyes didn't like that. He wished he understood his most enigmatic pack mate better.

'Do you have a suggestion for a new pack name?'

Weaver asked him, a glint in her eye. She knew the answer. Had she already seen this moment or a future one in which the pack's name was evident? Eyes smiled and nodded.

'The Lightning Lords,' he said, looking firmly at their new ally. Unchained Lightning opened his eyes and lifted his dragon-like head.

'That pleases me,' he crackled.

'I like it,' Stalker said, smiling and nodding appraisingly.

'Me too,' Weaver chimed in.

Eyes looked to Wind Talker, who simply nodded his approval.

'That settles that then,' Eyes said, with a sigh of relief. His nerves were jangled from the discovery of the intruder, but settling the pack name so easily felt like a positive accomplishment.

Wind Talker set about preparing some food, the others chipped in to help and Eyes sat at the table listening to their lively chatter as if through an invisible wall. He had felt it ever since they agreed that he would lead them, a distance suddenly present between him and the others. It was as if he could no longer be their brother, now he was their father. He was responsible for them and had authority over them. It immediately created a gulf. Somehow Fortune had managed to bridge that gap in the Blue Moon; he had been father, brother and friend to all of them. He thought carefully about how Fortune had achieved such a complex relationship with such ease, and doubted whether he could ever replicate that.

Sadness crept in at the edges of his thoughts and for a brief moment, Eyes allowed the feeling to step forward. He allowed himself to feel the loss. He saw Fortune's smiling face before him, felt his arms around him in a fatherly embrace and heard the pride in his voice at his ear. Eyes knew he would never get that back, Fortune was gone.

That night, Eyes stayed at Grove Street with the pack. Having to go home to his family had been a major barrier to his integration into the pack and he knew he was going to have to work extremely hard to find the right balance.

The four of them settled down on the cushions in the living room in their animal forms and slept until dawn.

Eyes woke to the vibration of his phone nearby. He shifted form and looked with bleary eyes at the screen lit up in the near-dark of dawn. He didn't recognise the number. He stood gingerly, making sure not to step on any paws or tails as he moved into the kitchen to answer the call.

'Hello?'

'It's Scribe,' the young voice said quietly. 'Apologies for the early hour.'

'Not a problem,' Eyes said, perking up. 'How can I help you?'

'Last-Breath-Echoes and I have made arrangements to hold the funeral on Tuesday the fourth, just before midnight in Crescent Park. I hope you can all be there.'

'Of course, yes,' Eyes said hurriedly. 'Do we need to do or bring anything?'

'No, just yourselves,' Scribe said softly, an edge of sadness to his voice. 'I am so, so sorry for your loss.'

'Thank you,' Eyes replied, wearily rubbing his face with his hand.

The line went dead and Eyes put the phone down

on the kitchen table. It was not quite 7am. There was no daylight yet and the house was still and quiet, but for the soft breathing of the three sleeping shifters in the next room.

Eyes took a deep breath, blowing out all of the tension and sadness that he was carrying. *Enough,* he told himself and set about making breakfast for his sleeping pack mates.

Chapter Nine

Stalker-of-Night's-Shadow

Stalker woke to the sound of sausages frying and the low rumble of voices in the other room. She stood up and shook out her fur, stretched her stiff legs and then shifted gracefully into her human self. Weaver was just waking up too, and the two of them moved into the kitchen together, arm in arm, without a word.

Eyes and Wind Talker stood at the counter making breakfast and talking quietly.

'Morning,' Stalker said sleepily. 'What time is it?'

'Just gone seven,' Eyes replied.

Stalker sighed. She had never been a morning person, though since her change it had been easier to survive on much less sleep. The last few nights her sleep had been restless and plagued by nightmares. Before the attack on the Blue Moon she had frequently dreamed of Rhys. Her thoughts went to the pained look in his eyes when she had stumbled away from him during their kiss. She had to try and make things right, she had to know if she still had a future with him.

She gratefully took a plate of bacon and sausages and lingered a moment next to Eyes as Wind Talker took two plates to the table for himself and Weaver.

'Eyes,' she said quietly. 'I need to do some damage control today. I was with someone the other night, when–' her words faltered. He nodded in understanding and placed a gentle hand on her shoulder.

'Do what you need to do. We can manage here.'

'Thank you,' she whispered and gave him a small smile. They joined the others at the small table and she ate quietly, thinking of what she was going to say to Rhys when she saw him. Assuming he would agree to see her.

Stalker waited for the sun to rise, out of courtesy, before sending Rhys the message, though she supposed he would already be up and on his way to work. Normal human life seemed such a distant memory to her, she had almost forgotten that at this time of year people trudged out to work daily before the sun came up. She knew that she would need to return to work in the next few days, and decided to go and see her boss, Ron, later too.

> Hi Rhys. I really hope you're ok. I was hoping you'd be able to see me today. Lunch? I really miss you and need to talk to you. Love A xx

She hit "send" and stared at her phone, waiting for the reply. The pack busied around her, tidying the breakfast things and making plans for the day. The next few minutes seemed to last an age, but finally her phone lit up with the reply.

Of course I can meet you. I'm so glad you asked. I really need to see you and see that you're OK. Same place as last time?

She breathed a sigh of relief and was finally able to smile. It seemed a lifetime since she had managed a real smile. She replied confirming their plans.

Stalker had a shower and changed her clothes, and anxiously waited to leave the house. Around her the pack buzzed like worker bees, though she didn't know what they were doing. She couldn't think about anything other than Rhys and the nervous knot in her stomach.

At last she stood to go and headed for the door. Wind Talker nearly bumped into her in the hall and she fumbled an awkward apology.

'Are you heading out?' he asked.

'Yes, I'm heading for the bus stop on the high street,' she replied.

'I'll go with you, I'm going that way myself.'

Stalker smiled and let him lead the way. She felt immensely private about Rhys, he was something from her old life and she felt instinctively that she needed to keep him separate from all of this. Somehow, letting her pack know about him felt like dragging him into their business. She supposed it was the same for all of them. None of them talked about their human friends or families. Even Eyes was very private about his wife and daughter.

Stalker and Wind Talker walked briskly through the biting cold to the main street a few blocks from their little terraced house. The traffic was heavy and the pavement was busy with people dashing about their business.

The two shifters strode purposefully towards the row of bus stops just down the street. People looked anxiously at them and gave them a wide berth. Stalker still wasn't used to the intimidating presence that she had. When she was on her own it wasn't too bad, but the more shifters you put together the stronger the effect.

She briefly wondered what a human would feel if confronted with the entire assembly of Odin's Warriors, her second shifter family. They were all fearsome warriors who had dedicated themselves to Odin, the god of war. There were over a dozen Berserkers in Caerton, and the gatherings she had attended before the disastrous attack on the Blue Moon had been somewhat lively affairs involving ritual combat and tattooing, as well as heavy drinking.

Stalker's hand went instinctively to the fresh tattoo on the back of her neck, though thanks to her rapid healing you wouldn't know that it was only a few days old. It was the rune that marked her as one of Odin's Warriors.

'This is my stop,' Wind Talker said, suddenly breaking the easy silence between them. Stalker looked up and noticed that buses from this stop went north, to the docks.

'Where are you going?' It suddenly occurred to her to ask.

'To see the Storm Riders,' he said quietly, glancing around at the passing people. 'How about you?'

'Oh, just into town to see a friend,' Stalker said, keeping it vague. 'I'll see you later.'

Wind Talker nodded and Stalker went on her way to her bus stop.

She did as Fortune had instructed when she first

changed and was sure to disembark the bus before entering Burnside, the territory claimed by the Glass Wolves. She walked from the edge of Chinatown south into the unclaimed city centre and made her way through the bustling streets to the café near the Central School of Martial Arts, where Rhys worked.

When Stalker walked into the café she felt a little prickle all over her body as she sensed him, he was already there, standing at the counter ordering something. She took a few steps towards him and she saw the moment he sensed her too. His head jerked and he looked around to locate her. The relief in his face was unmistakable and she closed the gap between them in seconds. He took her in his arms, holding her head against his chest and kissed the top of it.

'Thank God,' he whispered against her hair. 'I'm glad you're OK.'

'I'm fine,' she whispered back. It wasn't totally true, she wasn't fine, she wasn't going to be fine for a long time. But she was surviving.

The barista behind the counter cleared her throat and Stalker let go of Rhys so that he could pay for their coffees.

'Let's sit down with these and we can order food in a minute. Is that OK?' he asked. Stalker nodded and turned to find a table.

They got seated and Rhys immediately grasped her hands across the table and leaned close. 'I was really worried about you,' he whispered.

'I'm sorry,' she said, looking down at their entwined hands. She felt terrible. They had shared a passionate kiss up on the cliff in Fenwick the night before she changed for the first time and she had collapsed in his arms then. The next time they kissed she had felt the bond with her pack break and ran away from him. It must look so bad to him, yet here he was, holding onto her hands so tightly that she was sure her circulation would be suffering if she were normal.

'It doesn't matter. You're OK, that's what's important.' Rhys reached a hand out and stroked her face. She tilted her cheek into his hand and felt the warmth of his palm against it.

It felt so good to be with him, so right. She longed to feel his lips on hers again, preferably without any interruptions. She wished she could just let everything spill out though, that she could tell him everything about her life and explain why she had run away the other night. But she had to protect her secret life and it made her insides ache to withhold so much.

Reluctantly, she pulled away and took her jacket off. She turned around to hang it on the back of her chair.

'Oh,' Rhys said, startled. 'You got ink?'

Her hand went back to the tattoo on the back of her neck, exposed for the first time.

'Oh, yeah,' she said, smiling. 'Do you like it?'

'Yeah. Is it a rune?' he asked, frowning.

'Yeah,' she faltered, thinking furiously for a meaning that she could share. 'It means something to do with wisdom.' A half-truth. Odin was also a god of wisdom, as well as war. Rhys nodded in appreciation.

'Nice,' he smiled warmly at her.

They ordered food and lunchtime passed all too quickly before he had to head back to work. They walked out of the café together, Rhys's hand on her back right where her swords would be if she had them, but they were still at her flat. As they stepped outside she swung her jacket on and turned to face him. She didn't want to leave his company and return to the dingy house in St. Mark's and she leaned against him, resting her forehead on his chest. He stroked her back and stepped closer to her. She looked up into his dark eyes and he leaned close to kiss her. His lips brushed hers softly, his hand went to her cheek and she felt the butterflies swarming in her belly.

She broke the kiss reluctantly and gave him the best smile she could manage when it caused her so much pain to be saying goodbye.

'This was really nice,' she said softly.

'Yeah, it was,' he replied, returning the smile. 'Are you able to meet me on Tuesday night? I could cook dinner for you at my place.'

'That would be really, really great,' she grinned. 'All being well, yeah, that sounds like a good idea.'

Rhys kissed her again and Stalker's heart pounded so hard in her chest she thought he might hear it. As they parted, Stalker was smiling and their goodbye was a happy one, full of promise. Stalker didn't stop smiling all the way back to St. Mark's and if anyone gave her a wary look, she was blissfully ignorant.

She decided she needed to get off the bus at her flat and collect her dha. She had dropped the precious swords off at home on the day of the attack on the Blue Moon, which with hindsight, proved to be very fortunate. Her flat was just the same as always, gathering dust through lack of use. Her post was piling up and she spent a few minutes checking through it. There was nothing that seemed remotely important, not now. Bank statements and phone bills were the least of her concerns.

She hurriedly collected the swords from her wardrobe, where she kept them secure in their carrying case and left her flat. It hardly felt like hers any more and she had no real desire to return to it. The betting shop had become her home and now 32 Grove Street was. She had nothing tying her to this place now. Yet she was reluctant to let it go. Something inside her told her to keep a place of her own, just in case. *In case of what?* she asked herself. But there was no reply.

Stalker took the familiar walk from her flat to the dojo where she worked. It was high time she checked in there and made arrangements to return to work. It had been more than two weeks since she changed and the excuse of bereavement only bought her so much time. She needed to protect her income and more than that, she wanted to return to work and see her students. She had always loved teaching and she really wanted to go back to it. She just didn't feel ready yet. If the Blue Moon hadn't been destroyed then she would have felt ready, but the devastation was a serious blow. She had used the excuse of a bereavement to buy time and life had turned it into a reality. That was karma, she supposed.

She approached the familiar corner building, the abandoned electronics shop with the lively little independent dojo above it, and made her way up the narrow staircase inside. The office door stood open, as it usually did, and her boss, Ron, sat tapping away at his computer. She knocked on the door and he looked up, surprise and recognition lighting up his round, red face.

'Ariana!' he cried, standing up to greet her. 'How are you, love?'

She couldn't help but smile, and walked into his cluttered little office.

'I'm okay, thank you,' she replied and approached him for a brief hug. 'How have things been around here in my absence?'

'All right,' he said, sitting back down as she took the chair opposite him. 'It's not been easy, but we managed. We're really looking forward to you coming back.' He gave her a hopeful and cautious look, as if he was expecting her resignation.

'Oh me too, Ron,' she reassured him quickly. 'I can't wait to come back.' The lie tripped off her tongue too easily.

'Oh good,' he sighed. 'I've got your normal classes scheduled to start the day after tomorrow. Normal Tuesday groups through the afternoon. Is that okay?'

'Yes, that's fine. Thanks.' It would be a big day of normality for her, work, followed by a date. She stood to go and gave Ron a parting smile. Sadness tugged at her, though she didn't really know why. She was leading a double life, and somehow she knew that it was going to be incredibly hard.

Chapter Ten

Fights-Eyes-Open

Eyes looked out of the living room window anxiously as the street light outside flickered to life under a darkening sky. He knew that on the other side of the veil, somewhere nearby, there was a reasonably powerful demon snaking its way through pools of light, feeding off the energy of the lit streets. The Lightning Lords had a new ally who fed off power energy, all sorts of power, but chiefly electrical power. They also had an intruder. They needed to defend their territory and to do that they would need more allies.

He went to Weaver, who sat drawing at the kitchen table.

'The plague doctor again?' he asked, looking over her shoulder at her sketch.

'I can't get it out of my mind. This is a message from Artemis, I'm certain of it. It's a gibbous moon in the vision too, which is what it is now.'

He rubbed his eyes hard with his fingers. *One thing at*

a time, he told himself.

The front door opened and he looked down the hall to see who it was. Stalker walked in, looking like a weight had been lifted from her shoulders. She smiled warmly as she walked up the hall and entered the kitchen.

'Good day?' Eyes asked, curious to know where she had been and with whom.

'Yes thanks,' she replied.

Eyes hoped for her to elaborate, but he wasn't going to actively pry. He missed the pack telepathy that Grins-Too-Widely had granted them. Unchained Lightning hadn't given them the same power, Eyes didn't know yet what their new ally could do for them and given the state they had found him in, he doubted that even the fae himself knew.

'I collected my swords,' Stalker said, beaming.

She hoisted up the bag in her hand to show them.

'Oh,' Weaver said, looking up from her furious scribbling. 'I'm glad they're safe. I assumed they'd been in the shop.'

'No,' Stalker replied. 'I'd taken them back to my place the day that it happened.'

A dark flicker passed across her face, Eyes noticed, he felt it like a ripple around the three of them. Sometimes it felt like they were all trying too hard not to mention the Blue Moon and what had happened to them.

'Good timing,' Eyes said quietly. Stalker nodded and put on a brave face.

'So, what's happening?' she asked.

Eyes tried to find the words to answer. He knew they needed to act, and he had a hunch about what might work, but he wasn't certain and he was reluctant to come out with half a plan.

The front door opened and slammed shut with a bang as Wind Talker stormed up the hall, his face fuming.

'What's wrong?' Eyes barked.

'Weird fucking shit!' Wind Talker bellowed.

He walked to the corner cupboard and pulled out a bottle of whiskey and a small glass, poured himself a shot and knocked it back. Everyone watched him. Eyes studied him carefully.

'How did it go with the Storm Riders?' he asked tentatively.

Wind Talker barked with laughter that bordered on hysterical.

'Fine,' he said, his laughter stopping suddenly. 'Fine. I saw, I saw something in Hepethia.' Wind Talker poured another shot and knocked that one back too.

Eyes tried not to laugh. He didn't know Wind Talker nearly as well as he knew the women. He was something of an enigma.

'What did you see?' Weaver asked, moving closer to Wind Talker and gently sliding the bottle along the worktop away from him.

'Ha!' Wind Talker barked again. 'That's not really important. The more pressing issue is the Knights of St. Catherine's coming onto our territory to mug people. That is the real issue.'

Eyes felt his stomach tense up.

'Who are the Knights of St. Catherine's?' Weaver asked with an exasperated sigh.

'A human gang,' Eyes replied. 'I've had dealings with

them from time to time, in court.'

He remembered a case a year or so ago, involving a young lad who had been charged with aggravated assault. He had been the prosecuting barrister. Eyes had won.

'What were they doing on this side of the river?' Stalker asked.

'I don't know,' Wind Talker said, some calmness returning to him. 'I witnessed the mugging; they had this guy down an alley and knifed him. I chased them off and tried to get this guy to hospital, but he wouldn't go. So I walked him home instead. I don't know how bad it was, maybe it was just a scratch, but I could smell the blood.'

'We'll need to do something about the Knights, we need to keep them out of our territory,' Stalker said calmly. She still had her sword bag in her hand and Eyes noticed her thumb caressing the handle. She was right, and if his plan worked, it would be the solution to both the Knights and the intruder.

'I have an idea,' he said authoritatively. 'A couple of days ago I encountered a demon on our territory that might be able to help, if we can ally with it. Let's cross over now and see if we can find it.'

'OK,' Stalker and Wind Talker said at once. Stalker immediately got her swords out and strapped them to her back, where they disappeared; their magic melding them to her body until she needed them, in whatever form she might happen to be.

Weaver hung back a little and Eyes caught her arm and looked searchingly into her eyes.

'What? What is it?' he asked quietly.

'I'm not sure,' she whispered, shaking her head.

'Nothing, don't worry.'

Eyes reluctantly let go of her arm and marched to the back door. He trusted Weaver's judgement above any of the others, but she had to learn to trust herself too. If she wasn't going to open up and give him her opinion outright then he would have to go ahead without it.

The four of them crossed the veil and found Unchained Lightning making slow, lazy circuits of the small garden. He looked at them as they appeared and came to a gradual stop, his long body rippling. The whole garden glowed with his white light.

'We're going on a hunt,' Eyes told the fae. 'Would you care to accompany us?'

The elemental flexed and his light brightened for a moment, then he lifted his head and soared up and over the roof of the house towards the street.

'I think we can take that as a "yes",' Stalker said with a smirk.

Eyes smiled and led the pack back through the house and out onto the street. He stopped to close the door and placed a hand on the plain, black surface.

'Lock,' he commanded. Sure enough, there came the clunking sound of a bolt followed by the rattle of a chain. Hepethia had obliged with some basic security. 'Wow, I wasn't sure that would work.'

Weaver smiled and gave him a little wink.

Unchained Lightning swooped over the roof and up into the sky towards the clouds. Eyes watched for a moment as the bright white flared up against the dark sky and then disappeared through the clouds.

'He'll be back,' Eyes said, half to reassure the others,

who looked on with worried and quizzical expressions, half to convince himself.

The four of them set out from the house, walking cautiously up the middle of the road with Stalker taking the lead. Her senses were sharper than the rest of them, so she was the obvious choice to track.

Hepethia always made Eyes uneasy. The streets were usually too quiet and he could feel the buildings and shadows watching them. He didn't have the first clue how to find the dragon-like demon that he had seen, he just hoped that it would find them.

They walked for a few minutes, trying several different streets. Eyes was just beginning to wonder if he needed to do something to attract the demon's attention when Stalker held up a hand to halt them. Eyes heard it then, a moaning sound and a softer, slithering sound. He moved up next to Stalker and they took a few cautious steps forwards towards the street corner.

Eyes peered around the corner and saw the demon making slow circles around a lamp post. He indicated to Wind Talker, who came up and looked carefully around the corner of the building.

'Its name is Holds-to-the-Light,' he whispered.

The demon stopped in its tracks. It turned towards the four shifters huddled at the corner and sniffed its way towards them. Eyes took a breath and stepped out of the shadows to confront Holds-to-the-Light.

He had intimidated the thing once already and he hoped that it remembered and would be subservient to him. It was bigger than he remembered; it lifted up at the front and towered over him. A lump rose in his throat and he felt Weaver and Wind Talker just behind him, there to back him up.

'Holds-to-the-Light.' He greeted the demon with as much command to his voice as he could muster. 'We are here to enlist your help in protecting this territory, our territory. We will ensure good street light coverage in exchange for your assistance.'

The demon regarded him for a moment and Eyes felt a glimmer of hope, just for an instant. Then the attack came.

The dragon lunged at him and would have swallowed him whole if he hadn't just managed to dive to the side in time. He shifted form with a roar and leapt up to fight. The others shifted too and began the assault, four impressive Agrius, snarling and ready for action. Eyes jumped onto the dragon and dug his claws into its back. The demon roared and reared up. Eyes was thrown down onto the street and he rolled reflexively away and up onto his feet.

The dragon had no feet and sort of hovered a few feet above the ground. It twisted around and repelled attacks from the others as Eyes watched for a few seconds to assess the situation. Stalker came bounding across the street and drew her swords.

The dragon swiped at Eyes and knocked him to the ground, it pounced on him, pinning him down and Eyes struggled against his enormous bulk as the huge, black teeth lowered slowly towards him. He was vaguely aware of the chaos around him but all he could see was the orange light shining from inside that mouth, and then he felt the teeth sink into him and everything went black.

Chapter Eleven

Stalker-of-Night's-Shadow

'No!' Stalker growled. She leapt forwards and drove both swords into Holds-to-the-Light's neck. It released its grip on the Alpha and recoiled away from them. Her swords left two long rips in its body, and glowing, orange ichor spilled out onto the road.

Wind Talker and Weaver pounced, ripping into the gashes left by Stalker's swords and pulling scales off the dragon. Stalker slipped under the dragon and sliced at its belly with her swords as it twisted and writhed around, trying to shake them off.

Weaver went flying and landed with a crunch on the road, and Wind Talker slid down the dragon's side; his feral claws were still digging into it and they ripped it open as he fell. The demon roared and backed away from them.

Stalker sensed rapid movement above her and looked up into the black sky. Racing down towards them was a lightning bolt, Unchained Lightning. He hurtled down from the sky and struck Holds-to-the-Light. Stalker felt the impact vibrate through the ground and up into her body, and the electrical discharge filled the air, erecting all of the hair on the shifters' bodies. Holds-to-the-Light slunk slowly away up the street, dripping its orange blood as it limped away. Smoke rose from the ground where Unchained Lightning now stood.

Wind Talker stood nearby, panting. Weaver dragged herself to her feet and limped over to them. Eyes lay unconscious on the floor, his blood spilling onto the tarmac. Stalker ran to his side, shifting form and sheathing her swords fluidly as she ran.

'Well, that worked well,' Wind Talker scowled.

'We have to get him back to Grove Street,' Weaver said authoritatively.

The three of them hoisted Eyes up off the ground and carried him awkwardly back around the block to the house. The locked door opened for them as they approached and Stalker stared at it as they squeezed through the narrow passage with Eyes propped up between them.

They crossed the veil and carefully laid Eyes down on the sofa. His body had morphed back into his human form and was trying to heal itself, but he hadn't regained consciousness yet. They watched and waited. Wind Talker paced a lot and occasionally bent over Eyes to examine him.

Stalker felt utterly useless. Their Alpha was seriously wounded, it was by far the worst injury she had seen since she changed, and she had no clue how to help him.

'Wind Talker?' she asked at last. 'Can you summon a healing fae to help him?'

'Yes, of course.' He rushed away to fetch supplies. Stalker wiped sweat off Eyes' face with her sleeve. He was so hot and his body suddenly began to convulse.

'Hurry!' She called out. 'It's not looking good here.'

She heard heavy footsteps thundering down the stairs and Wind Talker burst back into the room. He passed Stalker a green candle and Weaver a white one then sprinkled some peppermint oil onto Eyes' torso. Eyes winced as the tiny drops of oil made contact with his open wounds. Wind Talker ran to the kitchen and came back with a bag of salt, which he split open and scattered all over the floor.

Wind Talker lit the candle that Stalker was clutching, his hands far more steady than hers, his face impassive. He went to Weaver and lit her candle too, then moved across the room and turned to face them, so that they formed a rough circle. He raised his hands and began to stamp a rhythm with his foot, which Weaver and Stalker quickly copied.

'I call upon the beings of healing, those who live to mend bones and heal wounds. Hear us and grant us audience.' Wind Talker's voice was steady and commanding, but Stalker saw hesitation in his eyes; he was nervous. He was normally so composed and difficult to read that she often forgot how newly changed he was himself, and that he was just a beginner with these rituals.

The circle throbbed with energy, however, and she felt the veil ripple softly. She was suddenly acutely aware that they were in the human world, not Hepethia, and she worried about the neighbours hearing anything they shouldn't.

The veil parted and through it came a floating column of shimmering light, right into the centre of their circle.

'Greetings,' Wind Talker said and bowed his head.

'Can you help us?' Stalker asked, feeling the urgency of their situation. The strange light swirled around slowly to face her and Eyes, who lay gasping for breath on the sofa. A beautiful sound filled the air, like wind-chimes, and Stalker felt calm wash over her. The shape before them began to change, slowly becoming more humanoid. It lacked facial features and the whole thing still shone brightly.

'Yes.' Its voice was soft and musical. Hands appeared out of the light and rested on Eyes for a moment. The angel-like fae stepped back and began to change again. The light faded slightly and a face took shape, a cruel, mocking face in darkness, like a photographic negative. 'I will heal him, but I require payment.'

'Anything,' Wind Talker said urgently. Stalker flashed him a worried look.

'I live to heal,' the creature said. Stalker was no longer certain that this was a fae; it had taken a demonic turn. 'I require injured bodies in order to live. Send one to the hospital for me to heal. That shall be your payment.'

'Done,' Eyes croaked. Stalker's gaze darted to him. She had thought he was unconscious.

'We'll do as you ask,' Wind Talker said. 'Please heal him now.'

The demon moved to the Alpha's side and placed its hands upon his chest. It flared up bright again and threw its head back. Eyes shone too, filled with healing light, and he took a sudden gasp as his chest was lifted towards the ceiling. Stalker watched in awe as his visible injuries healed in moments.

The demon released him and he dropped back onto the sofa. It moved away and re-took its slowly spiralling column form. Eyes sat up and felt his side where Holds-to-the-Light had bitten him. Stalker watched in awe as they all realised that his injuries were completely healed.

'Are you okay?' Weaver asked, taking his hand and touching his face.

'Yes,' he replied. 'I feel fine. Thank you,' he said to the demon with such depth that it turned towards him and seemed to bow. 'We'll fulfil our side of the bargain as soon as possible.'

The shimmering column of light glowed even more brightly for a moment and then spun suddenly across the veil. Stalker placed a hand on the Alpha's shoulder, relieved that he was healed, but guilt gnawed at her insides already at the price they would have to pay.

Chapter Twelve

'WHAT WERE YOU THINKING?' Stalker said quietly, a dark edge to her voice as she stared down Eyes and Wind Talker. 'We cannot possibly be seriously planning to go out and deliberately injure people in order to feed this healing demon's desire.'

'That was the price for healing the Alpha,' Wind Talker replied, as cool as ever.

'Eyes was dying, Stalker,' Weaver said gently. 'We had to take what we could get and this is the way it works sometimes. Demons, angels, everything in between, all beings in all the realms ultimately need to feed, and a healing angel feeds on healing. It can't do that without sick and injured people. That's the way the world works.'

'We just need to find someone who deserves to be hurt,' Wind Talker suggested. Stalker could not believe what she was hearing and she threw her hands up in the air.

'Who the hell are we to dish out judgement like that?

Who decides what crimes are punishable by a good beating?'

'We do,' Eyes said calmly. 'We do it all the time in our dealings with demons and fae. What about that gang? The Knights of St. Catherine's? We could track down one of them and give him a taste of his own medicine.'

'Eyes!' Stalker shouted. 'You are a barrister! Is that the kind of justice you seek in court?'

'This is totally different.' He sighed, rubbing his forehead. Stalker watched him carefully for a moment and decided that he was trying to convince himself of that. 'We'll head out this afternoon to track down a Knight and just hurt him enough to get him to the hospital. It's not like I'm advocating killing anyone.'

'Agreed,' Wind Talker and Weaver said together. Stalker looked around at them incredulously. It seemed she was outnumbered, and she grudgingly succumbed to the will of the pack and the authority of her Alpha. She felt sick to her stomach, though. Today they were plotting to beat up a gang member. What would it be tomorrow? She could see what a slippery slope they were on and it was with a very heavy heart that she went along with the plan.

'Everyone get some rest now,' the Alpha commanded, and they all obeyed. Stalker didn't sleep, she sat on the sofa watching the others and fought her heavy eyelids. Her mind churned with recent events and she felt the weight of it all.

After a few hours the others woke and they all ate a quick meal in uneasy silence.

'Stalker,' Eyes said softly as they moved towards the front door. 'I know how you feel about this. Thank you for agreeing to come. Please could you take a useful tracking form to help us find one of the people that we're looking for?'

Stalker scowled at him and didn't reply. She shifted into the form of a bloodhound and pushed past him to get to the front door.

They set off towards where Wind Talker had witnessed the attempted mugging the previous day. It was late afternoon and the streets were busy with traffic. When they reached the alley, Stalker had a good sniff around. She picked up four scents, one of them was her pack mate. She followed the scents out of the alley and tried to focus on sorting one from another. She could tell that the four people had gone off in pairs in different directions, so she followed the pair that did not include Wind Talker. Just as predicted, the trail led towards the river and across a bridge to the north. They crossed into St. Catherine's and Stalker led the way, trying to keep hold of the dissipating scent as the sun set.

She rounded a corner and was immediately struck by the strong smell of dozens of men. She looked up and saw that they were across the street from a lively biker bar. Loud music filled the air and people were shouting and laughing outside. Most of the men were wearing leather jackets and some had balaclavas tucked into back pockets or even perched on top of their heads. This was Knight territory, they were safe from the law and the general population were too scared of them to do anything, so they could wear their uniform openly here.

'What do we do?' asked Weaver.

'We wait for one or two to break away from the group,'

Eyes whispered, his eyes fixed on the crowd. 'We can't let them identify us when it happens.'

His caution hung in the air and they all exchanged nervous glances. The weight of what they were doing settled on all of their shoulders.

They waited just around the corner in a secluded alley for what seemed like hours, though Stalker knew time passed strangely when she was in non-human form. Night fell and the lights from the bar lit up the street. She spotted two gang members saying their goodbyes. They crossed the road, heading straight towards the waiting shifters. She alerted the others with a whimper and Eyes shifted into his wolf form in the shadows. Weaver and Wind Talker held back a bit, their animal forms were less helpful in a fight and they couldn't risk shifting into their Agrius forms and being seen.

The Knights strode towards them, laughing and talking loudly. As they approached, Eyes sprang from the cover of the alley and sank his teeth into one of the men.

There was a flurry of screaming and yelling. Instinct took over, and Stalker lunged for the other man and bit into his calf. He yanked his leg away from her and ran as fast as he could back towards the bar. She knew this was about to get very messy and gave a short, sharp bark as she set off away from the scene.

The others didn't follow and she skidded to a halt to look back. Eyes was pinning the other guy down, snarling threateningly at him, while Wind Talker approached him carefully from behind, a large chunk of brick in his hand. He raised the brick and brought it down hard on the man's head, knocking him unconscious. Stalker watched in shock as Wind Talker quickly rifled through the Knight's pockets and pulled out a mobile phone.

The rest of the pack ran quickly towards Stalker, who stood in stunned silence as they approached. Wind Talker had the stolen phone to his ear as they fled.

'We need an ambulance,' he was saying hurriedly as the four of them jogged back towards St. Mark's. 'A man has been attacked in an alley opposite The Dog and Spoon in St. Catherine's, he needs an ambulance.'

He hung up without leaving his details, then hurriedly scrubbed his finger prints off the phone and tossed it into a rubbish bin.

Stalker didn't go back to Grove Street with her pack. She went back to her flat without a word, and in the safety and comfort of her own little space she broke down in tears.

She showered and changed her clothes, renewed tears breaking out every few minutes with the horror of what she had been a part of. She lay down on her bed and cradled her phone; she was desperate to reach out to someone and the words of Shadow's Step came back to her. *Sometimes you will need those who loved you before to remind you of all that you are.*

With a shaking hand, Stalker tapped out a message to her best friend, Ben.

> Hi there stranger. Did you have a good time in Rome? I can't wait to hear all about it. Feels an age since I saw you. Love Ariana xx

Then another to Rhys.

Hi. How are you? Been a weird few days. Would love to chat, if you're free.

She instantly regretted it. There was nothing she could tell him about her life now. She had no one outside her pack to confide in, and it stung. Her phone buzzed and made her jump. She opened a message from Ben.

Rome was amazing. OMG! It was so romantic. I thought Marcus was going to propose at one point, but he didn't. I was a bit disappointed at first but I dunno, I think I was caught up in the mood. I don't really want to get married and settle down yet anyway lol! How the fuck are you anyway?

Stalker laughed a little and wiped her face. She remembered her old life, her friends, her old name. She felt nineteen again, if only for a moment.

Glad you enjoyed it. Phew, good job he didn't pop the question then, really. I'm OK. Miss you though. Drinks some time soon?

She watched the screen, waiting for the reply.

Defo! Bit busy catching up at work this week, but am free on the 11th.

Stalker grinned and hurriedly replied.

Sounds good. TTFN x

A moment later a new message came through from Rhys.

Hi, so sorry to hear you're having a hard time. Are we still on for dinner tomorrow night?

Stalker had forgotten their plans and groaned when she realised she was also due to return to work the next day.

> Absolutely. Looking forward to it. I'm working until 5.30. Can get to your place for about 6.30. That OK?

The reply came just moments later.

> Yeah, perfect. See you tomorrow xx

Stalker tried to smile. She was exhausted. She hadn't slept in two days and it hit her now. Just as she was drifting off, her phone rang and with bleary eyes she looked to see who was calling. It was Eyes. With a sigh she answered.

'Hi,' she said, trying not to sound too negative.

'Hi. Are you okay?' he asked.

'Yeah. Look, sorry for disappearing on you. I have to go back to work tomorrow, so I just need some time to myself to regroup and feel more human.'

'Yeah, I understand. I'm back at work tomorrow too. I'm heading home myself tonight. It's the funeral tomorrow. In all the chaos I forgot to tell you. We're meeting the others at Crescent Park just before midnight.'

Stalker groaned and ran a weary hand over her face. Tomorrow was shaping up to be another eventful day.

'Okay. Of course. I have plans for earlier in the evening. Can I meet you there?'

'Sure. I hope you have a good day. Sleep well.' Eyes spoke with heaviness and Stalker sensed that he was feeling the weight of everything they had been through just as much as she was. He was her brother, she loved him dearly and she did understand that he had done what he needed to do. He needed to survive. Not just for their pack, but for the Blue Moon, for their sacrifice to mean something and for his human family.

She turned her phone off and lay down. Sleep took hold of her in minutes. She dreamed of Shadow's Step. She saw him as clearly as if he were really there in front of her. They were sparring in the basement of the betting shop. His tiny rune scars glistened on his torso and his face passed in and out of the shadows as they danced around each other. She saw Fortune watching them and felt his fatherly love touch her heart. She became afraid; she felt she had disappointed her mentors, though she wasn't sure which of her actions were responsible.

It was mid-morning when she woke, by far the longest she had slept in weeks. There was a strange tapping noise coming from the kitchen and she became alert in an instant. She slipped out of bed and crept silently to the bedroom door. She peered carefully out into the open-plan living area. The noise was coming from the window in the kitchenette, a rapid tapping and scratching sound. Slowly she made her way towards it and was startled to see a huge raven pecking and scratching at the window. She went to it and quickly opened it. The bird hopped in and landed next to the sink. It squawked at her and shook its wings. Tiny black feathers dropped onto the worktop and she watched in amazement as they arranged themselves into words.

Crescent Park, tomorrow at 9pm. Odin is calling.

It was a message from Odin's Warriors. Two evenings in a row at the same place. She had passed it many times in her human life and never noticed anything about it, other than its distinctive shape. Clearly it had significance to shifters, however.

With a parting croak, the raven hopped onto the window sill and flew away. Stalker closed the window and drew a deep breath. It was going to be a long, taxing day.

Chapter Thirteen

Stalker arrived at work with a knot in her stomach. She walked past Ron's office and could hear him talking on the phone. She went into her studio and started dragging mats from a pile in the corner and set them up for her judo class. Her mind was racing with everything that had happened in the last few days, and the weeks before that. Her life had turned upside down and being here, in this ordinary place, made her extremely uncomfortable.

At 3.20pm her students started to arrive, fresh from school and stamping out the wet and cold from their feet as they entered. The noise made Stalker flinch, her heightened senses assaulted by the volume of the teenagers as they spilled into the quiet room.

She slapped on a smile and greeted her students warmly.

'Welcome back!' A young boy called brightly, and several others joined in. Two girls rushed over to her and caught her in a tight embrace. Stalker laughed and hugged them back. Warmth filled the room and she felt more at ease.

'Thanks, guys.' She beamed. Most of this class were not much younger than her, and before she had changed she had counted some of them as friends. 'Come on now,' she called out, turning on her teacher voice. 'Shoes and coats off, please. Find a space and take a knee.'

Stalker got the class doing warm-up drills and assessed them for any sloppiness that had crept into their practice during her absence. She didn't know who had been teaching them, but she could see that a few of her students had started to develop bad habits. Soon she was into the swing of things and it was as if she had never been away. She walked around the class as they practised some simple throws, correcting a few people here and there.

One boy was struggling to get his partner over his shoulder and she stepped in to help. 'You can do this, Joey,' she said, gently parting the two boys. She moved Joey aside and stepped into his place. 'You need to get yourself a little lower, bend the knees so that your shoulder is just here.' She pointed to the chest of the other boy and grasped hold of his judo jacket. He was so light, and as she lifted him and threw him over her shoulder everything felt wrong. He dropped to the mat with a sickening *thunk*.

The class had stopped and all eyes were on them. Stalker dropped to her knees, panic pumping through her veins.

'Are you all right?' Joey asked, kneeling at his friend's side.

'I am so sorry,' Stalker said, deep worry filling her as

the kid gasped for breath.

'Yeah,' he choked, trying to sit up. 'Just a bit winded. I see your muscles haven't atrophied while you've been away.'

Everyone laughed and Stalker smiled with relief.

'No, I guess not.' She stood up and helped him to his feet. She decided it would be best not to do any more practical demonstrations if she could help it, and got the group doing more drills.

Stalker had to get through two classes that afternoon. She tried to avoid contact with her students as best as possible and had to hold back when she did have to get in and demonstrate something. It was incredibly difficult for her, and as she talked to her Bando class about the cobra system she had to fight away the images of Shadow's Step transforming into a cobra in front of her in the basement of the betting shop.

At the end of the day, she didn't linger long to chat with her students. She made a slightly hasty exit and went home to get ready to see Rhys. She didn't have a lot of time and rushed to find clothes that were comfortable and just a little bit sexy. She listened to the radio as she applied a little make-up and hummed along to an upbeat song to try and get into a good mood. She wasn't planning to spar with Rhys, so her super-hero strength shouldn't be a problem, but she knew that she was going to find it hard to keep her mind on him given that she was leaving him later to go to the funeral.

She considered cancelling her date, but then what would she do to pass the time instead? She knew she would sit around growing more anxious and dwelling on things that she couldn't change.

She rushed out of her flat and jogged to the bus stop, only just reaching it in time. She watched the bright lights and bustling streets of China Town through the window, and got off the bus before passing into Burnside. It was a short walk directly across the city centre to where Rhys lived, and as she approached her mind flooded with the memories of when she had last been there.

She walked quickly up his street to his door and paused for a moment on the step; she composed herself and firmly pushed aside the feelings that threatened to overtake her. She took a deep breath in order to gather her resolve, and then rang the bell. She heard movement inside and a moment later the door opened. Rhys smiled warmly down at her and scooped her up into his arms.

'Hi,' he breathed into her hair.

'Hi,' she said with a smile.

Rhys released her and led her inside. The front door opened right into the living room, which was full of books, CDs and DVDs. A sofa sat in the centre of the room facing a wall-mounted TV, and a door at the back of the room led through to the kitchen.

'Come on in, let me take your coat.' Rhys fussed around her and she sensed that he was nervous. She stifled a small laugh and let him help her out of her coat. He took her hand and led her through to the back room. A delicious aroma and the sound of something simmering met them as they entered the kitchen. A small table and chairs sat against the wall; it was neatly laid, with a candle in the centre.

'Oh, this is lovely,' Stalker said, taken aback.

Rhys returned her smile and hung her coat on a hook in a little alcove, where a staircase led up.

'It's not much,' he said modestly. 'I hope you like stew.'

'I do,' she replied. She took a seat and watched him potter about the kitchen. He looked so at ease, this was the most comfortable she had ever seen him. 'It smells great.'

He glanced at her and gave her a satisfied smile before turning back to the stew. She watched him adding a few herbs and stirring. He began dishing up two portions and brought them to the table, then turned off the main kitchen light. The candle light was just right and Stalker gazed at him across the table as she waited for her stew to cool a little.

'How are you doing?' he asked solemnly, his kind eyes fixed on her. She looked deep into them and for a second felt as if he knew everything that had happened. She felt a wave of sadness and wanted nothing more than to leap into his arms and pour her heart out. Rhys blinked and that apparent depth of understanding vanished. Stalker shook her head a little, ridding herself of the tears that threatened to spill; and tried to smile.

'Not bad, thank you,' she replied. 'Work has been a bit stressful and it's been hard not seeing much of any of my mates. Ben was away and has been too busy with work to catch up since he got back. So I was going a bit stir crazy.'

'I know that feeling. Sometimes it feels like I spend all my waking hours working.' He picked up his spoon and dipped it into his stew. Stalker copied him, suddenly remembering her food. She took a mouthful; it was delicious.

'Lovely,' she said, smiling at him. She was an atrocious

cook and had survived on convenience food and eating out before she had changed. Now there was usually someone around to share the cooking with, and she had managed to disguise her ineptitude relatively well. She tucked in, pausing between mouthfuls to chat about what little she could share with him. He talked to her about his work and their shared music and film tastes.

After they had eaten, they moved to the sofa and sat facing each other, chatting animatedly. It was so easy and Stalker began to feel almost human. Rhys held her hand and stroked it as they talked. Every now and then his other hand went to her shoulder or leg and each time he touched her she felt sparks. She longed to kiss him and gradually they inched closer together.

Eventually their conversation began to dwindle and Stalker could feel the tension building between them. Rhys twisted his fingers in hers and looked down at their joined hands. His other hand went to her face and gently cupped her cheek. She tilted her face into his caress and closed her eyes. Their faces drew closer, his entwined hand released hers and snaked around her back. He grasped her and pulled her closer, planting his lips on hers in a passionate kiss.

Stalker sank into the moment, losing herself utterly. She threw all caution to the wind and manoeuvred herself onto his lap, still kissing him. Her hands twisted into his hair, his hands gripped her hips and their kiss became frenzied.

Stalker broke the kiss in order to breathe, and she held his head firmly, her eyes fixed on his. She needed to see into his soul. For a brief second his eyes were totally open to her, just as they had been just before they ate. She could see right into him. Suddenly that door slammed shut and he grabbed her, throwing her roughly back onto the sofa before climbing on top of her. She grinned, welcoming a little roughness, and wrapped him up in her arms and legs as they resumed their passionate kissing.

After a while, a sense of unease began to prickle at the edge of her awareness. Stalker broke the kiss and pushed him gently away. She looked around the room for a clock, but couldn't see one.

'What time is it?' she asked, her voice a little husky.

Rhys frowned a little, but tugged his phone from his pocket and checked it.

'Just gone 8.30. Why? Do you need to be somewhere else?'

'No,' she replied quickly, seeing his slightly hurt feelings. 'Sorry, come back here.' She grinned and pulled him back down onto her body.

Hands roamed to more intimate places and Stalker longed for more and more. Yet something tugged at her senses and she wasn't quite able to get back into the mood. She fought the sensation with all her might, but a voice popped up in her mind cautioning her not to ignore her instincts.

With a burst of strength, Stalker flipped Rhys over and onto the floor, landing on top of him and grinning wickedly. He grinned back and pulled her head down to resume kissing her. She pinned him to the floor and surreptitiously looked around the room while his eyes remained closed. She couldn't see much while sprawled on the floor with her lips locked to his but she didn't think there was anything to see anyway. She didn't quite understand the feeling, but it still gnawed at her.

She broke the kiss and locked eyes with him as his flicked open.

'Are you okay?' he asked, frowning again.

'I think so,' she replied, distracted. She reached out with all of her senses and tried to latch onto the strange feeling. She looked into his eyes, searching again for that openness. But it eluded her, his eyes were just ordinary eyes.

'It sometimes feels like you're a million miles away,' he said quietly, his eyes searching hers this time.

She slid off him and lay down next to him, propped up on her elbow.

'Sorry,' she whispered.

'No, it's okay. If there's anything you want to tell me, you can. But you know, if there are things you can't tell me, that's fine too.'

She looked at him quizzically. She felt again like he knew everything and was being extremely sympathetic.

'That goes both ways, you know?' she said, stroking his chest idly with her fingers.

There was the strangest moment, like he wanted to tell her something, but it quickly passed and again he closed up. Stalker knew in that moment that there was something between them that couldn't be spoken; a mutual understanding that they both had secrets and were honour-bound to keep them. A quiet acceptance settled over her. She had no right to judge him for holding something back. The secret she was keeping was enormous. Whatever his secret was, it couldn't possibly match her own.

She leaned in for a more gentle kiss. His hand caressed her face and he returned the tender gesture. When the moment passed, they lay staring at each other. Stalker took a deep breath and closed her eyes. She remembered where she needed to be in a few short hours and sadness settled on her heart.

'Shall we put a DVD on?' Rhys asked quietly. She nodded, opening her eyes, and he helped her back up onto the sofa.

'Something funny, please,' she requested, and he obliged.

They sat in easy companionship, watching a classic comedy and laughing at all the best bits. Stalker snuggled up against Rhys's chest and listened to his heartbeat. She drank in his scent and contemplated the day that she would fully claim him as her mate. But not today, not now. Her heart needed to be with her lost pack mates now, and as the final credits rolled it was with great sorrow that she said goodbye and parted from his company. He saw her out of the door with such quiet sympathy, again she got that feeling from him that he knew where she was going, and as she walked slowly up the street his door stayed open as he watched her go.

Chapter Fourteen

Stalker approached Crescent Park with a deep sadness clinging to every pore. There was a white van parked on the street right in front of the big, wrought iron gates that stood sentinel at the entrance to the park by the river. As she drew level with the van, Eyes pulled up in his smart, black car. She stopped and waited for him to get out, and greeted him with the warmest smile she could muster.

'How are you?' Eyes asked as he approached.

'Okay, given the circumstances,' she replied. She was relieved when he leaned in to give her a hug.

'Let's go in,' he said quietly, glancing at the van.

They walked into the park together. Tall trees lined the perimeter just inside a tall iron fence. Lamp posts were widely spaced, with deep shadows between the pools of orange light. The path wound its way downhill towards the river. Trees were scattered on the hillside with pale-coloured rocks and small, bare bushes filling the spaces

The whole park was crescent shaped and at the bottom of the hill, surrounded by incredibly old and tall trees, was a small, equally crescent-shaped lawn. It was perfectly sheltered; totally private.

Stalker felt a strange calm settle over her as they approached the bottom of the slope, like still water. She suddenly realised that there was no veil here, no border between worlds. In this one small space you could be in all of the realms at once. It was deeply unsettling and yet calming at the same time; the ultimate contradiction. There were no demons or fae here, no bleeding between realms. It was a perfect still point, a place of peace.

Standing on the grass were Scribe-of-the-Fallen and Last-Breath-Echoes, with a large, lidded wooden box. Stalker felt sick, she knew what was in that box; her family.

Footsteps on the path behind them got Stalker's attention and she whipped around to see who was coming. Weaver and Wind Talker walked briskly down the path.

'Hi,' Weaver greeted them warmly and gave Stalker a gentle hug. 'Everything okay?'

Stalker nodded and the four of them set off across the lawn to meet the Scroll Keepers.

'Is anyone else coming?' Stalker asked, not sure who would answer.

'These things are usually a pack affair,' Scribe replied. 'We're here to officiate and to bring... the bodies,' he said, faltering slightly. Almost all eyes flickered to the box.

'Just one box. Not separate coffins?' Stalker asked, a little offended.

'There wasn't much left,' Echoes said dreamily. 'It was difficult to separate out...'

'Okay!' Stalker snapped, interrupting her. 'I get the idea.'

'Let's get started, shall we?' Scribe said, breaking the tension.

He handed black candles to each person, and lit them in turn. He guided the shifters into a circle around the box and stood in the space between Echoes and Eyes. Scribe raised his arms and clapped over his head three times. Stalker watched in amazement as a pale blue light radiated out from his hands and spread slowly out, forming a dome around them. She had never seen anyone cast a ritual circle this way before. The blue light shimmered slightly and seemed to block out the world beyond it. Stalker suspected that it was concealing them from human eyes.

'Welcome to the circle,' Echoes said, breaking the silence and bringing all focus back to the task in hand.

'We call upon Osiris, Lord of the Underworld, and Anubis, Guardian of the Dead, to witness our ritual.' Scribe was holding a long, thin knife, pointing it to the ground, and Stalker saw small, blue drops running down the blade and dripping onto the grass. 'We ask that you safely guide these fallen shifters to the underworld or afterlife, each according to their beliefs and wishes.'

Scribe turned to Eyes and invited him to place his hand in his own outstretched palm. The Alpha did so, and Scribe slowly pricked the tip of Eyes' finger with the knife. Scribe turned Eyes' hand over so that his palm faced the ground and a single drop of blood fell to the grass. Scribe set off around the circle, pricking Weaver next, then Wind Talker and finally Stalker. He held her eyes for a long moment as he held the knife just over her finger. He didn't need words to convey his deepest sympathy to her, and she gave a short nod of thanks.

The knife pierced her skin and Scribe turned her hand over to drip.

Echoes escaped the blood-letting and Scribe resumed his place in the circle.

'The survivors of the Blue Moon give their blood freely in honour of their lost loved ones, and I invite them now to each say a few words.' Scribe gave Eyes an encouraging smile, indicating for him to go first. Eyes cleared his throat.

'The Blue Moon was an honourable pack, they took us all in when we turned and immediately became our family. Fortune was my Alpha, my brother and my father. He died defending me and I will endeavour to be the shifter and Alpha that he would want me to be.' There was a small crack in his voice and he went quiet.

Weaver reached over and gave his hand a brief squeeze.

'The Blue Moon shared much with us,' Weaver spoke up. 'They guided us, protected us and tried to prepare us. They set us on a path and it is now ours to follow, or to stray from. Like orphan children coming into adulthood, we are now out in the world without our parents' guidance. May Artemis now guide us and shine her light on the correct path for us, the Lightning Lords, to follow.'

Stalker felt a tear prickle at her eye and sniffed it back. Weaver sounded so mature and rational, yet there was a hint of sadness to her wise words. The candle that Weaver was holding shook slightly and the light flickered eerily across her face. Stalker wanted to rush across the circle and hug her pack sister, but felt she wasn't supposed to break the ritual circle.

'We were only part of the Blue Moon for a short time,' Wind Talker said, breaking the silence and diverting Stalker's attention to him. 'But we grew as close as family in that time and they will be missed. I personally vow to uphold their honour and avenge their deaths.'

'Seconded,' Eyes said firmly.

Stalker looked around at the others. Scribe looked thoughtful, Echoes was impossible to read. Weaver was nodding solemnly.

'Me too,' Stalker said, with a slight crack in her voice. She felt eyes all around the circle fall on her. It was her turn to speak. She didn't know what to say, whatever she said it was going to hurt. She looked down at her candle and focused on the flame. She didn't want to look at any of the others. 'I didn't grow up with shifters. When I changed I had no idea what was happening to me. The Blue Moon were there for me, they took me in, protected me. Shadow's Step was,' she faltered and tears began to fall down her cheeks. 'He was like a brother to me, and the others, all of them, they truly were family and I loved them all even though I only knew them for a couple of weeks.'

She ran out of words, though there was so much more she wanted to say. There was no way to express the loss she felt, at times she was drowning in it. She wiped the tears from her face, though they continued to fall.

Scribe cleared his throat gently and stepped towards the box.

'Thank you for sharing your thoughts and feelings. We honour the fallen here tonight. Please all step over to the box now.' Scribe ushered them over and they gathered around the coffin. Scribe placed one hand on it and touched the point of the knife to the centre of the lid. Stalker looked around uncertainly, as one by one they all placed a hand on the box. 'In the tradition of the Scroll Keepers and our ancient Egyptian ancestors, we will now leave an imprint upon the box; stories of those we bury tonight. Please focus your thoughts on your lost loved ones, think of a memory, or an impression of their character.'

Stalker pictured Fortune first, standing in the kitchen of the betting shop, laughing his big, belly laugh and pulling her in for a warm hug. She remembered Speaks-With-Stone sitting close to her and asking her if she was really okay, the day after she first changed. She thought of Flames-First-Guardian casting a circle and grinning when she showed him her dha. And Shadow, her brother in darkness, her mentor, shifting between a fox and a snake. She saw the pride in his eyes when she passed the initiation rituals of Odin's Warriors. Fresh tears spilled and dripped down her chin onto the box. Weaver was crying too, as was Eyes. Wind Talker sniffed loudly, she suspected he was holding back tears.

Stalker watched in amazement as shapes began to appear on the wood. Pictures emerged, Fortune laughing just as she had pictured him, and the others. There were runes too and English writing. She spotted the rune for Odin's Warriors, which Shadow had tattooed on his hip. The writing looked like Weaver's handwriting and was appearing in front of her as her mind projected it onto the wood. Stalker tilted her head to read it but the writing was too small. The box was soon completely covered in images, runes and writing; it looked beautiful in the flickering candle light.

Scribe lifted the knife and stepped back. He indicated for the others to do the same. Stalker wiped her face and took her place in the circle.

'We bury four shifters from varying traditions and paths tonight, and ask that Anubis guide each of them carefully to their chosen destination. Flames goes to the Underworld to greet Osiris, Shadow to Valhalla and the hall of Odin. Stone and Fortune return to source, to mother Artemis's belly and Sol's guiding light. We bury them all in accordance with shifter tradition, by sending their burning bodies to the ground.'

Scribe used his candle to set fire to the box, Echoes did likewise and the Lightning Lords each stepped forward to add their flames to the fire. They stepped back quickly as the box burst into a bright blaze, and Stalker felt the heat on her face, drying her tears. Scribe raised his hands to one side and swept them across his body. A huge hole appeared in the ground and swallowed the box, burying it instantly. Stalker was shocked and looked at the ground for evidence of the burial, but there was none.

'The Blue Moon now rest in Hepethia and will be protected there,' Echoes said softly. 'There will be no marking of their grave, for their own protection.'

Stalker knew that there was great power in shifters, and even in death that power could be used. It made sense that shifters would not mark the graves of their loved ones, in case anyone wanted to steal the remains and use that power. It made her sick to think about it, and she firmly swept the notion aside.

'Thank you Osiris and Anubis for your guidance and protection. Farewell.' Scribe crouched down and placed his hands on the grass. He stood slowly, raising his hands and as he did so, and the blue dome was gradually lifted from around them, disappearing into a point above his head.

'The circle is closed,' Echoes said, and a sigh seemed to ripple through the park. It made Stalker shiver slightly.

Weaver moved over to Scribe and spoke softly to him. Eyes and Wind Talker approached one another for a brotherly hug. Stalker went over to Echoes, who was staring absently up at the night sky.

'Thank you for this,' Stalker whispered.

'Not at all,' Echoes replied softly. 'It's our role, it's what we do. Are you all right?'

There was true concern in her voice and she made eye contact with Stalker for the first time.

'Not really,' Stalker replied. 'But I will be.'

'Wind Talker,' Scribe said, a little more loudly. 'We have something for you, in the van. Shall we all go up now?'

A few nods and murmurs of agreement went around and the six shifters set off up the hill back to the entrance of Crescent Park. Scribe unlocked the van and threw open the back doors. Stalker peered between him and Wind Talker and saw a coffin-sized wooden box.

'Is that the body of the dead Phoenix Guard?' Wind Talker asked.

'Yes,' Scribe replied. What shall we do with it?'

'It will fit in my car if I put the back seats down,' Eyes offered, quietly. They all helped to move the box to his car. Stalker felt deeply uncomfortable handling the box, like touching it made her dirty. It contained the remains of an unseen enemy that she hated. She didn't want to know what Wind Talker wanted it for. That thought made her feel unsettled as well.

When they had finished they bid farewell to the two Scroll Keepers. Last-Breath-Echoes climbed up into the driver's seat of the van and set off back to Fenstoke, the territory of her pack, The Hand of God.

'I'm heading in the opposite direction,' Scribe said, pointing towards the river.

'Which is your pack?' Eyes asked, his voice full of curiosity.

'The Hellsclaws,' Scribe replied. 'Over in South Stoke.'

Stalker had never heard of them before, South Stoke was on the other side of the city from St. Mark's and she had never had a reason to go there. Eyes gave a small nod of acknowledgement but said nothing.

'Thank you,' Weaver said and approached Scribe for a hug.

'No problem,' he replied. He turned and set off at a brisk walk.

'I have room for one passenger,' Eyes said, pointing at his car. 'Wind Talker? Do you want to accompany the box?'

'Yes, please, if no one minds?' he replied.

Stalker and Weaver agreed and the two of them set off walking towards China Town as Eyes and Wind Talker got into the car and set off.

'That was emotional,' Stalker said quietly as they walked.

'Yeah,' Weaver replied. They hardly spoke all the way back and dawn was approaching by the time they arrived at Grove Street. Eyes and Wind Talker were asleep when the women arrived. They shifted into their animal forms and curled up; exhaustion took over and Stalker slept deeply right through the morning.

CHAPTER FIFTEEN

 Eyes had slipped away early to work and the others were still sleeping. She went to the kitchen and put a pot of coffee on. Weaver's sketches lay strewn all over the table and Stalker leafed through them. The plague doctor featured over and over again and she decided this needed their undivided attention now. The last time Weaver's visions had been this focused on one thing, the Phoenix Guard had invaded their territory and slaughtered their pack.

As she was pouring herself some freshly brewed coffee, Stalker heard the television in the front room come on. She had never known the others to turn it on and wondered who had done so. She took her coffee back to the front room and found Weaver and Wind Talker just waking up and stretching out their animal bodies. She felt their confusion, obviously neither of them had switched the TV on.

Stalker felt a slight hint of static through the veil and the television started changing channels rapidly.

'It must be Unchained Lightning,' she said. Weaver and Wind Talker shifted form and the three of them watched the screen attentively. It finally settled on a news broadcast. A distressed-looking correspondent was standing in front of police tape and behind him was a gaping hole in the middle of a road.

'Hey! I know that street, it's not far from here,' Wind Talker said, and he leaned forward and turned up the volume.

'Everyone here is surprised at the discovery. Routine road works don't usually unearth ancient burial sites,' the correspondent was saying. 'We're waiting now for experts to finish their initial investigation, but I heard from one of them just now that preliminary thoughts are that the site may date back to the plague of the seventeenth century.'

Stalker felt a sickly sinking sensation inside her, and she looked over at Weaver, who was sitting with her head in her hands.

'The Plague Doctor,' Weaver whimpered.

'We need to go and investigate.' Wind Talker was already pulling on his boots.

'Let me call Eyes first.' Stalker pulled out her phone and quickly found the Alpha's number. It rang for what seemed like an age before she gave up and ended the call. 'Okay, we investigate but let's try to avoid a conflict, shall we?'

Wind Talker gave a curt nod and Weaver murmured her agreement. The three of them set off for the nearby street. Stalker felt a painful jerk as they rounded a corner to find police tape strung across the road and a gaping hole in the tarmac. It was too familiar.

'Focus on the road works,' Weaver whispered, patting Stalker on the shoulder.

Stalker swallowed the lump in her throat and did as Weaver suggested. She looked at the cones, diggers and tools that lay abandoned around the work site. The hole was neatly dug, not the result of a massive explosion. There were people everywhere; a crowd of onlookers, the media and workmen, all jumbled together, bumping into one another and chattering loudly.

The three shifters approached cautiously, edging through the crowd, towards the plastic barrier around the pit. As she peered into it, Stalker saw layers of rock and earth, pipes and tubes and wires scattered throughout, and just visible, deep down, were bones. The shifters walked along the edge of the hole, following the course that the forensic experts had been digging after the initial discovery of the remains. They had already uncovered several bodies, there were scraps of shrouds preserved and layers upon layers of the dead.

'This is horrible,' Stalker whispered.

'I believe it was common during outbreaks of the plague,' Wind Talker whispered back. 'So many died and people were so afraid of contact with the bodies, that they just piled the dead into these great pits, rather than taking the time to make individual graves.'

'It's like the pictures you see of the concentration camps,' Weaver said, her voice tinged with sadness. 'Something has been unearthed. Can't you feel it? There's something missing here.' Weaver looked around anxiously.

'It must have fled quickly.'

'Or was taken,' Stalker mused. 'The demon won't have been buried here in the human world, maybe this didn't unearth him, maybe he was around already. Couldn't the Plague Doctor be responsible for the humans finding this site in the first place? Maybe he was here waiting when they found it and was able to take what he needed as soon as it was found.'

She felt a shudder go right through her and felt eyes watching them. She looked around, her vision sharp, but saw nothing distinct in the sea of faceless people. 'We need to get out of here,' she whispered.

'Agreed,' said Wind Talker and the three of them moved quickly back through the crowd and jogged back to the house.

'What do we do about this?' Stalker asked when they got back. 'Something's been dug up on our territory and there's a demon of the plague on the loose. How do we even begin to deal with this, or find out what was stolen and why?'

She couldn't disguise the panic in her voice and Weaver stepped over to give her a reassuring hug.

'We'll figure it out. Artemis sent me the vision for a reason, there must be something in it to help us. We didn't manage to stop it from happening, but that might not have been the point of the vision.' Weaver patted Stalker gently on the back and released her. Stalker felt calmer. Her pack sister had the unique ability to say just the right thing.

'I have to work soon and then there's a meeting of Odin's Warriors tonight. Will you two keep working on this and come up with a plan?'

'Of course,' Weaver replied.

They hurriedly prepared some food and Stalker dashed out of the door with toast in her mouth.

Work was just as difficult as it had been the previous day, with Stalker having to hold back in order to avoid hurting her students. She hadn't fully appreciated that her new abilities gave her such added strength even in her human form, and if she wasn't careful her supernatural nature would be exposed. Her students expected a trained martial artist to be strong, of course, but not so strong that she could easily throw one of them right across the room.

She finished work feeling exhausted and questioning whether it was even going to be possible to keep her job. She retrieved her dha from her locker and strung them across her back, where they disappeared from human sight, blending into her body until such time that she might need them. With a meeting of Berserkers, you never knew when weapons might be drawn.

She set off through the chilly night, there was a clear sky and the stars were just about visible through the dull orange glow from the street lamps. Stalker walked south out of St. Mark's and into China Town. The streets were bustling. Stalker loved the vibe of this part of Caerton, it was always busy and little stalls lined many of the streets. She stopped on her way to pick up something to eat and tried to enjoy the walk through the markets.

She remembered what Fortune and Shadow's Step had said about China Town, it was something of a mystery to Caerton's shifter population. No one knew who claimed it, no one had ever encountered signs of any shifters here, but it was not out of control in Hepethia like St. Catherine's was. She and Weaver had walked through China Town after the funeral in the early hours of the morning, and had had no trouble. If anyone did claim the area, they clearly didn't object to other shifters moving through it. She glanced around cautiously, suddenly wondering if she was being watched. She quickly shrugged away the feeling and went on her way.

It was approaching 9pm when Stalker reached Crescent Park. It was as dark as it had been the previous night, but not so quiet. Cars sped past on the main road and a few people walked hurriedly past the entrance to the park. There was no through route, so no random, passing humans entered the place that was so sacred to shifter-kind at this time of night. It was likely that teenagers and the homeless would find their way into the park, but Stalker suspected that the odd feeling of the place was a fairly effective deterrent.

She walked in through the wrought iron gates and set off down the path towards the lawn. She tried not to dwell on the reason for her previous visit, and as she neared the bottom she heard loud voices and sensed the shifters gathering just out of sight. She heard footsteps on the path behind her and glanced over her shoulder. A dark figure waved and she paused to see who it was. As the figure entered a pool of light from one of the few street lamps along the path, she recognised Fire Talon, the young father from her first meeting with Odin's Warriors. He had shoulder length, blond hair and wore a long leather coat. His footsteps were heavy and as he drew close to her she saw dark circles under his eyes.

'Hi,' he greeted her warmly. 'How are you doing?'

There was genuine sympathy in his voice and she knew at once that he was referring to the loss of her pack.

'As well as can be expected,' she replied. 'How's fatherhood treating you?'

'It's challenging,' he said. There was something sad about his smile, but Stalker didn't feel she could probe further. They resumed their course down to the waiting gathering and walked in silence.

It looked like most of the Berserkers were already assembled. Ragged Edge and Red Scythe stood in the centre of the group, and she saw First Strike and Crimson too among the gathered shifters. As they reached the lawn someone pushed past Stalker from behind; her hackles immediately rose and she saw that it was Fury, her rival from the Wrecking Crew. Stalker let a snarl escape her curled lips. This was the first time she had seen a member of the Wrecking Crew since they had made a grab for more territory on the northern border in Redfield, the night that the Blue Moon were killed.

Fury turned and grinned at her, walking backwards into the group and disappearing amongst them. More than anything, in that moment Stalker wanted Shadow's Step at her side to stop her from reacting to the provocation. It was Fire Talon who placed a gentle hand on her shoulder.

'Not now,' he whispered.

Stalker nodded in agreement. She would have her moment with Fury, but it was not now.

The last stragglers arrived and Red Scythe called them all to order.

'We'll be moving on to a secure location in just a few moments.'

'You can feel the oddness of the place, right?' Fire Talon asked in a whisper, taking her arm and leading her gently towards the middle of the crescent-shaped lawn. She nodded. 'Plant your feet, feel the earth beneath and feel everything else. All worlds pour into this one place, like a drain. If you focus carefully you can even see the other realms, you can see into Asgard.'

She looked at him in alarm. He had an expression of awe upon his face.

'Why does nothing spill through?' Stalker looked up, as if something might fall out of the sky at any moment.

'It's a perfect still point. Although there's no veil here and everything could just cross between realms, somehow they don't. We don't know why.'

Stalker took a few seconds to feel her feet pressing into the grass; she looked down at them and allowed her eyes to slip out of focus. She lifted her head slowly and let her eyes see beyond the human world. She saw Hepethia before her, and it was perfect, undisturbed crystal with jagged forms jutting up from the ground. As she stared into space it was as if she could see further, like a telescope refocusing on something more distant. She saw fire and shadow, chaos and death. The world was ablaze and demons bigger than anything she had encountered before romped across the volcanic landscape.

With a gasp she shook her head and her vision cleared. Panic threatened to overwhelm her, but Fire Talon grasped her shoulders and shook her firmly back into the human world. 'Are you all right?'

'Yes,' she said, nodding. 'That wasn't Asgard.'

'Did you see Muspelheim, the fire realm?'

Stalker nodded, still feeling shocked and shaken.

'I wasn't trying to, I didn't know what I would see.'

'Your mind was on the demons, you were worried about them being able to cross into this world, so that was what your mind showed you when you looked out.' Fire Talon released her shoulders and gave her a small smile.

'It was awful,' Stalker said with a shudder.

'We're moving on now,' Red Scythe called out. 'We're convening at The Station, just a short walk from here. Please try not to be too conspicuous, travel in small groups, keep the noise down.'

'It's like being on a school trip,' Stalker whispered as she and Fire Talon set off up the path behind a few others. He chuckled.

The column of Berserkers filed out of Crescent Park and drifted apart for the short walk into the city centre. The Station was once a fire station, but it had been sold and converted into a night club about ten years previously. On the weekends it was a thriving hub for young clubbers, but mid week it was dark and empty. It stood on a quiet back street, a short distance from where most of Caerton's busiest night spots were jumping every night of the week.

As they approached the huge block of a building, Red Scythe was already there, and holding the small side door open for the pairs and small groups as they arrived. Fire Talon held his hand out for Stalker to enter ahead of him. The door opened into a dark, narrow corridor. There were posters lining the walls and the floor was concrete. A light was hanging from the ceiling towards the end of the corridor, and Stalker followed a dark figure towards it.

She stepped under the light and out into the club. It

was a vast, open space with one massive dance floor, a raised booth for the DJ at one end and a long bar at the other. The Berserkers were gradually filing into the club and First Strike was ushering people into a circle. He caught sight of her and gave a friendly smile and wink. She waved back and moved over to join the circle. Glancing around, she caught sight of Crimson, the stunning red-head, and Stalker moved to take a place next to her.

'Stalker.' Crimson greeted her with an elegant dip of her head. 'I heard about the Blue Moon. I am so very sorry for your loss.'

'Thank you,' Stalker said, trying to smile. She realised she was going to face a lot of this and tried to accept the courteous words without letting her feelings overwhelm her.

First Strike came over and drew her into a warm embrace. She wrapped her arms around him and pressed her cheek against his hard chest.

'Are you all right?' he asked, releasing her.

'Yes, I'm okay, thanks, pulling through. The funeral was last night.'

'I know,' he said with a sigh. 'Scribe informed a few of us so that we could hold our own observances if we wished. Shadow's Step was my brother too, a dear friend who I had known for more years than I care to count. I raised a howl for him in Hepethia at the appointed time.'

'Thank you,' Stalker said. She had been so wrapped up in her own grief that she had almost forgotten that her pack mates had other friends who would miss them as much as she would.

Ragged Edge strode over to them, leaning heavily on

his staff. He wasn't in his ritual robes tonight, he wore a battered, brown leather coat that fell almost to the floor and his long grey hair hung across his wide shoulders. A marginally younger-looking shifter accompanied him. He was tall and broad, like so many of their kind. He wore his long hair in a heavy braid and his long beard was intricately braided and beaded. His eyes were electric blue.

'Stalker,' Ragged Edge said in his gravelly voice. 'I am so glad to see you. I wasn't certain that you would come, what with Shadow...' He looked to the floor and his voice disappeared into an indistinct mumble.

'Of course,' she said firmly. 'I didn't just join Odin's Warriors because of my mentor. I am as much a Berserker now without him here as I was before.'

'Of course,' the elder said with a small smile. 'Forgive me, this is Mjolnir.' Ragged Edge indicated his companion.

Mjolnir held out his arm and she took it, they grasped each other's arms just below the elbow, as was customary among their group.

'Pleased to meet you. Your initiation was something of an event.' His voice was deep and warm and there was a distinct twinkle in his blue eyes. Stalker laughed, remembering her vicious fight with Fury that had ended in them being dragged apart.

'Yes, I suppose it was.'

'Stalker,' Ragged Edge interrupted with a firm, but quiet voice. He took her elbow and led her a short way from the others. 'Tonight, well you will soon see, but I wanted to let you know personally that we do not take this action lightly and I hope that you will understand the gravity of the situation.'

Stalker felt an uncomfortable lump in her throat. She didn't understand what he was talking about but was suddenly afraid that she was going to be asked to leave or told that there had been some terrible misunderstanding about her membership. He didn't give her a chance to say anything, however, as he gave her a brief, sympathetic smile and pat on the shoulder before striding back to the circle. She followed him and took her place between Crimson and Mjolnir as the rest of the Berserkers fell into a circle around their leader, Red Scythe, who stood with the huge weapon that was his namesake at his side. He struck the concrete floor with the wooden end of the scythe and the crowd fell silent.

'Thank you all for coming,' he called out. 'As I am sure all of you know, the shifters of Caerton suffered a very serious loss last week.'

Stalker felt eyes all around the circle flick over to her, it was immensely uncomfortable. 'The Blue Moon, one of our city's oldest packs, was almost entirely obliterated.' The leader went on. Stalker felt irritated. Half of them had survived, they may be young, but they still counted. She fought down her chagrin and listened attentively. 'A force of Furies crossed into our city and took out the Blue Moon in one strike. One of our very own, Shadow's Step, was taken down with three of his very experienced pack mates. This was an act of war. As Odin's Warriors it is our duty to see such aggression countered.'

Stalker felt energy soar through her at his words, all around the circle people were twitching. A few people murmured noises of assent.

'Hell yeah!' Someone shouted and Stalker looked

around to see who it was, several people laughed and a young man a few places to her left was being shoved jovially.

'We are not going to sit and wait for more Furies to raid our city!' Red Scythe shouted.

'Yeah!' The shout rang out around the circle from at least half a dozen Berserkers. Stalker felt fired up. This was exactly what she wanted to hear. The rage that her fellow shifters felt about her pack's destruction was touching, in a way. 'You are each charged with seeking out and killing at least one Fury, with or without your pack's cooperation. Your duty is to Odin. The Phoenix Guard of the Furies shed first blood and now they must pay. We will not allow Caerton to be taken by those who seek to expose our kind to humanity! They want a war, we will give them a war. Let them feel the might of Odin's Warriors!'

Everyone was getting fired up now, even the crystal cool Crimson beside Stalker was pumping her fists and snarling. The energy in the club was coming to a peak. Shouts rang out around the room and almost everyone looked about ready to burst into their Agrius forms.

Stalker's heart was pounding and she felt the frenzy building around her. It was intense and empowering. First Strike erupted and shifted form, quickly followed by the youngster who had first shouted out.

It was like dominoes, quickly each and every Berserker in the club shifted and fights broke out all around the room. Not serious combat, it was camaraderie and adrenaline that resulted in some shoving and a few punches being exchanged. Stalker was swept along in the moment and her body changed with no conscious effort on her part.

She looked around for something to hit. Fury was heading directly towards her, shoving other shifters out of her way. Her long braids rippled behind her like whips. Stalker snarled and ran towards her, her feet pounding on the concrete floor. She drew her fist back and swung it towards Fury's face, but Fury easily dodged the brazen attack and slipped around behind Stalker.

The two of them circled each other for a moment, but Stalker was not in the mood to fight intelligently, she had no patience with this thirst for combat clawing at her throat. She launched herself at Fury and pushed her to the floor. Stalker punched Fury hard in the face several times before the prone shifter gathered the strength to shove her away. Fury started to get up, blood pouring down her jaw, but instead of attacking Stalker she shifted down into her human form. Stalker was surprised and stopped in her tracks, watching carefully for Fury's next move.

'Stupid bitch,' Fury spat. 'I have a message for you; information.'

Stalker shifted form and moved closer so that she could hear Fury over the noise all around them.

'I thought you were going to attack me,' she said, almost apologetically.

'Maybe I was,' Fury smirked. 'But that's beside the point. A Witch has been crossing your territory a lot recently. We thought you lot probably hadn't noticed, what with being a bit pre-occupied.'

Stalker snarled at her. She was appalled at Fury for approaching her just to make such obviously derogatory remarks.

'Right,' Stalker hissed. 'Where do you get your name

from, anyway? Bit of an odd choice.' She cocked an eyebrow, challenging her rival to explain herself.

'It's Furious Vengeance, if you must know, and as you well know we don't choose our own names, they're within us already, waiting to be found. Do you think I like having a name associated with those fanatics?'

Stalker flinched, embarrassed and regretful at her hostility towards Fury.

'You need to control your territory if you want to claim to be a pack. Do something about it.' Fury snapped.

'We will!' Stalker yelled. 'Now that we know about it. Thank you.' Stalker put on a mocking voice. The two of them stared at each other as the chaos began to subside around them and people began shifting back and laughter replaced roars. 'Look,' Stalker said in a more calm and rational voice. 'Is there anything else that you can tell me that might be helpful here?' It was an honest appeal for cooperation and Fury looked momentarily surprised.

'I don't know,' she said, looking uncomfortable. 'I guess, well, the Witches seem to be connected to this property in Fenwick, a sort of new age shop. The Witch that's been passing through our territories has been tracked back to it by one of ours.'

'Okay, and where is she going?'

'I don't know, we haven't followed her across *your* territory.' Fury snapped and stalked away.

'Everything all right?' Fire Talon approached Stalker cautiously and she looked at him carefully for a moment. He had blood on his hands and face. She looked down at her own hands, her knuckles were bloody but any minor grazes that she may have received from pummelling Fury's face had already healed .

'Yeah, I think so. Thanks for asking.' She smiled at him and he gave her a gentle punch on the shoulder.

'So, war,' he said, almost wistfully.

'Yeah,' she replied. She tried to smile, but couldn't. The initial fire from Red Scythe's speech had worn off and now she felt a strange coldness seeping through her.

'Try not to think of it as being for you,' he said. His words caught Stalker off guard. She hadn't thought anything like that, but now she did.

'What do you mean?'

'Well, they like you, the elders, but the war isn't *for* you. You know?'

'Yeah, I never thought it was.' She frowned at him.

'Oh, well that's okay then. Sorry.' He looked sheepish and walked quickly away.

Stalker watched from the sidelines as people talked animatedly and exchanged information. All of Odin's Warriors were going to war over the destruction of her pack. Despite what Fire Talon had said, or perhaps because of it, she felt strangely flattered and unnerved by it. She felt almost responsible. She had vowed at the funeral to take the fight to the Furies, and again tonight. On some level it truly was what she wanted, she wanted revenge, she wanted the Witches and all of their allies to pay for what they had done. But the blood pounding in her ears was not just a battle drum, it was a warning siren.

Chapter Sixteen

 The events of the gathering buzzed through her mind, her heart raced and she kept breaking into a sweat. She was the last to rise the next day. Weaver and Wind Talker were in the kitchen talking animatedly and Eyes was sitting on the sofa with piles of paperwork stacked around him.

'Morning,' Eyes said quietly as Stalker shifted from her fox form into her human one.

'What are you doing here?' she asked, not intending to sound so hostile.

'I'm working on a case here today, I wanted to be around to talk to everyone, catch up.'

'Sure,' Stalker nodded. 'Good to have you here. It's hard, juggling work with all of this. Isn't it?'

'You could say that.' He looked up from his work and gave her a melancholy smile. 'How was your night?'

'Interesting,' she said, cocking an eyebrow. 'We'd best

get the others in here for this conversation.'

'Sure,' Eyes said, then placed his thumb and finger under his tongue and whistled loudly, and Weaver and Wind Talker came through from the kitchen, looking curious. 'Pack meeting, please folks.'

Everyone took a seat and Eyes held his hand up to Stalker, giving her the floor.

'So, Odin's Warriors have declared war on the Furies.'

'Oh my goddess,' Weaver said, clapping a hand to her mouth.

'Yeah, so we have all sworn to take the fight to them. I didn't think any of you would object.' Stalker looked around and saw nothing but support in her pack mates' faces. 'Also, I saw Fury, from the Wrecking Crew. She told me that one of the Witches has been crossing our territory.'

'What?' Eyes snapped.

'She's been coming through Runmead and down into St. Mark's. The Wrecking Crew haven't tracked her into our territory. That's something at least, what with the history between us.'

'How did we miss this?' Eyes asked.

'We've been busy and this is a big territory,' Wind Talker said solemnly.

'We should see if we can track her, see where she's going and what she's doing.' Eyes gave Stalker a hard look. She knew that tracking was her forte and that the Alpha expected her to be able to do this.

'Of course,' she said. 'I have to work this afternoon but we can try and pick up her scent later.'

'Fine,' Eyes said with a sharp nod.

Stalker looked at Weaver and they exchanged

concerned expressions. Stalker felt angry at the intrusion on their territory and overwhelmed at the task ahead. Searching for the intruder would be difficult, she didn't know where to start.

'In other news,' Weaver said, clearing her throat. 'We've been researching the Plague Doctor. We don't have much, but we think that it stole a body from the plague pit, possibly to draw energy from, but it may have been looking for something to tether itself to.'

'Demons can be vastly more powerful in Hepethia and the human realm if they have something physical to connect to,' Wind Talker explained. 'They're from Muspelheim, or Hell, or whatever you want to call it. Different religions call it different things, but it's the realm of fire and demons. It costs them a lot of power to travel into one of the other realms and they're usually sort of diluted when they get here. The demons we faced at the betting shop site were able to crawl here through the hole in the veil; they were pure. But crossing the veil takes a toll and most of the demons we've faced have been in a weakened state.'

Stalker thought about the things she had seen and fought; and she shuddered. Some of them had seemed very powerful to her. She dreaded to think what they would be like in their most powerful forms.

'When they're here for a purpose, rather than just having been drawn here by strong emotions or big events, they need strength and energy to remain here,' Weaver said. 'It helps them to tether themselves to something.'

'Like a corpse,' Stalker added. It was a grim concept.

'Exactly,' Wind Talker replied.

'How did it get here?' Stalker asked. 'I mean, there hasn't been an outbreak of plague to draw it here.'

'No,' Wind Talker said, shifting his weight uncomfortably. 'No, indeed, that's the most disturbing part. It's very likely that he was summoned here by someone.'

Stalker felt something cold and sickly spread over her skin. She glanced at Weaver, who looked gravely worried and then at Eyes, who wore a deep frown.

'That really doesn't bear thinking about,' Eyes said quietly.

'Could it be the Spiral Hand?' Stalker asked.

'I hope so,' Wind Talker replied. Stalker looked at him in alarm. 'Well if it wasn't, it means some other unknown agency is at work.'

'Very true,' Eyes said, rising from the sofa. 'Okay, well, let's stay vigilant. Tonight we sort out that Witch.'

Stalker could see in his pained expression that he was feeling as overwhelmed as she was and she put a gentle hand on his arm. He looked at her and met her eyes. Stalker wanted to tell him that everything would be all right, but she barely believed that herself.

Chapter Seventeen

 for the afternoon, Eyes went into chambers and Stalker went to work. It was starting to get easier, just a little, as she began to get used to how much of her strength it was safe to use with her students.

She finished work at 6pm and decided to head straight for the eastern border of their old territory, rather than going all the way west to Grove Street. She approached Fenwick with caution, unsure of what she would find there. On her way she sent Eyes a text message to tell him what she was doing. The reply came quickly.

Be careful. We'll meet you at Redfield Park x

Stalker tucked her phone away and slipped up a dark alley to shift form. She slunk back out as a fox and jogged to the border. There was still just the faintest trace of her deceased pack mates where they had marked the boundary quite thoroughly. It would soon fade completely. She decided to mark it herself and did so at regular intervals all the way north towards Redfield Park. There was no way that they could control all of their old territory yet, but she wanted to send the Witches a message. They had to know by now that their fellow Furies had failed to eliminate all of the Blue Moon, so it should come as no surprise to them to find this border marked.

When she reached the park she went more carefully. The Wrecking Crew's stench was all over this border from where they had snatched the park for their own. Stalker tried to get past that smell to pick up a foreign scent. She had been searching for quite some time when she sensed her pack mates approaching. Weaver was in her cat form, the others human. Stalker acknowledged them with a nod of her head and continued searching for the Witch's scent. The Wrecking Crew's markings were too strong and so she decided to move further into her own pack's territory, away from the stench of their neighbours. The others followed and Weaver helped.

After what seemed like hours, Stalker picked something up a few blocks south of the park. It was a female shifter, vaguely familiar but only as part of the mix of Witch scents that she had picked up before. Weaver trotted over to where Stalker was sniffing carefully and the pair of them tried to follow the trail.

Eyes and Wind Talker followed a few metres behind as they weaved their way through narrow back streets across St. Mark's and towards the river. The Witch had been keeping to the quiet, dark places and was apparently taking some care to avoid the areas that most strongly smelled of the Lightning Lords. They followed the scent down streets that Stalker had never gone down before.

As they approached the river, the trail led out onto one of the major roads through the city. Traffic roared past them and bright lights assaulted Stalker's fox senses. She flinched against the stimulation and put her nose to the ground to focus on the scent. It led to a bridge across the river, not Red Bridge, a smaller one further north and she led her pack mates across it. Weaver stayed hidden in the shadows as best she could and the others kept a safe distance behind so as not to draw too much attention to the odd group.

They crossed into St. Catherine's and the trail became easier to track. Once she had crossed the bridge, the Witch had taken far less care about her route; it was clear she had followed the same path many times as her scent was so strong. Stalker was able to break into a jog and hardly needed to dip her head to the pavement to keep the trail. It led about a quarter of a mile from the river straight to a block of flats. It was a rough neighbourhood, like most of St. Catherine's, and the building was in need of repair, with crumbling walls in places.

Stalker sniffed around the main entrance while Weaver slipped into the shadows and returned in her human form. There was a small porch area and on the wall next to the door was a smashed panel of buzzers to individual flats, clearly no longer in use. Eyes and Wind Talker caught up and examined the situation.

'So, this is where she's been coming?' Eyes asked. Stalker replied with a low whimper.

Wind Talker reached out and opened the door, he held

it open and they all filed in. Stalker slipped ahead of the others and followed the scent to the stairwell. There was a lift, but a sign hung on it declaring it to be out of order. The stairs stank of a hundred humans, of urine and sweat, and the scent of the Witch was hard to follow. At the top of each flight of stairs was a landing with a set of lift doors and a corridor leading to several flats. The walls were thin and Stalker heard televisions chattering, raised voices and crying children.

They climbed five flights without seeing anyone. On the sixth floor Stalker rounded the corner onto the landing and stopped in her tracks. The scent of the Witch was overpowering. She was standing in the corridor just a few metres away, wrapped in the wandering arms of a young man with a familiar balaclava tucked into his back pocket. The young pair were attached at the lips, kissing passionately.

Stalker's breath caught in her throat and at the same moment the Witch broke from the kiss and locked eyes on her.

'Stay back!' the Witch yelled at her boyfriend, giving him a shove and stepping between him and the Lightning Lords. She was so young, Stalker noticed, easily younger than she was herself. Her long blond hair hung over her shoulders and she was dressed in tight jeans and a too-big leather jacket that had to belong to the boy.

'We just want to talk,' Wind Talker called down the corridor.

The Witch shoved her boyfriend backwards.

'Get out of here, now!' she yelled, and reluctantly he turned and fled down the corridor.

The Witch started to shake, and shifted into a huge Agrius beast, filling the narrow corridor. She bounded towards them, snarling.

Quick as a flash, Stalker shifted to match her and was the first to strike the Witch. The others shifted a moment behind her and the concrete building echoed with the snarls and sounds of the mockery of a fight. The Witch was severely outnumbered and outmatched, and Eyes soon had her grappled. She writhed in his massive bestial arms and whimpered in frustration. Stalker sensed her losing control of herself, she saw the girl's limbs shaking violently as she struggled against Eyes and a light went out in her eyes as the beast took over. She roared and lifted her feet off the ground, tipping Eyes back a little. She slammed her feet down and the floor gave way below her. She and Eyes fell through the floor and Stalker ran to the hole to look down after them, through clouds of dust and sparks from torn electrical cables that spat angrily. The Witch had managed to force a hole through every floor below them, all the way down to the ground floor lobby. *That shouldn't be possible,* a voice inside Stalker whispered.

Wind Talker and Weaver approached the edge carefully and looked down. Stalker glanced at the pair of them before leaping into the hole. She plummeted most of the way, but a few feet from the bottom her talisman kicked in and she floated gently to the ground. Eyes was crouched in the falling dust, shaking his head. The Witch stood right in front of Stalker, breathing hard and trying to regain control. But the rage was too much for her and she launched herself at Stalker to attack.

Stalker easily dodged and landed a counter blow to the

Witch's back; she felt and heard ribs crack. Eyes got to his feet and tried to grab the Witch again, but she ran around him and managed to hit him in the back of the head. He reeled in agony from the blow and staggered forwards, almost crashing into Stalker.

Wind Talker and Weaver burst into the lobby from the stairwell and joined the fray. They had the Witch backed up against the wall and Weaver shifted into her human form, holding out her hands.

'Can we calm this down?' Weaver asked.

But the Witch roared at them, still lost to the beast and beyond reason. She lurched towards Weaver, and Stalker darted in to intercept, plunging her fierce talons into the chest of the Witch. Her face froze for a moment before she shoved Stalker away. Stalker stumbled backwards into Eyes and Wind Talker strode forward to punch the Witch hard in the face in an effort to render her unconscious.

She slammed into the wall and slumped to the floor. Her form shifted back into human and blood trickled from her mouth. Her eyes were glazed, her skin drained of colour.

'Ian,' she croaked. 'Mother.'

Her breath rattled and stopped.

Stalker shifted form, as did the others.

'Oh shit,' Stalker cried. Her heart was pounding and she was covered in debris. She tried to make sense of what had happened. How had they gone from tracking to killing this girl?

'We have to leave, right now!' Wind Talker shouted, and he ran for the door. Weaver and Eyes followed him, but Stalker lingered to look at the dead girl. She was wearing a necklace, an animal's fang-like tooth on a leather lace. Stalker reached out and touched it gently. Some instinct told her to take it, a trophy for the kill. She pulled and the lace snapped and came away from the girl's neck.

'Stalker!' Eyes yelled from the door. She looked up and ran after him.

People were standing in the street, drawn by the terrible sounds of a building being wrecked and the ferocious animals fighting within. Sirens could be heard approaching and the four shifters hid their faces as they fled the scene. As soon as they rounded the corner they all shifted into their animal forms and split up to return home.

Stalker clutched the Witch's necklace in her mouth as she shifted into an owl and took flight. She soared over the city, scared, angry and confused by what had happened. She kept an eye on her pack mates as they made their way back to Grove Street, ensuring they got there safely. She was the last to return to the house. She landed in the little back garden and shifted back into her human form to enter the house through the back door.

The others sat in silence in the living room.

'How did that happen?' she asked, slumping down on a cushion on the floor.

'We did what we had to do,' Wind Talker replied, his face cold and hard. 'She was beyond reason, she attacked us and had to be put down.'

'She wasn't a rabid dog, Wind Talker!' Stalker shouted.

'Yes she was,' he replied, his big eyes unblinking.

There was a charge of static throughout the room and all of them looked around for a sign of their ally. The television flicked on and the screen filled with fireworks and an excited crowd.

'We have a winner!' cried an over-enthusiastic presenter as the final results of some tacky celebrity reality show were broadcast. The channel hopped to footage of a flock of ravens flying across the sky, and then the screen went black.

Everyone looked at Stalker.

'I guess that means you were the first Berserker to fulfil that war oath.' Eyes placed a gentle hand on her shoulder and Stalker felt sick. Revenge and war were not so sweet after all.

Chapter Eighteen

 The look on the face of the Witch girl as Stalker killed her was burned into her mind and surfaced again and again in her dreams. She dreamed of running through the city, chasing Pursuit-of-Midnight-Solitude through the shadows. She woke several times in the night, her pack were sleeping all around her, even Eyes, who normally went home to his family.

Finally, before the sun was up, Stalker got up, sick of sleeping so badly. She stretched and slipped into the kitchen. Even though it was early, she felt restless and needed to act on the events of the previous night, so she picked up her phone and called Last-Breath-Echoes.

'Hello?' Echoes asked sleepily when she answered the call.

'I'm so sorry to trouble you so early,' Stalker said, keeping her voice low. 'There was an incident in St. Catherine's last night. I was hoping you could keep an eye out for the victim coming through your department, a teenage girl.' She chewed her lip while waiting for the reply. Echoes was quiet for a long moment.

'Of course,' she said at last. 'That's what I'm here for.'

Stalker wasn't entirely sure if Echoes was being sarcastic or genuine, her tone was hard to judge over the phone.

'Thank you,' Stalker replied. 'If there's anything I can do for you to return the favour, do please ask.'

'Thank you, but I don't think that will be necessary,' Echoes said sleepily. 'Take care, see you soon.'

'Yeah, see you soon.' Stalker hung up the phone.

She paced the kitchen anxiously for a few minutes, unsure what to do with herself. The sound of Eyes' phone ringing brought her to a halt. She wandered to the front room and found Eyes shifting from wolf to human. He looked at his phone with a frown and then answered.

'Hello? Martin Davison speaking.'

Stalker moved closer to listen, she could hear a woman's voice on the other end of the line.

'This is Warden, from the Watch. Would you please meet with me on the southern edge of St. Mark's by the river?'

'Yes, of course. What time?' Eyes asked.

'As soon as possible.'

Eyes looked at his watch and rubbed his face.

'Okay, I'm working today, so I can pass that way at eight. Is that all right?'

'That's fine,' Warden replied. 'You may wish to bring another of yours.'

Eyes looked anxiously at Stalker. Stalker nodded

to let him know that she could hear both sides of the conversation and could go with him.

'Does that mean I get to hitch a ride in your fancy car?' she asked with a grin. He stifled a laugh and nodded.

'Fine,' he said to Warden. 'We'll see you by the river in just under an hour.'

'Thank you.' Warden hung up without waiting for any further reply.

'Well this is odd,' Eyes said, frowning at his phone. Weaver and Wind Talker were waking and shifting form. 'Do you know anyone from the Watch?'

'Yeah,' Stalker replied. 'Ragged Edge is a Berserker, one of the elders. He conducted my initiation. I met a pack mate of his the other night too, Mjolnir. I've never met their Alpha though. I'm guessing that was her?'

'Yes. Can you be ready to go by then?'

'Yes. I just need to eat something.' She had showered off the blood and dust when they got home the previous night. Her clothes had been protected from the worst of it as she had been in her Agrius form. But she had felt they were tainted by association and didn't want to wear them again. She was grateful for the little stash of her things that she had at Grove Street. She went upstairs to freshen up for the day. When she came back down, Wind Talker was cooking sausages and he passed her a plate of them as she entered the kitchen.

When they had finished their hurried breakfast, Eyes and Stalker dashed out of the door and got into his sleek car. It only took a few minutes to drive to the meeting place. Eyes found somewhere to park just south of Red Bridge and they got out of the car.

'I wonder if we'll recognise her when she approaches,' Stalker said, looking around.

'I think we will,' Eyes said, indicating the riverside path. Stalker looked and saw an odd couple approaching. The woman was fairly short, only slightly taller than Stalker. Her dark hair was slicked back in a tight bun and she wore a neatly pressed skirt suit and flat, sensible shoes that slapped the pavement as she walked briskly towards them. The man with her had unruly black hair, stubble on his jaw and wore a simple suit that didn't quite fit properly. He looked really awkward, his cheeks were flushed and he kept glancing warily at the woman. She had a sour expression and kept looking at her watch.

They drew close and came to a stop.

'Fights-Eyes-Open?' the woman asked, looking pointedly at Eyes.

'Yes,' he replied and reached a hand out. She took it and they shook hands. 'This is Stalker-of-Night's-Shadow.'

'Warden-of-Stones,' the woman said, shaking Stalker's hand. 'This is James.'

'Hi,' the man said, looking at them all carefully, before extending his hand.

'How can we help?' Eyes asked as he shook James's hand.

Stalker sensed that James was a shifter, but shiny new by the looks of things.

'James needs a pack,' Warden said bluntly. 'I hate to burden you with the responsibility, when you are all so newly changed yourselves, but I thought perhaps you would welcome your numbers being bolstered.'

James looked incredibly embarrassed and Stalker felt

for him.

'Okay,' Eyes said slowly. 'Why can't he join The Watch? No offence, James.'

'None taken,' James replied. He had a slightly hoarse voice.

'We hold to an old tradition, I'm afraid, we only take werewolves.'

Stalker looked at her, her jaw dropped in surprise and she quickly closed it.

'Really?' Stalker asked.

'Really,' Warden replied.

'I'm originally from St. Mark's,' James said, breaking the tension. 'I've been living over in Old Town for a few years and my business is there.'

'It really would be best if you found new premises,' Warden said sharply.

James gave a shrug.

'Okay, well thank you,' Eyes said with a heavy sigh. 'Of course you can join the Lightning Lords, James, we'd be happy to have you.'

'Lovely,' Warden said without a trace of warmth. 'Well, I shall leave you to it.' She turned and strode away.

'Charming woman,' James said sarcastically, raising an eyebrow.

'Well, this is awkward,' Eyes said, looking around.

'It's fine,' James reassured him. 'Look, honestly, I just changed two weeks ago. The Watch were looking after me but they made it clear right away that I couldn't stay with them. I think they were waiting for an opportunity to move me on to another pack.'

'I'm sorry,' Stalker said. 'That's not the smoothest start

to this life.'

'I gather you haven't had a smooth transition either,' James said, giving her a sympathetic look.

'I'm sorry about this, James, but I have to get to work,' Eyes said, running his hands through his hair. 'Stalker, can you take him back to Grove Street and get him acquainted with the others, please?'

'Yes of course.'

'And we need to find that boy from last night. Can you get everyone onto that today?'

'Okay. Why?' Stalker felt her face flush. Memories from the traumatic fight filled her mind and she felt suddenly vulnerable.

'The Witches might be after him. It's entirely possible they had no idea what that youngster was up to, and once they find out they'll want to know who he is and what he saw. He saw us. As it stands they may not know who was responsible for her death, I'd like to keep it that way.'

Stalker nodded in agreement. 'Thank you,' Eyes said. 'Good to meet you, James. I'll be able to get to know you properly tonight.'

'Sure,' James replied.

Eyes got into his car and drove off. Stalker watched him go, struggling with the vivid memories swimming in the forefront of her mind.

'So,' she said abruptly, turning to face her newest pack mate. 'What moon did you change under? Obviously not a full one if The Watch won't have you.' She raised an eyebrow and he half smiled.

'No, a half moon.'

'Cool, so you're an owl then?'

'That's right,' he said. He looked immensely uncomfortable.

'Let's go,' Stalker said, gesturing back the way she and Eyes had come.

They walked quickly, it was raining, though only lightly, and there was a stiff wind. Stalker led them on the most direct route across St. Mark's, though it wasn't far. 'What's your business?'

'I'm a private investigator.'

'No way?!' she said, looking at him. He grinned. 'That is so handy.'

'Handy?' he replied. 'That's not the response I usually get.'

'Ha, you'll see.' She beamed at him. She was thinking of all of the mysteries they had facing them and how lost without clues they were. A PI was the perfect gift from Artemis. As her thoughts raced over the new situation something else dawned on her. With the arrival of James, the Lightning Lords would be a pack of five, one member born under each phase of the moon.

Stalker and James got to 32 Grove Street and as she opened the door, Stalker called out to announce their presence. Wind Talker appeared at the top of the stairs and stood stock still, looking down at them. Weaver stuck her head out of the living room door, a smile frozen on her face.

'Hi,' Weaver said, uncertainly.

'Guys,' Stalker said. 'Come and meet James.'

Wind Talker walked slowly down the stairs, an unusual expression on his face. Stalker stifled a laugh when she realised that he was trying to look friendly.

She led James through to the living room, Weaver had her sketches spread out on the floor and was tidying them away. 'James, this is Weaver-of-Sky's-Loom.'

Weaver gave him a warm smile and then looked at Stalker expectantly. Wind Talker walked in behind them, a pile of papers in his hand.

'Hello,' Wind Talker said.

'This is Wind Talker,' Stalker said. 'Guys, this is James and he's going to be joining the Lightning Lords. Some little issue with The Watch being stuck in the dark ages.'

'Hi,' James said, shuffling his feet and looking very uncomfortable.

'Look,' Stalker said, turning to him and catching his eye. 'I know this is all kinds of weird, but you are totally welcome.' She put an arm around his shoulders and turned him to face Weaver. 'It's meant to be. Weaver will back me up on this. Weaver, James is a half moon.'

Weaver's eyes bulged.

'Oh my,' she said. 'That is quite special.'

James looked around at them, a puzzled expression on his face.

'We now have one member of each phase. Owl, cat, badger, wolf and fox,' Stalker said with a broad grin.

'Sort of,' Weaver said with a smirk.

'Well, yes,' Stalker said, releasing James. 'I was born under a new moon, but not strictly of the fox.'

'Okay,' James said, looking at her carefully and in utter confusion.

'Stalker is unique,' Wind Talker said, as he picked up his bag from by the sofa and started looking for something inside. 'We haven't found an animal yet that she can't shift into. I've been researching your condition by the way. There's no record that I can find of any other shifter who can take multiple forms from the day they change. Not outside of legend and myth, anyway.'

'Oh, right,' Stalker said, suddenly very self-conscious.

'Artemis has great plans for us,' Weaver said, patting Stalker on the shoulder. 'She's given us the two of you.' She looked at James and gave him a beautiful smile.

'Let's cross over,' Wind Talker said, heading through to the kitchen without waiting for them. They followed and all crossed the veil into the garden.

Unchained Lightning was there, circling around the little space, glowing brightly. Stalker watched James for his reaction. He hesitated in the doorway, looking mildly alarmed.

'Is that a bolt of lightning?' James asked.

'Sort of,' Wind Talker said, smiling. 'This is our ally, Unchained Lightning.'

The power fae flared up and crackled.

'You wish to join the Lightning Lords?' Unchained Lightning's voice hissed like static on the air.

'I do,' James replied firmly.

'Very well,' the fae said.

There was a moment's pause and then he launched himself upwards, drew level with the top of the house and then discharged his power down into the garden. The small space glowed with electric blue light and static filled the air. All of their hair stood up on end and Stalker felt her skin tingling. She felt James connect with her, with all of them. Unchained Lightning couldn't grant them telepathy, as Grins-Too-Widely had done, but he was granting them empathy. It seemed as though he had been waiting for James to arrive. He was her brother and they were now a blessed pack, perfectly balanced as if Artemis herself had hand-picked them to be together.

CHAPTER NINETEEN

'Thank you, Unchained Lightning,' Wind Talker said and bowed his head slightly to their ally. There was a ripple of energy and then the fae shrunk back to its normal size and resumed circling the garden.

'Eyes told me to track down the boy from last night and stop the Witches from getting to him. We need to know if he's spoken to the police, as that could be bad for us,' Stalker said as they filed back into the house and across the veil.

'Are you working this afternoon?' Wind Talker asked Stalker.

'No,' she said, shaking her head. 'It's my day off. Interestingly, James here is a private investigator.'

'Are you able to check police records, James?' Wind Talker asked, not missing a beat.

'Yes,' James replied cautiously. 'But I need you to tell me what's going on. I can't just hack into any old thing without considering it.'

'Of course,' Stalker said, giving him a reassuring smile. 'We wouldn't want you to leap right into compromising your integrity. Last night there was a fight in a tower block in St. Catherine's, a girl was killed, and part of the building came down. There was a witness, a boy of about sixteen, he was a gang member. He had a Knight's balaclava in his back pocket. We need to know who he was and what he told the police, if he could identify any of the parties involved.'

'Would those parties happen to be you guys, by any chance?' James asked, wearily rubbing his forehead.

'Yes,' Wind Talker said bluntly.

'Okay, there are three options here,' James said, with a little more enthusiasm. 'I can call a contact of mine who may have those details, I can try to hack into the files or I can track him down and question him myself. I would prefer the first option, but if you need to keep this way under the radar then it might not be the right route. The problem with the second option is that if I get caught, well, that could inflame the situation. The third option relies on having some more information on the boy in order to find him, but I wasn't there last night so he can't identify me and won't know of my connection to you guys.'

'We know where he lives,' Stalker said. 'The fight happened in his block, or at least it looked that way. When we arrived they were stood outside one of the flats. It was probably his.'

'It's got to be that option,' Weaver said firmly. 'We need to talk to him in any case about things the police won't understand.'

'He never saw my human face,' Stalker said. She felt a hard knot forming in her stomach. She had a feeling where this was inevitably going to end up. She would have to go with James to show him which door it was, to positively identify the boy and as back up against anyone else who might be sniffing around the place. She felt sick at the idea of returning to the scene of the fight, the murder. She had to fight the urge to run and hide though, she had to be part of fixing this. 'I'll come with you.'

'Okay,' James said, looking her over. 'Do you have a suit?'

She raised an eyebrow at him.

'No. Why?'

'A PI needs to look the part.'

'I have a jacket. Will that do?' She looked him over in return and noted again the poor fit of his suit and the rumpled shirt, loose tie and dirty shoes. James glanced over his body and cleared his throat as he hurriedly straightened his tie and tucked in his shirt.

'Yes, that will be fine.'

Stalker went upstairs to find her smart jacket. This was going to be hard, she knew it. She pulled the necklace she had taken from the girl out of her pocket and ran her fingers over it. The tooth was old. It was smooth and slightly yellow. It looked like it probably came from a wolf. Stalker lifted it by the leather lace and tentatively tied it around her neck. The tooth came to rest on her chest, next to her feather pendant, and it suddenly occurred to her that the tooth almost certainly had mystical properties too. She thought of the way the girl had broken right through all those levels of the building and shuddered. She hurriedly took the necklace off. If that was what this pendant did she didn't want that kind of strength. She could hardly control her own supernatural strength right now, never mind adding to it so significantly. Stalker shoved the necklace into her pocket, grabbed her jacket and bounded down the stairs.

As she reached the living room, Stalker's phone began to ring. She pulled it from her pocket and recognised the number as belonging to Last-Breath-Echoes. She answered the call.

'Hello?'

'Hi, I have the body on the table. This is Angela Carter,' Echoes said, as if the name were significant. Stalker looked around the pack and switched the call to speaker phone.

'Should we know that name?' she asked.

'Carter is the surname of the Alpha of the Witches,' Echoes replied.

Stalker felt as though she had been punched in the gut. She looked around at the ashen faces of her pack mates.

'So this is her daughter?' Wind Talker asked. He looked genuinely worried.

'I would guess so,' Echoes replied.

'Did she have ID on her?' James asked.

'Yes,' Echoes replied. 'Do I know you?'

'It's okay,' Stalker said quickly. 'He's one of ours.'

'Okay,' Echoes replied, sounding reassured.

'Do you have the police report there?' James asked.

'Yes,' she said. 'Why?'

'Do they name any witnesses?'

'No, it says there were none. But I can tell you they're wrong.'

Stalker looked at the phone and then at James, who was frowning.

'Oh?' Stalker said.

'There was a boyfriend, Ian White. I have certain ways of knowing what she saw before she died, so I know he was there. Besides, his DNA is all over her and he has a criminal record. I haven't put that in my report yet. Should I leave it out?'

'Yes please!' Stalker and Weaver said in unison and they looked at each other with relieved smiles.

'Okay. Well, I have a lot to do here, but I can clean the body so that the Witches don't get a whiff of who did this when they claim the body.'

'Will they do that?' Stalker said, alarm rushing through her mind and body. 'Enter the city to get her?'

'No, not literally. Or at least, I don't think so,' Echoes replied. 'It'll come through as official looking paperwork from a funeral arranger and the body will be moved to Fenwick. The police will be notifying the family about now. I thought you should know.'

'Thank you,' Stalker said.

'You're welcome,' Echoes said and ended the call.

Stalker put her phone away and looked around at her pack. Weaver was chewing her lip and Wind Talker looked more concerned than he usually did.

'We killed the Alpha's daughter,' Stalker said, feeling even more sick than she had before. How could this be happening? Her life was spiralling so far out of control and she was petrified of never grabbing hold of it again.

'It would appear so,' Wind Talker said. 'You two get going. As soon as she knows she'll be all over this. Get the boy, make him talk and do whatever you need to do to stop him talking to her. I'll phone Eyes and update him.'

Stalker shot him a cold stare. Was he telling her to kill the boyfriend? She wouldn't do it. Not if there was any other way. She turned and strode from the house, James scurried behind.

'We'll get on a bus,' she said, not looking at him. 'We don't want our scents all over this.'

'I have a car, it's parked in the city centre.'

'Perfect,' Stalker tried to smile.

They ran to the main street and got in line for a bus to the city centre. James looked deeply worried and Stalker could feel his apprehension coming through their empathic bond. 'I'm sorry,' she said quietly.

'It's okay,' he replied, waving a hand dismissively. But his face remained set in a deep frown. 'It's not your fault. Who was that on the phone? One of our people?'

'Yes,' she whispered, aware of the humans standing either side of them. 'Someone in a very useful position.'

'Hmm, very,' he replied.

The bus pulled up a few minutes later and Stalker paid their fares. The bus took a direct route out of St. Mark's, south through China Town, where they disembarked and walked the rest of the way to the city centre. James led her to his car, which was parked in a multi-storey behind a shopping centre. 'I haven't driven it since I changed,' James said as he unlocked it. 'I was parked here that night and haven't been back since. This is going to cost me a small fortune in car park fees.'

There was something familiar in his voice and the look in his eyes. Stalker knew how he felt. That loss and longing for an old life, now inevitably left behind. They got into the car and drove slowly to the exit, where James paid at the machine with a grimace. James drove carefully out of the city centre and west towards St. Catherine's, crossing the river near the castle. They were taking a route right through Old Town, territory of The Watch, and Stalker watched James's face carefully for signs of strong reactions. His cheek twitched a few times and she wondered if they passed the place where he changed or any landmarks he knew from his weeks with the old and strange pack that claimed this area of Caerton. But he didn't volunteer any information and she wasn't going to ask.

They turned north, out of Old Town and into the unclaimed territory of St. Catherine's. Stalker directed James towards the block of flats. It was midday and the street was busy. There was police tape all over the place and press were still milling around, but no one was being prevented from entering or leaving the residence. They decided it was best to be subtle about this though and James parked at the back, where there was a place for the bins to be collected and a service door at the rear of the building. They got out of the car and headed to the door.

Stalker led James inside. It had been cleared up substantially. The rubble was gone but there were blood stains on the wall and floor and the gaping hole in the ceiling remained. There were signs declaring "caution" everywhere. In a different neighbourhood the building might have been evacuated, but this was St. Catherine's. The residents were accustomed to their homes and businesses being vandalised, falling into disrepair and their lives being otherwise disrupted and the police didn't care one bit about the residents.

Stalker and James climbed the stairs. On each floor the holes had been fenced off but in more than one place the fences had been knocked over to form precarious walkways across the holes. When they reached the sixth floor, Stalker led James cautiously along the corridor to where she had found the couple kissing the night before.

'This is the place,' Stalker whispered.

James gave her a quick wink and knocked sharply on the door. They waited, there was movement inside but no one came to the door. James knocked again, but his face looked grave. Stalker knew no one was going to answer. The building stank of fear, she could even smell it with her useless human nose.

'There's definitely someone in there,' James whispered. 'What do you want to do?'

'Try calling out. They might think we're the police.'

'Hello?' James called through the door. 'I'm looking for Ian White. I'm not with the police. I'm working for Ms Carter's family.'

Stalker looked at him in alarm. If Angela was keeping Ian a secret from her family, he may not take James's cover much more kindly than a police intrusion. There was total silence inside. They looked at each other for a moment. They had only just met, but they were bound together as siblings and could sense each other's strongest emotions. They seemed to think alike too, Stalker had warmed to him immediately. She nodded at him, knowing without the need for telepathy what he was planning to do. She granted him permission and a moment later he reached inside his jacket and pulled out a lock-pick.

'You are so useful,' she whispered, and they exchanged smiles. James set to work on the lock, which was at shoulder height. Stalker kept watch both ways down the corridor; the building was quiet, much quieter than it had been the previous night. There was very little movement and not much sound coming from the flats around them.

There was a satisfying click as James unlocked the door. They looked at each other for a moment and then he opened the door and they moved quickly inside. The door opened into a small living space, with a kitchen at the back. It was dark, curtains drawn tight against the daylight. On the sofa was the boy from the night before, asleep or unconscious. Hovering over him was a hunched figure, who looked up in alarm as they entered. It was a man, or at least a rough approximation of one. He had sickly pale skin that hung off his face rather alarmingly, and was dressed in a black suit and top hat. His eyes were absolutely black.

Stalker stood frozen and James twitched nervously beside her.

The demon smiled a sickly smile and blinked eerily, thin white lids over black eyes. Its long white fingers stretched out towards them, turning into blades.

'Greetings,' the demon said, its voice dripping.

'Who are you?' Stalker asked, edging slowly into the room towards Ian.

'Scourging Agony, at your service,' the demon replied. 'And you would be two of the shifters responsible for the mess out there.' The demon's eyes and blade-fingers flickered towards the hallway.

'Not me,' James said, a little defensively. 'I had nothing

to do with it.'

'Are you working with the Witches?' Stalker asked, inching closer to the boy.

'I would have thought that was obvious,' the demon said silkily, bowing his head slightly. 'And I'm afraid that now that you know that I can't let you leave here.'

Stalker had almost reached the sofa. Ian was breathing faintly. Scourging Agony lunged for her with his bladed fingers and Stalker drew one of her swords. She swung the blade down and took off one of the demon's hands. Black blood flew from the wrist as the hand exploded and disappeared. Shocked, Stalker stood for a moment. The demon was screaming but there was something deeply unnerving about the expression on his face. He was enjoying it.

Stalker lunged her sword straight through the demon's chest and retracted it a moment later. His face froze before he dropped to the floor. The body shattered like black glass but the pieces vanished. Stalker felt the veil ripple.

'He's not dead,' she said. She didn't know how she knew, she just sensed it. 'Maybe that's what happens when demons are killed on this side of the veil.' She looked at James, but he looked as confused as she felt. 'Grab the boy, we need to get out of here. We'll have to take him home to question him.'

James nodded and moved over to the sofa to pick up the unconscious teenager. Stalker got her phone out and called Wind Talker. He answered quickly.

'Stalker?' he asked on answering.

'You need to summon and hold a demon, Scourging Agony, right now,' she said in a rush. 'We have to stop it reporting back to the Witches. We attacked it but it disappeared across the veil.'

'Okay, I'm on it.' Wind Talker replied and ended the call.

Stalker moved quickly to help James carry Ian and they left the flat as quickly as they could.

Between them they got the boy down the stairs and out through the back door. Stalker checked that the coast was clear before they moved out past the bins and to James's car. They put Ian across the back seat and drove away.

Chapter Twenty

Stalker and James stumbled into the hallway at 32 Grove Street, with Ian propped up between them. Weaver ran to them from the kitchen.

'What happened?' she asked, trying to help but the lack of space in the narrow hallway made it impossible. Stalker and James lurched awkwardly down the hall towards the living room.

'Did Wind Talker get the demon?' Stalker asked as they heaved Ian into the living room and onto the sofa.

'Yes, we need you in Hepethia now.'

They left the human boy there and crossed the veil. Out in the back garden, Wind Talker stood with his arms raised. Light shone all around him and little sparks filled the garden around the dark, spindly figure of Scourging Agony hovering in the centre of a cage of light. His bladed fingers twitched and clicked, the hand that Stalker had sliced off had already been neatly regrown. His face was a grotesque mask of pain.

Wind Talker was straining to contain the demon within the mystical cage, he was sweating and his face was beetroot red.

Above them, Unchained Lightning circled, casting an eerie white glow over the scene.

'Did you question it yet?' Stalker asked Weaver quietly, afraid of breaking Wind Talker's concentration.

'No, we've only had it held for a few minutes.'

'Scourging Agony, did you report back to your mistress yet?' Stalker called out. The demon's attention fixed on her, his black eyes piercing right through the cage and into her.

'No,' it hissed. Its voice was sharp, like splinters.

'Good. What can we do to convince you not to?' James asked, stepping forward. Suddenly, there in the light of their ally's power, James began to radiate with the calming aura that Stalker had always felt from Speaks-With-Stone, her half-moon pack mate from the Blue Moon. He was calm but authoritative, and the demon responded immediately by relaxing and releasing a long, rattling breath.

'I wasn't expecting that,' the demon said, locking eyes with James. 'I thought you were going to kill me.'

'Not if we don't have to,' James said, straightening his tie and tilting his chin up defiantly. 'Ultimately, we don't want the Witches to know that we are in any way connected to what happened to that girl. We will prevent you from returning to them if we have to, but it would be better for all concerned if you could be persuaded to tell us everything you know about them.'

Stalker and Weaver exchanged discrete appraising

expressions as James spoke. He had only been with them a matter of hours but he was already stepping up and taking his place among them admirably.

'Pain,' Wind Talker said. It wasn't immediately clear whether he meant that he was in pain or something else. He was buckling and Stalker ran to him to support him. She leaned against his back, propping him up, and squeezed his shoulders. She focused her energy on the cage, drew deep breaths and drew upon what little casting ability that she had. It seemed to help and Wind Talker was able to relax enough to speak. 'You're a demon of pain, aren't you?'

'I am,' the demon said silkily, turning to Wind Talker.

'We can offer you opportunities to inflict pain.'

Stalker's eyes closed and she let out a barely audible sigh of exasperation. But she didn't speak, they had to appear united in front of this demon if they hoped to settle this without further bloodshed.

'Oh no,' the demon said, smiling eerily. 'I don't inflict it, I enjoy watching others inflict it upon themselves.'

Stalker shuddered, repulsed by the creature.

'Do the Witches do that? Do they hurt themselves for you?' James asked, his voice quiet and thoughtful.

The demon drew a rattling breath and its sigh was disturbingly sensual. Stalker flinched away from it, hiding behind Wind Talker.

'Oh yes,' the demon smiled and looked right at Stalker over her pack mate's shoulder, as if it could sense her discomfort and took pleasure in it.

Weaver walked quietly over to Wind Talker and drew his knife from his belt. She walked right up to the shimmering cage, held out her arm and drove the knife hard into the flesh just below the elbow. She winced, and as she pulled the knife down her arm towards her wrist she whimpered in pain. Blood ran down her arm, all over the knife and dripped onto the floor.

Scourging Agony's black tongue darted out and he twitched all over, his eyes flickered and almost seemed to roll back in his head a little. It was perverse and Stalker watched with utter revulsion coursing through her.

'We could find you a place,' James said, cutting through the sick tension. 'Somewhere where people go to hurt themselves. You could live there and feed off the pain there. We could promise to ensure that no human authorities interfere and cut off your source of energy.'

Scourging Agony considered James carefully, his fingers flexing slightly and clicking against each other.

'What do you want from me? Besides not returning to my mistress?'

'Information about them,' James replied.

The demon drew a breath and straightened up. He waved his hands and the cage disintegrated from around him. Stalker and the others immediately went on the defensive. Wind Talker looked confused and frustrated.

'Calm down, fleshlings,' the demon croaked, and a half-forgotten memory stirred in Stalker's mind. The memory of her initiation entombing and the demon in the dark, whispering to her. 'It was a good prison, it held me while it needed to. I'm not going to hurt you. I like you and will do what I can to help. Provided you fulfil your side of the bargain.'

'Of course,' James said, relaxing. 'Tell us about the

leader.'

'Jessica Carter,' the demon said, sitting itself down, cross-legged. 'She is ruthless and ambitious.'

'Tell us about her connection to the girl who was killed,' Wind Talker said, his eyes ever sharp.

'Mother and daughter,' Scourging Agony said with a sinister smile. 'Well done.'

Stalker twitched. She wanted to jump forward and punch the demon right between the eyes. 'The girl has a twin,' Scourging Agony continued. 'A human.'

Weaver was nursing her cut arm but she looked up sharply at this and locked eyes with Stalker. There was something in Weaver's eyes that made Stalker extremely uneasy, it was something so dark, almost vicious.

'Did you know?' Stalker mouthed. Weaver shook her head and returned her attention to her wound. Weaver had spent two days held captive by the Witches while they tried to convert her, they had begun to treat her like family. Clearly they hadn't revealed everything.

'But it's the rite mistress you should be mindful of,' the demon said, his voice dripping. He leaned forward, seeming to stretch across the little garden towards the gathered shifters. 'Spinner-of-Crystal.' The words dripped from his black mouth like little diamonds.

Wind Talker stepped carefully towards Scourging Agony.

'Is she special?'

'No,' the demon replied. 'She's another puny fleshling. But she's good, quick and clever. She's been casting circles since before you were born, boy.'

Wind Talker laughed and turned away. The demon

stopped him in his tracks with a click of his fingers. 'You don't truly understand it yet. You were surprised when I broke free of your pretty cage. Magic is just symbolism, that's all it is. The moment I decided to ally with you the cage was no longer necessary and so it ceased to function. Once you fully comprehend that fact you will stand a chance of becoming half the ritualist she is.'

Wind Talker's face twitched, caught between anger and appreciation. His eyes narrowed and he turned slowly to face Scourging Agony.

'I will be twice the ritualist she is.'

'We'll see,' the demon said, smiling.

'Thank you,' James said quickly, stepping forwards and placing a steadying hand on the shoulder of his seething brother. 'I have an idea for a place for you. Let me discuss it with my pack and we'll speak to you again in due course. What reassurance do we have from you that you won't betray us?'

'The way I betrayed them just now, you mean?' Scourging Agony spat. 'You just have to trust me.'

The demon winked at James and disappeared.

'Oh well that's just great,' Stalker said with an exasperated sigh. Trusting a creature like that ranked on a par with beating up gangsters.

'What's your idea, James?' Weaver asked, a slight crack in her voice that only Stalker seemed to notice.

'I know of a tattoo and piercing parlour not far from here,' James replied. 'They do these extreme piercings and this scarification stuff. That demon was getting a high off self-inflicted pain, so I figured he'd enjoy the vibe in a place like that. Plus, it's perfectly legal.' He smiled and caught Stalker's eye. She returned his smile.

'That sounds promising,' Weaver said quietly.

'What's it called?' Stalker asked.

'Red Drop of Ink.'

CHAPTER TWENTY ONE

FIGHTS-EYES-OPEN

THE PHONE IN HIS LAP LIT UP WITH AN INCOMING CALL from Wind Talker. The third in fifteen minutes. He couldn't answer, and felt frustration mounting. The interview he was sitting in on was taking far longer than anticipated and he felt like he had nothing to contribute. His familiarity with the case was scarce and his mind was firmly fixed elsewhere. He watched his phone until the screen went black again.

Finally his colleague drew the interview to a close and Eyes excused himself swiftly. He gathered his files and snatched up his phone, hitting redial as he dashed out into the lobby of his chambers. The phone only rang once before Wind Talker answered.

'Hi,' Eyes said quickly. 'Sorry, I was tied up in a meeting. What's the problem?'

'I think we have it under control, but we need you to get back here now if possible. We have the boy here and need a plan.'

Eyes looked around the lobby. It was bustling with people coming and going. Sharp suits and briefcases, clicking shoes on the marble floor and the noise of the street outside each time the door opened.

'Okay, sure. I'm finished here for the day. I'll be back in twenty minutes.' Eyes hung up and walked briskly to the parking garage. It was quiet, and in the stillness Eyes felt as if he was being watched. He stopped by his car and put his briefcase down on the floor. There was a prickle down his spine and he sensed movement nearby.

Theodore Harris appeared from behind a pillar and Eyes breathed a sigh of relief.

'Mr. Davison,' Theodore said smoothly. He walked slowly towards Eyes, a small smile playing on his lips, his hands tucked into the pockets of his crisply pressed trousers.

'Mr. Harris,' Eyes said, a little cautious and uneasy about being approached like this. 'I didn't expect to see you here.'

'No, I'm sure you didn't. I apologise for startling you. I just wanted to catch up with you, see how you're getting along.'

'Fine, thank you,' Eyes replied. He wanted to like the Alpha of the Glass Wolves, but he couldn't for a moment trust him; everything about this situation screamed at Eyes to be cautious.

'I gather your family has a new addition.'

'Well, I see news travels fast.'

'Congratulations.' Theodore smiled, showing too many teeth.

'Thank you,' Eyes replied. He knew there was something else that Theodore wanted and he decided to wait it out rather than press for it.

'I have a matter I need to discuss with you, but perhaps here is not the best place. Would you come to my office first thing in the morning?'

'Certainly. Is there any particular reason for you requesting this meeting in person rather than picking up the phone?'

Theodore cocked his head and looked carefully at Eyes.

'Just trying to be friendly.' He flashed that awkward smile again and Eyes gave him a slow nod of acknowledgement while reeling inside with disbelief.

'Okay,' Eyes said after a moment. 'Well, it was great to see you. I'll see you again in the morning at 9am.'

'Excellent. You take care now.' Theodore turned and strode away.

Eyes got in his car and set off for Grove Street. He couldn't get Theodore out of his mind the whole way back. It was such a show of dominance, such an obvious attempt to intimidate. It had worked. Eyes was keenly reminded that he worked on Theodore's territory and that the experienced and connected Alpha knew far more about his comings and goings than he could ever hope to know in return. How had he known about James so soon? Had someone from The Watch told him?

He drove too fast, but wasn't stopped and soon arrived at 32 Grove Street. He went inside and heard urgent, whispering voices in the kitchen. He went straight there and found the pack assembled and all talking over one another.

'Hi,' he interrupted. 'What's going on?'

'Hi,' Stalker greeted him first, the others gave nods and smiles of greeting. 'We'll have to fill you in properly later. Right now we have an unconscious boy on our sofa who will probably come around any minute now and we need to decide what to do with him.'

'I was saying that we should take him and leave him in an alley,' Wind Talker said, his voice rising a little above a whisper until Weaver shushed him. He lowered his voice. 'Leave him in an alley and then James should find him, the boy hasn't seen his face. He can befriend him and find out what he knows. Then we can decide what to do with him.'

'Or we could just take him to the hospital,' Stalker hissed. 'He's been unconscious the whole time. I don't think he knows anything, and if he did see anything last night then his mind will have messed it up.'

'What about the Witches?' Eyes asked, looking from one face to the next. 'What if they get hold of him? They could torture him for information. Even if he doesn't know anything they could still do it and he would suffer terribly.'

'Last-Breath-Echoes said something this morning about knowing what someone was doing right before they died,' Weaver said, her voice low and steady. 'What if the Witches can extract subconscious information in a similar way?'

'Echoes also said that she had removed all trace of us from the body and wouldn't report Ian's existence. The Witches may never know his identity. We are NOT killing this boy,' Stalker hissed again. She was so angry and was struggling to keep her voice down. Eyes had rarely seen her this way and was taken aback. 'I will not allow it.' She snapped, her voice rising.

'With all due respect,' Wind Talker said coolly. 'It is not your decision to make. We do what is best for the pack, or whatever the Alpha tells us to do.'

All eyes fell upon Eyes. He tugged at his collar, suddenly unbearably uncomfortable.

'James? I appreciate that this is your first day with us, but I would appreciate your opinion.'

'Well,' James paused, rubbed his temples and sighed. 'I think Stalker is right. I don't think we can justify killing an innocent human. My only reservation is that a quick death might spare him if the Witches go after him. But that's a big "if".'

Eyes watched his pack mates for a minute. He had missed so much and felt disconnected from them all. Wind Talker was so cold at times, ruthless one might say, but he undoubtedly felt strongly about what was best for the pack. Stalker and Weaver had changed, though he couldn't quite put his finger on what was different about either of them. James was a stranger to him still, yet he felt connected to him through Unchained Lightning, and trusted his wisdom and judgement.

'We take the boy out of the house, we don't want him to be able to identify this place. We wake him up, just one or two of us so as not to frighten him, and find out what state he's in. Then we make a call. We might be able to protect him.' Eyes looked pointedly at Stalker, who looked about ready to start throwing punches. She calmed down but still looked sullen. 'James, you and I will handle this.'

Eyes needed cool heads on this one and he wanted

the chance to get to know his new brother. The two of them went quietly into the living room and Eyes looked down on the unconscious teenager. He looked so young, his whole life still ahead of him. His girlfriend had been brutally killed by terrifying monsters, his home wrecked, and then he himself had been rendered unconscious and kidnapped. The poor boy's life was turned upside down and it would be a miracle if he was able to recover from this.

Eyes and James lifted Ian carefully, Eyes taking his head and shoulders, James his feet. Weaver went ahead of them and opened the door, she checked that the street was clear and then ushered them outside. They put him in the back of Eyes' car and climbed into the front. James kept an eye on the boy while Eyes drove east, towards St. Catherine's.

'There was a demon,' James whispered after a long silence.

'Oh?'

'Stalker and I found a demon with him in his flat. It had done something to him to knock him out and we interrupted. Wind Talker summoned it and we convinced it not to go back to the Witches.'

'How did you manage that?' Eyes asked in surprise.

'By promising to let it feed off self-inflicted pain on our territory.'

'Oh, I see.'

'It was able to tell us a little about the Witches too, we got some helpful information and I expect we can get more.'

'What happens if it betrays us?'

'I'm not sure,' James said, glancing at Eyes with unease.

'Well, let's hope we never have to find out.' Eyes tried to smile, but his face wouldn't cooperate.

They reached a quiet part of St. Catherine's and Eyes parked the car. They carefully pulled Ian from the back seat and dragged him into a dark alley. Night had fallen and Caerton hummed with its usual nocturnal activity, but here in this spot it was relatively secluded and quiet.

Eyes crouched in front of Ian, who they had propped against the brick wall. He gave the boy's shoulder a firm shake. 'Hey, are you all right?'

The boy stirred and Eyes shook him again. He looked up at James and beckoned him down. James crouched down and touched Ian's shoulder.

'Are you all right, mate?' James asked, raising his voice a little.

The boy's head rolled from one side to the other and back again and a whimper escaped his parted lips. His eyes flickered open and looked around blearily. Eyes waited and watched, giving the boy a chance to come around. James gave him another gentle shake when his eyes didn't open fully. 'Hey, come on, wake up. Are you okay?' James asked, his voice becoming noticeably more anxious. Something was wrong.

Ian's eyes slowly opened, his head still lolled on one side and a low moan escaped his lips. His eyes were glazed and he just sat and stared into the mid-distance.

'He's not right,' Eyes whispered.

'No, he really isn't. We need to get him to hospital.'

Eyes nodded in agreement and they helped Ian to his

feet. He stood up but was uncoordinated and continued to stare passively right through them. They got him back into Eyes' car and drove him back across Caerton to St. Mark's Hospital. Eyes felt his stomach turn in knots as they approached.

'We don't want to end up getting involved in this.' Eyes said reluctantly.

'No, but we can't just leave him, we have to get him some help.' James said solemnly.

They pulled into a drop-off space in front of the Accident and Emergency entrance and pulled Ian from the car. Eyes took the bulk of the boy's weight and James went ahead to grab a wheelchair from just inside the entrance. Eyes lowered the boy carefully into the chair and wheeled him into triage.

There were rows and rows of chairs filled with waiting patients, low moans were being emitted from some, a child was crying and a man on the far side of the waiting room was talking loudly into his mobile phone. A harassed-looking woman sat behind the desk with a queue of half a dozen people waiting to be logged in.

'We can't wait with him,' Eyes said in a low whisper. 'We need to get back to the house.'

'If the demon did this to him, the doctors won't be able to figure out what's wrong with him, will they?' James asked very quietly.

'No,' Eyes replied. 'We need to speak to the demon. That's the only way we'll get answers.'

'He'll be all right here,' James said, an edge of uncertainty in his voice. Eyes glanced at him, unsure how to respond. He didn't know if the boy would be all right, or if the Witches would find him. He crouched before Ian and looked into his glazed eyes, his head still lolled to one side and drool was hanging from his parted lips. He stood and looked around him, two paramedics were striding out from a corridor leading to cubicles, heading towards the main exit. Eyes moved into their path and held out a hand.

'Please, can you help this man? We found him in the street in St. Catherine's and brought him here. We don't know him and can't stay any longer.' He looked imploringly into one pair of eyes and then the other and the paramedics exchanged glances before nodding and turning their attention to Ian.

'Hello? Hello, can you hear me?' one of them said as he bent to examine Ian, in that loud voice reserved for the injured, the elderly and the hard-of-hearing. Eyes and James walked backwards a few paces then turned and made a hasty exit. They got back into the car and Eyes set off back to Grove Street. The relief was enormous, though he was reluctant to let go of all caution.

'The demon must have done something to him before we got there,' James said as they drove back to the house. 'He was already unconscious, but I guess we got caught up in stopping the demon going back to the Witches and didn't give the boy too much thought. I'm sorry.'

'It's okay, it's understandable.'

They arrived back at the house and found the others waiting anxiously for them. Stalker leapt up from her chair in the kitchen when they walked in, immediately firing questions at them.

'What happened? How did it go? What did he say when he woke up? Where is he now?'

'He was damaged, I think,' James said, voicing what Eyes had been thinking.

'Either the trauma or something the demon did to him,' Eyes continued. 'We need to get that thing back here and find out.'

Wind Talker strode out into the garden without a word and crossed the veil. Eyes followed him and the others trailed after him. Wind Talker drew his knife and stuck it right through his hand. Blood squirted out and trickled down his arm. Eyes didn't even flinch, the blood-letting was becoming so commonplace that he barely noticed it any more.

'Scourging Agony!' Wind Talker bellowed through gritted teeth.

The demon appeared in front of them. It was the first time Eyes had laid eyes on it and he suppressed a shudder of revulsion at the loose skin and black eyes and mouth.

'Ooh, that looks painful,' the demon said, sneering at Wind Talker.

'What did you do to that boy?' Wind Talker shouted.

'I thought you would never ask.' A grotesque smile formed on the demon's face. 'I extracted his memories for my mistress.'

Stalker and James reacted immediately, clearly ready for a fight. Eyes caught Stalker's arm and her head snapped to him, her eyes glowering at him. He shook his head in warning and gently pulled her to his side. 'That's right, calm your dog down. I didn't take the memories to her. I was intercepted by this rabble and have been true to my word to them.' Scourging Agony said with contempt.

'Do you still consider her to be your mistress?' James

asked, tension in his voice.

'No, I suppose not. Old habits die hard.'

'There's a place for you, half a mile from here,' James explained. 'It's a place where people go to deliberately inflict pain upon themselves, they decorate and mutilate their bodies with needles. Does that sound adequate for your needs?'

Scourging Agony drew a long, rattling breath and clicked his fingers against one another. His black eyes moved slowly from shifter to shifter as he considered their offer.

'I believe so,' he replied. The demon grinned at them, his black mouth distorted and grotesque.

'What about the boy?' Eyes asked, a tremor in his voice. 'Will he recover? How much did you take from his mind?'

'Everything,' the demon replied, as if it were the most obvious answer in the world. 'I took everything, all of his memories. He will remain as he is now unless I put them back. I can put them back if you would like.'

'No,' Eyes said quickly, before anyone else could speak. Stalker tensed at his side and he held her steady. 'No, I don't think that would be wise. Best he not remember anything of this business.'

'What happens when the Witches summon you?' James asked.

'If I ignore them they will either think that I have perished, or will know that I have betrayed them.' Scourging Agony looked thoughtful, but not concerned. 'They may use stronger magic that I cannot ignore and drag me to them against my will.'

'Don't ignore them,' Eyes said, his voice barely above a whisper. His thoughts were spinning as he tried to puzzle a way out of this mess. 'You'll have to answer their call and lie to them. Can you do that?'

'Of course,' the demon said, bowing his head slightly. 'What would you have me tell them?'

'That someone else had beaten you to it,' Eyes replied. 'You found the boy in a catatonic state with no memories.' He didn't know if it would work, he knew he couldn't trust this demon's word for a second but it was worth a shot. He wondered if they were making a terrible mistake and whether they would be better off killing the demon. But he knew what Fortune would have done, he knew he would have tried to turn the situation to his advantage. 'You'll report back to us and give us any information we ask for about the Witches. Do you understand?'

'I do,' the demon replied frostily. 'I had better go to them now, in that case, in order to prevent any suspicion.'

'Do it,' Eyes replied and in the blink of an eye Scourging Agony was gone.

Stalker snatched her arm from Eyes' grip and slapped him hard across the face. Eyes instinctively put a hand to his cheek and recoiled from the attack, but he had known it was coming and it didn't so much as sting.

'How could you do that? How could you make that kind of deal with that thing?' she shrieked. 'This is not good. Not good for the boy, obviously, but for us too. I'm worried about the things we've done. At least the boy won't be talking any time soon but that's really beside the point. The Witches we can handle, the police we can handle. Becoming the type of creatures that would allow an innocent person to end up like that? Can we handle that?'

She turned and stormed away without waiting for a reply. Eyes heard the front door slam and looked cautiously around at the rest of the pack. No one spoke. Stalker's question hung in the air around them for a long, silent moment.

'We'll have to,' Eyes finally whispered.

Chapter Twenty Two

Stalker-of-Night's-Shadow

The door slammed shut behind her and rattled in its wooden frame. Stalker glanced at it and considered going back inside to talk things over with Eyes. She was too angry, she needed to cool off, so she shifted into an owl and flew off into the night sky. The tumultuous clouds swirled overhead and rain began to fall. Somewhere nearby there was a shriek and a dark shape rose up from the street and snatched something out of the air. Hepethia was dangerous, even for shifters who belonged there, and Stalker swiftly crossed the veil back into the human world. She headed straight for her flat, which was a few blocks away.

She landed on a windowsill and shifted carefully into the form of a moth. It was difficult to make her body so small and it took a great deal of concentration. There was an air vent above the window and she crawled inside, right through into the kitchen.

Fluttering down from the vent, she shifted into her human form and landed smoothly on the floor. It was almost pitch black and the shadows seemed deeper and darker than they should. Stalker shivered, the emptiness of the place was palpable. She flicked a light on and it flooded the kitchen. She closed her eyes for a moment, recoiling from the sudden brightness. As her eyes adjusted, she opened them again and looked around. The surfaces were gathering dust.

Stalker moved into the living room and turned on another light. Something on the table caught her eye, a little package wrapped in brown paper and tied with thick string sat all on its own. She went to it and hurriedly unwrapped it. A small vial of water on a black string tumbled out. The vial was full to the brim and sealed with wax, there was not the slightest air bubble inside and she turned it over in her hand in confusion. She looked at the paper and saw small writing scrawled over the inside.

My dear Stalker-of-Night's-Shadow,

Congratulations on fulfilling your oath to Odin to take the fight to the Furies. Please find enclosed Still Waters. This talisman will help you to keep a cool head and calm nerves. Odin gifts us with furious fire when we need it, but he is also infinitely wise, and the All Father knows that sometimes we need control and this will help you with that.

It is my firmest wish to see you achieve great things in this life. Please do not hesitate to contact me for any support you may need.

On behalf of all of Odin's Warriors,

Your brother,
Ragged Edge

Stalker smiled. She placed the talisman around her neck, carefully folded the piece of paper into a small square and tucked it into her pocket.

She picked up her post and sat down at the table to go through everything that had mounted up. It was dull and tedious, but the vial of water against her chest felt cool and calming and her fingers kept drifting to caress it. She was concerned about paying the bills for a place she rarely visited and never stayed at, and considered giving up her flat. But as tonight had demonstrated, it was a valuable bolt-hole, a place to go when she needed her own space.

It occurred to her that she didn't know what would happen if she crossed the veil here. Hepethia was another layer of reality that existed alongside the human world. Sometimes it resembled the human world, if shifters had moulded it to do so. She could mould this place to suit her needs. She crossed the veil, holding her breath in anticipation. She dropped suddenly, falling rapidly towards the empty street and a few feet from the ground she stopped falling and floated gracefully down, thanks to her pendant. She was at the edge of the maze that the Blue Moon had created. The ground beneath her feet was cobblestones that stretched away to the south into a misty haze. Behind her was a huge, red brick wall that marked the edge of the maze. It was a relief to find that crossing the veil at her flat, her own private territory, led her to a place outside of this demon trap.

She crouched down and placed a hand on the smooth,

wet cobbles. She thought about what she would like this place to be; secure, safe, hidden and comfortable. The ground moved slowly, rumbling and vibrating. A mound began to rise beneath her and she wobbled slightly before finding her balance. A small hill formed against the brick wall, the cobbles broken apart slightly with grass sprouting up between them. It looked perfectly natural and Stalker wondered what she had created.

A moment later, she felt herself sinking slowly into the ground, like sinking through quicksand, but she didn't feel panic, she felt as though she were being wrapped in a thick duvet and drawn into an enormous bed. The ground swallowed her up and closed over her, hiding her perfectly. She blinked in the darkness and slowly light began to fill the space. It was warm, yellow light, like a hundred candles, and in the little hollow beneath the hill she found mounds of cushions, and set into the earth around her were shining crystals.

It was beautiful and everything she had wanted. Now she would have to keep her flat, it was the doorway into this place and only she could enter. With a smile she crossed the veil again and found herself back in the living room.

Finally she felt ready to return to the pack. She walked slowly through the rain, feeling every drop on her hair and skin.

She entered the dark, quiet house. She crept up the hall and peered into the living room. Wind Talker was curled up in front of the electric fire in his badger form, breathing heavily. James was scrunched onto the small sofa with a blanket over him. Stalker was struck by this, she had grown accustomed to shifters sleeping in their animal forms and seeing James, who didn't yet have a shifter name either, sleeping like a normal human seemed odd.

Weaver was awake, furiously sketching in the low light from the little fire. She looked up at Stalker and gave her a small smile.

'Hi,' she whispered. 'Are you all right?'

'Yeah,' Stalker replied. 'Has Eyes gone home for the night?'

Weaver nodded in reply. Stalker was relieved and moved into the room; she pulled off her boots and sat down next to Weaver. Her sketches were of the Plague Doctor and a hoard of huge rats. It made Stalker shudder. She didn't care for rats.

Stalker watched Weaver drawing for a long time, neither of them spoke. Stalker thought about the way in which Weaver had sided with Wind Talker and been so happy to go along with the plan to ally with Scourging Agony. It was a side to Weaver that she hadn't seen before. She was sure that it was to do with the Witches and what they had done to her when they held her captive. Weaver had a vicious streak when it came to dealing with them now. Stalker wanted vengeance for the destruction of the Blue Moon, she felt furious anger towards the Witches and the Phoenix Guard, but there was something else to Weaver's pain. It was something that Stalker couldn't quite identify and didn't relate to.

She didn't want there to be distance between her and Weaver, she wanted to go back to how things used to be when they used to sit up late talking and go sneaking around getting into trouble. It felt like she was thinking back on a lengthy childhood many years ago, yet it had only been a few weeks. Stalker put her head on Weaver's shoulder in a silent gesture of affection. Weaver tilted her head so that her cheek touched Stalker's head and Stalker smiled to herself. Perhaps all was not lost.

CHAPTER TWENTY THREE

FIGHTS-EYES-OPEN

EYES EXAMINED HIMSELF IN THE MIRROR. His suit looked good and he filled it well. His hair was never immaculate, it was too wild to tame, but he carried it off well. He had dark circles under his eyes and his cheeks looked a little drawn in. The stress under which he was living was written clearly on his face.

Chloe came up behind him and snaked her arms around him. He welcomed her warmth and turned to face her. She wasn't dressed yet and her hair was still tussled from bed. Eyes ached for her and stooped to kiss her deeply. With regret, he pulled away and stroked her hair gently.

'You look sharp,' she said with a smile.

'Thank you,' he replied with a grin. 'I have an important meeting this morning.'

'On a Saturday?'

'I'm afraid so.' He turned back to the mirror and

straightened his tie for the fourth time. 'I should be home this afternoon though. I'm looking forward to spending some time with you and Amy.'

'I'll hold you to that,' Chloe said over her shoulder as she swept away towards the bathroom.

Little feet came racing down the hall and an excited squeal yanked Eyes away from his reflection.

'Daddy!' Amy ran into the bedroom with her arms stretched above her head. 'Up!'

Eyes scooped her up into his arms and spun her around, grinning like a fool as she squealed and laughed with delight. How simple it was to make everything right in the world of a three-year-old. He fell with her onto the bed and they snuggled up together. He examined her carefully and tried to stifle a laugh at what he found.

'You, munchkin,' he said with mock seriousness, 'have glitter all over your hands and in your hair.'

'Yeah,' she said with a grin. 'Mummy said bath tonight after more glitter fun today.'

'You can help with that,' Chloe called from the bathroom and Eyes felt a small laugh bubble up his throat. What would Wind Talker say if he saw any of this? Not a lot, Eyes decided, but if looks could kill then his most certainly would.

'Can I? Oh great, I'm looking forward to it.' He stroked Amy's hair and gave her a kiss on the forehead. 'Daddy has to go to a very important meeting now with a very important man.'

'Who man?' Amy asked, full of innocent curiosity and not a hint of negativity.

'A man who just might be secretly in charge of the

whole city,' he whispered with a conspiratorial wink.

'Oh, Daddy, that's a very big job.'

Eyes kissed her again and stood up from the bed. His tie had been jostled loose and his suit rumpled but with a heavy sigh he decided it really didn't matter.

'I will see you later and we'll make glitter butterflies.'

'Yuck, no Daddy!' Amy shouted. 'Glitter monsters.'

'Of course,' he said. He smiled in wonder at her and went to the bathroom door. Chloe was brushing her teeth so he contented himself with a quick hug from behind and kissed the nape of her neck. 'See you later.'

She grunted a goodbye and he left her to it.

The drive into the city was relatively quiet but by the time he had parked and set off walking to Harris Intermediaries the streets were starting to feel busier. It was only a few weeks until Christmas and so Caerton was starting to feel festive and fill up with shoppers.

Eyes reached Free River Tower a little before 9am. The revolving door was locked and the lobby was dark. Eyes went to the buzzer system and found the button for Harris Intermediaries at the top. He pressed it and waited. After a moment there was a click and an unfamiliar male voice greeted him.

'Harris Intermediaries. Can I help?'

'I have a meeting with Mr. Harris, it's Martin Davison.'

'Of course, come on up.' The intercom went silent and the revolving door started to turn. Eyes made his way through the door and across the dark lobby to the lifts. At the push of a button, the doors glided open immediately and Eyes stepped inside. The ride up there in the lift was slow. Finally the lift slowed to a halt and the doors slid open almost silently.

The double doors opposite the lift were open and Theodore sat at his desk. He stood and ushered Eyes inside.

'Martin, do come in. Thank you for coming.'

Eyes looked around cautiously before entering the office. Theodore came out from behind his desk to shake Eyes' hand. Footsteps approached from the hall and a young man in a nice suit entered with a tray of coffee. He was human and his hands shook slightly as he put the tray down on the desk.

'Thank you,' Theodore said, a little too loudly. 'You can go back downstairs now. I'll be heading out after this meeting.'

The young man nodded, mumbled something polite and closed the doors carefully as he went.

'New assistant?' Eyes asked, taking a seat.

'Recruited for this morning from the insurance division downstairs. Useless, they're always useless. They scurry around in abject fear all the time.'

'You have no idea why?' Eyes said, raising a sceptical eyebrow. Theodore looked at him sternly.

'Of course I understand why,' he replied with a scowl. 'But I need someone who can overcome that and do the damn job without tripping over themselves.'

Theodore passed Eyes a cup of coffee and the two of them sat in slightly awkward silence for a moment. Eyes wondered what on earth he was doing there and burned with questions about the Glass Wolves, and about how Theodore had managed to build such a successful business whilst living as a shifter with all of the responsibilities that carried. He guessed that Theodore was several decades old and had had a lot of time to acquire wealth and success. It was unlikely that he also had a family to attend to in addition to everything else. That was what took its toll most on Eyes.

'What did you ask me here to discuss?' Eyes asked at last.

'Right, yes,' Theodore put his own coffee cup down and moved some papers around on his desk. 'I'm involved with a project and could use your expertise.'

'What kind of project?' Eyes asked. He was curious and cautious in equal measure.

'It's rather grand, but I have for a long time now wanted to see Caerton develop an underground rail system. After I don't know how many years, I have finally got all of the right people to approve it. I have politicians, city planning officials, architects, engineers, financiers and safety experts all working on it. What I need is a legal expert.'

Eyes swallowed a mouthful of his coffee and looked at Theodore carefully. He couldn't quite decide if Theodore was serious or a dreamer. He had never had the powerful Alpha pegged as a dreamer before, though he was clearly ambitious.

'I'm a criminal barrister,' Eyes said slowly. 'I would assume you need a solicitor versed in contractual law. You must have an entire legal team here.' Eyes indicated their surroundings.

'I need one of *our* people on this and you are the only such person.' Theodore's eyes were fierce and deadly serious. Eyes felt extremely uncomfortable and rather lacking in choice. 'I can bring you in-house, get you out of chambers. It's one less alibi for you to worry about. You can tell me when your territory needs you and never need to worry about how many sick days you take.'

Eyes loosened his tie slightly, his throat felt tight. Theodore made a good argument but something inside him was telling him to be careful here. Theodore already knew too much about Lightning Lord business, what he was proposing would give him unparalleled access to a rival pack.

'I would retain my autonomy, yes?' Eyes asked.

'Of course. You would remain the Alpha of the Lightning Lords and be in no way tied to the Glass Wolves, although I would hope you would count us as your allies. I will better your annual salary and give you few fixed working hours. As long as you can attend the meetings I would need you for and get the work done on schedule then you can call your time your own.'

'I need some time to consider it,' Eyes said, watching Theodore's face carefully for his reaction. He didn't so much as twitch.

'Of course.'

'I'll get back to you on Monday. Is that agreeable?'

'Absolutely.'

'Why are you doing this?' Eyes asked, suddenly struck by the peculiarity of the situation. 'Why build an underground railway?'

'Caerton needs one,' Theodore said smoothly, standing up to indicate the end of the meeting. Eyes stood slowly, still thinking furiously.

'No, there's something more to it than that. What's in it for you?'

'Curious man, Martin,' Theodore said with that smile of his that showed too many teeth. 'But if I told you I'd have to kill you.'

Eyes swallowed a nervous laugh. Theodore spoke with a smile but he was absolutely serious. Eyes left the office feeling like he had been trampled by rhinos. This was not going to be an easy decision to make.

He arrived at Grove Street soon after, to find the others assembled in the kitchen eating breakfast, James sitting at the table with a laptop open in front of him.

'Morning,' Eyes called in greeting as he entered the kitchen. 'What are you doing, James?'

'Looking for an office to rent in St. Mark's. The pickings are slim.'

'We'll help you find somewhere,' Stalker said, leaning over his shoulder and blinking sleepily at the screen. 'How about this one? It's only about ten minutes' walk from here, near the high street.'

'It's too expensive. Don't worry, I'll find something.'

Wind Talker handed Eyes a bacon sandwich and propped himself back against the counter to eat one of his own.

'Who are you trying to impress?' Wind Talker asked between mouthfuls of food.

'I just had the strangest meeting with Theodore Harris,' Eyes replied. He loosened his tie and sat down at the table. 'He offered me a job.'

'Okay,' Wind Talker said slowly. 'Why?'

'He's building an underground rail network and needs a legal advisor.'

'An underground rail network?' James repeated, his

voice full of curiosity and confusion. 'Why?'

'It's weird, right?' Eyes asked, before tucking into his food.

'I take it he's got human approval and whatever else he needs for it?' Wind Talker asked. He crossed his arms over his chest and leaned against the counter, his face set in a deep frown. Eyes nodded, his mouth full of food.

'It's an ambitious project, sure,' Stalker said, a frown on her brow. 'But why are you so suspicious?'

'I'm not sure,' Eyes said, having swallowed. 'It just doesn't feel right. Our kind don't normally do this. We're not normally big power players in human affairs. We just control the demons and try to stay alive. This sort of interference strikes me as very unusual.'

'But we do have people in key positions though,' Stalker said. 'I mean, there's Last-Breath-Echoes in the morgue.'

'One of the Glass Wolves is a police officer,' Weaver spoke up and everyone looked at her. 'Vengeance-of-Steel, or Sergeant Rachel Snow as she's otherwise known.'

'That's interesting,' Eyes said, raising an eyebrow.

'Warden-of-Stones is the curator of the museum,' James said. 'And she's a city councillor.'

'Really?' Eyes said, looking more and more intrigued. He knew a few politicians in the city, but not every councillor.

'It's like chess,' Stalker muttered.

'Hmm,' Wind Talker murmured. 'It is rather. Why do I get the feeling that someone is assembling pieces into critical positions?'

Everyone looked at him and silence hung in the air.

'By someone, do you mean Theodore?' Eyes asked. Wind Talker nodded. 'What is his shifter name? Does anyone know?'

'No,' Eyes replied. The others shook their heads. 'He always calls me by my human name too, even when we're alone.'

'Are you going to take the job?' Stalker asked him.

'I think I have to, it isn't much of a choice. He's offering me a very appealing deal which will radically simplify my life, and it may give us the opportunity to find out more about him and what he's up to.'

'We could do with knowing more about this railway business,' James said.

'Oh!' Stalker exclaimed, sitting bolt upright in her chair. 'I have a friend in the Development and Regeneration department, or something. I'm having lunch with him on Tuesday!'

'Perfect,' Eyes said, grinning at her. 'How do you know him?' He couldn't help but marvel at her connection and was intensely curious about how it had come about. He wondered if this was the person she was always sneaking off to see and who she sometimes smelled of.

'We went to school together. We moved to Caerton together straight from school and he got an internship with the council. He's just like an admin person, not high up or anything, but he might know something.'

Eyes nodded along, pleased at her openness, and something told him that this was not her secret. He wished there were no secrets in the pack, but on reflection, he knew that they were inevitable and perhaps, given the intimacy of pack life, it was no bad thing to keep some things for themselves. He felt that way about his family, after all.

'What else do you know from your time with The Watch, James?' Eyes asked, changing tack.

'Not much, they kept me separate from pack business.'

'Do you know anything about their allies?' Wind Talker asked.

'No, nothing. I didn't even really know about that stuff until I met Unchained Lightning.'

'Too bad,' Wind Talker said with a disappointed sigh.

'But I did hear things,' James said, looking uncomfortable. Eyes watched him carefully, waiting. 'Things I don't think I was supposed to. I got the impression that they are really worried about something and I heard mention of a missing king.'

'The King-of-Glass-and-Steel,' Wind Talker said, nodding his head. 'The city's soul, basically, he's missing. I expect The Watch are heavily involved in working out that particular mystery, seeing as it's their job to serve and protect the city.'

'I don't know,' James said. 'It seemed like they were taking it pretty personally. Could he have been their ally?'

'Oh my god!' Stalker shouted. 'Yes. I knew that. I'm sorry, I forgot all about it. Shadow's Step told me once. I thought it was odd at the time, Ragged Edge must have already known that the King was missing and didn't want to say because he didn't want his pack to appear weak to the others. Red Scythe asked him to ask his patron, that was the word he used, about the demons being restless and disorganised, and Ragged Edge got all sort of flustered and wandered off. Shadow told me that the embodiment of the city was a close ally of The Watch.'

'So The Watch tried to hide the disappearance from the rest of us at first, but they must have told the other packs about it because Theodore told me about it that first day after the Blue Moon–' Eyes' voice trailed off and they all exchanged troubled looks.

'I found a place marked on the map that might be worth checking out,' Wind Talker said, breaking the uneasy silence. 'It's labelled The Watchtower, maybe there's something there that can clue us in to what's going on with the city.'

'Good idea,' Eyes said.

Once they were all ready to face the day, Wind Talker led them south, in Hepethia. They negotiated the tangled maze of brick houses and emerged onto a crystalline plain, the ground smooth and shining with the occasional formation of jagged quartz sticking out of it. Ahead was a bluish haze and Eyes squinted, trying to make out any landmarks.

'It should be around here somewhere,' Wind Talker said, his voice barely above a whisper. 'It's hard to map Hepethia, but it didn't look far from the maze.'

Stalker pointed and took a few steps into the fog.

'There,' she said. Eyes followed her, looking around cautiously. He caught sight of James and saw the anxious expression on his face.

'You okay?' he asked. James nodded, but Eyes didn't believe him. 'Is this your first trip out into the wilds of Hepethia?'

'Yeah,' the new pack member whispered. His hand patted his jacket tentatively and he breathed a sigh of relief. Eyes cocked an eyebrow, bemused by James's odd behaviour.

'Checking you didn't forget your keys?' Eyes asked, a smirk slipping onto his lips before he could stop it.

'No,' James said, surprised. He opened the left side of his jacket and Eyes glimpsed the grip of a handgun holstered there.

'What do you have that for?' Eyes spat. His reaction surprised both of them and James stopped walking. Eyes stopped and faced him. 'I'm sorry, but seriously, why do you have a gun?'

'I had a close call a few years ago, I was shot on a job. Obviously, I survived, but it stopped me working for a while. I lost my confidence and my psychiatrist, that they made me see, suggested arming myself.' He was scowling at the memory of being forced into therapy, and Eyes suppressed a smile. 'I don't think this is quite what she had in mind,' he shrugged. 'But it was what I felt I needed to do to be able to get back to work.'

'Those small handguns are prohibited, you must know that.'

'Yes I do.' James straightened his jacket and lifted his chin. Eyes let it go. Now was not the time and who was he to call his new pack mate on breaking the law after the things he had done recently?

'What's the delay?' Wind Talker asked, striding over to them. Eyes looked around at him and saw Stalker and Weaver a short distance away, waiting.

'Nothing important, we're coming,' Eyes replied. As they walked on through the strange mist, a shape began to emerge just ahead, a dark tower loomed overhead, suddenly very close. Breath caught in his throat and Eyes looked up at it. It was a little taller than a three storey house, made from old stone bricks that weren't uniformly shaped, and parts of the tower were crumbling and covered in moss. The Lightning Lords crept inside the circular tower through an open arch in the base that was just a little too low for Eyes to walk through without stooping. Inside was overgrown with weeds, and fallen leaves were piled several inches deep. Half of the roof was long since gone and a stone staircase spiralled up around the inside of the walls. Eyes led the way cautiously up the steps onto a landing near the top that covered half of the width of the tower; above was open to the sky.

In the centre of the space was a stone chair, and in it was an ancient looking fae in rusted armour with furs about his shoulders and long, tangled brown hair and beard that trailed all around him. Ivy was growing all over the throne and it twisted up over the wizened fae and into his hair, seeming to become a part of him. A cold gust of wind accompanied the Lightning Lords into the throne room and blew dry leaves across the floor. The figure in the throne looked at them wearily from under hooded eyelids.

'Autumn Reaper,' Wind Talker said quietly, addressing the fae. 'Greetings.'

The fae drew a long, slow breath. It lifted its head slowly and then dropped it again with a loud sigh. James stepped forward, exuding his steady aura that sometimes seemed to contradict his own disposition.

'Do you know anything about the disappearance of the King-of-Glass-and-Steel?'

'We are in disarray,' Autumn Reaper said with a

sigh. 'Neither here nor there, unsure of the path forward without our king. Not unlike yourselves.'

Eyes felt a stab of indignation at the cutting remark, undoubtedly the fae was referring to the missing heir of Caerton and Eyes resented the idea that the shifters need a monarch to lead them.

'Do you know where he is?' James asked, an edge of impatience in his voice.

'No,' Autumn Reaper replied. He closed his eyes and seemed to settle back to sleep.

Eyes moved to the wall and looked out over Hepethia. They were above the fog and below was a blanket of the grey-blue substance. Far away to the north the red light of the telecoms tower blinked.

'We're not going to get any more from him,' Eyes said quietly, turning back to the others. 'I think he might be hibernating or something.'

'Let's cross the veil and see where we end up,' Weaver suggested.

They made their way back down the crooked steps and out of the tower. Eyes held his breath, it was a risk to cross somewhere unknown, they could emerge in the middle of a road right in front of a crowd of people, but shifters had made this place for a reason; they must have done so somewhere safe.

He stepped across, his pack mates at his side. They found themselves in the empty lobby of a small office building. There were a few vague sounds of life somewhere above, and there was noise from the street outside, but otherwise it was quiet. Eyes strode to the door and opened it. The bright sunlight from outside spilled in through the doorway and he blinked against it. He stepped into the street and turned to look at the building as the others filed out after him. The street was rammed with cars and pedestrians, and right where the desolate stone tower stood in Hepethia was the modest office building they had stepped out from. It was part of a terrace, built mostly of sandstone, with a large sign plastered to the front, declaring "First Floor Space To Let".

It was like a giant invitation addressed directly to them and Eyes couldn't help but laugh out loud.

Chapter Twenty Four

Stalker-of-Night's-Shadow

Stalker glanced at James, who was staring at the building in disbelief.

'You have to enquire,' she urged him. 'It has to be a sign from Artemis. You came to us from The Watch, and the Watchtower in this world happens to have a vacant office when you need a new one.'

He looked at her with a raised eyebrow.

'I'm not sure I believe in signs from deities,' he murmured.

Stalker gave him a gentle shove.

'You're a shapeshifter. You need to start believing, James.'

Weaver patted his shoulder and nodded in agreement, and James looked between their smiling faces. With a sigh, he took his phone from his pocket and dialled the number that was displayed on the sign. He walked away from the others to talk and Stalker looked again at the building.

'No wonder we never noticed it before,' Weaver said. 'It's just so normal.'

'Where are we?' Eyes asked, under his breath.

'Right on the southern edge of St. Mark's,' Stalker replied, recognising some of the surrounding shops. 'I pass this way sometimes. China Town is about a block that way.' She pointed up the street. They weren't far from her flat, if she had just led the pack a few hundred yards to the west when they emerged from the maze in Hepethia, she would have led them right to her bolt-hole.

James returned to them after a minute, a huge smile on his face.

'It's within my budget. The agent is going to meet me here in half an hour to show me around.'

'That's great news,' Stalker said and she gave him a quick hug.

'I think we all have our own things to do,' Eyes said. 'But let's reconvene at Grove Street tonight.'

Everyone agreed and went their separate ways. James was going to wait for the agent and check out the neighbourhood, Eyes returned to his family for some quality time, Wind Talker and Weaver went back to Grove Street to continue researching the Plague Doctor and Stalker headed across St. Mark's to work.

She had three classes to teach that afternoon and the vial of cool water around her neck seemed to help her to balance her strength and keep her cool immensely. She actually felt good to be working, for the first time since she had changed she felt calm and in control. As she left the studio at the end of the day she lifted the vial to her lips to kiss it, thankful for its protection.

She returned to her flat to freshen up and collect clean clothes, and while she was there she wrote a short note to Ragged Edge, thanking him for the vial and his kind letter. She paused before signing it, trying to decide whether she should say anything about the King-of-Glass-and-Steel. She decided against it and quickly signed and folded the letter.

Stalker pricked her finger with a sharp knife from her kitchen and let a few drops fall on the letter. She didn't really know what she was doing, she was just following her instincts. She went to the window and opened it. A blast of cold air rushed in and she had to brace herself slightly against it. Stalker rubbed her bleeding finger along the window sill and watched the dark sky.

A black shape appeared and drew closer. She had a moment of concern about what she had done, unsure of what she had managed to summon, but as the shape came closer she was relieved to see that it was indeed a raven.

The bird cawed as it approached and came to land outside her window.

'Hi there,' she said kindly, unsure of how well it could communicate. 'Can you take this letter to the shifter known as Ragged Edge, please?'

The raven cawed again and grabbed the letter in its claws.

'Ragged Edge of The Watch,' it squawked, catching Stalker off guard.

'That's right,' she replied. With a quick shake of its feathers, the raven hopped off the window sill and flew away with the letter. Stalker watched it circle overhead and then set off south-west towards Old Town. She just had to trust that the letter would reach him. Stalker rubbed the blood off the sill and shut the window. With one last check around her flat, she set off for Grove Street.

It was a busy Saturday evening and the ten minute walk took her along some streets alive with human revelry. She kept her head down and walked as fast as she could. Grove Street itself was a quiet residential street and Stalker reached number 32 without incident.

There was loud banter coming from the kitchen and she headed straight for it. Everyone was there already, and Eyes was pouring wine into plastic cups.

'Hello!' Several voices called out in greeting and Stalker took the cup that was thrust towards her.

'You took the office?' she asked James, who was sitting on the worktop with a drink in his hand.

'Yep, we're just about to toast it, we were waiting for you.'

'To James and his new premises,' Eyes said, raising his cup. 'At 14 Specula Row.'

Stalker frowned, the name of the road seemed important and sounded unusual.

'It's Latin,' Weaver said, grinning. 'City wall, or watchtower.'

'No way!' Stalker nearly spilled her wine. 'That's the name of the road?'

'It must have been where the city wall was when the Romans held Caerton,' Wind Talker said. 'A lot of the roads around there have Latin names. I think you were right, Stalker, it was a message from Artemis.'

'I may be starting to believe,' James said, with a smile just for her. She returned it and tilted her cup to him. They all drank and an easy silence fell on them for a moment.

'Where are we on the Plague Doctor?' Stalker asked. Weaver's smile slipped from her face.

'There's nothing,' she said softly. 'We can't find any references to him in any of Flames's notes. We're going to have to call on outside help I think.'

'We need to know where he might be hiding, who he's working with, what he wants. He's tethered himself here for a reason, he's not just here in passing, he has a purpose.' Wind Talker spoke with surprising passion. Stalker gave him an appraising nod.

'I'll take a patrol around the territory on my way out tonight,' Eyes said. 'I'll have a look out for any possible hideouts for a demon of disease. I can think of a few restaurants that ought to be shut down, one of them might suffice.' He snorted with laughter and Stalker felt her cheeks tug upwards despite the worry that gnawed at her, like a rat.

They drank some more and tried to enjoy the respite, Stalker put aside any concerns that she had about whether they could afford it or not. Eyes left a little after midnight and the rest of them settled down to sleep.

The room was rich red and black, with shadows that reached deep into the core of the many realms, seeping through and dividing them at the same time. There were four chairs on a dais and withered old figures sat in them, three of the people had long white beards and they all sat hunched over, seeming to blend with the chairs and the floor and the room around them. They each had a blue spotlight on them, as if on a stage. They were a part of the place, not merely inhabitants of it. Were they kings? They were old and infirm, they had shawls about their shoulders. All around them were small tables and more little hunched figures. Moving in between them were the spectres of nurses. Standing hidden in the shadows, almost invisible, was the Plague Doctor.

Stalker woke with a start and looked around the dark room. Weaver was sitting bolt upright, panting hard. Wind Talker and James were stirring too, James rubbed his face and looked around in confusion. Stalker shifted from fox to human and crawled over to Weaver.

'Are you all right?' she whispered.

'Yes,' Weaver replied. She wiped her sweating hands on her legs and drew her knees to her chest.

'I think I just shared your vision,' Stalker said, glancing at the others. 'How is that possible?'

'I don't know,' Wind Talker said. 'But with your unusual traits who knows what else you're capable of.'

'You didn't see it? The vision?' Stalker asked.

'No,' Wind Talker replied. James shook his head. 'The screaming woke me.'

'Screaming?' Stalker looked at him in alarm.

'I think that was me,' Weaver whimpered.

Stalker put an arm around Weaver's shoulders.

'It's all right, we're right here with you. I can't say it was just a dream, because we all know that's not true. But I can say that we'll tackle it.'

'What did you see?' James asked quietly, coming closer.

'It was like a throne room, but then it was like an old

people's home.' Weaver's voice was trembling.

Wind Talker stood up suddenly and left the room. Stalker heard his heavy footsteps on the stairs. A moment later he came thudding back down and came back into the living room with a map pinned to a cork board. He turned the light on and propped the board up on the sofa. The four of them crowded around it and Stalker looked at all of the strange markings on it.

'Flames-First-Guardian was keeping this record of trouble spots,' Wind Talker explained. 'I've been trying to keep it up-to-date and have spent some time examining it. There's a known problem here.' He pointed to one of the crosses with tiny runes next to it. It was about half a mile north of Stalker's dojo, and just about visible underneath Flames-First-Guardian's markings were the printed words on the map, *St. Mark's Retirement Home.*

'The runes say that it's a Rat King nest,' James said, squinting slightly. Stalker was surprised that he could read them and looked at him quizzically. He noticed and shrugged. 'The Watch didn't totally neglect me while I was with them, and I pick up things like this quickly. I have a photographic memory.'

'That is really useful to know,' Wind Talker said with a wink. 'Can you memorise this map, please?'

'You know, it doesn't really work like that.' James laughed and leaned closer to examine the map carefully for a few minutes. 'There are no guarantees, but I think that should be good enough for now.'

'We'll need to go and investigate the site,' Wind Talker said. 'But right now we should probably all try and get some more sleep, it's only 3am.'

They all agreed and settled back down to sleep. Weaver and Wind Talker resumed their animal forms, James went back to the sofa and Stalker watched him in bemusement as she lay down next to Weaver and stroked her cat head. Weaver purred and began to relax. Stalker wanted to help her sister to sleep, she wasn't worried about herself. She listened to everyone breathing and sensed the moment that she was the last one awake. The room was dark and the shadows were deep. Stalker couldn't rest, she could feel a familiar tugging sensation in her gut. She was being called out to hunt.

She got up quietly and crept from the house. She shifted silently into her fox form and sniffed out Pursuit-of-Midnight-Solitude. It didn't take long. The elusive demon caught her eye just a few metres from the house, and dashed off into the early morning, teasing Stalker and urging her into the chase.

She ran, more free and more at peace than she had been in days. She remembered her true nature, that of a solitary nocturnal predator with a thirst for this endless quest. The chase took her to the river and across into St. Catherine's, then north to the docks and into Storm Rider territory. She ran swift and silent, clinging to the shadows, her scent suppressed by the demon she hunted.

She crossed the river again into the industrial region of Northgate, and her paws pounded relentlessly on the wet tarmac in between the noisy factories that never slept. Pursuit-of-Midnight-Solitude led her through the north of Caerton, towards Redfield Park. Two weeks ago this would have been her pack's territory, but now it belonged to the Wrecking Crew and Stalker skidded to a halt at the boundary. The stink of the neighbouring pack was all over the place and she had enough previous experience with them to know not to cross. Pursuit-of-Midnight-Solitude slipped away from her into Wrecking Crew turf, and Stalker paced back and forth in frustration. She knew she couldn't follow. Almost any other territory she wouldn't hesitate to sprint through, but not this one.

Reluctantly, Stalker abandoned the chase and headed home. The sun was just touching the horizon as she entered the house, and the others were waking and getting breakfast.

'Hi,' Weaver said as Stalker entered the kitchen. 'Where did you go?'

'For a run, I couldn't sleep.'

'I was thinking,' James said as he buttered some toast. 'We need to check out the old people's home. Why don't we go in as prospective clients. I can say I'm looking around for my dad.'

'I like it,' Stalker replied with a smile. A flutter of anxiety niggled at her. She shouldn't feel so relieved at her pack mate coming up with a plan that didn't involve harming anyone. The recent actions of the Lightning Lords had caused her a great deal of moral strife, but if she was being absolutely honest with herself, the twinge of disappointment that she now felt was in part because she wanted to hit something. She was thirsty for a fight. When she felt like this there were two options, go out and find something to pick a fight with, or touch base with her humanity.

'I'll call them later and arrange a viewing for tomorrow.' James swept out of the room to go and freshen up.

Stalker took out her phone and was disappointed to have no messages. She quickly typed a message to Rhys.

Hi. Missing you. Can we get together later?

It was a while before he replied, though to be fair it was still early on a Sunday morning.

Hi, sure. I've been missing you too. Come to mine? I'll be home all day so whenever.

Stalker grinned to herself and quickly replied to confirm.

'Stalker,' Wind Talker said gently from behind her. She turned to face him. 'Can you help me with some research, please?'

'Of course,' she replied. She followed him upstairs into the bedroom. He had set up a computer and there were notes scattered across the floor. Stalker could hear the shower running in the bathroom next door.

'I want to find out a bit about the history of the building before we go there. There must be a reason for its infestation. There are no coincidences in Hepethia.' Wind Talker started up the computer and rifled through his notes.

'Is this what you do all day?'

'Pretty much. I'm going to need an income though. You and Eyes can't support the whole pack.'

'James has his own business too, don't forget that.' Stalker leafed through some of the notes. He had lists of names and places, diagrams, maps and a piece of paper with *Is TH Spiral Hand?* written at the top. 'Who's TH?'

she asked.

'Theodore Harris,' he replied.

James appeared in the doorway with a towel around his waist, he saw them and immediately looked embarrassed.

'Sorry,' Stalker said, hiding a smile. 'Small house.' She looked around quickly and spotted a pile of his clothes next to her own bag and passed them to him. He padded back to the bathroom and she exchanged a small laugh with Wind Talker.

James returned a minute later, dressed but with wet hair, and he sat on the bed to put his socks on as Wind Talker started trying to make the computer do what he wanted.

'What are you trying to do?' James asked.

'Research the retirement home,' Wind Talker replied, his lips curling in frustration at the slow pace at which the computer was connecting to the internet.

'Let me see what I can do,' James said. He took over and a few minutes later, having performed some sort of technological magic on the ancient system, everything seemed to be loading much more quickly. The three of them hunched over the computer as they searched the internet for useful information and James was in his element. 'I can probably hack into some useful systems, but would prefer to be using my own kit.'

Eyes arrived mid-morning and came to see what they were doing. Weaver hovered in the doorway and Stalker felt the warmth of having the whole pack together. She couldn't help but feel more positive about everything.

'Go back,' Wind Talker snapped, pointing at the screen. James went back to the previous page. 'There.'

Wind Talker tapped on a link and James followed it.

'Nice, we've found a history of the building going back hundreds of years here.' James said, grinning around at everyone.

'There,' Stalker said, looking carefully through the text. 'It was a hospital from 1660 to 1666, owned by Doctor Cornelius Wentworth.'

There was a link from his name and James clicked on it.

'He died of bubonic plague in 1666.' James read the short entry quickly. 'One of the last to die in that outbreak. He was buried in a plague pit in St. Mark's, Caerton.'

Stalker exchanged worried looks with the others. The pieces were clicking into place.

'It must have been his body that got dug up and taken,' she said. A shiver ran down her spine.

'So now a demon of plague has taken up residence in a former plague hospital and has used the corpse of the plague doctor to root himself in this realm.' Eyes paced the room, rubbing his temples.

'I was hoping to spend time today fashioning a new talisman for myself,' Wind Talker said. 'It should help when we visit the retirement home tomorrow.'

'Okay,' Eyes said with a firm nod. 'Go ahead. I want the territory patrolling this afternoon.' He looked pointedly at Stalker.

'I'm sorry,' she said, a stab of guilt hitting her throat. 'I have plans. I did a lap of the north before dawn.'

'Fine,' Eyes said, with no trace of resentment. 'Weaver and I will patrol. James, can you stay here and see what else you can find on the house, the actual doctor and the plague?'

'Sure,' James replied. 'We're due at the residential home at 10am tomorrow. I also get the keys to my new office and need to move my things. I've contacted Warden-of-Stones and have permission to take a van into Old Town. Can anyone be spared to help me move?'

'Yes, I'm sure we can all help. I don't need to be in court tomorrow, so I can be around too.' Eyes smiled. Stalker knew it must be hard for him, with so much to juggle. At least as Alpha he could delegate. In that moment she saw Fortune in him, in the way he was dishing out tasks and arranging patrols. She smiled at him. There was just the slightest physical resemblance too, in the way he paced and ran his hands through his thick hair. It was a little more than a passing resemblance and just for a moment her thoughts lingered on that similarity.

'Are we all going to the home? Or would a smaller party be wise?' Weaver asked.

'We'll all go,' Eyes said with no hesitation. 'We can masquerade as siblings.'

There were nods and murmurs of agreement. Stalker was looking forward to spending more time together. Her phone buzzed in her pocket and she quickly pulled it out to read the new message.

> Hi. Any idea what time you'll be here? I'm just having lunch. Looking forward to seeing you, R xx

Stalker glanced around the room, the others were talking and paying no attention to her. She held her phone close and replied.

I'm leaving in a few minutes. See you soon xxx

'I'm heading out soon. I'll be back tonight,' she told the pack.

'Where will you be?' Eyes asked.

Stalker glanced at the curious faces of the others. She had come this far without ever mentioning Rhys to anyone, not the Blue Moon or anyone else in the shifter world. She clung to her secret, reluctant to give him up to the scrutiny of her pack.

Weaver was watching her with a curious smile on her face. Stalker felt her cheeks burning.

'Erm, just with a friend. In town.' She bolted out of the door before her treacherous cheeks could do any more harm. She heard Weaver laughing and the men making confused noises behind her as she jogged down the stairs.

She left the house and headed straight for Rhys's house on foot. It was a cold day, with a clear sky; the first clear day in what felt like months, and she pulled her jacket tight around her against the biting cold. Winter had arrived.

She arrived at Rhys's house and knocked eagerly on the door. He answered quickly with a broad smile on his face.

'Hi,' he said, holding the door open for her. She stepped inside and he pulled her into his arms as the door swung closed. He captured her lips in a passionate kiss and she melted into it. He made her feel so alive and so human. They stumbled blindly across the room and onto the sofa, hardly drawing breath. They sat facing each other, kissing intensely and grabbing at each other.

Stalker tugged Rhys's t-shirt up and slid her hands

underneath it and across his back. She could feel the subtle difference in texture where the ink of his tattoos weaved across his skin. Gently, he brushed her hands out from under his top and placed them either side of his face. He held her face and kissed her so tenderly that her chest ached.

He broke the kiss and stared into her eyes, still cupping her face in his hands. 'I thought maybe we could go out, it's such a nice day. We could take a walk. Maybe we could drive back up to Fenwick and check out the sunset later.'

Stalker remembered their date, only a few weeks ago, the night before she had changed for the first time. It was a tempting offer. But she couldn't go into Fenwick any more. He couldn't take her to the museum either, that was on Watch territory. Future dates would need to be carefully planned and approved. She felt a little disheartened.

'It's surprisingly cold out, actually,' she said. She moved away from him slightly and his hands slid slowly down from her face and neck, over her shoulders and down her arms. 'Can't we stay here?'

She smiled seductively and leaned in for another kiss. She had one thing on her mind, the one thing she really needed in order to feel connected to another human being. He returned the kiss but Stalker felt like he was holding back and she let the kiss end. 'Is something wrong?'

'No,' he said a little too quickly. Stalker pulled away from him and looked him in the eye. She felt frustrated and confused. 'You're amazing, you're the most passionate and warm person I have ever known. I have to literally pinch myself on a regular basis to check that I'm not imagining you being in my life.' He seemed absolutely sincere and

Stalker began to relax again. His words made her blush.

'But you *are* holding back,' she said, not willing to let this go.

'Yes.'

'Is it something about me?' Stalker had been worried that it would be difficult to have a relationship with a human since the very first day of discovering her true nature. Fortune and Shadow, even Stone, had all warned her that it might not be possible. Humans often felt uneasy around shifters, knowing on some level that they were in the company of something supernatural. Rhys stifled a laugh.

'No, there's nothing about you that's putting me off. I just don't want to rush this. I don't want to dive into something physical without a solid emotional foundation first.' He lifted her hand and kissed her palm.

Stalker released a slightly frustrated sigh. She wasn't a kid, she was a woman and she had needs. Yet, he made a good point and was being more of a gentleman that any man she had ever been with before.

'Well, thank you for being honest and for being a real gentleman.' She looked into his dark eyes and saw that wonderful openness that she sometimes glimpsed. It held for a long moment without suddenly vanishing like it usually did.

I'm scared of the day I lose you.

Stalker shook her head at the intruding thought. She wasn't entirely sure who it belonged to. Rhys seemed undisturbed, though he looked at her a little strangely, and she tried to laugh in order to break the tension.

'Okay,' she said and she pushed him against the sofa

cushions and straddled him. He grinned and grasped her hips. 'This is how it's going to be, I'm going to kiss you again and you're going to enjoy it and you're going to relax and not worry so much. What will be will be.'

He looked like he wanted to protest so she quickly placed a finger on his lips. 'I agree with you, I think a strong emotional foundation is a good idea and I promise not to coax you into doing anything more intimate than you're comfortable with.'

She released her finger from his lips and brushed her lips against his instead. It was a soft, lingering kiss, filled with yearning and a promise of what was to come.

Chapter Twenty Five

Fights-Eyes-Open

Monday morning rolled around and the Lightning Lords assembled early for their day of productivity. They drove to the retirement home in Eyes' car. It had been a good weekend for Eyes, he had spent some quality time with his family and been able to catch up properly with the pack too. He knew that he was going to accept Theodore's job offer, but had yet to summon the courage to make the call. He would do it later. They needed to investigate the rat nest first and make a plan for taking down the Plague Doctor. He needed his attention on this task, Theodore would have to wait.

The retirement home was towards the east of St. Mark's in a slightly more leafy and affluent area. James directed Eyes and pointed to a driveway on the right. The gates stood open and a high wall with tall trees behind it hid the property from the road. Eyes turned into the drive and followed it carefully as it swept in a curve through lightly wooded gardens. The trees gave way to a gravelled car park in front of a huge and very old manor house.

It was built from dark grey stone and had two round turrets front and centre over a grand entrance with steps leading up to the wooden doors. It was quite an imposing building and as they all piled out of the car and looked up at the dark windows, Eyes couldn't help but shudder.

James took the lead and Eyes fell into step just behind him. He glanced back at Wind Talker, who was walking with the others and had a hand hovering nervously over his new talisman, which was hidden away under his shirt.

They entered through the main entrance into a brightly lit lobby with a large reception desk. The windows were small, so the space was lit with artificial lights, and the dark wooden floor gleamed. A woman's fast footsteps echoed down the wooden hallway and Eyes turned to see her approaching. She was late middle-aged, with neat, greying hair and a crispness that punctuated her appearance and demeanour.

'Hello? Can I help?' she asked as she neared them. James stepped forward and raised a hand.

'James Harper, we spoke on the phone yesterday?'

'Yes of course, about your father?' The woman extended a hand and James shook it.

'That's right,' James replied. 'This is my family. We all wanted to look around and make sure we're all happy with where Dad will be.'

Eyes nodded along and was quietly impressed with how James was doing.

'Of course, this way please.' The woman led them down the hall. James walked up front, listening to her spiel, answering her questions and asking plenty of his own. Eyes hung back with Wind Talker, while Weaver and Stalker pretended to look interested in the facilities.

'What are we looking for?' Eyes whispered, half to himself.

'We'll know when we see it,' Wind Talker replied.

Eyes looked at him and noticed a slightly glazed expression in his eyes.

'Are you all right?'

'Fine,' Wind Talker replied absently, his concentration fixed on something in front of them. 'The place is a fortress in Hepethia, but deserted. The infestation must be downstairs, in the basements.'

Eyes looked at his pack mate carefully. Wind Talker reached out and grasped Eyes' arm as they walked, as if he needed steadying.

'That must be disorienting,' Eyes whispered. 'Seeing both sides of the veil at once.'

'Very,' Wind Talker replied.

They slowed down as they passed an unmarked door on the right, and Eyes checked behind them. There was no one in sight and they slipped through the door into a narrow stairwell. It was dimly lit with walls on either side, the stairs leading down. Eyes went first, with Wind Talker's hand lightly touching his shoulder for guidance.

At the bottom of the stairs a narrow corridor stretched before them with small doors leading off it. They followed it to the end, where it turned right into a wider corridor with exposed pipes and a few twists and turns.

'Rats,' Wind Talker gasped. 'Everywhere.'

Eyes peered into the dark, there were no rodents in the

human world.

'How many?'

'Hundreds, a swarm of them. Crawling up the walls and along the pipes. He's down here, I can feel it. We need to leave, he could be on either side.'

Wind Talker reached into his shirt and tugged the talisman out, breaking its contact with his skin. He gasped and pressed a hand to the wall. His eyes lost that glassiness and returned to their normal colour and focus.

'Okay, let's go find the others and get out of here. We'll need a plan before we try to tackle this situation.' Eyes led the way back upstairs and opened the door into the hallway carefully, checking that there was no one there to see them emerge from the cellar. The coast was clear and he stepped out into the well-lit hall, Wind Talker right behind him, apparently desperate to escape the narrow, rat-infested corridors.

They jogged after the others, catching up to them in a large dining hall. The woman was talking about the entertainment that they provide for the residents. Eyes gently took Stalker's arm and led her a short distance away.

'Where were you?' she whispered.

'Checking the basement,' he replied. 'It's infested on the other side. He's definitely here and has a whole host at his control. We'll need a careful plan. He may know we're here.'

'Let's get out of here,' she whispered. There was no trace of panic in her voice, just calm authority.

'James,' Eyes called out, interrupting their tour guide. 'I just took a call from the carer, Dad's in a bad way. We should go.'

'Oh my, I'm sorry to hear that,' the woman said.

She hurriedly showed them back to the reception. 'I'm just at the end of the phone if you have any further questions or need our services.'

'Thank you,' James said as he shook her hand. 'You've been very helpful.' James was the perfect front man, calm, polite and just emotional enough to be believable.

They piled back into Eyes' car and set off towards the van hire place that James needed to get to to collect his rental van.

'It's a stronghold on the other side,' Wind Talker told them. 'Like a castle. It's old, older than the house. It could be that shifters built the house in order to have access to the place they created in Hepethia. But there were pipes in the basement, it looked almost normal down there, except for the rats everywhere.'

'What do we do?' Stalker asked. 'Do we try to attack it? If so, how will we infiltrate it?'

'We could come back here and cross over inside, that might be the only way in,' James suggested.

'We should do some more reconnaissance first,' Weaver said, her voice anxious. 'We need to be prepared.'

When they arrived at the rental place, James got out and went to collect his van. Eyes got out to stretch his legs and to call Theodore's office. The phone only rang twice before he answered.

'Harris.'

'It's Martin Davison,' Eyes said. There was a long pause.

'Good to hear from you,' Theodore said at last. 'How

can I help?'

'I've given your offer due consideration and would like to accept.'

'I am very glad to hear it.' Eyes could tell Theodore was smiling at the other end of the phone, though whether that was genuine happiness or satisfaction that his plan was unfolding correctly, Eyes couldn't tell.

'I'll need a week to clear my case load.' Eyes couldn't quite believe he was doing this. He ran his free hand through his hair and clung to the back of his tense neck.

'Of course, whatever you need. Welcome on board.'

'Thank you.'

Eyes ended the call and leaned heavily on his car. Stalker climbed out of the back seat and placed a hand on his shoulder.

'Are you all right?' she asked.

'Fine,' he replied wearily. 'I just made a deal with the devil.'

'There's no going back now,' she said with a smile. 'Let's get James moved, shall we?'

The rest of the day was spent emptying James's small office in Old Town into the back of the van and moving it all to his new place in St. Mark's. It was a bigger office, with a small reception hall and a door into his office with a frosted window in it, just like in the old movies featuring private investigators. Eyes wanted to see a well-dressed receptionist in stockings, doing her nails and waiting for the phone to ring.

They all laughed about it as they unloaded boxes of files and moved a desk and cabinets up the stairs into the first floor office. Eyes dipped in and out to make phone calls. He was shifting as many cases as he could over to colleagues and starting the wheels turning to get him out of chambers and into Harris Intermediaries. He was met with a number of surprised reactions to the news, which he tried not to let bother him. He knew it must look odd, such a dramatic change in focus, but it was no one's business but his own.

Around dinner time he went out and picked up a takeaway for them to eat in the office and Weaver poured out a round of fizzy drinks into paper cups for a toast.

'To James and his business. May it thrive here in St. Mark's.' Weaver lifted her cup.

'Hear, hear.' Eyes joined the toast, happy to see smiles on all of the faces around him. He leaned closer to Wind Talker from his perch on the desk, as the others started chatting animatedly. 'Could I please borrow that talisman of yours?'

'Of course,' he replied. He lifted it over his head and passed it to Eyes. Eyes took the necklace and looked at it. It was a small copper eye styled like something from ancient Egypt and it hung on a black bootlace. Eyes lifted the lace over his head and let the pendant rest on his chest under his shirt. It was the most bizarre sensation, like wearing glasses with pictures on them.

'This is so strange, I know I'm sitting in the office, but I can see the Watchtower clearly at the same time, right through the walls and ceiling where there's no ceiling in Hepethia.'

He wobbled from his perch on the edge of the desk and Stalker laughed as she quickly grabbed him and steadied him again. Wind Talker laughed too and Eyes felt content that the rift between them was on the mend.

He stood and walked from the office onto the landing, his hands outstretched like a child playing blind man's bluff. Straight ahead, where there was a door into another set of offices in the human world, in Hepethia the ancient stone Watchtower lay before them, and sitting on the throne, tall and proud, was a new figure with a crown of ice upon his head. Frost ran all down his body, over the stone throne and spread out from his feet across the floor. The roofless tower opened right onto the night sky, crystal clear and filled with stars, the waning crescent moon shone down on the tower, causing the frost to glisten.

Eyes smiled and removed the talisman, his vision returned to normal and he passed it carefully back to Wind Talker.

'Beautiful,' he said with a serene smile. 'Seems winter has arrived.'

They returned to their feast and unpacking boxes. Life was good, if only for a few hours.

Chapter Twenty Six

Stalker-of-Night's-Shadow

Stalker sat in the café, anxiously playing with a napkin on the table while she waited for Ben to arrive. She wasn't sure how she was going to bring up the subject of the underground railway or explain how she knew about it, and the whole idea of using her oldest friend to get information was a touch unpalatable.

Ben arrived with a gust of ice-cold wind and he swept through the little café with a flurry of noise and activity. He dropped down into the chair opposite her.

'I could murder an espresso,' he huffed.

Stalker got the attention of the waitress and ordered a drink for Ben.

'Stress at work?' He had provided her with the perfect opening gambit and she sipped her latte as she waited for him to take off his coat and settle himself.

'Yes,' he replied. 'You would not believe what they expect. It's like they want everything done yesterday.'

'What are you working on?' Stalker asked. The waitress returned with Ben's espresso and he took a careful sip, wincing slightly against the heat.

'I wish I could say,' he gave her a reluctant smile.

'You can tell me, I mean, it's not a breach of confidentiality if I already know from someone else. Is it?'

Ben looked at her quizzically and she gave him a playful expression.

'True,' he said slowly. He looked around at the half empty café and leaned across the table. 'Do you know something?'

'Maybe,' she whispered back. 'I know something really massive is being built and I was wondering if you were involved with it.'

Ben leaned back in his seat and crossed his arms over his chest.

'How do you know that?'

'I have my sources,' she teased. The slight upturn at the corner of his mouth betrayed him, he was playing at being upset. 'So is that what you're working on?'

'I nearly told you about it a few weeks ago.'

'You did?' She was surprised and searched her memory for a clue. 'When?'

'It was the day after the Halloween party. We had coffee and there was a guy following you so you were totally distracted and didn't take the bait I offered you.'

Stalker swallowed her coffee. That had been Fortune following her, it was before she changed.

'Oh yeah,' she said, fighting back thoughts of her old pack.

'Did he ever bother you?'

'No,' she said, too quickly. 'No, not at all. Never saw him again.'

Ben watched her carefully for a moment. The silence was interrupted by the waitress coming over to take their food order. As she left again, Ben leaned across the table.

'So I'm helping to draw up the plans for the underground. We have to go through all the city blueprints, all the sewers, cabling systems and everything to map out the access points, where the work will be done, set out a timetable and everything. Back when I was first put on the project they gave me this massive file, right, it goes back years. Someone has been planning this for years. Then about a week ago they gave me a new file and said the layout needed to change. I guess they found something while doing the tunnelling and have had to change direction.'

'What did they find?' Stalker asked, intrigued.

'I don't know, I'm just guessing at the reason for the changes. Someone higher up sends down the orders and we follow them. We're not really supposed to ask too many questions. For whatever reason we have to change the plans and we are being nagged hourly to get it done. It's going to set the whole project back, and someone up top doesn't want any delays.'

Stalker suspected she knew exactly who it was "up top" who was changing the plans.

'So the work is already under way?'

'Yeah, it has been for ages. This is massive, Ariana. They're projecting completion of the initial tunnel work by next summer.'

'Who's funding it?'

'A conglomerate, with some subsidies from the

government and the city council.'

'So is it someone from the private sector dictating these changes?' Stalker knew the answer in her gut. She didn't know how long Theodore had been involved, maybe since the beginning, but he was certainly calling the shots now.

'I have no idea, I guess it could be, though I don't know why they would be involved. They're basically just the bank. I get my instructions from my boss within the council.' Ben took a sip of his espresso and sat back in his chair with a satisfied smile.

'You feel better for telling me, don't you?' Stalker asked with a smirk.

'Absolutely. You have no idea what it's like for me, I am awful at keeping secrets, just awful.'

They ate their lunch and laughed about old memories. Ben told her all about his trip to Rome and the near-proposal. It was nice, Stalker felt happy and relaxed and more like her old self than she had in a month.

Reluctantly, she parted from his company when he had to return to work and made her way to James's new office to meet him and help him finish unpacking. She saw him walking down the street towards his building and waved to him as she approached. He saw her and stopped at the door. He was holding a sandwich and greeted her with a warm smile.

'I just popped out for some lunch. There isn't much left to do.'

'Okay, well, I'll come in with you anyway and see if I can help.'

They went inside and were chatting away as they

stepped off the stairs and into the reception area of James's office. Stalker stopped laughing as she set eyes upon a strange man sitting cross-legged on the floor in front of the office door. He had small facial features and a thin moustache, his eyes darted about and he twitched nervously.

'Can I help you?' James asked.

The man scrambled to his feet and looked at Stalker with narrowed eyes.

'Can we speak privately, please?' the man asked in a small voice.

'We'll step inside my office. This is my colleague, Ms Yates. You can speak freely in front of her.'

James moved forward with his keys out and the man stepped aside so that he could open the door. The three of them filed into the office and took seats around the desk. 'How can we help?' James asked.

Stalker felt uncomfortable, the man didn't smell human and he was entirely too rat-like in his features for her liking. He looked at them both suspiciously for a moment and his eyes kept darting to the door.

'I need your help,' he said at last. 'I can help you in return.'

James looked at Stalker, caution all over his face.

'Can you be a little more specific?' he asked.

'I know who you are,' the man said, sounding a little threatening. 'Lightning Lords.'

Stalker glanced at James again, he was totally un-phased.

'And?' he said coolly.

'I know what you're trying to do and I'm willing to help

you. I have no love of the Doctor and his grand ambitions, but it is the Red Minister that I want to see perish.'

'Who's the Red Minister?' Stalker asked, taken aback by news of another player.

'A leader of my kind. If he is dispatched, I move in to his place and a thousand of my kind are diverted from the Plague Doctor's army.'

'So you want our help in taking down the Red Minister, and in so doing we weaken our enemy?' James asked, laying it all out clearly.

'That's right.'

'We'll need to speak to the rest of our pack,' Stalker said. She didn't trust this man one jot and was not going to allow them to commit to anything without checking with the others and trying to verify this man's story.

'Of course,' the rat man said with a bow of his head.

'What's your name?' James asked.

'Raigo,' he replied, twitching uncomfortably.

James stood up and Raigo nervously copied.

'Meet with me later, in the Tap and Barrel with the rest of your kin, and we can discuss the details. I already have a plan.'

'Okay,' replied James. 'I know the place. We'll meet you there in two hours.'

Raigo nodded and scurried from the room. Stalker followed him and watched him run down the stairs and out of the door.

'Well?' she asked.

'He was telling the truth.'

'Is that your PI experience talking?'

'No,' he gave her a small smile. 'My gift from Artemis.'

'Well you are just full of useful surprises.' Stalker grinned at him. 'So we head over to Grove Street and run this by the others and then head to the pub?'

'Yeah. This could be just the break we need.'

They left again, locked up and headed for home at a brisk walk. Stalker wanted to believe that they had caught a break, but she couldn't shake the feeling that there was something amiss.

They got back to Grove Street and found Weaver and Wind Talker working in the garden, doing more of the work that Stalker had started when they first moved in. Eyes was at chambers for the day. Stalker called him and was relieved when he answered his phone.

'Hi, we have a significant lead and need everyone together for an important meeting. Can you get away?' she asked.

'I'm just finishing up here, I can be there in about an hour,' he said and hung up the phone.

James filled the others in and his enthusiasm was infectious. By the time Eyes arrived, the four of them were buzzing with optimism.

'We'll need to hear what his plan is and have some sort of assurance that he'll keep his army out of the fight when we hit the Plague Doctor,' Eyes said. 'But it does sound promising.'

The five of them headed back out at 4pm and walked to the nearby pub, the Tap and Barrel. They went inside and found Raigo sitting at a table with two other similarly ratty figures, and hung back slightly.

'He didn't say anything about friends, but I guess it's only fair. There are five of us,' James said quietly.

James led the way over to the table. It was a proper "old man's" pub, that served real ales, had exposed beams overhead, low lighting and smelled of tobacco and old fashioned cologne. A few people sat at the bar and a solitary barman was stacking glasses; they were all chatting loudly to each other.

'Thank you for coming,' Raigo said, standing to greet them. 'Won't you please join us?'

Everyone began to sit down, but Wind Talker remained standing.

'Shall I get a round of drinks?' he asked. Eyes and James asked for whatever was on tap but Stalker just wanted water, she wanted a clear head for whatever lay ahead.

'I'll give you a hand,' Weaver offered and went with him to the bar.

They sat in awkward silence and waited for the others to return with the drinks. When they did, Weaver had a bottled fruit drink, and they tried to make themselves comfortable on the small wooden stools. Stalker tried not to laugh at the strange group sat around one small table.

'So,' James said, looking Raigo in the eye. 'What's your plan?'

'There is a body of great importance. The Red Minister is charged with protecting it at a separate location to the Plague Doctor's nest. We can ambush him and destroy him,' Raigo replied.

'A body?' Eyes asked sharply. Stalker glanced at him, his face was unreadable but she knew he was thinking the same thing she was: the body of the doctor that was taken from the plague pit. It was almost certainly the thing that was helping the Plague Doctor to remain in this realm, rather than being sucked back into his demon realm, Muspelheim.

'A body,' Raigo repeated. 'I don't know why it is significant, only that it is.'

'Where is it being held?' Stalker asked.

'The Circle,' one of the other rat-men replied.

'Ugh. Why?' James asked, dropping his head into his hand. The Circle was a particularly horrible part of St. Mark's. It was an old, abandoned block of flats that stood in a circle with a courtyard in the centre. It was frequented now by drug users and prostitutes, and the inhabited neighbourhood around it was no better. Even the police never went there if they could help it. There was a sick irony that it was the last place you passed through on your way to Crossway, the wealthy neighbourhood where Eyes lived.

'It is secluded and your kind never go there,' Raigo said with a smirk.

'Fair enough,' Eyes said. 'When do we strike?'

'Tomorrow night,' Raigo replied. 'We will meet you there, just outside, and lead you to the Red Minister.'

'What sort of numbers will we be facing?' Wind Talker asked, sipping his beer.

'A small contingent, probably a dozen or so of those of us that can take human form. There will be half a dozen larger combatants and a small swarm.'

Stalker looked at Eyes with raised eyebrows. *A small contingent?*

'Those numbers don't sound so small,' Eyes said pointedly.

'Perhaps not to your kind, but to us they are. We normally count our number in hundreds, I am having to think quite carefully about my words in order to give you accurate information.'

'What sort of capabilities do your kind have? Is there anything you can tell us that'll help us to make this a swift fight?' Stalker asked.

'Focus on the Red Minister, he is the leader. Take him out and the rest will fall into utter disarray and follow me away. Watch out for the bite of the hybrids, they are poisonous.' Raigo was smiling a sickly sweet smile that showed his large front teeth. Stalker didn't like it one bit.

'Thank you,' Weaver said, nodding at all three of them. 'Why are you doing this? Isn't this a betrayal?'

'No, the Red Minister has betrayed our kind by falling under the thrall of the Plague Doctor. We are simply trying to set our own house in order.' Raigo's voice became more of a vicious hiss that set Stalker's teeth on edge.

'Very well,' Eyes said, his voice steady but firm in an apparent attempt to ease the sudden tension. Stalker took a deep breath and flexed her fingers, surprised at the amount of stiffness in them. 'And we have your word that you and your followers will not turn on us in this combat, or when we strike the Plague Doctor?' Eyes asked, his eyes sharp. James was watching Raigo carefully and Stalker kept her attention on the other two. Their faces were absolutely unreadable.

'You have my word,' Raigo replied.

James gave Eyes a slight nod to let him know that Raigo was telling the truth.

'Very well,' Eyes said after a moment's consideration.

'We'll agree to this temporary alliance.'

'Excellent,' Raigo said with a smile. 'We will meet you outside The Circle at 8pm tomorrow.'

He and his fellows stood and took their leave.

'I don't like it,' Stalker said quietly when they had gone.

'Neither do I,' Eyes said. 'But we'll take what we can get and proceed with great caution.'

'Weaver, try this, it's really good.' Wind Talker passed Weaver his beer and she took a sip.

'Hmm, yeah, that is good.' She took another gulp and then passed it back.

They all sat and finished their drinks while they quietly talked over the plan.

They moved back to Grove Street and stayed up late talking and drinking. It was great to spend time together and Stalker fell asleep in the small hours just as Eyes was heading home to his family. She felt Weaver shift and curl up next to her, Wind Talker likewise slept on the floor with them and James again fell asleep in his human form on the sofa.

When Stalker woke she sensed something was wrong before she was fully conscious. It was the noise first, and then the smell. She opened her eyes and looked around. Weaver was lying next to her clutching her stomach and moaning. Wind Talker and James were nowhere to be seen, but she could hear them both in the kitchen being violently sick.

Chapter Twenty Seven

Stalker shifted form. She felt fine, except for the standard passive nausea that she felt whenever she was around anyone who was sick.

'Weaver,' she whispered, reaching out and gently touching her pack sister's shoulder. Weaver looked up at her through milky eyes. 'What's going on?'

'So sick,' Weaver moaned. Stalker stroked Weaver's hair and slowly stood up and made her way to the kitchen. James was hunched over the sink and Wind Talker was slumped in the back doorway.

'At least you both made it out of the living room,' Stalker said with a wry smile. Wind Talker turned his head to look at her. He looked like the living dead. 'So, poisoned?'

'Poisoned,' groaned James from the sink, his voice echoing around the metal basin.

'Don't drink the beer,' Stalker chided. 'I'll go check out

the pub. Back soon.'

Stalker left the house and jogged to the Tap and Barrel. It was still early in the morning and the place was dark and quiet. She slipped around the back and shifted into a sleek, grey wolf. Sniffing her way, she found the entrance to the cellar; it stank of rats. She looked around, there was no one in sight and the cellar entrance was hidden from the road by a high wooden fence around the small courtyard. Stalker shifted into a bear, and with a huge fist smashed open the cellar door. The wood splintered, barely hanging on at the hinges.

She shifted back into her wolf form and crept cautiously down the stone steps into the cellar. A couple of rats skittered away from her into the pitch black shadows and she stopped in her tracks. The only light came from the murky early morning daylight spilling in through the shattered door. She listened and sniffed for a moment. There was no movement, the only sound was the slow, monotonous *drip, drip, drip* of a leaking barrel. Aside from a handful of seemingly mundane rats, the cellar was empty.

Inching slowly across the cobblestone floor, Stalker found her way to a row of massive beer barrels. There was a distinct and unpleasant smell of demonic rat all over each barrel, just one by the smell of it, and it wasn't Raigo or any of his friends. She found the leaking one and sniffed the little pool of beer that was forming underneath. It was tainted with blood, poisoned rat blood. Who knew how many humans had drunk the contaminated beer.

Shifting back into the bear, Stalker slammed her fist into the nearest barrel, shattering the wood and spilling the beer in a cascade all over the floor. She rampaged around the cellar, destroying every barrel. The floor was soon a foot deep in the foul smelling liquid and she lumbered to the stairs, shifting form as she scrambled up them. As she burst out into the courtyard Stalker realised that she needed to alert the police. She looked around and saw a battered old pay phone on the corner outside the courtyard. She went to it, looking around anxiously, and hurriedly left an anonymous tip about the contamination. She hung up the phone before any awkward questions could be asked and walked swiftly away.

She was almost back at the house when her phone rang. It was Eyes.

'Hey there,' she said in a falsely bright voice. 'How are you feeling this morning?'

'Like the dead,' he groaned. 'I take it you guys are all sick too?'

'Not me,' she said, a little too cheerfully. 'I didn't drink the beer. It was poisoned. I've dealt with that already but it looks like we'll need to find a cure for you guys.'

'I'm going to head over to the house now, if I can stop being sick for twenty minutes.' Eyes made a strange noise at the other end of the phone, somewhere between a cough and slurp, and Stalker grimaced.

'Nice,' she said. 'See you when you get here.'

She hung up and entered the house a minute later. Everyone seemed to be slightly improved. James had dragged himself to his laptop to research what kind of poison it might be.

'The beer barrels were contaminated, I smashed them all up.' She reported back to the pack.

'The question is, who's responsible?' Wind Talker said, no trace of surprise in his voice.

'Not Raigo,' Weaver said from her curled up position on the sofa. 'He seemed to genuinely want our help. It makes no sense for him to have poisoned us.'

'The smell wasn't him or either of his companions,' Stalker told them. 'It was another rat.'

'It must have been the Red Minister,' Weaver said with absolute certainty. 'He must have got wind of our meeting and tried to intervene, take us out of the equation.'

'I agree,' Wind Talker said.

'We have to get you lot in fighting form in time for the ambush tonight. It's the last thing the Red Minister will expect.' Stalker fetched Wind Talker a bottle of bleach for him to clean up after himself and James, then went to sit with Weaver while she lay shaking on the sofa.

'I'm all right,' Weaver said weakly. 'I haven't been as sick as them.'

'You look awful,' Stalker said as sympathetically as she could manage. 'We need to know if this is a straightforward human disease or poison, or if it's demonic. What do you think?'

'It'll be demonic, and our bodies should burn it off in a few hours. It's the humans who were drinking there that we should worry about. They might not recover without a spiritual cure. Human medicine might not help at all.'

Stalker drew a slow, deep breath.

'Right,' she said. 'Honestly, I don't know what we can do about that. We have so much on our plates already.'

'We have to do something,' Weaver said, reaching out for Stalker's hand. 'You know we do. We're responsible for protecting the humans on our territory from demons. That's our primary purpose for being.'

Stalker smiled weakly. She was glad to hear Weaver say something like that. She had been worried that her pack were slipping too far from their humanity. She didn't say anything, she didn't need to, Weaver squeezed her hand, knowingly.

James shut his laptop and looked up a short while later, looking grim but stable.

'I think it might be Lassa Fever,' he declared. 'When is Eyes getting here?'

'Any time now,' Stalker replied.

'I just hope he didn't get too intimate with his good lady wife last night.' James shook his head and plodded into the kitchen to help Wind Talker clean up.

Eyes arrived soon after, looking pale and clammy.

'I had to stop twice on the way here,' he complained. He went to the kitchen and poured himself a glass of water.

'How's your wife?' James asked.

'Fine,' Eyes said warily. 'Why?'

'If this is what I think it is, it's transmitted from human to human.'

'What?' Eyes snapped. 'How?'

'Bodily secretions.' James coughed and turned away. Stalker tried not to laugh at the typically male awkwardness on display. Eyes dropped his head into his hands and moaned.

'This is not good,' he whimpered. Stalker watched him carefully through the doorway. He didn't need to say it, she knew what had happened and the urge to laugh vanished. They had all been fine for several hours before the poison took effect. There was no way Eyes could have known he was contagious.

'James, how serious is this for humans?' she asked soberly.

'Very,' he replied. 'It can kill, cause deafness and miscarriages.' His voice trailed off.

Eyes looked at him sharply.

'Is there a treatment?' Eyes asked.

'Yes, an antiviral drug. I highly doubt local healthcare services will be able to dispense it quickly though. The disease is from West Africa.'

'Well I tipped off the police,' Stalker said, trying to reassure everyone. 'With any luck they'll test the beer, find the disease and get the drugs imported quickly, and be on the alert for people presenting with symptoms.'

'We should summon a healing fae and see what assistance we can get though,' Wind Talker said, grimacing at the stink of the bleach.

'Last time we tried that we had to strike a pretty harsh bargain to get Eyes healed up. I won't agree to those terms again.' Stalker kept her voice calm, but her pulse was racing.

'Neither will I,' Eyes said, staring straight at her, and a nod of understanding passed between them.

'I can try summoning a health fae,' Wind Talker said. 'Health, rather than healing.'

'What's the difference?' James asked.

'Hopefully a health fae won't require an increase in injured people for it to heal,' Wind Talker replied. 'It will get its rocks off by people being in good health, rather than fixing bones, which need to be broken in the first place.'

The pack was stirred into action. Stalker, as the only one not ill, was the one to go out to buy supplies. There was a health food shop on the high street, which she headed for, and bought up bottles of vitamins, boxes of herbal tea and some protein bars.

Wind Talker led them all across the veil and into the garden. Unchained Lightning was circling slowly above the garden, and looked down at them sleepily.

'Greetings, Unchained Lightning,' Eyes greeted the elemental formally.

'Poison,' he crackled.

'Are you poisoned too?' Stalker asked in surprise.

'What affects you affects me too,' he said slowly.

'We are so sorry,' Eyes said. 'How can we help you?'

'Heal yourselves and I will follow.' Unchained Lightning floated slowly up and over the house, drifting off into the grey sky.

'Oh great,' Stalker said, rolling her eyes. 'So not only did we get ourselves poisoned but we poisoned our ally too. I hope he forgives us when we fix this mess.'

'Okay,' Wind Talker said, clearing his throat. 'Start eating and popping pills while I cast the circle.'

They did as he instructed, and Stalker watched him walk around the garden, ripping open tea bags and scattering the herbs on the ground in a circle around them as he walked. The pack formed a loose circle and passed the vitamins around. Stalker chewed on a protein bar, it was foul, chewy and tasteless. She persevered and swallowed the mouthful she had already taken, and made herself finish it off in two more bites.

Wind Talker came to a halt and took his place in the

circle. 'We consume these goods in order to maximise our health and well-being, in honour of the gods and fae of healing, wellness and health. We honour our bodies as gifts from Artemis and thank her for giving us rapid healing abilities. We call now in this time of great need, for some extra assistance. Fae hear me and answer my call.'

There was a rushing sound overhead and Stalker looked up, searching for the source. A dark shape was hurtling towards them, and landed with a thud on the soft earth in the centre of the garden. The figure uncurled before them, taking the form of a tall man with enormous muscles and tanned skin. He had a full head of impossibly wavy hair and looked rather like a caricature made to mock bodybuilders. Stalker stifled a laugh and exchanged a glance with Weaver, who also looked amused.

'Fleshlings.' The fae Adonis greeted them with a broad grin, flashing them his bright white teeth. He placed his hands on his narrow hips and puffed out his chest. 'Did you summon me to marvel at my magnificence?'

'Perfection-of-Flesh.' Wind Talker addressed him with a slight bow of his head, and Stalker spotted a smirk poorly hidden on his lips. 'Thank you for coming. We are in need of your assistance.'

'Perfection-of-Flesh can do anything. Speak. What is it that you require?' The fae's voice boomed out and Stalker again tried not to laugh as he referred to himself in the third person.

'We find ourselves poisoned, the victims of sabotage. There may be humans who are also affected. We need to detoxify ourselves and the innocent bystanders.'

'Perfection-of-Flesh does not like this,' the fae said,

looking crestfallen. 'Children of Artemis, your creator greatly aided mine in a time of dire need. I shall return the favour.'

'Who is your creator?' James asked.

'Heracles, of course.' Perfection-of-Flesh grinned and shook his head so that his hair rippled.

'Of course,' James replied with a grin.

'My wife may be poisoned also,' Eyes said, his voice trembling slightly. 'I believe we will mend ourselves given time, but I am worried for her.'

'The disease within you is sometimes fatal to human bodies.' The fae's tone was blunt and Stalker blanched at its unsympathetic honesty.

'Can you help her?' Eyes asked, growing impatient.

'I can aid recovery, but I cannot directly heal. I can stay with her and aid her body in doing the job itself.'

'That would be great,' Eyes replied, the relief evident in his voice.

'What do you require of us?' James asked cautiously.

'Eat well, exercise regularly and get plenty of fresh air. Look after yourselves and I will look after your human.' The fae gave a firm nod and jumped high into the air, disappearing over the house.

'That sounds rather too good to be true, doesn't it?' Stalker said sceptically.

'I think we should be extremely thankful.' Eyes rubbed his face wearily as he spoke.

Wind Talker closed the circle and collapsed on the ground. Stalker rushed to his side, the others quick to follow.

'Are you all right?' she asked him.

'Yes, I'll be fine in a minute. That took a lot out of me.' Wind Talker stood up slowly and the pack crossed back into the human world and led him to the sofa to rest.

'I need to go home and check on Chloe,' Eyes said. 'Stalker, can you hold down the fort until tonight? I'll meet you all at the Circle. Assuming we want to go ahead?'

'I think we have to,' Stalker said. It didn't feel right, but they had little choice. They were so short of leads or any kind of plan. This was all they had. They just had to trust that Raigo was true to his word and that it was the Red Minister that had poisoned them. Eyes nodded in agreement and slipped out of the house. Stalker looked after her suffering comrades during the afternoon, hoping that they would be sufficiently recovered to face their fight.

Chapter Twenty Eight

WHEN IT WAS TIME TO GO, with the help of a nutritious meal and some of the herbal teas that Stalker had bought, everyone was feeling much improved. They drove in James's car to the Circle and parked half a block away. It had once been part of Blue Moon territory, but Stalker had never set foot near the place, and the Lightning Lords were not yet bold enough to try to claim territory this far east of the river.

It was dark; half of the street lights weren't working and ice cold rain fell upon the city in a fine drizzle. Stalker spotted Eyes pulling over a short way up the street and wondered if all of the wheels would still be on his car when they returned.

'How's Chloe?' she asked him as they all greeted one another.

'Fine, but she may not show symptoms for a few days if she has caught it. So we just have to watch and wait.

She knows I was sick this morning, so she's alert to the possibility of catching something, and I told her to tell me if she starts to feel ill.'

'I hope she doesn't get sick, I really do.' Stalker patted him on the shoulder and he smiled appreciatively.

'Okay,' Eyes said, shaking off the blues. 'Let's do this. Meet Raigo and get in and out of there as fast as possible. We're looking to take down the Red Minister and find the body.'

The five of them walked briskly up the road to the meeting point. The three rats were waiting for them. 'Raigo.' Eyes greeted the leader.

'Is everyone ready?' Raigo asked, looking them each over with his sharp, shrewd eyes.

'Absolutely,' Stalker replied. She felt fired up and ready for a fight, and was further reassured by Raigo's presence that he hadn't been responsible for poisoning them. If he had, and the appeal for an alliance had just been a ruse to get them drinking in that pub, then surely he would have expected them to be incapacitated and not show up.

'We will lead you into the courtyard and across the veil,' Raigo explained. 'The body is under ground, we will take you to it and divert the Red Minister's forces while you deal with the body and the Minister himself. Does that sound agreeable?'

The Lightning Lords murmured their agreement. The rat in a man's body twitched nervously, his eyes darting from one face to another and around their surroundings. Stalker watched him carefully as they set off towards the Circle. The rats led the way, Stalker just behind them. The rest of the Lightning Lords followed, with Wind Talker taking the rear and watching for anyone following them.

The rats led them through a tunnel under the towering flats above. The Circle stood six storeys high and the walls were crumbling in places. Stalker looked overhead as they passed through the tunnel, the ceiling looked solid enough. There was graffiti all over the walls, and a strong smell of urine. She wrinkled her sensitive nose.

They emerged into the vast central courtyard. It was almost pitch black as there was no lighting here, and very little that could reach from the lit areas outside the Circle. The sky above glowed orange with light pollution from the surrounding areas and that was their sole source of light. Stalker looked cautiously around, checking for movement on any of the balconies that ringed the courtyard. It was still and silent.

'We cross the veil here,' Raigo whispered. Stalker glanced back at Wind Talker, who was wearing his new talisman. He nodded, giving them the all clear, and Stalker stepped across the veil behind Raigo and his companions. The rest of the shifters followed. The Circle in Hepethia was an exaggeration of its human equivalent, being even more dark and dilapidated. The courtyard was overgrown with long grass and moss climbed up the walls of the building. There was old graffiti peeking out between patches of moss and bits of the towering concrete circle had crumbled away and lay smashed on the floor. Movement caught Stalker's attention high up on the Circle and her gaze snapped to it. It was just a trickle at first, but it quickly became a blur of motion all around them on the balconies.

'Movement,' she hissed. Everyone became alert and cast their eyes up. It was too dark to see anything clearly.

Stalker felt a rush of air beside her and her eyes darted to Raigo and his friends. They were sprinting for the centre of the courtyard, two of them shifting form mid-stride into small rats. Raigo scurried behind the others and glanced back over his shoulder at her before disappearing into the darkness. 'Raigo!' Stalker snarled.

'Where did they go?' Eyes whispered. 'Back across the veil?'

'No, not so much as a flutter from the veil.' Stalker ran after them, Eyes hot on her heels. As they reached the centre, Stalker spotted a manhole cover and heard it clunk into place. She skidded to a halt over it and looked around in the blackness. There was no other sign of Raigo and his friends. 'They must have gone down there.'

'The son of a bitch double-crossed us,' Eyes growled.

Wind Talker, Weaver and James caught up to them, and the five of them immediately turned their attention to the buildings around them. The walls were crawling with movement. Stalker snarled in frustration; her human eyes were totally inadequate. She shifted form into a brown barn owl and flapped her wings to hover just above the pack.

There were rats everywhere, a vast swarm pouring out of every doorway, off every balcony, and heading straight for them. She searched the swarm for anything that stood out. Amongst the normal-sized rats were several bigger creatures, rat-like monsters roughly the size of large dogs, with massive jaws and glinting teeth. Scurrying down one of the huge pillars was a human-sized rat creature in a red coat.

Below her, her pack had figured out what was

coming and were readying themselves for a fight. Eyes, Wind Talker and Weaver had shifted into their Agrius forms. James had drawn his gun. Stalker rolled her eyes, exasperated by her new pack mate's reluctance to take non-human forms. Stalker swooped down to the ground and shifted to match most of her pack. The first wave of rats was just a few metres away on all sides.

A rat leapt into the air straight at Eyes and he easily swatted it aside with one massive, clawed hand. The small ones were easily dispatched, but their numbers were significant. One of the large, dog-sized wererats bounded right at Stalker and she slashed at it with her claws. At her back, James was buffered by Weaver and Wind Talker while he bided his time. Just as Stalker ripped the head off the wererat that had jumped at her, a shot rang out behind her, then another. Wind Talker stepped out slightly from the pack to give himself room as he grabbed hold of one of the big creatures and swung it around, clearing the floor of the normal rats briefly. Stalker drew her swords and strode forward to meet another big rat creature, slicing it neatly in three with her blades as it leapt into the air.

She searched the swarm for the Red Minister, but there were too many of them and she couldn't find him. She continued cutting down the wererats and stomping on little ones, feeling their bones crunch beneath her monstrous feet. She was aware of James firing shots somewhere behind her and heard the snarls and grunting of her pack mates as they each did their share of fighting. It all seemed pointless though; the rats just kept on coming. They needed to find the Minister.

Stalker broke rank and waded out into the swarm,

searching for the leader. She had seen him from above, he had to be here somewhere. She circled around, careful to avoid James's line of fire, and took out as many wererats as she could.

Suddenly there was an impact on her back. She felt sharp claws digging into her fur and skin and tried to shake the thing off. She roared and writhed around, but its grip on her was tight. She couldn't let it bite her and risk being poisoned.

A shot rang out and the scrabbling, scratching at her back stopped suddenly. The wererat slid to the floor and she wheeled around to look at it. A clean gunshot wound scarred its ugly head and blood spattered its fur. She turned to James, who was still aiming his gun her way. She gave him a quick nod of appreciation and he returned it before turning and taking aim at his next target. Perhaps his gun *was* useful after all.

She saw him then, the Red Minister, just beyond James and making straight for him. Without the ability to warn him verbally in this form, Stalker howled and charged towards him, bounding over the rats covering the floor and leaping over Weaver as she grappled a wererat and ripped its throat out. Stalker pounced with her swords raised straight at the leader of the swarm. She landed with a thud before him and he raised himself up to his full height. He easily matched her for height, but was much more wiry. His face was cruel and pointed, his fur black, and his red coat was splattered with blood.

Stalker went to strike but he dodged and spun behind her. She turned to face him and slashed again, this time he caught hold of her sword in his hand and pulled it towards him, dragging her with it. She lurched forward and headbutted him, sending him reeling, forcing him to release both her and her sword. Stalker went in for a low blow and managed to swipe one of his knees before he leapt out of her reach. Blood sprayed out onto the floor and he roared in pain as he went staggering backwards.

There was a gunshot and the Red Minister's eyes darted to his stomach. A pool of blood was appearing there and he dropped to his knees, staring at the wound.

Stalker pounced, plunging one of her swords into his chest and ripping it upward and out through his shoulder. His torso split in two and fell apart, like a banana peeling and out poured a dozen or more regular-sized rats. Stalker jumped back as his body fell to the floor and the blood-soaked rats climbed out of his remains and retreated towards the building.

A terrible shriek filled the courtyard, a million rats squealing at once, and all of them turned tail and fled for the cover of the buildings. Stalker stood panting and looking around at the fleeing vermin. The others ran over to her and she shifted back into her human form. She had scratches all over her body and her head was throbbing like crazy, but she felt energised, exhilarated from the fight.

'James, you were absolutely amazing!' she cried, grabbing him and pulling him into a tight hug. He let out a brief laugh and patted her back.

'No problem.'

'Who needs claws, eh?' Eyes asked, grinning at their newest pack mate.

'Not when you have claws of lead,' James said. He

lifted his pistol and blew across the barrel, just like in the old Western movies, and they all laughed. A strange, serious expression replaced James's grin and he looked around at them. 'Claws-of-Lead, why do I feel like that's my new name?'

Chapter Twenty Nine

The Lightning Lords stood in the middle of the Circle, congratulating Claws on his name. Nearby there was a choking, gurgling sound among the piles of rat bodies. They all looked around, searching for the origin. Weaver broke away from the group and moved swiftly and smoothly across the corpses to one wererat that was holding on to its life with rattling breaths. She grabbed hold of it and dragged it over to the waiting shifters.

Stalker examined it briefly. It had a broken leg and huge gash in its chest and was fluctuating in form between giant rat and man.

'That is so disturbing,' Weaver said quietly. 'We should question it.'

'Not here,' Eyes said, looking around cautiously. He grabbed the wererat roughly by the scruff of its neck and dragged it from the courtyard, back down the tunnel they had entered through. They crossed the veil and Stalker ran silently to the mouth of the tunnel to check that the coast was clear. Claws joined her and they looked up and down the street. A couple of cars swept past, and less than a hundred yards away there were three young women in skimpy clothing waiting on the street corner.

'I'll get my car,' Claws said, and quickly ran for it. Stalker got the others to stop in the shadows and they waited for Claws. A minute later Claws' beaten up old estate backed up to the tunnel entrance and the boot popped. Stalker ran to it and lifted it up and a moment later Eyes and Wind Talker were hoisting the rapidly shifting body inside. Stalker and Weaver climbed into the back seat. Eyes and Wind Talker went to Eyes' car and they drove quickly back to Grove Street in convoy.

They hastily moved the creature into the house and crossed the veil, not wanting any noise it might make to attract attention from their neighbours on the narrow terrace. It groaned with every movement and was bleeding profusely. Wind Talker dropped it down on the kitchen floor.

'What the hell happened in there tonight?' he snarled. The creature on the floor writhed in pain and coughed up a huge glob of blood that splattered onto the linoleum. Stalker gagged a little at the stink, but forced herself to ignore the stench and crack on with the task in hand.

'Do you know Raigo?' she asked, crouching down to get closer to it.

'Raigo?' the creature asked, a deep frown etched onto its jumbled features. 'We are all Raigo.'

Stalker glared at him and then turned and looked up at the faces gathered tightly around them. Everyone shared her confusion.

The creature seemed as confused by the question as they were by the answer. Stalker realised that these creatures did not live as individuals. The Raigo they had met with told them they normally counted their number by the hundred. She began to understand.

'Do you mean all of your kind call themselves Raigo?'

'Yes,' it said with a splutter.

'What about the Red Minister?' she asked the thing before her.

'He was our leader, he was Raigo until we made him our leader.'

'Is he dead?' Claws asked.

The thing on the floor looked up at him with a sneer on its shifting face.

'Yes, disintegrated. We all felt it happen.'

'Tell us about the Plague Doctor,' Eyes demanded, his voice impatient.

The creature coughed again, splattering more putrid blood over himself and the floor.

'Are your kind working with him?' Stalker asked more gently.

'Yes,' it hissed.

'There's a body, it's important to him. Why?'

'We protect the body, it gives him the strength to be here.'

Stalker exchanged meaningful looks with Weaver and Wind Talker. They had been right.

'What is he planning? Why is he here?' Stalker asked.

'Why would I tell you that?' the creature spat.

Wind Talker leaned over and pressed his thumb

into the wound on its chest. The wererat yowled in pain and squirmed around on the floor. Wind Talker held fast, increasing the pressure. Stalker looked away, uncomfortable with the turn that the interrogation had taken. In the corner of the kitchen stood Scourging Agony, a nasty grin smeared on his pasty face. Stalker ignored him and looked down at the wererat again.

'To spread plague,' it screamed. Wind Talker released his thumb. 'He can't create it, only spread it, so he needs a sample. I don't know where he's getting it from. Please, that's all I know. Let me go.'

Scourging Agony drew a rattling breath from the corner and smacked his lips together. Stalker glanced at him in disgust. Eyes wheeled around, seeing the demon for the first time.

'You,' he snarled. 'Enjoying yourself?'

'Absolutely,' the demon said, curling his lip. .

'How's the tattooist working out for you?' Claws asked.

'It is simply delicious, thank you for asking. You won't be getting any more out of that wretch now.' He pointed a bladed finger at the wererat, who shuddered and recoiled from the demon.

Eyes ran his fingers through his hair.

'We've got what we needed. Scourging Agony, would you be so kind as to take this thing and dispose of it?' Eyes asked, turning towards the demon.

'What?' shrieked the wererat. 'I told you everything you wanted to know. Please let me go.'

'I would be delighted,' sneered Scourging Agony, and before Stalker could intervene, the demon swooped towards the wererat, dug his blades into its chest and scooped it up. His mouth opened freakishly wide, his jaw expanding to form a gaping maw, and he shovelled the wererat into his mouth still alive and screaming.

Stalker felt sick to her stomach and she clasped a hand over her mouth to hide her revulsion and her shocked expression. Scourging Agony's mouth returned to normal and he gave them a sickening smile before disappearing.

'Eyes!' Stalker snapped.

'I never told it I was going to let it go,' he said with a shrug. He stepped across the veil and the others slowly followed. Except Claws-of-Lead. He stood looking at Stalker, his face full of concern.

'That was awful,' she whispered.

'Yeah, it really was. Are you all right?'

'I will be in a minute.' Stalker rubbed her face with her hands and then shook out her limbs, trying to rid herself of the horrible feeling coursing through her body. 'Nice shooting tonight,' she said after a minute.

'Thanks,' he replied with a smile.

'You saved my skin, literally.' Stalker looked over her shoulder and saw that the scratches had already healed.

'I do my best.'

'Well, thank you,' she said meekly. It wasn't often that she had cause to thank anyone for saving her life, surprisingly, given the life she now led.

'You're welcome,' he replied with a small nod. 'Shall we clean this up?' He indicated the blood all over the floor.

'Yes, definitely.' Stalker went to the sink and turned the tap, unsure of what would happen. Water did begin to flow, but it pooled in the sink for a moment and then rose up in the form of a water elemental. 'Oh, wow,' Stalker said. She watched in awe as the beautiful fae floated out of the sink and onto the floor. It sparkled as it spiralled around and around, its crystal clear body rippling softly. It slipped across the smooth surface and covered the blood, then moved to the door, stained pink. The blood was gone from the floor. The elemental slipped under the back door and Stalker quickly ran after it into the garden. It found its way to the soil and slowly soaked into the ground.

Stalker and Claws exchanged glances. That had been a remarkably easy clean up. Stalker resented having to do it at all, and as they crossed back into the human world and settled down for the night, her mind raced with the events of the evening.

The following day was Thursday and Stalker had to go back to work. She was relieved to get out of the house. Tensions were running high with the pack, but thankfully her vial of still waters was soothing her temper just enough to keep a huge argument from erupting. They all needed to rest after the big fight, so solving all of their problems was put on the back burner.

Claws and Eyes went off to work first thing in the morning, Weaver even went in to university to do some work on her PhD. Wind Talker carried on with his research and his work around the house. Stalker noticed a few home improvements when she returned from work in the evening, just minor repairs and a few homey touches added to the kitchen. There was no one else around when she got back, just Wind Talker pottering about in the kitchen. She still felt awkward about the previous night and approached him cautiously.

'Hey,' she said softly, leaning on the kitchen door

frame.

'Hey,' he replied, looking up from the washing up. 'Did you have a good day?'

'It was okay, thanks. You?'

'You know, so-so.' He looked at her for a moment and then returned to his chore. 'I was thinking about going to get a tattoo tomorrow. I wondered if you wanted to come.'

'Yeah, okay. What are you getting done?' Stalker replied, a little surprised.

'Something to honour the Blue Moon.'

Stalker nodded, though he wasn't looking at her to see. It was just two weeks since the Blue Moon had fallen. Some days she hardly had the chance to think of them at all. Other days she couldn't get them off her mind. It was almost the new moon too, her one month anniversary since changing. It felt like a lifetime.

'That's a really nice idea,' she said at last. 'I'll get something done for them too.'

'I'll call and make appointments for us both,' Wind Talker said, a sad smile touching his lips.

The following day, Stalker and Wind Talker set off for Red Drop of Ink. Stalker wasn't convinced that going to Scourging Agony's new abode for this was such a good idea, but it was their nearest tattooist, and Wind Talker was convinced that it was important in order to retain positive relations with the demon that could so easily go back to the Witches.

Wind Talker and the others seemed to be fully recovered from the poisoning now, thanks to the rapid healing ability that shifters shared. Stalker hadn't talked to any of them about sacrificing the wererat to Scourging

Agony, she felt it was best to let that one go, though a hint of tension remained. She and Wind Talker covered the entire ten-minute walk to the tattooist in silence.

Stalker thought about what she wanted, she tried to picture various options as they walked, and by the time they arrived she was reasonably sure that she had decided.

The shop was painted bright red and had black bars on the windows and door. A sign in the window indicated that the shop was open, so Wind Talker opened the door and they went inside. The walls were covered with posters of heavily tattooed bodies, and there was a strong smell of ink and metal. There were a few old plastic seats and books of templates to browse, but Stalker knew she wouldn't find anything she wanted in there.

A man emerged from the back room, wiping his hands on a cloth. He was very tall with long red hair in a pony tail and a long pointed beard. He wore a bandanna, and a sleeveless shirt, displaying full sleeves of tattoos on both arms. He had on ripped jeans and big black boots, and Stalker smiled; he ticked just about every stereotype box going.

'Hi there,' the guy said in a warm and welcoming voice. 'How can I help?'

'I called yesterday. We have custom designs we'd like,' Wind Talker said, and he pulled a sketch out of his bag. He passed it to the tattooist, who looked at it and gave an appraising nod.

'Okay, cool. I can do this. How about you?' He looked at Stalker.

'Do his first, I'll refine my ideas while I wait.' She took a seat and grabbed a pen and some paper from a small table near the window.

The two men disappeared into the back room and Stalker tried to draw what she wanted. She wondered if it might have been better to go to a shifter tattooist, but she was here now.

The time passed slowly, she wasn't used to sitting still for so long, her life had been such a chaotic jumble over the last month. She could hear the buzz of the electric needle and a little low conversation between Wind Talker and the tattooist. The street outside was fairly busy, cars chugged by, slowed by the large, light-controlled cross roads a few yards up the street. Stalker stared out and watched the world go by, occasionally looking back at her sketch and adjusting it.

Eventually, Wind Talker emerged from the back room with his shirt off and his new tattoos shining. He had four clusters of markings across his chest, one for each of their fallen pack mates, noting their names and their honour in the runes of their people.

'What do you think?' he asked, looking like he was seeking her approval. She smiled and nodded.

'They look great,' she swallowed hard against the grief. 'Are you going to wait for me? You don't have to, you can head back.'

'No, I'll wait,' he said and he took her seat by the window as she followed the tattooist through to the back room.

'So, have you had ink before?' he asked as he cleaned his things and fetched sterile equipment from a small unit next to the chair.

'Yeah,' she answered. She looked around at the

extremely clean and uncluttered room. The walls were painted pale blue and there was soft lighting around the edges with a large, bright movable spotlight in the centre over the chair. Stalker shrugged off her jacket and showed him the back of her neck.

'Nice,' he said and held out his hand towards the seat. 'I'm Red, by the way.'

'Ariana,' she replied, her human name sounding odd on her tongue. She sat down and passed him her rough sketch. 'I'd like this here.' She tapped her chest, right over her heart.

'It's beautiful,' Red said with a small smile. Stalker felt like he had picked up on the sombre mood of herself and Wind Talker, and although he wasn't going to ask for confirmation, he had a hunch of the general significance of their chosen tattoos.

Stalker lifted her top over her head, swung her pendants over her shoulder so that they hung down her back out of the way and got comfortable in the chair as Red got everything ready. He held the needle up and looked her hard in the eye. 'Are you absolutely sure?'

She simply nodded in reply. Without another word, Red began. Stalker watched the device move across her skin. It scratched, but the discomfort was nothing to her now. She turned her thoughts to Fortune; she remembered the way he hugged her and made her feel like the centre of his world. She thought of Speaks-With-Stone and her calm aura, her incredible strength and softness at the same time. Flames-First-Guardian was still the most unusual shifter she had met, striking and confident, blunt and stoic. And Shadow's Step, her brother, her mentor. He had taught her to fight, he had nurtured her secret ability to take any form and introduced her to Odin's Warriors. He had set her on the Path of Night and guided her through those vital early days with care and strength.

A tear escaped her left eye and rolled slowly down her cheek. She left it alone and felt it hang off her jaw, suspended above her heart, where Red was carefully working. 'Are you all right?' he asked, without looking up or pausing.

'Yeah,' she replied with a sniff. She wiped the tear from her jaw. 'I'm okay thanks.'

'I've never seen these markings before,' Red said. 'Your friend had the same ones. They aren't Sanskrit or anything I know.'

'No, they're like an ancient European runic language.' It was a half-truth, she couldn't tell him the whole truth. He seemed to accept it though and carried on with the delicate work. Stalker felt the veil ripple slightly as Red worked, and over his shoulder she caught a glimpse of the bladed fingers of Scourging Agony as if he were pulling back the veil to peek across at her. She tried hard not to react. She heard him draw a rattling breath of pleasure and she firmly shoved her revulsion aside. It was understandable that he would come to feed on this. The tattoo wasn't causing her physical pain, but she was willingly putting herself in a situation that drew out painful memories, just the sort of thing the demon enjoyed. She couldn't deny him his nature. After a few minutes he disappeared and the veil fluttered closed again.

When Red had finished he wiped away the last smear of blood and sat back to admire his work. Stalker looked down at it and pulled out her phone to take a picture so she could see it the right way up.

An eclipsed blue moon rested on her chest, half over the flesh of her breast. A solid, dark blue circle with a light blue glow around it. Around the edge of the moon were the shifter runes for Fortune, Stone, Flame and Shadow. She would keep them close to her heart for the rest of her life.

'Do you like it?' Red asked quietly.

'I love it, thank you,' she replied softly. She straightened her jewellery and put her top back on.

'You'll need to make sure it gets plenty of air so that it heals well,' Red instructed as they walked back out into the shop front.

'Of course, thanks,' she said, suppressing a smile. It would be healed by the time they got home.

'Can I see?' Wind Talker asked as he stood up to greet her. She grinned and pulled the neck of her top down to show him the work. 'That's really nice.' They exchanged sad smiles.

Red took their payments and said a friendly farewell as they left the shop. The walk back to Grove Street was more animated and Wind Talker slung a heavy arm around Stalker's shoulders as they walked. It felt as though a breach had been at least partially mended, which Stalker supposed was the reason he had asked her to join him. Stalker had to work that afternoon, but she did so with a happy feeling of anticipation about returning to the house afterwards, rather than dreading awkward silence and dirty looks. She hoped the feeling would last.

Chapter Thirty

Fights-Eyes-Open

The pack assembled at Grove Street around dinner time. Wind Talker had cooked a roast chicken, with a little help from Weaver and Claws. Eyes arrived feeling grim.

'I think Chloe is sick,' he said as he entered the kitchen.

'Is Perfection-of-Flesh at your house?' Wind Talker asked. Eyes nodded.

'Yeah, I think so. Chloe has been struck by a sudden urge to take vitamin supplements, when she never has before.' Eyes smiled weakly.

Stalker patted his arm and gave him a reassuring smile.

'Well, let's hope his help can pull her through without it getting too serious.'

'Can we try and get hold of some of the antivirals anyway? Just in case?' Eyes asked, looking pointedly at Claws and Wind Talker.

'Why are you looking at me?' Claws asked. 'I'm a PI,

not a drug dealer.'

'I know,' Eyes said. 'But I thought you might know someone.'

'It's okay,' Wind Talker said. 'I know a guy. I already put out feelers for this just in case.' He pulled a piece of paper out of his pocket and passed it to Eyes. Eyes unfolded it and read it quickly.

Ribavirin antivirals. Meet @ The Dragon's Den, South Stoke, 11pm. Cameron.

'Is this tonight?' Eyes asked.

'Yes.' Wind Talker replied. 'It's a club on Hellsclaws' territory. Do you want to call Scribe-of-the-Fallen and check with him that it's okay for us to turn up there?'

'Sure,' Eyes replied and immediately took out his phone to call their contact. It rang for what felt like a long time and just as Eyes was about to give up, Scribe answered the call.

'Hello?' he asked, sounding breathless.

'Sorry. It's Fights-Eyes-Open. Is this a bad time?'

'No, it's fine. Just a second.' There were some strange noises at the other end of the line and Eyes waited, trying not to listen too closely in case it was personal or pack business. After a moment it went quiet and Scribe returned. 'How can I help?'

'I was hoping to get permission for my pack to enter your territory tonight. We have an appointment at The Dragon's Den.' Eyes explained.

'Yes, of course. Cameron set it up, didn't he? We're already expecting you.' Scribe sounded mildly surprised.

'Oh. Is Cameron your pack mate?'

'Yes,' Scribe replied, a smile in his voice. 'Didn't Wind

Talker know that?'

'I guess not. Sorry to bother you. I guess we'll see you later.'

'Not a problem, see you later.' Scribe ended the call and Eyes looked at Wind Talker with a half-smile as he put his phone away.

'Cameron is one of us. Didn't you know?'

'No, I've never met him face to face. Flames used to get all of the drugs and herbs and stuff for rituals from him, and put me in touch. There's a dead drop in town for everything, with no personal contact, usually.'

'So, a night on the town then?' Stalker asked with a grin.

'Sounds good to me,' Weaver said. She did a little happy dance and bumped hips with Stalker, they both fell about laughing. Eyes felt irritation bubbling up inside his throat.

'It's business,' Eyes snapped and both women stopped laughing and looked at him.

'Sorry,' Weaver said, dipping her head.

'It's okay. I'm sorry for snapping. I'm just worried about my wife.'

'We know that,' Stalker said calmly. 'Let's eat and get going, shall we?'

They sat down around the little table and ate quickly, all eager to get out of the house. Weaver and Stalker ate particularly quickly and then dashed off to get changed. Eyes was still in his work suit. He had wrapped up his last case and was ending the week knowing that he would soon be working for Theodore Harris. He felt a mixture of relief and apprehension. He took off his tie and rolled it up neatly before tucking it into his pocket. The two women returned looking suitably dressed up for a night clubbing. He couldn't blame them, two young women who had had their carefree lives taken from them before they'd really had chance to live. He had done his share of drinking and late nights when he was their age, but he had settled down to have a family and develop his career years before he had changed.

Eyes caught a glimpse of a new tattoo on Stalker's chest, above her scandalously low cut top, but he didn't allow his eyes to linger. He just caught the rune for Fortune and felt a surge of mixed emotions. Pushing his feelings to one side, he led the pack out to his car and they set off for the club in South Stoke.

It was on the far side of Caerton from St. Mark's. They drove south, through China Town and the city centre, west across the river by the castle into Old Town and turned south again into South Stoke. It was a heavily industrial area of the city, but there were also lots of retail areas, some more successful than others. There were lots of low buildings with big car parks and glaring neon signs. The more residential parts were run down and poorly lit.

Eyes took directions from Claws to the club and drove past the front of the building that the website had directed them to. It was an old factory, long since closed, and there was nothing at all on the front to indicate that there was a nightclub inside. Eyes parked in a narrow back street between two red brick buildings, he wished he could camouflage his car in rough neighbourhoods like this one. There were people milling about in the street, smoking and drinking. They were all dressed for a goth club, with varying amounts of PVC and black eyeliner, crazy hair extensions and huge platform heels. And that was just the men.

The buildings on either side had black fire escapes snaking up them, much like the old betting shop had done. On the second floor of one of them was a narrow, steel door with a blinking green light above it. When the light was on Eyes could make out a small black dragon on the light casing. He pointed up, and without waiting for the others, set off up the fire escape. He led them up to the second floor and opened the steel door. He expected to be hit by loud music and smoke, but the door simply opened into a quiet, small room. They filed inside and approached another door at the back. There was a small window next to it with shutters across it and a crack of light down the centre. Eyes looked around his pack mates in bewilderment. This was by far the most unusual club he had ever been to.

He knocked on the window and it popped open. A young man sat on the other side, he had long black hair and a short beard. He glanced over Eyes' shoulder and raised an eyebrow. Eyes was suddenly acutely aware that most of their attire didn't match the club's target clientele. Stalker was possibly the exception, with her visible tattoos, low cut black top and skinny jeans with black boots.

'Five please,' he asked firmly.

The doorman silently counted out five stubs from a ticket book and looked at Eyes with deep scepticism. Eyes paid cash and the doorman handed over the tickets. Eyes nodded in thanks and led the way over to the door. There was a buzz and a red light on the door blinked to let him know that it would now open. He pushed the door and was met with the noise he had been expecting from the fire escape.

Loud music pounded out a relentless rhythm, the air was filled with smoke and coloured lights flashed and swirled around the cavernous space inside. They walked out onto a broad landing constructed from scaffolding and heavy, black metal mesh like the fire escape outside. Eyes walked slowly to the railing and looked down onto the club below. The dance floor was packed and hanging over it was a colourful model dragon. At one end of the club was a huge stage and at the other was a vast bar that was heaving with waiting patrons.

'This is fantastic!' Stalker cried out over the music. Eyes gave her a quick smile, he was genuinely pleased to see her happy, it was too rare. Across the other side of the club was another balcony, on it was a small, quiet bar area and booths of perspex with deep red couches inside. Eyes spotted Scribe sitting in one of them with a small group of people.

'That must be them,' he said, pointing across the club. The Lightning Lords made their way down the steps into the belly of the club and weaved through the crowd to the stairs on the other side. They got to the top to find a red rope across the stairs, and a burly bouncer stood with his arms crossed over his chest.

'Have you booked a booth?' he asked in a gruff voice.

'We're expected,' Eyes said and pointed over towards Scribe. The bouncer glanced over and then back at Eyes with careful consideration.

'One moment.' He strode over to the booth that

Scribe was in and another man stood to greet him. They exchanged a few words and the man looked over at the Lightning Lords. He gave the nod and the bouncer returned to lift the rope for them.

'Thank you,' Eyes said politely as they passed through, and he led the pack over to the booth. Scribe stood to greet them and shook Eyes' hand.

'How are you doing?' he asked warmly.

'Not too bad, thanks,' Eyes replied.

'This is Voice-of-Truth, my Alpha.' Scribe indicated the man who had granted their admittance. He was quite short, the top of his head barely coming level with Eyes' chin, and had tightly cropped, dark hair. He was dressed all in black, with dozens of wristbands and chains on his arms. His eyes were sharp and wise. He radiated calm, Eyes noted, making him a half moon, like Claws.

'Come in and take a seat,' the Alpha said, gesturing to the curved sofas around the booth. There were three other members of the Hellsclaws besides the Alpha and Scribe-of-the-Fallen. The two women were clearly sisters, they had a very close resemblance, but one of them stood out to Eyes. She had long dark hair with streaks of blue in it, piercing blue eyes and a stud in her nose. She was wearing a black PVC vest and extremely short shorts. On her right arm was an ornate tattoo of lightning running from her shoulder to her elbow.

Her sister was more plainly dressed. The other member of the pack was a young man, who sat with his arms stretched out over the back of the sofa, a smug expression on his face. He wore huge boots that came almost to his knees, and a sleeveless shirt with a heavy metal band logo emblazoned across the chest. As the only other male, he had to be Cameron.

Wind Talker led the others into the booth and they all sat down, Wind Talker taking a seat next to Cameron. Eyes observed the discreet handover of the drugs and was able to relax a little, knowing that Wind Talker had them. The booth door clicked shut and the noise of the club dimmed away to almost nothing, granting them some peace and a sense of privacy, despite onlookers being able to see inside.

The two packs exchanged trivial pleasantries. Eyes sat next to Voice-of-Truth, and the other Alpha called a waiter over by hitting a big red button in the middle of the table, which made the perspex around them glow with red light from above. A waiter entered the booth a minute later and they ordered a round of drinks. Eyes was confident that no one would try to poison them this time.

Idle chit chat filled the next few minutes until their drinks arrived. Eyes found it difficult to participate, he wanted to get down to business. They had come for the antivirals, but there was so much more they could talk about. It was possible that the Hellsclaws had information or resources that could help. After a few minutes, Eyes leaned closer to Voice-of-Truth.

'I was hoping you might have some information or suggestions for us on a critical issue,' he said. The other Alpha gave him a grave look.

'I see. What's the problem?'

'We're facing a demon of plague who has allied with the rats in Caerton. Has anyone ever dealt with anything like this before?'

'Scribe is the one to ask,' Voice-of-Truth beckoned Scribe over and he scooted closer, sitting on the table in the middle of the booth and leaning close.

'What's up?' Scribe asked.

'Do you know anything about the plague? Or diseases in general?' Eyes asked.

'Only a little,' he replied. 'Shifters were apparently instrumental in bringing outbreaks to an end in the past. Sometimes it's essential that there is an outbreak, as it restores balance, but the demons who thrive on it rarely end it voluntarily so our kind has had to step in. Why are you asking?'

'Is this related to the medicine you requested?' Voice-of-Truth asked.

Eyes nodded solemnly.

'There's a demon on our territory who's trying to start an epidemic.'

'Oh, that's not right at all,' Scribe said, looking worried. 'No demon should start it, it's a part of nature and happens from time to time, at which point the demons come for the all-you-can-eat buffet.'

'So we're right to try and prevent it?' Eyes asked.

'Yes, and it would be wise to establish how this demon came to be awake and working here,' Scribe said, his face grim.

'He's tethered here by the corpse of an old plague doctor,' Eyes informed them. 'But we don't know how he got here in the first place.'

'I need to know how this demon was vanquished last time there was an outbreak,' Wind Talker said, leaning in to join the discussion. 'If shifters banished it back to its own realm then maybe there's a record of how they did it.'

'Maybe, but it would pre-date any of the Scroll Keepers' normal records. If there is any information on that it'll be in the Scroll Archive,' Scribe explained.

'What's the Scroll Archive?' Eyes asked.

'A hidden archive of all of our records. But it's lost. Neither Echoes nor myself know its whereabouts. Flames almost certainly did.' He looked awkwardly at Wind Talker.

'Does no one else know? Perhaps someone who isn't a Scroll Keeper?' Eyes asked, unable to hide the desperation from his voice.

'It's likely that Father Ash knows,' Scribe said. Eyes noticed a quick glance between Scribe and his Alpha. Tension filled the air.

'Who's Father Ash?' Eyes asked. He didn't like that look between them, and as he said the name he felt a shiver down his spine.

'An outcast shifter,' Voice-of-Truth said quietly. 'He was a Scroll Keeper and one of the city elders. He was a very well respected hunter.'

'What did he hunt?' Eyes asked, not sure that he really wanted to know the answer.

'Spiral Hand,' Voice-of-Truth said in a voice barely above a whisper.

'So he was a hero?' Eyes asked, unsure where this was going.

'For a while,' the other Alpha replied. 'But the other elders suspected that he had been tainted and become Spiral Hand himself. He was cast out of Caerton.'

'Where is he now?' Wind Talker asked.

'He lives out on the coast to the west,' Scribe replied. 'In that big white house.'

Eyes knew the place, it was a notable landmark.

'Is he likely to welcome visitors?' Eyes asked.

'I have no idea, but I strongly urge you to stay away from him and find a solution from the present rather than looking too far into the past.' The two Alphas locked eyes, and Voice-of-Truth's expression was set in a deep frown. Eyes felt the seriousness of his concern, but he didn't see where else they could turn.

'The Scroll Keepers do need to learn the location of the Scroll Archive,' Scribe broke the tension gently. 'If you do approach him and he is able to tell you, please could you keep me involved?'

'Of course,' Eyes said. He had assumed that this would all go through Scribe.

Scribe patted him on the shoulder and moved over to Stalker and Weaver. Voice-of-Truth still looked grim, but he let the subject go. 'When it comes to taking down the Plague Doctor, can we count on your support?' Eyes asked.

Voice-of-Truth looked at him carefully for a moment.

'That's not normally how it works,' he said slowly. 'We can certainly share information, but we would not come to your aid in a conflict. It's your territory and your responsibility.'

Eyes felt frustrated, but he suppressed the feeling and nodded in understanding. 'You're all welcome to stay here this evening and enjoy yourselves. You might need the R and R.' The Alpha stood and placed a firm hand on Eyes' shoulder before leaving the booth and heading over to the bar. Eyes watched him move behind it freely and go through a back door and he realised, a little belatedly, that the Hellsclaws must own The Dragon's Den.

Eyes sighed and leaned back into the sofa. The girl with the lightning tattoo moved to sit next to him, too close to him, and he cast his tired eyes over her. She was incredibly attractive, though not his usual type. She leaned her head back to rest on the sofa cushion and smiled at him.

'I'm Lightning Claw,' she said. Her voice was like honey.

'Fights-Eyes-Open,' he replied.

'Did you get what you came here for?' she asked. Her fingers gently brushed a stray hair from her face and tucked it behind her ear. He looked into her pale eyes and realised that she was coming onto him. He glanced at her cleavage, but mercifully Chloe popped into his head and he moved away from her and cleared his throat.

'Yes, thank you. Nice to meet you.' He stood up and leaned across the table to Wind Talker. 'I'm going to make a move, I want to get those pills to Chloe.'

Wind Talker nodded and passed Eyes the small bottle.

'We'll get a taxi home,' Wind Talker said. 'I hope these do the trick.'

'Thank you,' Eyes replied and gave Wind Talker a brotherly one-armed hug. He said his goodbyes to the others and left the club. It wasn't his scene anyway.

He drove home across Caerton, determined to shake off the temptation of Lightning Claw and focus on his family. Chloe was long since asleep when he got home. She felt clammy to the touch and had placed a bucket by the bed. He hoped it was just a precaution. He placed the bottle on the night stand next to her and went to shower before tucking into bed beside her. He couldn't help feeling guilty for giving her this horrible disease. A tiny voice in his head, that sounded remarkably like Fortune, told him that this is why shifters didn't try to have human families. *They are fragile and a vulnerability,* the voice said.

I know, he replied.

CHAPTER THIRTY ONE

STALKER-OF-NIGHT'S-SHADOW

STALKER WOKE EARLY THE FOLLOWING MORNING, still tired from the late night. She could hear Eyes and Wind Talker talking in the kitchen; the others were stirring too. She shifted from fox to human form, stretched and wandered through to the kitchen, yawning.

'Morning. You're here early,' she said, looking pointedly at Eyes.

'We need to go to see Father Ash as soon as possible. I don't want to sit on this.'

'Eyes, relax,' she said, placing a hand on his arm. 'It's not even eight in the morning.'

The rest of the pack got up and they ate a sleepy breakfast together. Eyes had picked up baked goods on his way over and Stalker tucked into a stack of croissants.

When they were all refreshed and ready, they bundled into Eyes' car and set off for the coast. They crossed the river and drove through St. Catherine's and the suburbs beyond, passing right out of Caerton and onto the scenic coast road to the west. They hardly spoke and Stalker knew she wasn't the only one filled with apprehension. They were seeking out a shifter who had been exiled under suspicion of committing the worst crime possible for their kind, that of allying with the most dangerous demons with the intention of bringing about the end of the world. She didn't know what they would find, what kind of shifter he would be. But she felt in her gut that he was dangerous, regardless of whether or not he was guilty of the crimes of which he was accused.

Eyes clearly knew exactly where he was going, he drove with purpose and no hesitation. Stalker watched out of the window, staring at the tumultuous sea as it crashed against the cliffs further along the coast. She saw the house when they were about a mile away. It stood high on a cliff, stark white against a crop of fir trees. The road twisted and turned as it followed the shore and then wound its way up the steep hill, through dense forest.

They had lost sight of the house and Eyes slowed down to look for a driveway. He nearly drove right past it, it was tucked away on a blind bend on the right, just a narrow dirt track that you wouldn't notice if you weren't looking for it. Eyes slammed on the brakes and turned sharply into the drive.

'Are you sure this is right?' Stalker asked. It didn't look like a driveway befitting the magnificent house on the clifftop. Eyes drove slowly, the car jostled about on the rough track. Eventually the trees thinned and the track levelled out a little. They turned a corner and emerged from the woods, there before them stood the huge house, and just beyond it was the steep cliff down to the sea.

Eyes parked the car. No one moved, they all sat and stared up at the house. It was the biggest home Stalker had ever seen up close. It was built from white stone and had sweeping stone steps leading up to a balcony and the main entrance. To one side was a circular conservatory with huge windows facing out over the sea, and the house rose two storeys above that.

Eventually Eyes opened his door and stepped out of the car, and the others followed. He gave them all a look of fierce determination and led them up the steps to the front door. It was solid oak and next to it was an old fashioned bell on a rope. He rang it and Stalker held her breath, waiting for an answer. She could hear the waves far below and the gentle swaying of the tall trees behind the house.

A minute later the door slowly opened and before them stood a man of medium height and build, with very neatly cut white hair and an immaculate silver beard. He was wearing a dark blue silk robe tied at the waist, and white hair curled from his bare chest. Stalker felt the power radiating off the shifter. She had been in the presence of powerful elders before, and felt immediately subservient to them, but this shifter rivalled some of the most powerful fae and demons that Stalker had encountered, like the Lord-of-Storms-and-Rain, who was basically the god Thor.

Her breath caught in her throat and she felt the strong desire to run back to the car. It seemed the others felt much the same and they had all taken a step back when this shifter had opened the door.

'Can I help you?' His voice was steady and deep with a

genuine edge of curiosity.

'We're looking for Father Ash,' Eyes said. Stalker could tell he was trying hard to sound confident.

'Well, you've found him. It's not often I find five young shifters on my doorstep early on a Saturday morning. Won't you come in?' He held the door wide and stood back to admit them.

Stalker grabbed Weaver's hand and held her back. This didn't feel right at all. Weaver glanced at her and squeezed her hand to reassure her, and they followed the others inside. The entrance lobby was huge, with a marble floor and a grand staircase. Father Ash led them into a drawing room to the right and offered them tea.

'No thank you,' Eyes said quickly, speaking for all of them. Stalker swallowed hard, her nerves a knot in the pit of her stomach. It was probably wise not to accept any food or drink from Father Ash. She looked around at her surroundings. The room was spacious, with three huge, white sofas and several spindle-legged coffee tables. The walls were adorned with huge, framed paintings. The Lightning Lords sat down, taking up two of the sofas, and Stalker glanced at each of them in an effort to judge their thoughts. Everyone was nervous and she knew that Father Ash would be able to tell, as no one was hiding it particularly well. 'Thank you for inviting us into your home,' Eyes said. 'I apologise for the unannounced visit.'

'Not at all,' Father Ash said, waving a hand dismissively. He sat down in the centre of the third sofa and leaned forward on his knees. 'As I don't know you, I must assume that this is not a social call. Who are you and what can I do for you?'

He was so polite and well-spoken, his manner was easy and amiable. Stalker began to relax a little. She realised that she had been expecting someone rather different, someone cold and hard, battle-worn and bitter. He seemed to be none of those things.

'We are the Lightning Lords of St. Mark's and we need to find the Scroll Archive. We were led to believe you might know its location,' Eyes said. He spoke a little quickly, another sign of his nervousness. Father Ash sat up straight and drew a deep breath. He watched Eyes shrewdly for a moment and Stalker watched him. She tried to reach out with her senses and do what Shadow's Step had taught her, to look into someone's soul and find the thing that was most true to them in that moment. She knew they couldn't trust him, no matter how friendly he might seem, and one day it might be useful to understand him better. But she couldn't see inside him at all. It was as if there was a solid brick wall behind his eyes, blocking access to his inner most being.

His eyes flickered over to her and locked with hers. She knew at once that he had sensed her attempt to read him, but there was no hint of malice in his face, no warning to stop, just a simple acknowledgement. She looked away, embarrassed.

'The Lightning Lords? What happened to the Blue Moon?' the powerful elder asked. Stalker felt a stab to her chest for just a moment. All of the shifters in Caerton knew what had happened without them having to tell anyone. For some reason, she was surprised that this powerful shifter didn't know, but she realised how foolish that was, given that he was living in exile.

'They were killed by the Phoenix Guard of the Furies,' Eyes said, his voice steady and detached, which impressed Stalker. She didn't think she could speak like that of them yet.

'I see,' Father Ash replied. He looked at each of them briefly, reading their reactions. Stalker saw his cheek twitch slightly, the tiniest hint of emotion, but she couldn't tell what it was. 'Flames-First-Guardian is gone, then?'

'He is,' Wind Talker replied, coolly. There was a long, heavy silence.

'I do know where the Scroll Archive is,' Father Ash said suddenly. 'Why do you want access to it?'

'It's not for us, exactly. The city's remaining Scroll Keepers don't know where it is and they would like to. We're simply trying to help them.' It was Wind Talker who spoke and Stalker glanced over at him and Eyes on the other sofa. Eyes didn't seem to object to Wind Talker speaking up.

'Isn't that generous of you.' It wasn't a question. Father Ash looked at Wind Talker with scepticism written on his face. 'Is there nothing in it for you?'

'Perhaps,' Wind Talker went on. 'Perhaps all of Caerton's shifters would benefit from the information stored in there.'

'Perhaps,' Father Ash said with a knowing smile. 'I will share its location only with a Scroll Keeper, and only if you youngsters will do something for me.'

'What would that be?' Eyes asked, his voice edged with caution.

'You want something that is missing, well so do I. Find me the skull of a member of the Spiral Hand that I executed ten years ago.'

Stalker held back a gasp. She felt Weaver tense up beside her. Claws rubbed a hand over his face and Wind Talker and Eyes exchanged disbelieving glances.

'That seems an unfair exchange, with all due respect,' Eyes said after a moment. 'How on earth are we to find a ten-year-old skull?'

'How you do it is your business,' Father Ash said, his eyes twinkling slightly. 'That is my price.'

'What was their name?' Wind Talker asked.

'Spirals-of-Bright-Agony,' Father Ash replied with a flash of a predatory smile.

Chapter Thirty Two

Stalker and Weaver looked at each other discreetly. Stalker felt the hairs on her neck standing up and nerves fluttering in her stomach. She didn't think it would be wise to alert Father Ash to the fact that the name was alarmingly familiar, so she kept her cool. Eyes and Wind Talker also exchanged nervous looks. Claws looked none the wiser, he hadn't yet been introduced to the haunted painting at Grove Street.

'Right,' Eyes said at last. 'Well, leave it with us. Do you have a number that we could contact you on if we find the skull?'

'Of course,' Father Ash said with a smile. He moved smoothly over to a beautiful old bureau and returned a moment later with a small card, which he handed to Eyes. Eyes stood up as he took the card and the rest of them did likewise. Stalker was relieved to be leaving. As polite and friendly as Father Ash seemed, the situation was far from comfortable.

He showed them to the door and parting pleasantries were exchanged. The Lightning Lords climbed quickly into the car and Stalker looked out of the rear window to see Father Ash watching them go from the door.

'Do you think he knows?' she said suddenly, as they turned onto the main road.

'Knows what?' Claws asked.

'That Flames kept a part of Spirals-of-Bright-Agony in a painting in his attic,' Wind Talker replied.

'What?' Claws snapped.

'Maybe he disposed of the remains too,' Wind Talker suggested, voicing something that Stalker was just beginning to wonder herself.

'That's pure speculation,' Weaver said. 'We really don't know that for sure. Just because he had a painting with that shifter's madness trapped inside it, doesn't mean he had the corpse too.'

'No, I know,' Eyes replied. 'But it's the best lead we've got on what would otherwise be us looking for a specific skull in an unmarked graveyard of thousands of corpses.'

'I don't believe in coincidences,' Wind Talker said. 'I don't think he realised that we may have already come across something of the shifter, but he wants us on a quest, he quite possibly wants to lead us to an important discovery of our own.'

'Why?' Stalker asked, puzzled by this.

'I think he likes us and wants to teach us something.' Wind Talker shrugged.

Stalker considered the possibility. It sounded reasonable, it sounded like the sort of thing an elder of their kind might do. It sounded like an initiation task. But what might he be trying to initiate them into? The Spiral Hand?

They got back to the house and Wind Talker retrieved the painting from the attic. The five of them stood around the box, none of them willing to open it.

'Will it have, sort of, recharged?' Stalker asked, voicing the concern they shared.

'What are you talking about?' Claws asked, a deep frown creasing his brow.

'Open it,' Wind Talker said, pushing the box across the kitchen table towards Claws. Stalker watched Wind Talker carefully, trying to read him. She wondered what he was thinking and why he was leading Claws into this. She readied herself, knowing she might have to shift form to contain Claws if the painting did to him what it had done to Wind Talker.

Claws cautiously flipped the box open, exposing the dizzying painting. Stalker tried not to look at it, fixing her eyes on Claws. His face strained into a painful expression and his arms went totally rigid, his fists clenched hard. A low whimper clawed its way out of his throat and he began to tremble. Stalker quickly closed the box and got ready to grab hold of him; she noticed the others twitching nervously as well as they waited to see what would happen.

Just as she thought she was going to have to intervene, Claws took a slow, deep breath and the trembling subsided. His stubborn refusal to give in to the beast within had served him well, and he was able to retain control. He blinked a few times and pressed his fingers to his temples.

'What the fuck was that and why do I feel like I'm

coming off some very intense drugs?'

Stalker laughed and gave him a gentle shove.

'That was The-Madness-of-Spirals-of-Bright-Agony. You have now been formally introduced.'

'Huh,' Wind Talker grunted. He opened the box again and peeked inside with one eye closed. Nothing happened and he opened it all the way so they could all look at it again.

'You know, we might be able to use it to defend the house,' Weaver suggested. 'We could rig it so that it falls down in front of people who open the front door and it'll send them running.'

'Bit of a problem for any innocent bystanders outside though,' Eyes said with a smirk.

'I'm joking,' Weaver said with a smile, and Stalker couldn't help but chuckle.

'I'm amazed that you held yourself together,' Wind Talker said, eyeing Claws up carefully.

'He didn't do so well,' Stalker said conspiratorially and Claws let out a snort of laughter.

'Okay,' Eyes said, his tone very business-like. 'So, we have this. Where do we even begin looking for the body?'

'How about Crescent Park?' Stalker suggested hesitantly. 'I mean, if that's where our kind usually perform burials then maybe there are other remains there too.'

'No,' Weaver shook her head. 'The Blue Moon aren't really buried there, they were transported to another realm from there, using the place's unique quality. The idea is that no one knows where their bodies ended up so no one can find them on purpose.'

'That wouldn't happen with an executed enemy,' Wind

Talker said quietly. 'Bones have power, the Scroll Keepers understand that better than anyone. That's why Father Ash wants the skull. The body will be buried somewhere safe, somewhere where the hunters who caught him could keep an eye on it, protect it.' His voice dipped away at the end and almost as one, the five of them turned to stare out of the kitchen window.

'No,' Weaver whispered, her voice full of disbelief. 'It can't be.'

'It can't be that easy. Can it?' Stalker said, glancing around at the others.

'Let's find out.' Eyes strode to the door and they filed out into the back garden. The perfectly neat and well-tended square of earth in the centre of the garden was wet from the steady rainfall they had had. 'Which side of the veil?'

'Hepethia,' Wind Talker said, with certainty.

They crossed over, a real sense of urgency fuelling them. Stalker's heart was racing, though she wasn't sure how much of her anxiety was coming from her pack mates and how much originated with her.

Stalker began digging up the soaked soil with her bare hands and Wind Talker got down to help her. She became almost frenzied as she dug, hoping to find nothing, desperate to not have a dead body buried in their garden, and yet yearning for something in their lives to be simple and achievable. Her fingers scraped against wood suddenly and she stopped and looked at Wind Talker. They only paused for a moment before continuing with even more urgency.

'It's a coffin,' Wind Talker said quietly.

The others moved closer as Stalker scraped the soil away and revealed more of the wooden box. It reminded her of her initiation into Odin's Warriors, and a shudder went through her at the possibility that whoever was inside it had been buried alive.

As she and Wind Talker ripped up the lid her fears were put to rest, the poor fellow had clearly been decapitated before he was buried. His skull was resting in the middle of his chest.

Bones were all that were left. Stalker carefully picked up the skull and lifted it from the grave. There was a faint sigh all around them and she looked up in alarm. She felt the veil ripple slightly.

'What was that?' she asked, panic filling her. She scrambled up out of the grave and looked around anxiously. Everyone else was doing the same.

'I don't know,' Wind Talker whispered. Stalker usually counted on him and Weaver to know the answers to these things, but Weaver looked just as blank.

'Did we just release something?' Stalker asked.

'Maybe,' Weaver said quietly. 'But maybe that's not a bad thing.'

'Do we all think that this is the right skull?' Stalker asked, holding it up to examine it.

'I think so,' Eyes said. Everyone else agreed.

'Well, let's get this grave covered up again, shall we?' Stalker suggested. Everyone helped to refill the grave. The urgency was gone and Stalker moved slowly, suddenly exhausted, her limbs aching.

'Let's not let Father Ash know about this just yet,' Eyes said, his voice filled with caution.

'No,' Wind Talker said. 'We don't want to let him know it was quite so easy.'

Stalker rolled her eyes in disbelief. It was all about politics, so much game playing and she had no patience for it. If she had her way, they would get the skull straight back to Father Ash that afternoon and crack on with finding the Scroll Archive. Did they really have time to spare for these games? But there was no arguing with these two once they had set their minds on something.

Stalker showered before she had to go to work that afternoon. She hated to have to go back to her human life after the morning's events, but she needed the money and she wanted to keep that connection to her humanity. Even her vial of still waters didn't help much that afternoon. She felt anxious and was filled with adrenaline, which she tried to use to her advantage in teaching her more advanced students some more aggressive moves.

When she finished work, she didn't want to go straight back to the house. She had to run off some steam first, so she shifted into her fox form and ran the borders of the territory. She had hoped to see Pursuit-of-Midnight-Solitude, but she didn't feel her calling to her at all and had to content herself with a normal patrol. It was a clear night and bitterly cold. The stars pierced the slight haze but there was no moon. Stalker felt Artemis watching her, even with no visible eye in the sky. This was her moon, she felt stronger, faster, quieter and more connected to everything.

As she jogged down a back alley there was a rattle of bin lids that stopped her in her tracks. She turned and crept silently towards the cluster of metal bins on the side of the alley. One of them was overflowing and Stalker sniffed her way carefully, trying to get past the smell of the contents of the bins to get to whatever had made the noise.

She was a few feet away when a sudden movement stopped her; a regular fox darted out from between the bins into the alley right in front of her. She would have laughed if she was in human form. The fox stopped and looked her right in the eye. They stared at each other for a few seconds.

Suddenly the fox yelped and its middle scrunched inwards, like it had been crushed by a giant, invisible hand. Stalker leapt backwards, her breath quickened and her eyes darted all around. The fox dropped to the ground, dead, and as Stalker looked closer she saw that it was frozen solid.

She felt the veil ripple and an elemental of ice crossed over right in front of her. It was roughly the size and shape of a bear, but with edges like cut crystal and it radiated freezing cold. Its heavy feet pounded on the tarmac, cracking it and planting a rapidly expanding patch of frost under each foot. It sniffed the air and its white eyes landed on Stalker.

She shifted into her Agrius form and took a defensive stance. She hoped that a show of strength would make it back down. It wasn't her job to kill any fae or demon that crossed her path, simply to keep them all in line and out of the human world. This elemental fae took a step towards her and made a sound like a freezer door opening. The blast of cold air hit her full in the face and she stumbled backwards.

'Hungry,' came a whisper on the wind from the

creature.

Behind her, there was another ripple in the veil and Stalker wheeled around to see another winter fae crossing over. It froze a puddle in the middle of the street in seconds as it stomped towards her. She had a feeling this was going to end badly if she didn't act; these elementals were breaking the rules in crossing the veil in search of food. She leapt toward the new arrival and threw a punch at its head.

The impact shattered several bones in her bestial hand, splintering pain shot all the way up her arm and she recoiled from the fae. Her other hand went for one of her dha on her back. She drew it and sliced neatly through the elemental in one fluid movement, causing it to split in two and shatter on impact with the ground, sending a million shards of ice scattering across the road before disappearing back across the veil. The other one stepped backwards away from her, its eyes cast down to the ground in submission, and slowly it crossed the veil back into Hepethia.

Stalker swiftly sheathed her dha and shook out her throbbing, broken hand. She looked around anxiously for any sign that humans had seen anything they shouldn't. The coast was clear, so she shifted into her human form and sprinted back to the house, where the rest of the pack were sleeping. With a heavy sigh of resignation, Stalker settled down to sleep as well.

'The winter fae have gone crazy,' she declared to the others when everyone was awake the following morning. 'Two of them crossed the veil and attacked me while I was patrolling last night.' She clutched her broken right hand gingerly with her good one, it was mending but still painful.

'What?' Wind Talker said, visibly confused.

'Why would they do that?' Stalker asked.

'Did they say anything?' Weaver asked.

'One of them said "hungry".'

Wind Talker and Weaver exchanged troubled looks. Stalker looked from one to the other, waiting for a response.

'We need to appease them, offer a sacrifice in order to keep them favourable,' Wind Talker explained.

'A sacrifice?' Stalker asked. She was nervous about where this might be going.

'A sacrifice,' Weaver said, looking grim. 'All the packs have to do it, we have to honour the gods and the seasons. Now that winter is here, we have to honour that.'

'What kind of sacrifice?' Claws asked. Stalker looked at him and saw how uncomfortable he seemed.

'A life,' Weaver replied, a grim expression on her face.

Chapter Thirty Three

'So we kill a stray dog or something, right?' Stalker asked, looking from one face to another. No one replied. Weaver and Wind Talker exchanged uncomfortable looks. 'Not a dog?'

'Not a dog,' Weaver said quietly.

'Preferably a human,' Wind Talker said. There was the slightest trace of discomfort in his face. Stalker couldn't quite believe what she was hearing. She didn't *want* to believe it.

'You are joking?' Claws said, his voice a little elevated.

'People die in winter all the time,' Wind Talker said. 'They die of illness, cold, malnutrition. Winter claims them. When we don't offer a ritualistic sacrifice, winter claims more than its share. It's how we keep balance.'

'The best thing we can do, is find someone who is at greater risk of being claimed by winter anyway,' Weaver said. She sounded concerned and uncomfortable with the idea at least, but Stalker hated hearing her make the suggestion.

'Someone homeless?' Eyes suggested. His face was set in a grim but determined expression. He was going to sanction this. Stalker hung her head in her hands. Something unpleasant moved in her stomach.

'Too easy,' Wind Talker replied. 'The more effort we put into it, the more acceptable a sacrifice the winter fae will consider it.'

'An old person,' Weaver said, her voice barely above a whisper.

'I cannot believe you three are discussing this,' Claws said. He stood and strode from the room.

'I want no part in this,' Stalker said and followed Claws to the kitchen. 'I can't believe this.'

'It's abhorrent. I had no idea it would be like this.' Claws made a mug of strong coffee for each of them. 'Don't you ever wish you could just go back to being normal?'

'No,' she said. Surprising herself with the ease with which she could answer. 'We never were normal. We were always going to be this. When I changed it was like the blinkers had been taken off and I could finally see the world the way it really was. I never knew I was wearing any, but once they were gone everything made perfect sense. Isn't it like that for you?'

'No,' he replied, not looking at her.

'You don't like shifting form, do you?'

'No, I don't.'

She placed a hand on his arm and gave it a gentle squeeze.

'I've got an idea,' she said, suddenly inspired. 'Wait

here.'

Stalker returned to the living room. The others had been talking but fell silent and looked at her awkwardly.

'You okay?' Eyes asked.

'Fine. Wind Talker? Can I borrow your all-seeing-eye please?'

'Why?' he asked.

'Claws and I are going to The Watchtower. I'd like to be able to look across the veil before we cross over, just in case there's a welcoming party.'

'That's a really good idea,' Eyes said with an encouraging smile.

'Okay,' Wind Talker said, a little reluctantly. He took the necklace from around his neck and passed it to her. She was careful to only touch the lace that it was strung on and tucked it into her pocket.

'Thank you. We'll be back soon.' She thought about asking them to delay killing anyone until their return, but bit back the words. There was no need to cause an argument. She returned to the kitchen and knocked back her coffee. 'Come on, we're going to see if there is another way.'

She led Claws out of the house and they walked quickly to his office. He let them inside and led her up the stairs. Stalker carefully took out the necklace and placed the copper eye in her palm. It was a curious sensation, seeing both sides of the veil at the same time, especially in a location where the site in Hepethia was so different from the human world.

In Hepethia, the Watchtower was crawling with winter fae. The fallen leaves were coated in frost, and elementals of ice and wind were climbing the walls. There was a new figure upon the throne, the one Eyes had seen. He sat upright and alert, not half asleep as the Reaper had done. A sudden flurry of movement caught her off guard and she stumbled as she tried to orientate herself. Several of the fae had started fighting. It was like a bar brawl, vicious and dirty with other fae cheering and taking sides. She couldn't hear anything, only see it, but she got the gist. It was chaos and disorder.

'What do you see?' Claws asked. Stalker looked at him, suddenly remembering that he was there. She let the pendant fall from her hand, keeping hold of the lace so that her vision returned to normal.

'We don't want to cross over here.'

'They're going to do it, aren't they? No matter what we found here.'

'Yes,' she replied. The truth of it settled like a heavy shroud across her shoulders. She got her phone out and typed a message to Eyes.

> Winter fae in disarray, turning on each other. Looks nasty. Do what has to be done but me and Claws are staying out of it.

'Let's get drunk,' Claws suggested.

'Yes, let's.' Stalker had never felt the divide in the pack so strongly, but she was extremely glad to have Claws on her side. She couldn't see how they could possibly reconcile after this and the first shot of whiskey was filled with sorrow. Claws poured out a second and slid the glass along his desk to her. She scooped it up and knocked it back. It burned her throat; whiskey wasn't her favourite drink and she shuddered as it went down. The third went down more easily but with it came a tear that she couldn't prevent. Claws stared at his fingers splayed on his desk and let out a long, unsteady breath.

'How do you stand it?' he asked, his voice barely above a whisper.

'Stand what?'

'All of it. The violence, the utter insanity of the world. Sometimes I look at you and it's like you're turned on by it all.'

Stalker looked at him, puzzled. He was glaring at her.

'I'm here with you tonight, aren't I?' she snapped back. 'You were getting your thrills shooting up the rats, so I think that's a bit rich.'

Claws raised his glass to her and gave her a half-hearted smile.

'Fair play,' he said, then slowly downed his drink. 'So you haven't let go of morality, but there are things you enjoy about this life.'

'Yeah,' she smiled. 'I love shifting, I love what my body can do and I do like a good fight but that's nothing new. I wasn't just drawn to martial arts for the exercise.' She poured another drink but just stared at it as her mind slipped back to her life before her first change. 'But it's really hard. I had a nice, simple life that I had to leave behind, or should leave behind. I can't though, I can't turn my back on my humanity and I don't want to.'

She leaned back in her chair and let her slightly intoxicated eyes drift around the room.

'Yeah I know what you mean,' Claws said, taking another drink. 'You're getting behind, keep up.' He tapped her glass.

'Let's play a game,' she said with a grin.

'A drinking game?' he replied, looking at her with an eyebrow raised. 'Okay.'

'Do you know I Have Never?'

Claws snorted with laughter and nodded. 'Okay,' Stalker went on. 'So, I have never hacked into a confidential computer system.' Claws took a drink, keeping his eyes focused on her. Stalker grinned.

'I have never,' Claws said, pausing to think of something, 'fought another shifter.'

Stalker looked at him for a moment, trying to decide why he would bring that up. Slowly, she picked up her glass and drank. She had fought more than her share of shifters already, and even killed one. The guilt over that incident still gnawed at her. She looked around the room and her eyes settled on a framed picture on his desk, a young boy grinned out at her, he had the same thick, dark hair as Claws and the same bright eyes.

'I have never had a child,' she said quietly, watching him carefully. Claws slowly refilled his glass and drank. 'Sorry,' she whispered.

'It's okay.'

'Why haven't you mentioned him?'

'When has there been a chance?' Claws said with a sad sort of smirk. 'I don't see him, haven't seen him in years. His mum and I didn't work out. I'd like to see him, of course, but she made it really difficult for me. They moved away and she messed me about, mixing up dates when I was meant to visit, and poisoned him against me. Now he doesn't want to see me anymore.'

'I'm really sorry,' Stalker said, a lump in her throat.

'Turns out it was for the best, though, eh?' He shrugged and leaned back in his seat.

'Yeah, maybe,' Stalker replied, thinking of Eyes. 'The best way to protect the people we love is to keep them away from all of this.' She wasn't thinking of Eyes any more. Her thoughts drifted to Rhys.

'I have never had a secret boyfriend,' Claws said, a small smile playing on his lips.

Stalker's eyes snapped back to him and she felt her cheeks burn up. Reluctantly, she took a drink.

'I bet you have, I bet there's a whole alternative side to you buried under your layers,' she said, with a huff of indignation and playfulness in her voice. Claws laughed. 'I have never got so drunk that I urinated in public.' Stalker waited, watching as his face twitched. Claws lifted his glass to his lips and Stalker burst out laughing, she pushed away from the desk and her chair toppled over backwards, spilling her onto the floor. She automatically went into a backward roll and sprang to her feet, wobbled and fell sideways into the wall. Claws was chuckling and put down his drink.

'I've never done that either, I was teasing you,' he said with a wink. Stalker laughed and stumbled back towards the desk. Claws passed her a drink and she tipped it down her throat. The bottle was almost empty and they both looked at it with a mixture of regret and relief.

Suddenly, Stalker's phone broke the silence with an incoming message.

It is done. Come on home x

Stalker shook her head.

'No, I'm not going back to the house. I can't even look at them.' She passed her phone to Claws so he could read the message.

'I'm going back,' he said, his speech only slightly slurred. 'I don't want to sleep in my office.'

'You could shift and perch on the back of your chair,' she said with a wicked grin.

'I don't think so,' he replied, wrinkling his nose. He knocked back the last of his drink and slammed the glass down on the desk. 'Where will you go?'

'I need to clear my head,' she said, giving it a shake. 'I'll go for a run.'

'Alright, look after yourself and I'll see you in the morning. Okay?'

She nodded and gave him a hug. He patted her on the back and they went their separate ways. Stalker walked for a bit, letting the freezing cold night air fill her lungs and clear her head of the drunken fog. It stung her lungs to breathe, but it worked. She was half way through China Town before she even realised where she was, having walked aimlessly through the deserted, midnight streets.

As the alcohol finished burning its way through her system, clearing far quicker than it would in a human, she realised where she needed to be. She picked up her pace and broke into a jog, leaping over a fence that blocked her way and landing with a crunch on the gravel track below the overpass. She glanced up and saw how far she had jumped, and felt a tingle of excitement. She set off again, taking a more direct route rather than sticking to the main streets. She ran through a car park and easily clambered over the high wall on the far side, dropping into a scrap yard and resuming her run without breaking stride. The wooden gates back onto the road were no problem for her, she climbed them and swung over the top smoothly.

Stalker skidded to a halt outside Rhys's front door just a few minutes later. She rang the bell and stepped back onto the pavement to wait for him to answer. She paced anxiously. It was late, about 1am, but she had to see him. She needed him more than ever.

After more than a minute she sensed him on the other side of the door, and stood still on the step. Slowly the door opened a crack and his tired face appeared in the shadows.

'Ariana?' he said, sounding confused. He opened the door wider. 'What are you doing here? What's wrong?'

He was wearing loose pyjama trousers and no top, obviously not bothered by the cold night air. 'You're crying,' he said and ushered her inside. Stalker touched her cheek and felt hot tears fresh on her skin. She wiped them away and went inside. She didn't know what to say; she couldn't tell him the truth. He grabbed her and pulled her into a warm embrace.

'I'm sorry, thank you for letting me in.' She broke into renewed sobs as she thought about everything that had happened with the pack. Rhys held her tightly as she shook and cried, her face pressed against his chest. Her sadness switched to anger and she pulled away from him, fury boiling up inside her. She was angry with everyone, the others who had come up with this plan to sacrifice someone, and with herself and Claws for not putting up more of a fight.

She shrugged off her jacket and threw it across the

back of the sofa. There was a small clunk and she looked down to see Wind Talker's talisman on the wooden floor. She stooped to pick it up and held it by the lace for a moment, looking at it carefully. She glanced around the room, feeling that same discomfort that she had felt here before, and carefully she gathered up the lace and took the copper pendant in her hand. Her vision shifted and she looked around the darkened room. There were no lights on, just the orange glow from the street lamp outside the window and a little light spilling down the stairs in the short corridor between the front room and the kitchen at the back of the house.

On the other side of the veil it was just as dark, and the same eerie, orange light seeped in through the window. She saw markings all over the walls and on the inside of the front door. Shifter runes were carved right into the walls in deep gouges. They were the runes for *secret, hide, protect* and then over and over again, a million times in varying sizes, *human, human, human, human, human.* She tried not to react, though a hard lump had risen in her throat. Rhys was watching her carefully, a deep frown on his brow. She looked at him in disbelief. His tattoos were not solid, black, tribal swirls; they were an intricate string of the same runes, but more disturbing than this was the demon. Draped over his shoulders like a black cloak with a hood that covered his head and most of his face, was a demon of secrecy. It had red eyes that looked right at her, and as she stared, it raised a silky finger to Rhys's lips to silence her.

She shoved the pendant into the pocket of her jeans and tried to hold back the dizziness and nausea that was filling her body. What was happening? Rhys was her mundane port in the storm. What was he and did he even know about the demon cloaking him?

'What's the matter? Talk to me,' he pleaded.

'I can't,' she whispered. Slowly she walked towards him and took a deep breath. He smelled completely human, he didn't exude supernatural power. She looked carefully at his tattoos and as she drew very close to him she saw that the runes were just about visible without Wind Talker's talisman, hidden there in plain sight. Up close, even in very low light, she saw that the runes were inked onto his skin so tightly packed that from a distance they looked like solid lines. She reached out and touched one of them and he suddenly pulled away from her.

'Ariana,' he said, his voice filled with panic.

'Why do you have those tattoos?' she tried to sound casual, but wasn't sure she had achieved it.

'I can explain.'

'Please do,' she snapped, losing patience.

'I– I'm a shifter, like you.'

Stalker felt like the wind had been knocked out of her. She leaned heavily on the back of the sofa and groaned, fighting for air. Fresh tears stung her eyes.

'How can you be? Why are you hiding it?'

'I'm so sorry. At first I couldn't tell you, because you hadn't changed yet, and then I wanted to but didn't know how to even begin. I was terrified of losing you.'

Stalker's heart raced and her head throbbed. She clutched at her chest, desperate to breathe normally but she was hyperventilating. Rhys tried to touch her but she yanked away from him.

'Why are you hiding it?' she yelled. 'Most of us don't have houses and bodies graffitied with runes of concealment, or have demons riding on our backs to hide us.'

He stared at her, his mouth slightly open as if to speak but no words came out. Stalker felt fear building up inside her. She could think of one reason why a shifter would go to such lengths to hide from others. If they were a member of a secret cult, whose sole purpose was to destroy the world; if they were Spiral Hand. She ran past him and flung open the door.

'Stalker!' he called out, using her shifter name for the first time, a name he shouldn't even know. She stopped in the doorway, clinging onto the frame on both sides, her foot halfway to the step below. She closed her eyes and felt the weight of that name pressing onto her shoulders. 'We all have demons,' Rhys whispered.

Stalker stepped into the street, shifted into her fox form and sprinted away, feeling his eyes on her as she ran.

CHAPTER THIRTY FOUR

STALKER CREPT SILENTLY THROUGH THE HOUSE and into the living room, where the pack lay sleeping. Even Eyes was there, rather than at home with his family. Stalker wondered if he was there for her or because he didn't want to face his wife after what he had done. She was still shaking as she dropped to the floor next to the sofa. Claws stirred and rolled over to face her, though he didn't wake. She wanted him to. She wanted to tell someone what had happened and he was the only one who knew that she had a boyfriend, but she couldn't be sure how he would react to the news that Rhys wasn't what he appeared. How could she tell any of them? They would immediately worry about what he knew, what she had told him, and they would probably want to march straight over to his house to kill him. She burst into silent tears. She had fallen in love with Rhys without realising it, she didn't want him killed, even if he *was* a member of the Spiral Hand.

She was going to have to carry the burden of this secret with her. She could never see him again, not now that she knew what he was, but she didn't have to betray his secret to anyone in a position to do anything about it.

Slowly, her body morphed into that of a fox and she fell asleep on the floor. Her thoughts and dreams were less vivid in this form, and she was able to switch off her neocortex enough to sleep with only mildly disturbing dreams.

When she awoke, the room was still and dark. She lifted her head and looked around at her sleeping pack mates. She looked up at Claws on the sofa, his eyes were just flickering open and locked with hers. He looked so sad.

'Morning,' he whispered. She made a quiet snuffling noise in reply.

One by one, the pack woke and an awkward breakfast followed. Stalker's phone buzzed intermittently with incoming messages, which she resolutely ignored. She fished Wind Talker's talisman out of her pocket and slid it across the table to him.

'Thank you for lending it to me.'

'Did you see what you expected to?' he asked gently. Stalker shook her head. There were no words adequate to convey the poignancy of his question, he didn't need to know and she couldn't tell him anyway.

'We'll head over to Father Ash soon, with the skull,' Eyes said as he ate.

A knock at the door interrupted them and everyone looked curiously down the hall.

Wind Talker went to answer it and Stalker heard his

surprise when he opened the door.

'What do you want?' he said, barely restraining the anger from his voice. The others exchanged worried glances and Stalker made her way cautiously down the hall. Over Wind Talker's shoulder she saw a vaguely familiar face, and she clamped a hand to her face against the stench of tar and rot.

'Please,' Tar Peter said. His hands were raised in surrender and he clutched a white handkerchief in one of them. 'Hear me out, I come to parley.'

'We don't negotiate with, what was it? "Rubberneckers"?' Wind Talker snapped.

'I can help you with the Plague Doctor,' the demon said hurriedly. He glanced up and down the street.

'Let him in,' Stalker insisted and gently tugged Wind Talker away from the door. He glanced at her and then gave way. Tar Peter stepped into the hall and followed Stalker to the kitchen. Eyes and Weaver were on their feet. Claws looked puzzled and rose slowly to greet the strange visitor. 'Sit down,' Stalker ordered and Tar Peter took a seat at the table. The Lightning Lords gathered around him.

'What can you do to help?' Wind Talker barked from the kitchen doorway, his arms crossed defensively over his chest. 'And why would you?'

'His activities are interfering with my work,' the demon said, not even trying to contain his scorn. 'It's my job to keep the traffic flowing, but he's digging up roads and filling the sewers with rats, which blocks the under-city networks. It's a mess.'

'Wait,' Claws said. 'Who is this guy and what's going

on?'

'This scumbag stopped to gloat when the Blue Moon was destroyed,' Wind Talker snarled. 'We caught him at the site of the wreckage right afterwards.'

'I was not gloating, I had nothing to gloat over,' the demon replied defensively. 'I was merely looking. I'm sure you can understand. It was no different than the hordes of humans that assembled at the police cordon.'

Stalker had to give him that. They had been shocked and angry at the time, and had reacted strongly to his presence, but he wasn't really doing anything wrong.

'How can you help?' Stalker pressed, anxious to get back to the matter in hand.

'I can distract the rats for you when the time comes.'

'What do you want in return?' Eyes asked shrewdly.

'I just want the rat population reduced, which will happen with the destruction of the Plague Doctor. You don't need to do anything that you weren't going to do anyway. It's in both of our interests to end him.'

'So, you'll do something to clear the rats out of the Plague Doctor's lair, leaving the way clear for us to take out the big man?' Eyes asked.

'That's the idea. They won't all follow me, you'll have to deal with some of them too.'

'This all sounds rather familiar,' Stalker said, thinking of Raigo. 'How on earth can we trust you?'

'You don't have to,' Tar Peter replied. 'I'll do as I say, you can trust my word or not. Will it make any difference to what you do?'

Nobody answered. A few glances were exchanged. 'Well, that settles it.' Tar Peter stood up, brushed down his black suit and placed his hat upon his head. He carefully placed a card on the table. 'Call me when you need the distraction and I will provide it.'

He walked past Wind Talker and let himself out.

'He was telling the truth,' Claws said, breaking the silence. 'But after Raigo, I don't know, I guess demons can slip past my ability if they believe enough of what they're saying and steer clear of outright lies.'

'We'll be cautious,' Eyes said, his face set in a determined expression.

An hour later, the pack were pulling to a halt outside Father Ash's house. Stalker's phone continued to receive messages, buzzing as they approached the front door. Finally Eyes snapped.

'Will you reply or turn that thing off, please?' he hissed.

'Sorry,' she mumbled and turned off her phone.

The front door opened and Father Ash greeted them, wearing neatly pressed, grey trousers and a white roll neck jumper. Eyes held up the skull and Father Ash raised his eyebrows in surprise.

'You didn't expect us to be able to find it, did you?' Eyes asked, a smirk playing on his lips.

'Of course I did. I wouldn't have asked you to do something impossible. What would the point of that be? But I didn't expect you to find it so quickly.' Father Ash took the skull carefully and led the Lightning Lords inside. This time he led them into a room to the left and asked them to wait while he authenticated the skull.

They stood awkwardly in the dining room. A huge table dominated the room and Stalker wondered what it was like for the man to rattle around in a huge house like this on his own. She drifted over to a long cabinet against the wall and glanced at the photographs standing on top of it in silver frames. A familiar face caught her eye and she stopped dead.

'Guys,' she whispered. The others moved over and they all looked at the pictures. The same face appeared in several and Stalker let her finger brush one of them, as if that would reassure her it was real. 'Could he be her father?'

'It certainly looks that way,' Eyes said quietly. 'Is this her as a child?' He held up another picture of a pre-teen girl smiling awkwardly at the camera. There was a definite resemblance to Last-Breath-Echoes. The other, more recent pictures were all taken at a distance, like paparazzi shots.

'It's a little bit creepy,' Stalker whispered. They quickly dispersed away from the pictures, though Stalker wondered if he had shown them in here on purpose so that they would see them.

A few minutes later, Father Ash returned looking satisfied.

'It is indeed the correct skull. Wherever did you find it?'

'I believe that would be best not shared,' Eyes said. He locked eyes with Father Ash and Stalker watched the pair of them, waiting anxiously for one of them to back down. Finally, Father Ash smiled and turned away, looking around at the rest of them.

'You've got yourselves a strong Alpha there, folks.' He put his hand in his pocket and pulled out a phone. 'Now, who do I need to call?'

Eyes gave him Scribe-of-the-Fallen's number and they all waited while it rang. 'Hello? Is this Scribe?' Father Ash strode from the room to have the conversation. He returned a moment later and passed his phone to Eyes.

'Hello?' Eyes spoke into the phone. There was a reply that Stalker couldn't hear. 'Okay, thanks Scribe. I'll talk to you later.' Eyes passed the phone back to Father Ash. 'Okay, well I think that concludes our business. Thank you so much for your help.'

Father Ash offered a hand and Eyes shook it. Stalker watched everything carefully, taking in every little nuance of the power play.

'Any time.' Father Ash glanced at Stalker, who was still lingering near the photos. He gestured to them and looked down, as if he didn't quite want to make eye contact with Stalker. 'You know her?'

'We do.' Stalker nodded.

'How is she?'

'She's okay, as far as I know,' Stalker replied. She didn't like his attention being on her. Father Ash nodded appreciatively. 'Would you like me to mention that you asked after her?'

'Probably best not,' he said with a sad smile.

The Lightning Lords left and returned to the city, barely talking to each other on the drive back. Eyes dropped Stalker off at work, but Claws was the only pack mate that she was sorry to be leaving. They exchanged sad smiles as she closed the car door and she didn't wait to watch them go. The afternoon was a living hell. Her young students arrived for their judo class and she greeted them with little enthusiasm, though many of them were in a particularly boisterous mood.

'Settle down, please,' she called. Some of them took a knee and went quiet, but two young boys continued to laugh and joke between them. 'On the mat, now!' she shouted. She hardly ever raised her voice to her students and they instantly went quiet and knelt down on the mat in front of her. Stalker's hand went to her vial of still waters, but she wasn't feeling its cooling effects today.

She directed the class through some drills to warm up and tried to focus herself, to call on the discipline that she had prided herself on a few months ago. The boys kept acting up, however, and she struggled to contain her temper. 'If you can't behave in my class you can leave,' she snapped at them, and after that they settled down. She noticed several other students exchanging looks of surprise but chose to ignore it.

'Have a good Christmas,' one girl said quietly as the class was finishing up and Stalker blanched, suddenly reminded of the date. No wonder the kids had been so disruptive.

'Thank you,' she muttered meekly. 'You too.'

She packed away her things once everyone had left, and set off towards the stairs down to the street.

'Merry Christmas!' Ron called to her from his office as she passed.

'You too,' she replied with a bright smile, despite having no festive feeling in her at all. She had two weeks off work ahead and given the way she was feeling and the challenges that she knew lay ahead, she was very relieved.

As she left the building she found the courage to turn her phone back on. There were dozens of text messages from Rhys, she opened one to find him pleading for her to reply, but couldn't bear to read the rest. She deleted them all.

Stalker felt completely isolated. Her pack was going somewhere she couldn't follow, and now she couldn't trust Rhys. She didn't return to Grove Street, she needed some space and she walked slowly back to her own flat, even though the evening was biting cold. A small smile crept onto her face as she approached her building and saw Claws leaning on the wall.

'Hi,' he said with the same, small smile that she greeted him with. She unlocked the door and led him up to her flat. He was the first pack mate to visit her home since Shadow's Step had brought her back to collect clean clothes just after she first changed, somehow it felt right that it was him.

'How did you know where I live?' she asked.

'I'm a PI,' he said with a completely deadpan expression and she laughed.

'Of course. I wish I could offer you a drink or something, but there is literally nothing here these days.'

'That's fine. This is your bolt-hole, then? The place you're always sneaking off to?'

'Sometimes,' she said with a shrug. Claws raised an eyebrow and waited for her to go on. 'The secret boyfriend you guessed right about, I went to see him last night.' She stopped and glanced at him, he watched her, patiently waiting for her to say what she needed to say. She swallowed the hard lump in her throat and made herself go on. 'I thought he was human and last night I found out that he isn't, and now I don't know what to do about it.'

'I see,' Claws said. 'Does it matter? Is the lie more important than the man?'

'Maybe,' she said and collapsed onto the sofa. Claws came to sit by her and waited patiently for her to speak again. 'He's a shifter and I think he's Spiral Hand.'

'Ah. Wait, you *think* he is. You don't know?'

'Well, he was hiding his true nature, not just from me, by the looks of it, but from everyone, everything. Why would he do that if he weren't Spiral Hand?'

'Did you talk to him about it?' Claws asked, as if it was the easiest and most obvious thing in the world.

'No,' she admitted. 'I ran away.'

'Granted, I don't know much about them, but I got the impression that they had an agenda and were allied with demons. If this guy is hiding his nature from everything, even the demons, how could he be working with them?'

'He has a secrecy demon cloaking him. He *is* working with demons.'

'But a secrecy demon isn't chaos, fear, anger or greed. Isn't it possible that he's hiding from all of them too?'

Stalker sighed. His words made a lot of sense.

'Maybe I should hear him out. I just can't trust him anymore. Who's to say that anything he says now won't just be more lies?'

'Me,' Claws said, raising an eyebrow. 'I can detect lies, remember?'

'So you can.' Stalker smiled, there was a glimmer of hope. 'But look, I need to sit on this for a bit. We need to get the Plague Doctor dealt with. Everything else needs to wait.'

'Okay, whatever you think best. Do you want to go

back to Grove Street?'

'Not really,' she said, grimacing.

'We have to make things right with the others,' Claws said tentatively.

'Do we? I don't want to be part of a pack that kills old people. Do you?'

'No, I don't. But I don't think there's an alternative. The Watch was the same. I may not have been one of them, they kept a lot from me, but I could tell they were doing things that my silly, human morality would struggle with.'

'We could form our own pack!' Stalker said, lighting up with optimism.

'And last, what? A week?' The light quickly faded. Claws was right, there was safety in numbers. She had seen the things they had to face, and the two of them wouldn't last long on their own. 'We don't have to be okay with what they did, and we don't have to participate in anything like that. But we do have to stick together and try to get along. We might be able to prevent future incidents, now that we know about this side of it all. We might be able to change them if we work together.'

Stalker nodded. He was right, again. She was spotting a pattern here, Claws was always right. It was probably best not to voice the thought, it might go to his head.

The two of them slept at her flat that night, she let him sleep in her bed and she curled up at his feet as a cat. In the morning they got up early and went over to Grove Street. Stalker got up the courage to check her phone on the way. There were more messages from Rhys, though their frequency was reducing.

Please hear me out.

Please meet me.

I don't know what you thought, but I'm not a bad guy, please talk to me.

I want to work this out with you, please.

I'm crazy about you and I was crazy to hide this from you.

She deleted them all. She acknowledged to herself that part of her wanted to test his persistence. She wanted to know if he was going to give up. If he was evil then his persistence might go to extremes, she knew that the Spiral Hand were experts in manipulation and she refused to let him manipulate her. Everything would be on her terms and in her own time.

They arrived at the house to find Eyes on the phone, the others listening patiently. Eyes glared at them as they walked in and Stalker instantly felt bad about not letting them know where she and Claws were. Eyes finished the call and turned on Stalker.

'I'm glad you two are all right. A call next time would be nice. Right now, Scribe needs our help.'

Chapter Thirty Five

The Lightning Lords stood on a street corner in Northgate, north of St. Mark's. People bustled past in thick coats and bowed their heads low against the icy winter wind as they made their way to work. It was rush hour and the road was heavy with slow-moving traffic chugging out thick smoke. Stalker thought of Tar Peter and wondered what these conditions meant to him. It was the first time she had given much thought to how a demon lived.

They were a few blocks away from the heavy industrial area of Caerton, in a more commercial area. But it was a rough neighbourhood with many homeless people and a plethora of shelters, food banks and a thriving soup kitchen. The Lightning Lords stood outside the soup kitchen now, waiting for Scribe to meet them.

Stalker saw him walking briskly towards them through the throng of pedestrians, and they greeted each other warmly.

'Thanks for meeting me and allowing me to come,' Scribe said quietly.

'Not a problem,' Eyes replied. 'What are we doing here?'

Stalker looked over his shoulder at the building on the corner. The windows were boarded and the big wooden door held a sign declaring the place open. It looked like it had once been an office building, but had long since been abandoned as such.

'We're looking for a man called Henry Smith,' Scribe said, leaning close to the pack and keeping his voice low. 'He's a vagrant and known around here, he comes to this place most mornings for breakfast. He has the key.'

Scribe led them inside. There was a small lobby and a set of double doors stood open, leading through to a large hall. In the hall was a long serving station with heat lamps and a single volunteer positioned behind it. The hall was filled with long tables, where half a dozen people sat eating hot porridge. Scribe looked around and shook his head. 'He's not here.'

Stalker strode over to the serving station and waited while someone was served. The volunteer, a man in his fifties with greying hair and kind eyes, looked her up and down with a frown.

'Hi,' Stalker said with a smile. 'I'm looking for Henry Smith, I'm a friend of his. I heard he comes here for breakfast.'

The man looked at her carefully for a moment, considering her. He gave a small nod of approval.

'You just missed him. He left about ten minutes ago.'

'Oh, okay, thanks. Do you know where he was going?'

'He panhandles about five minutes from here, near the cash machine.'

'Thank you,' Stalker said and walked briskly back to the others to relay the information. They set off and found the cash machine easily enough but there was no sign of Henry.

'Spread out, he must be here somewhere,' Eyes instructed. They went off in pairs to search the surrounding streets and alleyways. Stalker and Scribe went together down a side street that was wet and strewn with rubbish. About halfway down the street was a little coffee shop and just outside it, in a boarded up doorway, was a hunched figure in an old coat with a small tin on the ground in front of him. Scribe gave Stalker a curt nod and came to a halt in front of the man.

'Hi Henry,' Scribe said gently. He crouched down in front of the greying old man. Henry looked up at him with watery eyes and a smile of recognition passed over his thin lips. 'Do you have something for me?'

Henry just gazed at Scribe, like he was an angel. Scribe glanced up and down the alley and then moved closer to Henry, placed his hands on the man's cheeks and whispered to him. Stalker could barely hear what he was saying, it sounded like a chant. She kept watch for passersby, but the street was empty. People dashed past the end of the street without looking down it, and the coffee shop was deserted.

Henry began to cough violently and Stalker's attention snapped back to him. Scribe kept hold of his face and whispered soothing words. Suddenly Henry leaned over and gagged, bringing something up and spitting it out into his empty tin with a clang. Scribe carefully fished it out and held up a very small key. 'Thank you, Henry,' he said and patted the man on the shoulder. Stalker quickly found some money in her wallet, a few notes of low denomination and some loose change. She stuffed it all into Henry's tin. He looked up at her, the glaze lifted from his eyes, and he blinked a few times. He looked into his tin and back up at her with surprise.

'Thank you, miss,' he croaked. 'That's very generous.'

'Not a problem, Henry,' she said kindly. 'Thank you.'

She and Scribe walked away, no doubt leaving Henry confused as to what Stalker was thanking him for. 'He had no idea he had it, did he?' she whispered to Scribe. 'He didn't really know you.'

'The spell on him allowed him to recognise any Scroll Keeper who approached him. Flames-First-Guardian hid the key with him for safe keeping until any one of us found him. Very clever.'

They met up with the others and Scribe led them to the bridge that connected Northgate to Old Port on the other side of the river. They jumped down from the footpath onto the bank and trudged carefully through the thick, wet clay under the bridge. There was a narrow door set into the wall, hidden away from human eyes. Scribe glanced around at them and held out the key.

'Try it,' Stalker urged. Scribe found a small lock and fit the key into it, he turned it and there was a loud click that echoed around the space far more than it ought to have done. Scribe opened the door, it was a little stiff and required a shove but as it opened a light flickered on inside; a wall-mounted torch cast a warm glow around the cavernous room in the river bank. Stalker peered inside and saw tiny writing all over the stone walls. Scribe stepped into the doorway and turned to face them.

'I can't let you inside, I'm afraid,' he sounded truly apologetic. Eyes gave a sympathetic nod.

'I can't say I'm not curious to see it for myself,' he admitted. 'But I understand.'

'Do I have your permission to come and go over the next few days while I work in here?'

'Of course, just do me the courtesy of a text message to let me know, please.' Eyes and Scribe shook hands. Wind Talker couldn't stop peering inside and Stalker felt drawn into the Scroll Archive herself.

The Lightning Lords drifted away, reluctantly. Stalker decided to patrol the territory, while Eyes and Claws had to work, so the pack all went their separate ways. Stalker set off along the river at a jog, weighed down slightly by the clay that clung to her boots. She traversed the territory with growing confidence, running carefully along railings and slipping through small spaces. All was quiet on the southern border and she reached the east before lunch time. She took more time and care as she moved north through Crossway, covering more ground in order to thoroughly check for signs of movement by the Witches. She found nothing and resumed experimenting with freerunning along the edge of Redfield Park. The patrol helped to clear her head, if only while she was running.

That evening, they ate together at Grove Street, waiting anxiously to hear from Scribe. No one mentioned the winter fae or the sacrifice, though Stalker thought of little else. Rhys punctuated her thoughts from time to time, and Claws glanced at her anxiously every time her phone buzzed with another incoming message.

They heard nothing from Scribe and decided to get some sleep. Eyes went home to his family, while the others took up their usual positions in the living room.

The following morning they woke to a knock at the door. It was still early, the sun was barely touching the horizon and Wind Talker went to the door rubbing his face and yawning. He returned with Scribe, who looked exhausted.

'Have you been up all night?' Stalker asked him.

'Yes,' he replied, a crack in his voice. 'I just left the Scroll Archive. There is an unbelievable amount of information in there.' He dropped onto the sofa and they gathered around him, waiting anxiously for him to share some useful information. 'Okay, so I found references to the Plague Doctor from a few hundred years ago. He was around during the last great outbreak and our kind managed to banish him from here and Hepethia, back into Muspelheim.'

'Did you find the exact wording of the ritual?' Wind Talker asked, his voice full of eagerness.

'No, but a fae called Winding-Breeze-of-Petals helped the shifters. She might be around today to help again.'

'How did she help?' Stalker asked.

'She inhabited masks the shifters wore, like the real plague doctors, masks filled with poppy petals. I guess she protected them from infection.'

'Okay, that gives us something to try, thank you so much for your help.' Wind Talker helped Scribe up off the sofa and patted him firmly on the back.

'You're welcome. I'm going to go home and sleep for three days now. Good luck.' They showed Scribe out and didn't waste any time.

'We won't easily summon a fresh air fae here in the city,' Wind Talker said. 'We might have better luck at the beach.'

'I'll let Eyes know what we're doing,' Stalker said, hurriedly sending a text to the Alpha as the rest of the pack quickly got ready to leave the house.

They drove swiftly to the coast in Claws' car, not quite as far out as Father Ash's house, and pulled up just as the sun was properly rising, casting a cool light over a frosty morning. The sand crunched under Stalker's boots as they strode out towards the gently lapping waves. The beach was deserted. Wind Talker grabbed a stick and began drawing a circle in the sand. The others took up positions just inside the line. Stalker took a small bottle of pine oil from Wind Talker and opened it as he cut his palm and raised it to the sky. She sprinkled the oil into the centre of the circle and carefully replaced the cap. 'We call upon the fae of fresh air, the breeze and cleansing breaths. Winding-Breeze-of-Petals hear our call.' Wind Talker called to the sky.

Stalker looked around them, checking that they weren't being observed, and for any supernatural activity. Everything was still and quiet and the air smelled of salt; she could feel the gentle spray from the sea on her face.

Suddenly the wind picked up and whipped around them. Stalker stumbled slightly against the gust to her back but quickly righted herself. In the centre of the circle a small hurricane swirled across the veil, it spun on the spot, whipping up the sand and lifting Weaver's long hair around her face. Stalker shuddered against the cold.

Wind Talker dropped his hands and looked a little disappointed. 'Greetings. Thank you for answering my call. We were hoping to find Winding-Breeze-of-Petals.'

'Not here,' the elemental whispered. 'Living in human form for a time.'

'Can you give us the name of the human?' Wind Talker asked, frustration creeping into his voice.

'Josie Ansell.' The elemental disappeared in a flurry and the pack were left staring at one another.

Chapter Thirty Six

'It's an unusual surname,' Claws said as the pack set off back to Grove Street. 'I can track her down.'

'Good,' Wind Talker said briskly.

'I'll be at my office,' Claws said. 'I have other work to do as well but this will be my top priority.'

When they got back to Grove Street, Claws left for work and Stalker found herself alone with Weaver and Wind Talker for the first time since their falling out. She gave them an awkward smile and went straight out into the garden. She felt frustrated and overwhelmed, she was going to have to find something to hit soon, the tension inside her was painful. She took a few minutes to read some of Rhys's messages. To his credit, he wasn't giving up, despite her lack of reply.

They were all much the same, pleading with her to hear him out, trying to reassure her.

> There is so much I want to say to you, but I'm not doing it by text message. Please meet with me. Not at my place if you don't want, I understand that. Anywhere you want. Please.

She felt a tear run down her cheek and she brushed it away angrily.

> I'm a bit busy ATM. With all that stuff I thought I couldn't talk to you about. Pending apocalypse. But I have read your messages and I am willing to hear you out. I'll be in touch.

She hit the send button.

> Thank you, thank you a thousand times over. I hope you're ok xxx

Maybe she was making a mistake. Maybe she should have continued to ignore his messages, delete them without reading them and wait for him to get bored and give up. If he was evil then she was putting herself and her pack in danger by agreeing to have contact with him.

'Are you all right?' Stalker looked up to see Weaver in the doorway, her arms crossed and her face full of concern.

'Not really,' Stalker admitted.

'I feel like you hate me,' Weaver said and moved over to sit down next to Stalker. She started pulling up weeds and Stalker set about the same task.

'I don't hate you, or Wind Talker. You're my pack mates, my siblings.'

'You're disappointed in us though,' Weaver said, not looking at her.

'I am.'

'Stalker,' Weaver's voice was insistent and Stalker felt her eyes on her, but Stalker kept working, not wanting to look Weaver in the eye. 'We aren't human, human morality doesn't apply to us and sometimes we just have to do things that we would never have contemplated in our old lives.'

Stalker narrowed her eyes and shook her head in disbelief.

'I can't believe you're bringing this up. I think it's best if we just don't talk about it.'

'We have to talk about it, we have to come to an understanding. We're about to go into battle together and need to be in sync.'

Stalker dropped her gardening trowel and looked hard at Weaver. She tried to read her face. Weaver was being honest and gentle, she was the same compassionate person she always had been, but with an edge. An edge that simply wasn't human.

'I won't lose myself,' Stalker said firmly. 'I will not forsake my humanity. I will always strive for a different solution and if that means that you and I will always clash, then I'm afraid that's the way it will be. But I will work with you to the best of my ability and as long as you aren't making cold-hearted plans to slaughter old people, then we should be able to get along fine.'

'If it's any consolation to you, the old man didn't suffer. It was gentle. He died in his sleep. We simply left a window open and allowed winter to enter. He was living in poverty and couldn't afford to heat his home.' Weaver's eyes were sad and Stalker got the feeling that she was trying to convince herself as much as Stalker.

'It was a mercy killing then?' Stalker asked, with sharp scepticism on her tongue.

Weaver got up and went back inside without replying. Stalker wanted her sister back, the one she could hug and cry with, the one she would have told about Rhys. Silent tears fell as she continued to work in the garden.

After lunch, Claws burst into the house.

'I've found her. Or where she works, anyway,' he announced. 'It's a club called Silk. I think she's a dancer there.'

'I think it's best if we don't find out how you know this,' Stalker said.

'Ha ha,' Claws said, mockingly. 'It was in the paper a few weeks ago for a big charity event they hosted. I found a picture of the staff and she was credited in it.'

'Where is it?' Wind Talker asked.

'Right here in St. Mark's,' Claws replied. 'Convenient, isn't it?'

'Too convenient, this isn't a coincidence.' Wind Talker wore a puzzled expression.

'Will there be anyone there in the day?' Stalker asked.

'We'll have to go and check it out,' Claws replied.

They set out for the club, which was a little north of Grove Street, in a bustling area of St. Mark's. It wasn't what Stalker had expected, she thought it might be a seedy strip joint, but it was a huge cabaret club with great big signs and show pictures on the front. Claws tried the front door but it was locked. 'Let's see if there's a staff entrance,' he said, and led them around the side of the building. There was an unmarked door half way down the side street and Claws tried it; it opened and he looked at the others expectantly.

'We have to go in,' Stalker said.

'Not all of us,' Wind Talker said. 'Stalker, you and Claws go in. We'll wait out here.'

'Okay,' she said with a shrug.

Stalker and Claws entered a well-lit, narrow corridor. The left seemed to lead to a door into the lobby. Right led backstage. They followed the corridor and found themselves in a wider corridor with dressing rooms off it, and one big communal dressing room at the end. There was no sign of anyone anywhere. They slipped past an office and heard movement inside, but seemed to mutually agree without the need for words that it was unlikely to be Josie. So they kept going and found their way to the backstage area. Music and voices came from the stage, where a rehearsal was in progress.

Stalker gave Claws a grin and led him up the steps to the wings of the stage. Half a dozen dancers were there in sweats, blocking a new routine. Claws came up beside her and peered out onto the stage.

'There,' he whispered. 'The one in grey shorts and a pink top.'

She was dancing up front, clearly the headline act. She looked only a little older than Stalker and had thick, glossy black hair pulled back loosely and falling free from the tie in places. She was wearing bright red lipstick and had a stunning smile. Stalker felt an unexpected stab of envy.

'Take a break!' Someone shouted from front of house. Josie and the other dancers dispersed, with Josie heading directly for Stalker and Claws. She caught sight of them as she stepped into the wings and came to a halt.

'Oh my gosh!' Stalker said, summoning as much enthusiasm as she could. 'I am such a big fan.'

'Thanks,' Josie said with a wary smile. 'How did you get in here?'

'Through the back door, I'm sorry, I know we shouldn't have. I just really wanted to meet you.' Stalker glanced sideways at two dancers passing them with curious looks.

'Come with me,' Josie said firmly, eyeing them suspiciously. She led them down the corridor and into a dressing room with her name on the door, which she closed firmly behind them. 'What do you want? Do you want to talk to *her*?'

Stalker and Claws looked at each other.

'Who do you mean?' Stalker asked carefully.

'I can tell what you are, or she can. Sometimes it's hard to tell the difference between what I know and what she knows.' Josie perched on the edge of her vanity station and crossed her arms.

'Okay,' Stalker said. 'So you know about *her* and us. That simplifies things, actually. We need her help.'

'What kind of help?'

'I think we would feel more comfortable if we knew we were talking to her directly,' Claws said delicately.

'You are,' Josie said. 'I am both Josie and Winding-Breeze-of-Petals. It's not like one of us needs to be unconscious for the other to be conscious. What kind of help do you need?'

'Someone has raised the Plague Doctor,' Stalker whispered, glancing over her shoulder towards the door. Josie closed her eyes and sighed.

'I see,' she said. 'And you need my help defeating him,

again.'

'That's right,' Stalker replied. 'We understand that you helped last time by protecting the shifters that fought him.'

'That's right. I will do this for you, but you must do something for me.'

'Okay,' Claws said quickly, and Stalker cast him a sideways glance.

'What do you want us to do?' she asked cautiously.

'Make the streets flow with flowers.' Josie smiled and locked eyes with Stalker. It was a challenge, Stalker realised, suitably vague so that they would have to be creative.

'We can do that,' she said with a grin. 'Will you help us the same way you helped before? By inhabiting masks?'

'Yes, any mask will suffice and I can provide the petals.' Josie grabbed a piece of paper and scribbled an address down, which she passed to Stalker. 'Come here when you need me and you have fulfilled your side of the bargain.'

'Thank you, we truly appreciate this,' Claws said as Josie showed them out.

'Don't thank me yet, do as I ask and then we'll talk again.'

Stalker and Claws left the building and met up with the others.

'We have a task to do, but she'll help us,' Stalker explained. 'I have an idea, come on.' She set off running and the others followed. A plan had formed in her head almost as soon as Josie set the challenge, she just hoped it would work as well as she was imagining.

She led the pack to a small supermarket and instructed them to buy as many bunches of flowers as possible while she ran for washing-up liquid. They met up back at the exit with their supplies, everyone looked confused and asked repeatedly what the plan was, but when Claws laid eyes on Stalker's purchase his eyes lit up.

'Genius,' he said with a grin.

'Thanks,' she replied.

They had to wait until late in the night to enact the plan if they wanted to stand half a chance of not getting caught. In the meantime, Wind Talker contacted Last-Breath-Echoes and went off to meet her at work. He didn't say what it was about, but returned late in the afternoon with a handful of surgical masks.

After dark, Eyes came to the house and Stalker filled him in on the events of the day and her plan. The pack made their way into the city centre and stood in the central plaza where the huge fountain stood. They were wearing the surgical masks and hooded clothes to hide their faces from CCTV cameras, and they hurriedly scattered the flowers throughout the pool of water. Stalker leapt up onto the wall around the fountain and emptied the contents of several bottles of washing up liquid. The fountain quickly churned up the water and started generating thick, white foam.

Stalker howled with laughter as she watched the foam fill the fountain and begin to spill over the sides. The flowers rose up on top of the foam and spilled onto the paving.

'Wind Talker?' she called. His eyes lit up and he barked with laughter. He ran for a wall at the edge of the plaza, in front of the museum and stood there, his arms outstretched as he focused his energy. Stalker felt the veil fluttering and then she felt the breeze pick up all around them, it built to a fairly strong wind and the gust blew the bubbles across the plaza towards the drains at the street end. The foam sank into the drains, taking some of the flowers with it.

The pack made a run for it, stopping occasionally to pour more soap and flowers down the drains. As they ran, the drains overflowed with bubbles and water carried the flowers down the streets. Over the course of the night they filled many streets in Caerton with soapy water and flowers, bringing people out to point and laugh. It was infectious, soon others were copying the prank and the pack checked the internet on their phones for news reports and Tweets about the chaos and fun in the streets.

It was more fun than Stalker had had in weeks, and for a short while she was able to forget her worries and enjoy being with her pack.

'Look!' Claws called out, his phone clutched in his hand. Stalker leaned over his shoulder and the rest of the pack gathered around. 'I found Josie on Twitter.'

Her latest Tweet was a photo of the foam in the street topped with flowers and the words *View from my flat! Love it guys. You're on!*

Stalker and Claws exchanged grins and Eyes patted her on the back.

'Good job, Stalker. Thank you.'

Stalker was content as she settled down to sleep, and she slept more soundly than she had in a long time.

Chapter Thirty Seven

The Plague Doctor moved silently through the dark maze, his shoulders were hunched and in his hand was a heavy metal case. Rats swarmed all around his feet. He passed torches in wall brackets that threw eerie shadows across his dark face and haunting beak-mask. He moved into the light and lifted the case onto a table. Emblazoned in yellow and black on the front was a bio-hazard symbol.

Stalker woke with a start and her eyes met Weaver's. Weaver lay totally still, her eyes wide with fear. As one they both shifted form, lying face to face as humans.

'He has it,' Weaver whispered. Stalker nodded. 'We need to act now.'

'Yes, we do,' Stalker replied. The two of them just stared at each other for a minute. Stalker's mind was blank and her body was numb. She felt lost and ill-prepared to face such a formidable foe. What would Shadow's Step say if he saw her now? She sat up suddenly, spurred into action by the thought of her lost mentor. 'Come on,' she urged Weaver.

The rest of the pack stirred at her sudden movement. Stalker called Eyes, not caring that it was only 6am or that none of them had had more than a few hours' sleep.

'What is it?' he answered, his voice thick with sleep.

'He has the plague sample, we need to act now. Meet us at Josie's flat.' Stalker relayed the address. Once they were all ready to go, they bundled into Claws' car and drove across St. Mark's to meet Eyes.

Josie lived near Crossway, not far from Eyes, in a nice apartment block. Stalker took the lead and rang the buzzer. Josie's sleepy voice answered after a minute.

'Hello?'

'Hi,' Stalker said, trying to keep her voice low enough to not be overheard but clear enough to be understood through the intercom. 'It's us, we need your help now, I'm sorry for the unsociable hour.'

There was a long silence, but finally the door buzzed and Claws pushed it open. They bounded up the stairs to the fourth floor and Josie met them in the hallway, dressed in pyjamas and a silk robe. Without a word, she led them up to the roof. There was a beautiful garden there, quite unexpected and in contrast to the surrounding area. Josie had covered the roof in wooden planters and was growing all manner of winter greens and flowering plants. A delicate string of white fairy lights was strung around the rooftop and at the centre was a tall Christmas tree decorated with coloured lights and scarlet flowers.

To one side of the roof garden was a workbench. Josie

led them to it and Wind Talker laid out the surgical masks he had collected from Last-Breath-Echoes.

Josie opened a box filled with bright red poppy petals. She laid a handful inside each mask and sprinkled scented water onto each of them.

'What will happen to you?' Stalker asked.

'I will leave this body and reside in these masks.'

'Will you be split into five pieces?'

'Only temporarily,' Josie gave her a sad smile.

'You'll never be able to return to Josie's body, will you?'

'Probably not, no. But that's okay.'

'What about Josie?' Weaver asked, her voice quiet but insistent. Stalker felt a lump rise in her throat.

'I'll be fine,' Josie replied, her duality never more evident. 'I'll carry on just as before, though perhaps with some memory gaps.'

'We are truly thankful for your sacrifice,' Wind Talker said solemnly. Stalker glanced at him, trying not to react to his choice of words. Josie nodded and then sat down in a lawn chair nearby. She closed her eyes and turned her face up to the slate-grey sky. The sun was only just above the horizon and thick clouds filled the chilly winter sky.

Stalker watched as Josie's body began to shudder slightly. She felt a ripple in the veil and saw Winding-Breeze-of-Petals lift gently out of Josie's body. The fae was a beautiful, wispy thing, fluctuating between all the colours of the rainbow and smelling of flowers. She drifted across the garden and settled over the table. She split smoothly into five smaller versions of herself and sank down into the petal-filled masks.

Stalker went to the human's side and checked her

pulse; it was fine, she was in a deep sleep but seemed like she would be all right.

'Is that it?' Eyes whispered.

'I think so,' Wind Talker replied. He picked up his mask and placed it over his face. Stalker did likewise. She could feel the fae against her face, moving ever so slightly, like a soft breath. Stalker removed the mask and held it gently in her hands.

'That's it, we need to go before Josie wakes up and finds us here. She may not have any recollection of us.' Stalker waited for the others to pick up their masks and then led them quickly back to the stairs.

They left Claws' car parked outside Josie's building and drove in Eyes' car across St. Mark's to the retirement home. As he turned into the sweeping driveway, Eyes glanced around the car at everyone.

'Has anyone ever taken a car across the veil before?' he asked, a glint in his eye.

'There's a first time for everything,' Weaver replied.

Stalker grabbed hold of the car door and gripped tightly. She closed her eyes as Eyes put his foot down hard. She willed them all to cross safely by this highly unorthodox method. When she opened her eyes they were in Hepethia, surrounded by twisted, dead trees and dark shadows. Weaver and Claws looked as alarmed as she felt, but Eyes and Wind Talker cracked up laughing.

'I cannot believe that worked!' Wind Talker cried.

Eyes drove slowly along the gravel driveway and stopped the car in the cover of the twisted old trees, out of sight of the retirement home. They got out of the car and quietly made their way towards the treeline. Stalker gasped when she caught sight of their destination. On this side of the veil the old manor house was indeed like a castle, just as Wind Talker had described. It was ancient, perhaps even older than the Watchtower, but not in ruins. It was well maintained, with battlements patrolled by huge rat-demons.

'Are we going to call Tar Peter?' Stalker whispered.

'Absolutely not,' Eyes replied. 'We're not falling for that again.'

They put their masks on and made their way through the trees around to the back of the castle. There were no guards on this side and the trees pressed almost up to the walls. Stalker led the Lightning Lords cautiously towards what looked like a cellar door down some steps, and they crept down them. The door at the bottom was black and heavy with huge locks all over it.

'How are we going to get through this?' she whispered in frustration.

'It depends if we want to remain stealthy or not,' Weaver said, peering over her shoulder. They exchanged glances and Weaver gave Stalker a wink.

Claws squeezed past Eyes and Weaver and fished his lockpicking equipment out of his jacket pocket.

'This might take a while,' he whispered. Stalker watched him work, while Eyes and Wind Talker kept watch at the back. Slowly, carefully, Claws tackled one enormous lock at a time. Some were padlocks, others were old-fashioned door locks. Just as the last lock clicked, the whole door gave a shudder and Stalker reflexively tensed up. Claws groaned and hung his head as a hundred new locks shimmered into existence all around the door.

'So much for stealth,' Weaver said with a sigh.

'Fine,' Stalker replied. Weaver and Claws stepped back, giving Stalker space to shift. Stalker's limbs lengthened and her muscles bulged as her skin sprouted thick hair all over. The surgical mask over her face stretched to accommodate her muzzle, and she felt the presence of the fae within easing her breathing in this small space. In her Agrius form Stalker was able to rip the padlocks from the door and smash the whole thing in easily, but the racket echoed around the little stairwell and she heard movement inside.

The narrow hall beyond the small doorway was empty and dusty, but there was a scurrying sound in the distance.

'Here,' Wind Talker called in a whisper from the middle of the pack. He passed a torch to Weaver, who shone it over Stalker's shoulder and they proceeded carefully inside. Stalker barely fitted into the hallway in her Agrius form, and she walked with her shoulders stooped and her clawed hands scraping the walls on either side of her. It was hard to see, but she reached out with her thoughts and connected to the darkness demons. She could feel them shielding her. It was almost impossible to be stealthy in Agrius form. Her breath rattled, though it was slightly muffled by the mask, and her feet thudded on the floor, but at least she could be partially hidden from sight.

The corridor opened up into a sort of boiler room, and rats scurried away into the corners. The room was hot and filled with steam; pipes hissed and the boilers clunked noisily. There was a dripping sound nearby, and Stalker crept as quietly as she could into the room, followed by the others. She caught the scent of oil and moved carefully to where it was leaking and forming a puddle on the dusty floor.

Suddenly the scent changed, tar and rot poured into the corner from the leak in an overhead pipe, and out of the pool rose Tar Peter.

'You didn't call me,' he hissed. Stalker shifted into her human form and the others gathered quickly around her at the sound of his voice.

'No, we didn't,' Eyes whispered. 'So what are you doing here and how did you know we were here?'

'You brought a car across the veil,' Tar Peter said incredulously. 'Every construct of roads, traffic, cars, mechanics and electronics felt it, you idiots.'

Stalker smirked inside her mask and glanced around at the others. Everyone's eyes looked surprised and torn between amusement and concern.

'Seeing as you're here, do you want to help?' Stalker asked.

'Of course, that's why I'm here. Wait here for my signal, then follow the stairs down in that corner.' Tar Peter pointed to a corner of the room and then disappeared back into the pool of oil. Stalker looked anxiously around at the others.

'We can't trust him,' Wind Talker whispered. 'Let's go now. That door is the only way out of here aside from the way we came. But let's not wait and give him time to warn anyone.'

Eyes gave a curt nod of agreement and they all followed him to the doorway. A steep staircase led down, right under the basement and into the earth. There were no man-made walls or steps, just bare earth and wooden slats pressed into the ground beneath their feet, creating rough stairs. They moved quickly and as quietly as possible. Just as they reached the bottom Eyes stopped dead and raised his hand to halt the others behind him.

Stalker listened, she heard scurrying feet and squeaks. Rats. Dozens of them. But they were running away from them, not towards them. She felt rather than heard the explosion. The ground shuddered and dirt rained down on them.

'What was that?' Wind Talker hissed.

'A signal?' Stalker said, her voice dripping with sarcasm.

Eyes glanced over his shoulder at her then set off at a run along the passage. It wasn't quite high enough for any of them to walk upright, even Stalker, who was the shortest of the bunch. So they all ran stooped over.

They burst out into a cave and Stalker just caught sight of the last wererat disappearing down another hole. There were half a dozen more passages leading off this cave and they looked around with no clue which way to go.

There was a scuttling sound to her right and a monstrous wererat burst out of one of the passages, running right into Stalker. It yelped as it stumbled backwards away from her. Another followed, tripping over its fellow and falling at Stalker's feet. Swiftly and silently she drew both of her dha and in one fluid movement took the heads off both creatures.

There were more noises and everyone readied themselves, Claws drew his gun and the others began shifting form. Stalker gripped her blades and pointed up the tunnel that the two wererats had burst out of. 'This way, come on.' She led the pack up the passage. It was almost pitch black, but for the torch Weaver held casting its eerie white light up the tunnel, broken by Stalker's shadow. Stalker could see just fine, however, and had to assume that her darkness allies were allowing her to see the way.

They entered another chamber and on the opposite wall was a solid, metal door. In the way, however, were half a dozen huge rat demons; all of them locked their red eyes on the intruders. They were far more monstrous than the wererats that the Lightning Lords had encountered before. These beasts were as big as their own Agrius forms and just as ferocious-looking.

A shot rang out and one of the demons dropped to the ground. Every eye in the place darted to Claws and his smoking gun, only for the briefest moment before utter chaos ensued. The air was filled with snarling, howling, biting and ripping, punctuated by gunshots. The stench of blood was overpowering. Weaver's torch lay discarded on the floor, and huge black shadows jerked and writhed across the light it cast.

Stalker shifted form mid-stride, still gripping her dha, and took out one of the demons with relative ease. The next was quicker and dodged her attack. It caught her arm with a massive claw and tore through her flesh. It stung like hell but healed in seconds. The next blow was more damaging; the demon slipped under one of her blades and tore into her thigh. Her leg buckled and a snarl escaped her lips.

Before she could react, the demon dropped to the ground and was dragged along by its leg. She whirled around to see Weaver yanking it away from her. She ripped the demon's leg right off and tossed it aside. The demon writhed around, yelping in pain. Stalker strode over to it and plunged both of her swords into its chest. It fell silent and its blood poured onto the dirt beneath it.

She looked at Weaver and nodded in thanks. The cave fell quiet and still. The demons were all dead, their bodies broken and scattered around the floor. Claws was leaning against the wall clutching his side and Stalker ran to him, shifting into human form as she reached him. 'Are you all right?' she asked.

Claws nodded and coughed as he tried to speak. He winced and clutched himself harder. Stalker could see blood all over his clothes and seeping out between his fingers.

'We have to get him out of here,' Weaver said quietly.

There was a loud clang behind them and Stalker spun around to see the metal door swing open. There was a lit room beyond it and Tar Peter stood in the doorway, blood and dirt all over his hands and clothes.

'You're going to want to see this,' he said.

Stalker moved towards him cautiously, Eyes and Wind Talker close behind her. She glanced past him into the room and saw a hole in the ceiling with tar dripping from it. Tar Peter had found his own way into the room, there were no other doors. The room was made up of metal struts holding up densely packed earth. An electric strip light was rigged up on the ceiling and in the centre of the small room was a metal table with a body bag on it. The zip had been partially undone and left hanging open.

'Have you been taking a sneak peak?' Stalker asked

Tar Peter. He shrugged in reply. Stalker edged closer and peered into the bag. A corpse lay inside, nothing but bones. Wedged into its chest between two ribs was a large wooden stake.

'What happens if we take that out?' Eyes asked, gesturing at the stake.

'I don't think we want to know,' Wind Talker replied.

'Hello?' They spun to face the source of the quiet, rasping voice with a slight echo to it. Before them stood the Plague Doctor. 'Have you come to pay me?'

'Pay you?' Eyes spat.

'I did what you asked, now it is time to fulfil your side of the bargain.'

Stalker looked at Eyes, he looked confused and torn between wanting to pounce on the demon and talk to it. Stalker felt the same. Her hand loosely gripped the hilt of her dha.

'Who do you think we are?' Stalker asked, her intention curious, not demanding.

'You raised me, brought me back.' The Plague Doctor looked at each of them, his huge eyes were empty sockets and yet he seemed to see everything. 'I have walked the lines, called the host and prepared the way. Give me what you owe me.' There was just the slightest edge to his voice now, the threat was clear.

Stalker's grip tightened on the hilt of her dha, ready to strike at the Alpha's command.

'We didn't raise you,' Eyes said incredulously. Wind Talker placed a gentle hand on the Alpha's arm.

'Of course you did,' the Plague Doctor said. He didn't sound confused, he was absolutely certain of it. Stalker felt terribly confused and looked from one face to another to try and work out what to do. Tar Peter stood absolutely still, his face unreadable. Weaver had moved into the doorway and was looking shocked and confused.

'You've got the wrong shifters,' Eyes roared and he leapt across the body on the table, shifting form as he vaulted and grabbed hold of the demon, wrapping his arms and legs around the thing. Wind Talker and Weaver were in there in an instant, punching and tearing with teeth and claws. The Plague Doctor writhed around, hissing and spitting. He folded in on himself and then burst outwards, pushing the three Agrius beasts off him as if they were rag dolls.

Stalker slashed at him with her dha but he dodged easily and put the table between them.

'I'm going to find my payment,' he hissed and then disappeared. The Lightning Lords exchanged troubled looks and slowly shifted back into their human forms again.

'What the hell was that about?' Eyes roared. He rounded on Tar Peter and grabbed his slick, black jacket. He pushed Tar Peter against the wall and shook him hard.

'What?' the demon cried, squirming. 'Why are you attacking me?'

'Was he talking to you?' Wind Talker said. He didn't shout, his voice was quiet and dark, full of the threat of thunder. 'Did you raise him?'

'Absolutely not,' Tar Pater said, his voice full of venom.

'He's telling the truth,' croaked Claws from the doorway. 'Grab the body, we need to go.'

Eyes released Tar Peter with a snarl, and he and Wind

Talker each picked up an end of the body bag.

The six of them moved quickly through the tunnels back to the boiler room, then up to the back door they had entered through. They ran quickly to the car, Stalker looking all around them for signs of trouble. They bundled the body into the boot of Eyes' car. There was movement in the woods around them and Stalker looked around anxiously. There was smoke rising on the other side of the building and Stalker's eyes settled on Tar Peter.

'What did you do? To draw them away?' she asked.

'Just caused a little accident. There are a thousand rats drowning in hot, molten tarmac over there now.' He had a sickening smile playing on his lips. 'Good luck with finishing that thing off.' Before anyone could stop him, Tar Peter melted into a pool of tarmac.

'Let's go to the telecoms tower. We might be able to get some information there about what the hell is going on,' Eyes suggested, and they climbed into the car. Stalker sat next to Claws and made him lean back so that she could lift his shirt and look at his wound. He'd been gouged deeply, but it was starting to heal.

'You'll be okay soon,' she reassured him. He tried to smile.

'Why did he think we had raised him?' Eyes demanded, turning on Wind Talker.

'He's a very old, very powerful demon,' Wind Talker replied. 'To him, all shifters are like the rats. Numerous and identical.'

'We are all Raigo,' Stalker said quietly. Everyone looked at her.

'Exactly,' Wind Talker replied.

'So what's his payment?' Eyes asked.

'Maybe the plague sample?' Weaver replied. 'My vision might not have meant that he already had it, but that he would have it soon. When he talked about the work he had done to fulfil his side of the bargain he didn't mention spreading disease. Maybe that's his payment. In exchange for these other things, he gets to spread the plague.'

Nobody spoke. Stalker shuddered at the thought. It seemed plausible. But the most terrifying thing that they had to consider was not the Plague Doctor spreading plague, but the fact that one of their own kind had clearly raised him. The Spiral Hand was at work in this and a sick sensation filled her stomach to think that it could be Rhys.

Chapter Thirty Eight

The car skidded to a halt at the foot of the vast tower.

'Claws, wait here, you still have some healing to do. Rest while you can,' Eyes instructed. Claws snarled but reluctantly sank back against the seat. Everyone else climbed out of the car. The dark clouds in the sky above looked ready to burst and high at the top of the tower, the Lord-of-Storms-and-Rain was circling.

Eyes strode over to the tower and placed his hands on the cold metal. He had blood all over them from the fight and he smeared it on the struts of the tower.

'What are you doing?' Stalker asked, looking around at the small elementals that scuttled around them, just out of sight.

'I'm not interested in the man at the top,' he replied. 'I want the communication spirits to make themselves known. We need to know if anyone is moving a sample of the plague across Caerton today. We need news broadcasts monitored, radio frequencies scanned, phone lines tapped, anything like that.'

Wind Talker hung back by the car and Stalker heard him open the boot. She watched Eyes carefully and kept a lookout for any sign of trouble approaching. Weaver circled the tower, and Stalker caught her eye a few times. She looked worried. Everything was far too still.

Movement in the sky caught Stalker's attention, and she looked up to see Unchained Lightning soaring towards them. He circled the tower and moved up to greet his father briefly. The Lord-of-Storms-and-Rain returned the greeting with a flash of lightning and a clap of thunder. Unchained Lighting flew to the ground and weaved in and out of the tower's supports, crackling slightly.

'Guys,' Wind Talker called out. Stalker turned just in time to see him pull the stake out of the corpse in the car. He turned to face them, a triumphant smile on his face.

'What did you do?' Stalker shouted and stepped towards the car.

'It's okay, I figured it out,' Wind Talker called. His smile dropped from his face as his eyes came to rest on something behind Stalker. She whirled around and saw the Plague Doctor striding towards the car.

'Pay me, now!' the demon roared and as he strode towards Wind Talker his form changed. His dirty, grey robes disappeared, the long beak-mask exploded and he rapidly grew to three times his former size. A huge, pulsating creature towered over Wind Talker, it was red and brown with sickly green slime moving just under the skin.

'C-Caerton Plague,' Wind Talker stammered.

The Demon reached out a massive hand, scooped Wind Talker up and tossed him against the tower. There was a loud crunch of breaking bones and he fell to the ground. Caerton Plague, formerly the Plague Doctor, grabbed Eyes' car and lifted it off the ground as if it were nothing but a toy. Stalker heard Claws yelling inside and ran forwards, with no idea how she was going to help him. The demon ripped the sleek, black, luxury car in two and threw the pieces away. The front of the car skidded across the dirt and crashed into the chain link fence that surrounded the tower. A few sparks flew and the engine caught fire. The back of the car landed with a thud at the demon's feet and he began clumsily searching it for the body.

'Stop it!' Weaver yelled at Stalker. She shifted form and charged towards the demon. Eyes was next and Stalker wasn't far behind. She bounded on all fours towards the huge demon and lunged at it, ripping into it with her talons. Thick pus poured out of the gashes she made and stung as it touched her. She recoiled but the pain continued and she stumbled backwards, watching in horror as her clawed hands smoked and the smell of burning skin and fur reached her nostrils through the mask.

Weaver ran around the demon and pulled the door off the car. Claws came crawling out, scrabbling across the dirt and away from the car and the demon. Eyes was laying into Caerton Plague, tearing and slashing at it, managing to ignore the pain of the poisonous pus. Stalker drew her dha and went in for another attack with her blades. The demon was huge and any attacks that landed seemed to result in nothing more than minor cuts and scrapes. Stalker did her best to get under its feet and managed to trick it away from the car, while Eyes tore chunks out of it. He couldn't maintain his assault, however, and Eyes soon stumbled away from the demon and collapsed at the foot of the tower. His whole body shook and smoked. Stalker looked around, Wind Talker had disappeared. She tried to keep the demon distracted whilst also looking for her pack mates.

Weaver and Wind Talker were dragging the body bag across the dirt to the flaming wreckage of the front of Eyes' car. Unchained Lightning swooped overhead and Stalker felt him charging up for an attack. She leapt out of the way as he discharged his power down on top of Caerton Plague, landing like lightning and scorching the ground. The demon roared and stretched out its terrible, tentacle-like limbs. It caught hold of Unchained Lighting and the two of them merged into this terrible, writhing ball of diseased flesh and bright white light. Sparks were flying in all directions and the ground burned and smoked everywhere that the two of them touched it.

Stalker sprinted towards the car; Weaver and Wind Talker were holding the body bag, hesitating as they watched the fight. Stalker shifted form as she reached them.

'What are you waiting for?' she yelled.

'What about Unchained Lighting?' Weaver asked, looking shocked and desperate.

'I don't think fire will hurt him,' Stalker said, grasping at straws. 'But even if it does, we have to do this, we have to destroy that body. I'll bet my life that fire is the only way to get rid of the demon.'

Wind Talker nodded solemnly. He and Weaver threw

the body onto the burning car, and as the plastic body bag slowly melted, the body inside it caught light.

Caerton Plague shrieked and hissed. Unchained Lightning managed to disentangle himself and slipped away from the demon. He looked hurt, his light had faded and he flickered feebly as he settled himself under the tower, next to Eyes.

The demon burst into flames, screaming and spitting poisonous pus all over the ground. The stench was terrible, even through the flower-scented mask on Stalker's face. They all just stared as Caerton Plague burned, gradually shrivelling away into a charred and smoking lump.

Once she was satisfied that the demon was dead, Stalker ran to Eyes. Claws had crawled over to him and was checking him over, despite an obvious head injury of his own.

'Are you all right?' Stalker asked. Claws nodded. 'Is he?'

'Yes, he's unconscious and badly burned, but he'll recover, he's already healing,' Claws said.

'He is going to be so pissed off about his car,' Stalker said with a sigh. She looked around and saw several big, black birds perched on the fence, watching them. They weren't ravens, they were something else, and their big eyes never blinked. Stalker shuddered and turned away from them.

Unchained Lightning flickered suddenly and then went dark. His dragon-like body lay still and black, coiled around the base of the tower.

'Oh my goodness,' Weaver said, pressing her hands to her face. She ran to the elemental and carefully reached out to touch him. She didn't receive an electric shock, nothing happened.

'Is he dead?' Claws asked.

'No,' Stalker replied. 'I don't think so; we're still connected. Can't you feel it? When Grins-Too-Widely was killed it severed the bond we shared. This is different.'

'He is alive,' boomed a voice above them. The Lord-of-Storms-and-Rain hovered just above their heads, a sad look in his ancient eyes. 'He needs to rest and recharge. Leave him here with me.'

Stalker sensed pride in his voice and allowed herself a small smile. The Lightning Lords slowly took off their masks. Claws carefully removed the one from Eyes' face and Stalker watched as Winding-Breeze-of-Petals floated out of them and reformed. She settled over the remaining husk of Caerton Plague, and there was a disturbing crunch as the beautiful fae crushed it and it turned to dust.

'Thank you,' Claws said. She flickered in reply and floated away, like spores on the wind.

'It burned our skin, but I don't think any of us inhaled anything life threatening,' Weaver said.

'It seems that way,' Stalker replied. 'Let's go home.'

Chapter Thirty Nine

Stalker sat on the park bench, a coat wrapped tightly around her against the cold, though she could barely feel it; the coat was mostly for show. There was the very distant sound of passing cars and the occasional noise from a bird or small animal in the trees and bushes. The crescent-shaped lawn in front of her sparkled with frost, and the last of the path lights flickered out; finally enough daylight reached into this sheltered place from the grey sky above to turn off the electric lights.

The sound of quiet footsteps on the path drew her gaze. Rhys walked slowly towards her, a heavy fleece done up to the neck. Also for show, she now realised. His breath was visible on the cold air and he came to a halt a few feet away. He didn't quite meet her eyes, looking slightly to her left instead.

'Thank you for agreeing to meet me,' he said. His voice had a slight crack to it and Stalker detected his nerves.

'That's okay,' she replied. She fought to maintain her composure, but inside she was a wreck.

'May I sit down?'

Stalker nodded and scooted along the bench to one end. Rhys sat down at the other end and turned sideways to look at her. She couldn't look at him, not yet. They sat in uncomfortable silence for what seemed like eternity. Stalker heard a few guttural noises from his throat, like he was about to speak and then changed his mind. She sighed and turned to him.

'Right, so you're a shifter.'

'Yes,' he said quietly. 'But I'm not in a pack, I never changed my name. I live entirely cut off from that whole life.'

'Why?'

'I was raised by my kin in a community in the forest, about fifty miles from here. I grew up in full knowledge of what they were. I saw them change, I saw them fight. I was being prepared, groomed, for changing myself.' He paused and took a deep breath. He still couldn't quite look at her, but she fixed her eyes on him, determined to detect any trace of a lie. For a second she wished she had brought Claws with her, but swiftly dismissed the idea.

'What happened?' she asked.

'They were killed. An enemy pack came through the forest and destroyed them all. That was when I changed for the first time. I fled and ended up here.' His voice was hard and strained, he was holding back the rage and sadness. Stalker almost wanted to reach out and touch him, to comfort him, but she held back. She thought over what he had said and an uncomfortable cog clicked into place.

'You were raised in the woods? To the east?'

'That's right.' Rhys looked at her properly for the first time. Stalker groaned and leaned back on the bench.

'So you were raised by Furies?' She didn't dare look at him.

'I was.'

'Caerton's shifters aren't too fond of your people.'

'I know, it goes both ways. I never questioned it when I was growing up. My family were members of the sect of Alecto, the Never-Ending. They hated Caerton's shifters, they taught me that the throne had been stolen and corrupted by soft, city-dwelling shifters of the moon. When I ended up in the city I hid from the shifters because I thought they would kill me on sight. I've lived here for over a decade now and have matured a lot. I'd never moved among humans before, I despised them. I believed they were like cattle, there to be controlled and used.' His voice trailed off and Stalker watched him carefully. His eyes were sad and totally open, his walls were right down and she could see inside his soul. 'But living among them changed me, saved me. I realised that my people had been wrong about humanity and they were probably wrong about the Chosen of Artemis too.'

He looked into her eyes and tentatively reached out a finger to brush her cheek. His touch felt warm. She wanted to believe him, but she still felt utterly deceived by him and she brushed his hand away.

'How can I trust anything you say? You hid your true nature from me, you live under the cloak of a demon. How do I know you aren't Spiral Hand?'

'Spiral Hand?' He blinked, his eyes full of confusion as he leaned away from her. 'Why would you think I was anything to do with them?'

'Because you sneak around in hiding. That's what they do.'

'No, they infiltrate. That's what I was always told. They work from inside shifter society. My family always said that the Spiral Hand were rife in Caerton, that was part of the problem. They were planning to cleanse the city of the "plague".' He raised his hands and made quotation gestures with his fingers.

Stalker grimaced and her breath caught in her throat. She began shaking.

'They used that word?' She wondered if it were a coincidence or if the Furies had been linked to what had almost been set loose in the city.

'Yeah. What's wrong?' He moved closer and tentatively touched her arm.

'I can't tell you, I'm sorry. I just can't trust you.' She shook her head and pulled her arm away from his touch. 'I'm sorry, I can't see you again.'

Stalker stood up and glanced down at him. He looked stung by her words, but nodded with acceptance.

'I understand that. I am so sorry. I never wanted to hurt you, I never wanted to break your trust. If I can ever earn it back, I will, I will never stop trying. But I'll give you space, if that's what you need.'

Stalker drew a deep breath and walked away, tears falling down her cheeks.

Later that evening, she stared into the fire, a paper cup of beer in her hand. The noise was deafening. She had never seen so many shifters in one place before, but the revelry passed her by in blur. It was a small park, neatly fenced off from the surrounding crystalline landscape, and the bonfire in the centre roared, the elementals dancing and singing their unearthly song. Shifters danced, drank and fought around the fire in various states of undress and drunkenness. Skin and weaponry were on display everywhere, with no humans to hide from.

The Watch had arranged everything, and kindly invited almost all of Caerton's shifters to their winter solstice celebration. Many had come, though the Glass Wolves were notably absent.

A dark figure dropped down onto the floor beside her, and Stalker looked to see Fire Talon smiling at her.

'Penny for your thoughts?' he asked, his voice slightly slurred.

'We killed a plague demon yesterday. We saved the whole city,' she shouted over the din.

'Shouldn't you be celebrating that?' Fire Talon asked, looking confused.

'I am,' she said with a half-smile and raised her cup. 'Cheers.'

'It takes more than a beer to be a celebration,' he chided. 'Why are you so sad?'

'I had to leave my boyfriend.'

'Oh,' he said, suddenly sobering. 'Oh yes, I know that one well.'

Stalker looked at him with a raised eyebrow. She knew he wasn't gay, but she couldn't resist the joke.

'You had to leave your boyfriend too?'

'No,' he replied. 'My girlfriend, and baby.' He knocked

back his drink and they sat in uncomfortable silence. 'I'm never falling in love with a human again.'

'Me neither,' Stalker said sadly, letting him believe that was the reason.

Fire Talon gave her a pat on the back and moved away. Weaver appeared by her side and lifted her to her feet.

'It's a party, come on. We won! We beat the bad guy. Enjoy it.' Weaver pulled Stalker over to the rest of the pack. Scribe-of-the-Fallen and Last-Breath-Echoes were standing with them, joking and fooling around, or as close to such behaviour as Echoes ever came. She exuded such stillness and serenity, yet a playful smile lingered on her lips and Stalker saw clearly the resemblance that she held to her father.

'Honestly,' Eyes was saying. 'We couldn't have done it without you. Thank you both so much.' Scribe thumped Eyes on the shoulder and the Alpha winced.

'Sorry,' Scribe said, looking concerned.

'It's okay, I'm still healing. I'll be fine.' Eyes reassured him.

'Are you having fun?' First Strike whispered at Stalker's ear, and she whirled around to face him. She laughed, enjoying the shock. He pulled her into a hug and she returned it. He felt warm and smelled amazing. He was topless and she let her hands linger a little too long on his smooth, dark skin. He pulled away, reluctantly, and Stalker knew she was blushing, she only hoped that the glow from the fire hid it.

First Strike gently touched her chest where her new tattoo was and she felt an intense spark run through her entire body. 'New ink?' he asked.

'Yeah,' she replied. Her heart was hammering and she felt confused and unsettled, but tried hard to overcome the feelings.

'Nice,' he gave her a sad smile. 'Lovely way to honour them.'

'Thanks.' Her voice came out a little cracked.

His finger was still resting on her skin and his eyes roamed. Stalker enjoyed it; just for a minute she allowed everything else to melt away so that she could enjoy the attention. Suddenly he cleared his throat and took half a step back. He smiled warmly at her and placed his hand on her shoulder; his thumb gently stroked her neck just for a second before he pulled away.

'Lovely Stalker,' he said with his wonderfully silky voice. 'Have a good night.' He walked away and she watched him go before internally scolding herself for being such a hussy.

It was almost dawn when the Lightning Lords returned to Grove Street. They were all very drunk and fell into the hallway laughing and tripping over each other. Wind Talker flipped the light switch, but nothing happened. He tried it a few times and suddenly the pack sobered up. Eyes led the way into the house, Stalker right behind him. None of the lights worked and the digital clock on the microwave was blank.

Stalker felt the veil blowing gently and led them into the back garden. Unchained Lighting lay curled up in the corner, still black but beginning to glow a little at his core.

'He must have drained the power from the whole house in order to cross over,' Wind Talker whispered.

The elemental groaned and crackled. A few small

sparks flew off him and he lifted his head.

'We cannot express enough how grateful we are for the aid you gave us,' Eyes said, his voice more humble than Stalker had ever heard it.

Unchained Lightning coughed and spluttered, sparks flying everywhere and dying on impact with the cold earth.

'Whelps,' he spat. 'You have taken me too much for granted. I am Power. I will be demanding more from you soon.' He suddenly reared up and threw himself against the wall. Thin strands of light erupted from all over his body and wrapped around him, sticking him to the wall, right in the corner of the garden. Stalker watched in horror, unsure of what she was witnessing. Everything fell still, the shimmering cocoon breathed gently and the Lightning Lords exchanged nervous glances.

Stalker was both impressed and unsettled. Their ally had never spoken to them like that before, it was his father's voice. She thought it would probably be best if he didn't spend too much more time with the Lord-of-Storms-and-Rain after he emerged from his cocoon, and she wondered what he would transform into.

The Witches may soon be knocking at their door, the King-of-Glass-and-Steel was still missing without a trace and they had the Spiral Hand to uncover. It was going to be a long winter. Let their patron sleep now and pray that there may be a calm before the storm.

Please Leave a Review

I hope you enjoyed *Ghosts of Winter*. I would really appreciate it if you could take a few minutes now to review the book on your favourite retailer. Independent authors rely heavily on reader reviews, they really are like oxygen. Reviews help other readers decide whether a book is a good fit for them or not. Much as I want everyone to love my books, I also know that it's important to find the right readers, so just a few words from you could help me to do that and reach other readers who will enjoy my dark and twisted tales!

Thank you!

About the Author

H.B. Lyne is an urban fantasy author, podcaster and bullet journal enthusiast with a knack for organisation and getting stuff done.

She lives in Yorkshire with her husbeast, two children and midwife cat. When not juggling family commitments, she writes dark urban fantasy novels, purging her imagination of its demons. Inspired by the King of Horror himself, Holly aspires to be at least half as prolific and successful and promises to limit herself to only one tome of The Stand-like proportions in her career.

Check out my website for all the latest updates and offers
hblyne.com

Follow me on Instagram
@hblyne

And on Facebook
facebook.com/authorhblyne

Also by H.B. Lyne

In the Shifters of Caerton series:

Fate of the Blue Moon

Ghosts of Winter

Demons of the Past

Rise of the Furies

Dark Echoes: Tales from the Shadows

From Ashes to Echoes

Lies the Dead Tell series:

In The Blood

Join my Tribe of Rabid Readers

Get short story collection *Dark Echoes: Tales from the Shadows* free when you sign up for updates via my website

hblyne.com